Like life itself, All Gone Awry, the story of a quest for fulfillment, for an authentic, honest identity, is layered and complex. Kumasaka addresses who gets to be an artist and looks at the transformative power that art-making can have. What does that art look like? What are the risks one is willing or required to take for it? How do family, ethnicity, and cultural history inform and influence our present? And what about romantic love? *All Gone Awry* is a sweeping story that welcomes contradictions; it movingly prods us to reflect on our own questions of identity, morality, and our place in the world.

—Patrice Vecchione, author of *My Shouting, Shattered, Whispering Voice: A Guide to Writing Poetry & Speaking Your Truth*

A literary treat awaiting readers who will enjoy this provocative novel narrating the evolution of Alex Arai from staid art history professor to obsessively driven graffiti artist. Risking everything to explore the Postmodern, alternative art world of graffiti, Alex aims to fulfill his dream of authentic self-expression, while wrestling with and redefining his own ethnic identity. But at what cost to his relationships, his career, and even his freedom? A psychologically fascinating debut novel by Andrew Kumasaka.

—Christine Z. Mason, novelist, author of *Boundaries, Weighing the Truth,* and *The Ancient Stone City*

2021 marked the 10th anniversary of one of the deadliest natural disasters of the 21st century, often referred to as 3/11, when a massive undersea earthquake struck off the coast of Japan, triggering a nuclear meltdown crisis and an enormous tsunami that brought more death and destruction than the quake itself.... Those living in Santa Cruz County at the time might remember that the tsunami was large enough to reach the West Coast of the United States.... The 3/11 tragedy is a compelling literal illustration of the metaphor at the heart of environmentalism, that a disruption anywhere globally can cause ripples locally. It's also the inspiration and jumping-off point of a new novel by writer Andrew Kumasaka.

—Wallace Baine, nationally syndicated newspaper writer, *Lookout Santa Cruz* correspondent, and author of *A Light in the Midst of Darkness*, *The Last Temptation of Lincoln*, and *Rhymes with Vain*

Deceptively engrossing, *All Gone Awry* is fun and perceptive, with an engaging cast of characters. The prose pulls you in, and the plot feels light-hearted. But Kumasaka is a very smart writer. By the time you're turning the pages as fast as possible, you realize there's a wealth of life here, as a series of complex and surprising events, ideas and revelations take hold. *All Gone Awry* tells one hell of a great story, to be sure, even as it dives deep into the role of art in any and every life. Kumasaka revels in the pleasures of dissonance, the distance between who we think we are and who we find ourselves to be. He takes us from a quiet life to bigger than life, from embarrassment and shame to joy and success so seamlessly that we as readers realize only afterwards that the journey is ours as well.

—Rick Kleffel, Monterey Bay radio host and podcast creator for *Narrative Species*

ALL GONE AWRY

a novel

Andrew Kumasaka

For information about permissions to reproduce selections from this book, translation rights, or to order bulk purchases, write: akumasaka27@gmail.com.

Cover art by Chase Kumasaka
Book design and publishing management by The Publishing World

Kumasaka, Andrew
All Gone Awry
978-0-578-31444-0

1. Fiction / Literary. 2. Fiction / Asian American. 3. Fiction / Own Voices.

Also for sale in hardcover and ebook formats.

GANBATTE! BOOKS

Printed in the U.S.A.
Distributed by Ingram

For...

my grandfather Yuji, a storyteller and mimic
my grandfather Matahei, who faithfully kept his "daily book"
my grandmothers, Tosa and Sadaye
my parents, George and Yuriko

"You wrote it once and a hundred people saw it.
You wrote it twice and a thousand people saw it.
By your hand, you were known."

—TAKI 183

1

Santa Cruz, California—Westside
A house on Escalona Drive

*U*p in the loft, hours pass as the distant bay congeals into night. With back turned to the picture windows, Alex Arai draws his musings to a close. He shuts his laptop, stands at his desk—shutters the tableau with a sweep of a tall *shoji* screen. In the now hidden alcove, he leaves behind three subtle changes to a lecture he's given so many times before.

Descending the stairs, he enters the hallway—heads for the master bedroom suite. After a shower, he dresses for sleep—props himself atop a worn blue comforter. A leftover warmth infuses him as he picks up the remote. Tapping in the news, he welcomes the glow from someplace on the opposite side of the world.

Here on the California coast it's a March night—just past 12. What pours into the room are fractured images of a highly distressed, ancestral Japan. *For godsakes,* he reacts—*I wonder if Lisa's watching.* Lisa's up in Portland this week, or is it Seattle?

Quick connections—Japan, northeastern Japan—Fukushima. Earthquake, tsunami, a "9" on the Richter Scale, that American invention for measuring destructive potential. A Fukushima nuclear power plant fills the screen—no *f* sound in Japanese. Just a *wh* sound like a *whoosh*. Like the sound of a large, lethal object flying overhead. Awestruck, Alex wonders how many people have already died. The reporter says maybe five hundred—but of course the number will climb.

The crestfallen Japanese ambassador to the U.S. speaks under a hot, bright light. Alex detects the sheen of shame on the man's downcast face—half expects the man to apologize for the mishap. Maybe he *should* apologize for his country having created so much trouble for the rest of the world. The news anchor raises the death toll to seven hundred, but says over nine thousand, five hundred people are missing in Sendai alone.

Through the electronic portal, Tokyo shudders and keeps shuddering. Over and over, the tsunami strikes—a cumulative impact on the psyche. Every time the loop replays, more people have died. What an embarrassment for a country so sophisticated in quakes and tsunamis, a country so expert at predicting the magnitude of the future.

Alex watches in horror as an explosion rocks a power plant. The electricity has failed—the diesel-fueled backups, knocked out. There's nothing left to calm the reactors. *Will there be meltdowns?*

Japan relocates citizens outside a ten-kilometer radius, trying to spare them the fiery flash of sudden death, the cold time-bomb of extended death. No one wants to become an atomic clock, measured out in his own half-lives. An oil refinery goes up in bulbous flame—an actual mushroom cloud portending nuclear doom. Godzilla soon to be reborn. Godzilla already alive? The reincarnation of Godzilla, the worst nightmare—the worst case memory for a diminishing, elderly few.

Reaching for the phone, he calls Lisa. No answer—but of course, it's late. As for the TV, changing channels does nothing to alter the breaking story. He continues to watch—can't stop. Only commercial splices disturb the ongoing tale of destruction. *It's only a matter of time before it happens here.* The prophesied dropping of California into the Pacific—Santa Cruz, San Jose. Another example of synergy—the tsunami now heading for the Central Coast.

* * *

After a turbulent night, Alex eases out of bed. Cursing the ache in his left calf, he calls his friend Carter.

"Hey—sorry about missing the last game. Should be fine in a couple days."

"Great news, Al—got us a tough one this week."

Although built more like a soccer player, Alex has always enjoyed Saturday night "hoops" with the guys. Given the ever-increasing wear and tear, maybe it's finally time to give it up. After all, he's a professor—an ivory tower type—pondering life at the cusp of fifty. Sadly slowing over the years, he's made adjustments—plays smarter. Still, basketball belongs to much younger bodies—a game for kids who continue to have "hops."

After a few stretches, Alex drives off to Coffeetopia. Past the pink doorway, he joins the cobbled customers—settles to a croissant and his usual medium roast. At the communal table, he finds copies of the *Guardian,* the *Mercury* and the local *Courier*—wades through coverage of last night's destruction in Japan. He wonders if any of his students will be stopping by to chat, something that happens from time to time. With a paper due on Surrealism, some could definitely use his help. But no one wants to compare Miró with Dalí, or Ernst with Magritte today. Instead, the lively little room buzzes with comments not only about events in Japan, but about those taking place along this stretch of California coast.

...A grizzled, white-haired man in worn leather jacket and olive cords—
I went lookin' at it—the tsunami. The upper harbor got hit pretty bad. ...'Round 11 this morning— musta been about ten of them surges.

...A young male student in black ski cap, plaid flannel shirt, and beige shorts—
Definitely I saw it. It was on YouTube. The decks kinda exploded, all in a row. ...Man, what would you do if you saw that thing coming after you?

...A young female student in orange tank top, denim cutoffs, and black leggings—

3

*And did you hear about some guy up north getting
swept away? ...He was trying to take some pictures
or something. Seriously, what was he thinking?*

...A muscle-bound guy in gray sweatshirt, blue cargo pants,
and skater shoes—
*Oh fuck it, man...I tried to figure out why it sank.
Might be a door wasn't closed. ...Could only be there
a half an hour before the police shut it down.*

Alex wonders if the man swept away near Crescent City
could possibly have been Japanese. Could the man be a part of
that ethnic strain who, instead of duck-and-covering, grabbed
their cameras and started clicking and recording? *What kind
of people are they?* In the midst of certain death, they seem
focused on the import, the significance of the moment—choose
to memorialize an already indelible point in time. To capture
the fleeting, the ephemeral—to record this grave moment before
toppling to the earth themselves.

Here at the coffee shop, the quake and tsunami are the
talk of the town. How many of these youngsters have actually
experienced a meaningful quake? How many were even alive
in '89 for Loma Prieta, a geological event a hundred times less
powerful? Alex heads for home after absorbing the energy,
the excitement of the morning. He notes how so many people
had proceeded the wrong way—had flocked to the shoreline in
response to the tsunami warning.

They had wanted to view the local water surging through
the narrow harbor. They had gone to view this once in a lifetime
occurrence—nature in all her power, the threat of the apoca-
lypse with just a slight slip of oceanic plates.

And as for his own lost, unknown relatives, he wonders to
himself about the eerie lack of bodies so far. Soon enough, they
would be washing ashore. In the midst of unspeakable horror,
the Japanese people seemed not to speak. In shock, no doubt
a strange, if not bizarre silence. Not exactly *shikata-ganai*, the
Japanese concept of "it can't be helped," but a stunning calm
radiating from the faces of so many victims, as Alex returns to
the TV and the flat black screen of his circumscribed life.

All Gone Awry

* * *

Porter College, University of California, Santa Cruz

On stage at the Media Theater, Professor Arai scans his audience, some two hundred students filling the lower bowl of the auditorium. The lights play off his high forehead, a crest of black, silver-flecked hair. Beneath lively eyes, shadows sculpt the angular cheekbones, his supple mouth primed for a smile. Overdressed by school standards, he wears a light gray suit, a blue shirt, and yellow tie. Strolling left from a bank of computers, he begins the next installment of his class, "From Impressionism to Pop: The Story of Modern Western Painting."

"As you recall, following World War II, the epicenter of the Western art world shifted from Paris to New York City. The first truly American-grown style of painting was called *Abstract Expressionism*. Go ahead anyone—give me the names of some artists associated with this style."

"Jackson Pollock," calls out a young man—his hand waving about as if demonstrating the technique of drip painting.

"Franz Kline," suggests a young Goth—slashes of black hair disrupting her stark white face.

"Helen Frankenthaler," asserts a sharp soprano—her raised arm sheathed in diaphanous colors.

Pleased with the return, Alex saunters back across the stage.

"These artists moved abstraction into uncharted territory. A painting was no longer considered just a product of the artist, but a kind of documentation of the creative process itself. With a strong belief in the unconscious—these artists expressed *not* the reality of the external world, but the reality of their internal, psychological world. Today, we will examine the paintings of Mark Rothko, a Russian-born Jew, who not only expressed his deepest truths—but in so doing, encouraged the viewer to embrace his or her own unique experience as well."

The lights dim. On the giant screen behind Alex looms the image of Rothko's *Untitled* from 1957.

"Like many of the Abstract Expressionists, Rothko preferred to work on a large scale. As you can see, the painting is composed of three vertically arranged rectangles on a red background. The harshly applied orange of the top form seems to fade to a thin veil of color in the bottom one. Between these two, a purple rectangle appears, rendered in quick up and down strokes. In this example of his *classic* work, Rothko demonstrates his mastery with the brush." Pausing—"Any reactions?"

"The colors seem to glow—they pulse."

"The rectangles look like they're floating."

"I feel a kind of energy, a kind of heat."

With instructions to experience each one intently, Alex projects a series of paintings, starting from the strongly-hued works of the 1950s to the so-called *black and gray* paintings of 1969-70.

Finished with the images, Alex turns the lights back up. He asks his students to share their impressions.

"Well, there were all these stunning paintings, and then the color went away. Gorgeous reds, yellows, and blues. And then he ends up with these dark works with nothing but black rectangles over gray ones. I don't get it."

Alex extends an open hand—"How did these changes make you feel?"

A second voice pops up. "It was with the contrast—the draining away of the color. It made me feel kind of gloomy, a real mood killer."

A third voice. "Truthfully, I got worried for him."

Alex enjoys the energy in the room. "Mark Rothko was truly a man of the Modern era, a time when the horrors of World War II, and the science that led to *the bomb*, lent great anxiety and uncertainty to the world. In his final paintings, he was able to express his relationship to that ultimate existential *void*. As such, these paintings represent a major accomplishment in the history of Modern Western art."

A quick glance at the floor—"I must also note that Rothko suffered from a number of internal demons as well, including episodes of severe depression. And, despite serious health problems, he continued to smoke and to drink to excess."

Dimming the lights once more, Alex displays the haunting image of one final black and gray painting.

"I recall attending a retrospective of Rothko's work. Whether the growing darkness of his palette reflected the return of depression was still open to debate. All I can say is that I found these paintings profoundly sad and disturbing. I also remember the day I attended a lecture and the speaker announced that Mark Rothko had died. Eventually, I read that the painter, one year separated from his second wife, was discovered dead in his kitchen after slashing his wrists with a razor. Blood reportedly everywhere. I can't help but believe, that with his life, as with his color—Mark Rothko gave fully of himself, then took everything away."

Stepping towards his audience—"How ironic it must have been to view that rich red blood covering his body and the kitchen floor. While submitting to the void, after these final dark paintings, what a color for him to leave us with."

Professor Arai restores the sheen of the lights. With somber eyes, he looks out at the rows of silent young faces. "Well, class is dismissed," he says quietly. "I'll see you back here in a week."

* * *

San Jose, California—1964
A modest bungalow on a tree-lined street—
Alex's childhood home

Kazuo Arai to his wife Sumi—

"When I finish teaching for the year, I'm heading for Seattle. First three days, I'll stay at George and Ayame's. After that, I'll find a hotel—two weeks total. George has a trip to Kansas City later in the year—the dedication of his new fountain. Oh my gosh, he's getting famous. I plan to learn a lot from him—see how he does it. He's even got a one-man exhibition going on in Tacoma."

"...Yeah, that's right—he was born in Seattle, too. Got drafted into the army, so he didn't end up in Minidoka. His family did. I'm pretty sure he met Ayame when he visited Tule Lake on furlough."

"...So, Henry can hold down the fort with you. He's a big boy. Just keep an eye on Alexander. I mean, for cryin' out loud—he actually ruined a sketch I made. And I don't care if he was just trying to help. Don't let him get near my things. And one last piece of advice—stop trying to encourage him—you know the boy can't draw. He's got no talent. He'll only be fit for what—cartoons?"

"...Well, I don't care how old he is. When I was his age, back in camp—I was already known as a prodigy."

* * *

Pacific Collegiate School—
  city league basketball, over-40 division

A smallish gym, close to the university—no windows, an off-white wall running down one side of the court. The smell of freshly varnished bleachers, the smell of distressed sneakers. The sound of basketballs slapping the beige linoleum floor.

Joey, the lanky old hip hop ref, comes jogging up to Alex. With long black shorts falling to mid-calf, his pallid legs look swaddled in drapery. Raptor eyes flank a beak-like nose—light brown stubble claims a weathered face.

"You guys showin' up tonight, or what?"

"Yeah, we're good," comes the reply.

Alex prefers simple gray shorts coupled with his classic Foamposites. Upending a well-worn canvas bag, he flushes out three vintage basketballs. Grabbing his favorite, he casually dribbles across the floor.

A tall slender black man enters the gym—doffs his jacket as he ambles toward Alex.

Extending a friendly fist—"Notice anything new?"

Alex glances at the baggy gold shorts, the long black socks. "Let's see, Carter. Oh, yeah—but I can't believe you went with the Kobe's—"

"Why, because I don't like the Lakers?" Sitting down on the three-point line, Carter begins his ritual stretching. "They're super light—look great."

"Especially that *pointillist* effect in purple and gold. Where did you get them?"

"On the way home from seeing my folks. Nita talked me into driving across the bridge. You know—Union Square."

"Sorry to hear that—"

"Don't be—my reward was going to Nike Town."

Alex dribbles, puts up a three, just as the rest of the guys arrive. As their team, the "Silver Backs," try to warm up, Joey decides to start the game. Always in a rush, he moves fast, talks faster, blows the fastest whistle in the league. The opposing team calls itself "The Posse." Made up of guys who just turned forty, they look forward to older, weaker, more laid-back competition.

Joey puts the ball up. The first few minutes don't go well for the Silver Backs. The team's center gets hacked every time he goes for a shot. As usual, he misses his free throws. Smooth Carter, or *Silk*, as he's known—plays the *three* and serves as the team's go-to guy. But every time he touches the ball, the Posse quickly doubles up. The team's off guard struggles to get open—can't establish a rhythm. Playing the point, Alex focuses on distributing the ball. What's starting to bother him, besides the score, is the excess physicality being shown by the Posse. Usually quiet, he tells Joey to *watch the fouls*. After all, this is a senior's league. By the end of the first quarter, the Silver Backs are down by fifteen points.

"Say Joey—my guy keeps pushing off, and you *still* call the foul on me?"

"Just keep on playin'—you're lookin' out of sync tonight."

Taking a towel to his face, Carter says—"Hey Al, if nothing's working just take the ball to the hole. We need you to create."

"I'll try—but I'm going to get killed. Joey's calling a lousy game—acting all spacey, you know?"

The second quarter starts off the same as the first. The Posse seems to rack up points at will. For the Silver Backs, only Silk can score.

Alex tries to drive to the hoop, but gets slammed hard every time. To make matters worse, the guy guarding him literally stinks—a hairy throwback whose uni-brow is only exceeded by a *uni-pit*—underarm sweat oozing from his entire chest. Repulsed, Alex forces himself back into the paint. As he clears his man, he feels his arm being raked by a set of unclipped nails. Losing control of the ball, and himself—

"What the hell, Joey! Didn't you see that? He's been doing that all night."

Trotting past—"Don't get so riled, man. Stay in the flow—it's a beautiful game."

Alex points a stiffened finger—"The game in your head is *not* the one being played on this floor!"

Scooping up the ball, Joey awards it to the other team. "We're all in the same game, bro. All us cats out here. It ain't cool to be talkin' like that."

Carter puts a hand on his teammate's shoulder. "Forget it Al. It's just Saturday night hoops."

Even as he takes a step toward the ref, Alex can't quite believe how out of character he's acting. On the other hand, he can't seem to stop.

Incensed—"You're out of your mind, Joey. You've always been. Maybe you fried your brain back in the *freaking* Mission!"

Joey blows his whistle—signals a technical foul. "All right, man—now you're bein' disrespectful. Nobody talks shit about San Francisco. Fact is, you're messin' with the flow." Now the whistle's blown a second time. "Somethin' in my head just told me to give you *two* technicals. That means you're outta here, Professor *A-wry*—"

Mixed in with the anger, Alex feels like a total idiot. *What a complete and public loss of control,* he thinks. He hasn't gotten so pissed in a game since he was back on his high school team in San Jose. From over his shoulder, he hears some Posse members laughing. As he strides toward the bench, a concerned Carter trails behind.

"It's okay Al—Joey should be canned by the league."

"Thanks, Silk." Still amped, Alex fumbles through everyone's gear while gathering his sweatshirt and keys.

"Try some breathing exercises," suggests his friend.

"Don't worry, I'll be fine." Alex marches off, then turns. "Say—what are you doing after your faculty meeting tomorrow?"

"Nothing."

"Want to get together for lunch?"

"Sounds great."

"How about in front of the Media Theater?"

"I'll be there."

"Give me a time—"
"A quarter past?"
"Works for me."
Punching open the metal doors—Alex exits the gym.

UCSC Campus

*P*erched atop a knoll, a tall grid of translucent panels defines the boxy front of the lecture hall. Facing the building, a cluster of thirty-foot coastal redwoods rises from a circular planter rimmed in concrete.

A few paces along a grassy ridge stand a couple of old wooden picnic tables. Arriving first, Professor Sessions takes a seat—leans his back against the worn tabletop. An unusually rainy spring, he always carries a Gortex shell in his briefcase. But the sun is out today—perfect weather for a crisp, burgundy cotton shirt. Stretching out, he all but inhales the expansive view of the bay.

"Hey—" comes a voice from up the hill.

"Hey—" comes the reply. A simple call and response from two men who could bill themselves as *The Two Baritones*, if only they could sing. For over fifteen years, Carter and Alex have been best friends, colleagues, and teammates. Four years younger, Carter returned to California after earning his doctorate at Columbia.

"Thanks for the support last night."

"You had me worried, Al. That was kind of a first for you."

"Can't believe I blew it—"

"Authority issues," Carter chuckles.

"That's for sure. Joey and me—what a joke."

"Try not to beat yourself up—"

"Hard not to."

Sleeves up, tie loose, Alex parks himself on the same side of the table. "I got us a couple burritos from that new place at Porter. *The Slug Café*, I think."

"And I brought the apple juice and blueberries. You know you're going to kill me with that food."

Exchanging treats—"So, how did your meeting go?"

Carter lets out a prolonged sigh. "Just the usual political bullshit. Who gets this, who gets that. What do I need to teach next fall—"

"The students love your social psych classes."

"Yeah, but I want to crank things up a notch. Frustrating, really."

"'The Ethnic American Narrative: Self Determination.' As I've said before, I got lots of material sitting in on your lectures."

"Thanks," says Carter, taking a tentative bite out of Alex's offering. "But I wanted more time for cutting-edge issues—the controversial stuff."

Happily munching now—"I've always liked how you don't just focus on the African American experience. And all my stuff about *collective memory*—my study of memorials owes a lot to you."

"Well, we've been good for each other over the years."

"Especially that stretch when I was stuck teaching ethnic art."

"A pretty bleak time—"

"No one would dare entrust the Western canon to someone of Asian descent."

"Of course not. And just look at all those white academicians hailed as experts on *Oriental* and African art."

"Precisely."

Speaking of Asian American artists—how's that intro coming along—the one for your father's upcoming retrospective?"

"Oh yeah—I'm working on a draft right now." Alex motions through a grove of redwoods to his right. "In two years—the twentieth anniversary of my father unveiling 'The Big One' up there. The memorial that got him on the map. I've got no clue how to make it special enough for him. In fact, he's still unhappy with the last article I wrote. Didn't do him enough justice, he said. It just irks me—pisses me off. You know what I think of my father."

"I wouldn't trade places with you on that one. So much history between you two. I think it's beyond time you break away from all that crap. Just think of what else you could do," smiles Carter—"like playing more hoops with the guys."

"Thanks for saying that. All this intrigue with my father and his reputation. Now *that's* the game I'm sick and tired of playing."

* * *

From the San Francisco Guardian *September, 1993—*

Amidst redwoods on a pristine bluff over Monterey Bay, the University of California, Santa Cruz welcomed a major new memorial this past summer. San Jose sculptor, Kazuo Arai, joined school and local government officials for the festive unveiling at the Porter College site. The memorial, dedicated to Japanese Americans illegally interned during World War II, was inspired in part by the twentieth anniversary of the book, "Farewell To Manzanar," by Jeanne Wakatsuki Houston and her husband, James Houston.

The twenty-foot-high sculpture, "Forever Manzanar," consists of a novel amalgam of materials. The stainless steel rectangular base is reminiscent of David Smith's "Cubi" series. When struck by the sun, the highly buffed surface dematerializes, lending a sense of levitation to the forms above. Three bronze figures stand atop the base, representing a grandfather, a mother and a young child. According to the artist, these figures signify the three generations of Japanese interned in the camps.

Certain of Arai's techniques evoke the work of the French sculptor, Auguste Rodin. The vigorous modeling of the surface and the strenuous gestures produce a dramatic ensemble. Anguish and displacement are expressed by the twisted arms of the 'parents' as they reach skyward. At the same time, these larger figures form a protective shield, arching over the 'child.'

Unique to the use of materials is a blue-green skein of glass that wraps itself like a veil about the bodies of the internees. The creases and folds blend smoothly together as they ascend the sculpted forms. At times, the effect is that of classical Greek cloaking. At other times, the glass suggests the flowing of a river, a sense of movement that further serves to soothe, contain and to unite the participants. As Arai notes, the sand used for the glass comes from the actual Manzanar site. He adds that the glass represents change and transformation, from a "gritty substance to a thing of great clarity and purity." Once again, depending on the position of the sun and the angle of light, the glass allows the sculpture to glow.

The new memorial on the UCSC campus is not only a welcome esthetic addition but serves to remind us all of the struggles and triumphs inherent to the Japanese American narrative. Sculptor Kazuo Arai can be lauded for his innovative use of materials. His dramatic work, "Forever Manzanar," crystallizes the Japanese American experience and resultant identity in a powerful, unforgettable image.

—Professor Alexander Arai, Department of History of Art and Visual Culture, UCSC

* * *

Collage of ironies

Alex to his students—Spring, 2011

"So, what have we seen to date? The narrative of Modern Art—the story arc. Spanning roughly the 1860s through the 1960s. Birthed by the Enlightenment, embodied by the avant-garde—a celebration of the *new*, of the revolutionary. Artists broke free of rigid constraints regarding technique and subject matter."

Phone call from Kazuo Arai to George Tsutakawa—Summer, 1990

"I want to do something different with my sculpture. I want to express the heroic struggles of our people. I'm frankly tired, you know—there's nothing but abstraction out there. Of course, I'm not talking about *your* work. Your fountain sculptures capture the elegance of water—movement in time. I plan to add some fluid glass features to my bronze figures—create some flow of my own."

Alex—

"No longer was subject matter restricted to myth, allegory, history, or religion. As we've seen earlier—there's Manet's seminal *Luncheon on the Grass,* Monet's paintings of water lilies and haystacks. Picasso's *Les Desmoiselles*—a brothel scene."

Kazuo—

"We've been quiet enough through the years—the *model minority*. What we really need are better memorials to the Japanese Americans interned during the war.... Yes, George, I know you caught flack in '83 for the one you did. But, I'm going to pursue it anyway. I even think I've found a style that unites the whole history of Modern Art in my work. At least, that's what Alex says. I'll take the best of Rodin and put it on an industrial base. Nothing like this has been done before."

Alex—

"The Modernist era was propelled by various *movements*. In addition to Impressionism, we have Expressionism, Futurism, Constructivism. And, of course, Cubism and Surrealism, Abstract Expressionism. Artists jostled for position within the art world, keenly aware of their place in history."

Kazuo—

"Got my letter? Yes, I can't believe it—my first big commission. The University of California. I won the competition, even with some big-time players involved. It's that memorial I was telling you about. The twentieth anniversary of that Manzanar book by Jeanne Houston. They want to put it in her hometown of Santa Cruz—right up on campus.... Yes, for gosh sakes, I think it's pretty funny—same place Alexander teaches. He's up for tenure about the same time. I'm sure he'll write an impressive review for me."

Alex—
"The narrative of Modern sculpture entwines with that of painting. Just as an aside here—for those of you who will still be on campus this fall, I'll be teaching my course on Modern Sculpture titled, "From Rodin to Minimalism: The Story of Modern Western Sculpture."

"All right—questions anyone? Okay, the young fellow with the colorful scarf.... Oh, I see—someone always seems to ask me that. No, I'm not the *Arai* who created the memorial up at Porter College. I'm glad you like it—that sculpture was done by my father, Kazuo.... Well, you'll just have to stay tuned and find out. I'm not saying if I'll grant my father any special treatment, beyond what I'd give to, say—Brancusi, Calder, Moore, and...."

* * *

The house on Escalona Drive

It's one of those evenings that pulse with the stuff of future memory. Just the kind of night that forces a person out for a walk, to take stock—to salvage. A restless night full of found objects for creating an assemblage or an installation. It's all about an artistic urge to leave a mark—to make a personal statement, even though Alex might not know what it is. Wearing dark sweats and basketball shoes, he clambers down his steep driveway—takes a long trek through the Westside. In the cool, ocean-tinged air, he feels compelled to head downtown to the Pacific Garden Mall.

Beginning his stroll along the historic street, he takes in the *gestalt*—surveys what's become the most sincere memorial to a tragedy that took place some twenty-two years ago. He passes vibrant shops and restaurants, the old Del Mar Theater—a hodgepodge of architectural styles. He scans the surviving 19th-century sandstone façades, the latest Postmodern multi-use structures. Two plots of land remain empty—lingering victims of that last geological insult. Tonight, the recent disaster in Japan resonates with the Loma Prieta quake of '89. Alex looks for connections between the events. The vivid TV images mesh with his own memories. In the soft gray pall of the coastal layer, he can detect the foreboding smoke he once saw rising from this very street on that October day. He remembers the random deaths that littered the cultural center of town.

Acutely uneasy, Alex presses forward, doused in light spilling from street lamps shaped like ginger jars. He's aware of a mounting pressure inside his head. Maybe it's from departmental whispers about subject matter he could be forced to teach. Maybe it's from his father's incessant emails. Swirls of pedestrians buffet his senses—college kids, skaters, hipsters, Goths, young couples of every persuasion. He wants to yell out to them—remind them how the fragile earth is not solid, but simply a network of fissures. Instead, his attention turns to a ragged woman pounding away at a set of congas. From across the street, a tall young man in a black derby plays heart-wrenching blues on his guitar.

Making a break, Alex takes a sudden left down Church Street, then another left into a back alley. A half block in, everything goes quiet. To the side, he notes a fine skein of streetlight that's found its way to a wall. Attacking the store's logo, the tortured scrawl of a graffiti vandal bursts into view. Alex stops—tries to make out the stylized letters or numbers, or whatever. Even in the semi-dark, he recognizes the color *red*. Maybe gang related, maybe not. Below the tag lies an abandoned can of spray paint. Breath quickening—*Maybe the vandal fled the scene. Maybe he was chased. Maybe....* Alex looks left down the alley—looks right. Looks left again. And then, in a scene that seems shot in slow motion, a scene in which he watches himself—he stoops to grab the can. Straightening, he hears it rattle to life. In a single decisive moment, he raises what feels like a hard fist—squeezes the cap—releases a hissing stream of red paint across the tag and down the wall. Heart pounding, he drops the can and runs.

Racing through the alley, he feels light and free—a sense of relief. His eyes hurdle every shadow, ears reverberate with the sound of his own breathing. Over and over, his lungs explode— far beyond the level of exertion. Alex runs, skin tingling— laughs to himself as he merges with the night.

3

*I*t's a clean bus, relatively clean. But inside, Whitney B can still smell traffic—stale flannel and fleece—last night's or this morning's weed. Job section from the *Courier* in hand, she stares out a big scuffed window, as River Street pivots left onto Hwy. 1. Another dawn of *marine layer*, euphemism for "fog." *So, why does it always start off like this?* Kind of like how she's feeling right now. The gray light takes away all the colors, makes all the edges soft and fuzzy. A bracing swim by the field house would help, stuck as she is on another lurching trip up to campus for a lecture.

The cell phone rings.

"Hey Julie, go back to sleep. Yeah, I've got you covered."

As an artist, Whitney wonders why she's awake so early just to hear some old guy talk about the art of even older, even *dead* people. When she gets off at Porter College, she ought to head straight for the studio. She's got work to do, has painterly concerns—the *only* concerns she cares about today. A text message—*It's Mario*, the morning check-in. *Maybe an update on that journalism project he's doing.* Nothing could be worse than getting sidetracked, and the whole morning feels like a big distraction. She thinks life should be all about the idea in her head right now, the eerie magenta she wants to smear all over that pretty face on her canvas.

Oh shit! What about that paper due today? She'll just have to Google the topic this afternoon—change a few words, add a brief editorial, then hit *send.* And then it's off to the studio where she plans to duke it out with her so-called subject.

But Whitney feels like a captive of sorts, being hauled off to some distant outpost where none of her interests lie. She might as well be leaving town, it seems so far away. What a waste of time—her eyes dulled, her fingers feeling restless and out of touch. *How annoying. How stupid—*

But all of this thinking makes her antsy as well. She needs to do something—needs to take matters into her own hands. Reaching into her quilted vest pocket, she finds a hair clip wedged between a wrapped piece of blueberry muffin and a set of keys. She wants to make this a good day, an *excellent* day. Taking a heap of her chestnut hair, Whitney twirls it into a tight bun—her personal version of rolling up her sleeves. She's decided to skip today's lecture and focus on her own art instead.

* * *

Bill's Wheels Skateshop, Eastside Santa Cruz
"Serving skateboarders since 1977"

A young teen in a blue plaid shirt and baggy shorts runs loose in a display room as colorful as any candy shop. Flashy-looking decks circle the walls overhead, while others cluster like decorative murals. The boy ricochets past racks of clothing, a helmet display—several glass cases of wheels, trucks, and other accessories.

Alex approaches the skinny cashier at the counter. Dressed in a black T-shirt and matching pants, the young guy peers at Alex through a tussle of dark brown hair.

"Say—is Joey around?" asks Alex. "Joey Miletich—"

"Yeah, he's here—but he's not workin' the counter."

"So what's he doing today?"

"He's paintin' the wall outside."

Pausing to think—"What wall?"

"The graffiti wall."

"Really? I didn't see him when I parked my car."

"Must be takin' a break."

Thanking the young man, Alex steps outside—hangs a right into the huge, rectangular parking lot. The two-storied side of the main building stretches some one hundred feet along the right. For over fifteen years, the owner has provided a *legal* wall where some of the best graffiti writers in the Bay Area have come to render their creations.

Before Alex can absorb it all, he hears the sputter of an approaching car—some tarnished, non-descript sedan. Finished parking, Joey unfolds his boney frame—runs a hand through shaggy hair—pops the trunk. Out come a heavy can of house paint, a roller, and Joey's little boom box.

Spotting Alex—"Hey, Professor—what brings you here?"

Alex shoves both hands into his pants pockets. Looking more than a bit sheepish—"That last game, Joey. I'm really sorry I got so upset."

Joey smiles—"Is that a fact now, Professor A-wry?"

"Yes—yes it is," says Alex. "And I'm particularly sorry for what I said about you."

Setting down his supplies—"Oh—about my brain bein' off?"

"Yes—"

"And bringin' my hometown into it?"

"Yes, I apologize."

"You know, I'm San Francisco, born and raised."

"I was aware."

"Holly Park Court Projects—"

"Once again, I'm sorry."

Joey laughs. "So you came all the way from the Westside—just so's you could apologize?"

"I did. And, it won't happen again. Not at the game tonight—not ever."

Joey fiddles with his boom box—the same one he brings to the gym. Looking up—"I appreciate that, but you know somethin'?"

Alex eyes Joey with a bit of suspicion. "What?"

"I could really be usin' some help today." After passing on tracks by Q tip and Master Flash, Joey settles on Public Enemy. "I ain't got a crew, man—I'm independent. If you got the time, could you lend me a hand? I'll consider us squared, if you do."

Glancing down at his Dockers and deck shoes, Alex pauses. "Well—well—okay, I suppose. But, what do you actually want me to do?"

"No worries—I'll get you a roller from the trunk." Joey scans the mural, the product of a half-dozen guys, representing days of concentrated work. "Before we buff this wall—you oughta be takin' one last look."

With an open hand, he revels in the vast expanse, covered with intricate, highly stylized, colorful letters and figures. Not waiting for a response, he struts in the direction of a pink cartoon character who's pointing at a futuristic blue and purple city. Just beyond, a ferocious green lizard's face drips blood over a silver-masked, grim reaper.

"Man," he says, reverently. "There's some crazy-ass shit up here. I mean, these guys can really rock it—know what I'm sayin'?"

Joey gets the second roller and hands it to his new partner. Staring at the implement, Alex reminds himself he's not even one for home improvements. As Joey pries the paint can open, Alex takes in his first whiff.

"This is all the rejected stuff," says Joey. "Got tons more in the car. I wanted black, but all they had was dark gray. Cheap stuff, though."

Alex decides to lie to Joey—says he's got a meeting to attend before the game tonight. He'll hang around and help for a half an hour at most. Then, folding up the sleeves of what is still a pristine yellow broadcloth shirt—he dips his roller into a fresh pan of enamel.

As time passes, what strikes him hardest, besides the paint drop on one of his cuffs—is the sheer beauty of the various designs. He finds himself fascinated by the structure of the letters, the detail of the characters, the use of vibrant color, the rhythm of the composition—the surprise of embellishments. *What a shame,* he thinks to himself—to cover over, to destroy the work of another artist— *Of whom? An artist,* most definitely. *But what kind of practice is this? What kind of artist would create works so temporal in nature? Beyond gaining recognition, doesn't every artist want a measure of immortality?*

Thoughts keep churning in his head, not at all unusual— but this time, to a hip hop beat. *Wow, I wonder if Joey's mind always pounds like this.* Noting the time, he feels rather guilty that Joey's far outstripped his contribution to *buffing.* However, he reminds himself, Joey is the pro at this—makes Alex wonder about the man's life as a graffiti artist.

"Hey, I'm sorry, but I've got to go."

"That's okay, you've done enough." Dropping his roller to the side—"All is forgiven, man. You did good today."

"Oh, thanks. I enjoyed looking at all the art. By the way, I didn't know you painted graffiti. How did you get this—gig?"

"Well, for one, we're called *writers*—ever since the early days back in the '60s, back in New York, and Philly before it. I first did this wall in '98. Since I've been workin' here—I thought it could use another update. So, I asked Bill—"

"Sounds good—how long have you been writing?"

"Well, I'm what now—forty-one years old? I *got up* a lot back in the '80s. Back in San Francisco, I painted me some major walls like Psycho City, Franklin Auto, Norfolk alleyway, Silver Terrace, Cayuga Park—Crocker Park. Yeah, I hung with some great writers. I was taught by a guy named CRAYONE. A great dude—a great teacher. Generous, you know what I mean?"

"So, you've been writing ever since?"

"Nah, man, I took some time off—a whole bunch of years. I'm just gettin' back into it. Somethin' I just gotta do."

"That's interesting," says Alex, wondering about the timing. "Maybe one of these days we can talk a little more about graffiti." Taking another look at his watch—"Well, I really do have to go now. See you later this evening."

"That's fine, Professor A-wry—Alex. But just remember, the way I call the game tonight, it's how I'm feelin' it. Kinda like the flow in one of these pieces."

"That's understood." Stepping back, Alex surveys the area where Joey's new work will go. Then, he scans the rest of the imposing wall. "You know, I'd kind of like to come back sometime. That is, to watch you put up your design. Would you mind?"

"Not at all, I'd be honored, man. Try me in a coupla days—gotta work on my sketch some more. Plan to go bigger than I thought."

"That's great," says Alex, carefully setting his roller down.

With mind pulsing, he thinks to himself—*There's something about this graffiti art—certainly a form of Contemporary Art. Would it qualify as Postmodern?* Heading for his car, he starts to shake out his right hand and arm. And then it hits him. *Dammit to hell,* he silently curses. *That Joey—I bet he knew this would happen. My arm is all messed up—my shooting arm. I'm going to be totally useless tonight.*

* * *

From memory

Alex—

It was back at *The Farm*, that's where we met. In the dorms—Gavilan House in Florence Moore. I was sitting in the dining area—good light, you know. It was fall quarter, junior year. Thought I'd stretch myself a little and take a class in architectural design. The first day, there were nothing but guys, and some of them had slide rules hanging from their belts. Real off-putting, and the instructor seemed kind of inarticulate. Visual thinker, I guess. But the assignments were great—a lot of fun.

Anyway, I was sitting there in the dining area with all my stuff laid out. I had balsa wood, wire, dental floss, contact cement, and a huge assortment of balloons. The challenge was to design and build the lightest possible tripod that could support a six-pack of beverages six inches off the ground.

I was really struggling. I blew up one balloon after another. The problem was—they didn't seem uniform in length. I'd put together a triangular base made of wire—planned to attach a balloon to each of the corners and have them meet at the top to form a pyramid. But since the balloons didn't match, I kept on blowing until three tables were completely covered. The worst part was that dinner would be starting in half an hour. Already, a couple guys had filed past on their way to go *hash*.

I was sorting through the balloons, but they all kept scattering. Just as I lunged to one side, I heard a funny voice asking if I needed some help. Funny, I say, because the voice sounded sweet and a little husky at the same time. This girl was standing over the table in front of me—she looked tall. And without waiting for an answer she started collecting the fallen balloons.

I said something like, "Thanks, I'm part of tonight's floor show."

She said, "Oh, so you're an entertainer. What are you—some kind of clown?"

"Yeah—" I said, "after this, I plan to continue my graduate studies in clown school."

The girl wished me good luck on my career choice—asked me, "Do you plan to drink that whole six-pack of beer yourself?"

So, she was nice. It's not like I hadn't noticed her before. Long, dark brown hair, pretty hazel eyes—kind of lanky. She told me she'd transferred from a school in Pennsylvania, a sophomore business major. We probably exchanged names then—told me her name was Lisa. I explained the project—even shared the secret feature I planned for later. Just like that, she found three balloons that were perfect matches. Then she helped me tie the balloons to the base. Jostling the top ends to form the apex, one of them suddenly popped. I must have looked stunned.

She said, "You've got to find stronger materials than these."

I muttered something about just having run out of condoms.

"Oh," she said, "so you're some kind of bad boy, are you?"

I didn't have time to figure out if she was serious or not.

Eventually, I found a replacement balloon. With Lisa bunching the top ends together, I took the six-pack of Heineken and carefully set it atop the apex. As the weight registered, the legs of the tripod started bowing out—completely unstable. I was so frustrated, and students were starting to pass by on their way to the cafeteria. I got a lot of laughter and comments like, *When's the party start?* and, *Too many balloons and not enough beer!*

Lisa could tell I was pretty upset—embarrassed, really.

I remember her voice going soft—she said something like, "Why don't you take some of your dental floss and make a sling for the beer—then hang it from the apex? The loop could also keep the balloons together."

I thanked her for what turned out to be a great idea. Lisa deflected credit, said it was just a refinement of my basic design.

"Besides—" she said, "you're the really creative one. When you finally get these balloons filled with helium, I'd pay to be there at the weigh in. I'd love to see their faces when your little project goes floating off the scale."

4

Porter College, office of Professor Arai

With a hint of a shrug, Whitney B. Willis takes a seat. Lamp light brings out the peach in her skin. Subtly-shaped Asian eyes glow green-gold over an unhappy mouth. Tucking her head between her shoulders, she examines the office. Somehow, it feels more claustrophobic than her rental unit downtown.

With a bob of his head, Professor Arai extends a welcome. A gentle smile displays both restraint and an eagerness to connect. As usual, the professor wears a dress shirt and tie.

"I appreciate you coming in for office hours, Ms. Willis."

Nodding in return, Whitney squirms inside her oversized sweatshirt.

"So," continues the professor, "are you from this area, or did you have to move in order to discover paradise?"

Not smiling. "I'm from Torrance, south of L.A."

"And I believe this is your junior year. How've things been going for you?"

"Fine—" Whitney watches the professor's eyes.

"Well, I just asked you to come in for a little chat. Are you taking this course as a part of your major?"

Raking a hand through her wayward hair—"I'm a painting major. I need your class to get into senior studio next year."

"Interesting relationship—studio art and art history. Many young artists think it best if *never the twain shall meet*. I personally like to engage artists—like to show how art history can be of help in their development."

"Yeah—yes. Well, I really don't know about all that."

Pausing, the professor's brows push creases into his forehead. Whitney's brows immediately mirror a response.

"I'm sure you're aware—you'll need a 'B' average in your elective classes."

"I'm—going to get a 'B' in your class, aren't I?"

"Well, do you recall what I said at the beginning of the term?"

"You said for an 'A' we needed to produce some serious work, and you outlined the criteria. If not, we could write an extra credit paper on how the content was meaningful to us. That was for a 'B.'"

"So, you know exactly what to do. It's just that, over the years, I've made it a practice to invite students in—those who might be having issues with the class. I want to know if there's something not right with the material or the presentation. I just want to make sure I'm attentive to the needs of my students."

"Well, you're not doing anything wrong—so don't worry." Glancing up at the perforated ceiling tiles, "Like—what makes you think I'm not into your class?"

With a concerned gaze—"I had an issue regarding your main Internet source for the last paper, the one on Surrealism. You were mostly appropriate in paraphrasing things, but a couple of pages caught my attention. For starters, the language seemed to shift."

"I thought the ideas in that source were kind of different to begin with. I might have repeated a phrase or two. That source was a little on the obscure side."

"I know," says Professor Arai sternly. "I know it was obscure—I was the one who wrote it."

Whitney's mouth flies open. "Seriously?" Her startled eyes flash bright in a look of horror.

"It was one of my first publications as a grad student. Quite an honor at the time, but not exactly the pinnacle of my scholarly work."

"I am SO sorry. I can't believe it. I should have paid more attention. Sloppy job, but— Oh-My-God...."

"As you know, Ms. Willis, representing another person's work as your own is considered plagiarism. Your appropriation could be viewed as academic misconduct."

"But I didn't mean to steal your words, like—*rip you off*. I was in a big hurry. It felt more like *borrowing*."

"Violating the Code of Student Conduct can lead to serious consequences."

"But it was only a couple paragraphs, max."

"How about a total of one full page?"

"Really? It's hard to remember. I must have been stressed!"

"Well, pursuing a matter like this is a bit of a judgement call...."

"But I've never done anything like this before. And I swear, I'll never, ever, do it again. I can't blow my parents' money like that—and everything else they've done for me."

Alex studies Whitney's eyes. "For some reason," he says, "I find myself believing you. How about this? If you agree to rewrite the paper, I'll let you off with a letter of warning this time."

"Thank you—thank you SO much!" Shoulders starting to loosen, Whitney shakes out her hands. "It's really amazing," she says. "I guess you remember everything you write."

With a wan smile—"Just put it this way—never use the phrase, 'the schizophrenic chic of Max Ernst' again."

"I promise," says Whitney, grimacing.

"Okay, so enough about my forgettable paper and the history of Modern Art. Why don't you tell me something about your painting."

Bowing her head, Whitney's hair tumbles forward—hides one half of the blush she feels in her face. "I actually do a lot of things, a lot of things with my painting."

"So, who have been some of your chief influences?"

"Well, I really don't have any obvious influences."

Coaxingly—"Who are some of your favorite painters?"

"The usual. Matisse, Van Gogh, Picasso."

Leaning forward—"And, what do you like most about those painters?"

"Well, I mean there's a lot to like about them. But really—I keep my own work separate from everyone else's."

Perplexed, but not exactly surprised—"Wouldn't it help to know what's gone before you?"

Whitney's cheeks flare hot again, but this time not because of embarrassment. She's heard this line of questioning before. "Look Professor Arai, I want to be respectful and all. But to tell you the truth, I believe the only thing that counts is what's going on inside *me* at the moment I paint."

"It sounds like you could claim the Abstract Expressionists as your artistic parents. That is—I assume you've been attending all the lectures."

Volume rising, "I really don't think I have parents—that is, I don't have *artistic* ones." Sitting straighter—"So what if Jackson Pollock drips paint all over the floor? That's his creative moment—not mine. What happened fifty years ago— that's half a century—doesn't affect me."

"So, you don't really care—"

"It's irrelevant to me what happened back then. It's not even interesting."

"You think you create in a vacuum?"

"I *am* in a vacuum when I create.

"But the rich history of your medium...."

"I don't need all that history. All that counts is right now. Look, I'm sorry, but it's all a dead thing to me. I *do* art—I don't study it."

The professor inhales, exhales slowly. "I apologize for upsetting you. Of course, you're right. For the artist, it's truly *your* vision that counts."

Whitney stands, squeezes past the desk and steps to the door. "I know I'm way out of line saying all this stuff to you— but it's what I believe. Sorry to mess up your afternoon."

When the door shuts, Alex pushes his chair back, striking the bookcase. So, there it is again, that old saw—"Those who can, do. Those who can't, teach."

And all this from some little *hapa* girl. *I wonder what the Asian part of her is,* he muses. Alex stares at the stack of books on his desk. Certainly not the first time he's heard such uppity words from a snot-nosed, student painter. So what does she plan to do with her lofty truth, her creative moments? Paint her little heart out—paint her way to fortune and fame? But with this generation, the so-called millennials, there's no such thing as planning. Leaning forward, he reaches for a recent MOMA catalogue. Muttering to himself—"I'm just surprised her cell didn't go off."

* * *

The house on Escalona Drive

From the Westside cliffs overlooking the bay, a shelf of land extends inward. After some two miles of quiet neighborhood, the remnants of a second set of cliffs arise—a geological formation much older than the first. Once there, the traveler discovers rolling hills, wide swatches of grassy fields, and campus architecture nestled in a redwood forest. Running just below the long ridge, Escalona Drive features an eclectic collection of fine houses.

Alex makes an urgent call to Lisa's cell phone. "Leese? I just got home and checked out the new retaining wall. You won't believe it—the damn thing's off line by nearly a foot."

"Well," says Lisa, cautiously, "does it really make that much of a difference? I mean, the wall's over twenty feet long, isn't it? Twelve inches over twenty feet?"

"Yeah, but you can really tell because it's not completely parallel to the deck."

"Is it that obvious?"

"It is to me," he snaps. "Anyone can see it, if they just look."

"Even if they do, no one will really care."

"But *I'll* know it's wrong—"

"I suppose you can have them do it all over again. It's cinder block—labor intensive. It'll probably more than double the cost."

"Exactly. I guess the joke's on me—this mistake is literally set in concrete."

"Oh, Hon, go easy on yourself. This kind of stuff happens with contractors. It's happened to us before."

"But I feel bad. I was supposed to be on top of it. And this time we're both paying for the project. I'm sorry."

"Don't be. I'll be home in another hour. You can show me how it looks when I get there."

Alex revisits the back deck, glowers at the uneven gap between redwood planks and the new retaining wall. *How did I let this happen? I signed off on the plans, was here last week when the crew got started....* Four to six feet tall, extending across the back of the yard—the structure reinforces the hillside rising up to High Street. Spring rains had soaked the heavily wooded terrain and caused a slide—several elm and madrone now threatening to crush the deck. Alex continues to ream himself. The times in his life when he's admitted to a mistake, he always managed to pay twice. First, for the impact of the actual error, and second, for the endless rounds of self-castigation.

Turning his back to the project, he slumps into a patio chair—studies the dark redwood siding of the house he and Lisa bought some twenty years before. Having lived together, they decided to take another step in the level of their commitment. Lisa might have preferred marriage, but Alex wasn't quite ready—thought buying a house would be a nice preliminary move, a safer bet.

Of an otherwise perfect house, he had only one major misgiving. A broad, overbearing live oak stood directly in front of the bank of living room windows. The stately old tree obliterated the view from the main seating area. And because of its southern placement, it always managed to block the sun's arc, casting shadows into the room. Lisa opined that the tree be cut down, but as much as he resented it, Alex couldn't bear the thought of destroying the oak. The solution? He decided to build upward, adding a third story perch that would clear the top of the tree. Lisa thought it was a huge waste of money, so Alex paid for it himself.

Upon its completion, they both enjoyed entertaining in the spacious, airy loft. In one corner of the room, behind a tall *shoji* screen, Alex set up a drafting table where he kept his art supplies. When sufficiently moved, he let himself draw—even though he never let his guests scrutinize or critique the results.

In order to set things right with the imperfect wall, Alex must now create a new concept—a fresh way of viewing it.

After a week of troubled sleep, he arrives at an idea. Behind the cinder block, atop the compacted dirt, he will specify a raised platform to be built at one end. From there, seated guests will have a better look at the small creek bordering the property. The width that the pad encroaches on the main deck will provide just enough space for an additional chair. Now, the offline wall makes sense—is conceptually correct. Alex feels both satisfied and relieved—is more than happy to use his own funds to finance the extra work.

* * *

Office of Professor Arai

"Once again, I apologize, Ms. Willis—or Whitney, as you prefer. I realize I was pushing you too far last time. You *are* the artist, without whom there would be no art."

"Thanks," she says, while reaching into her backpack. "I felt kind of bad, too. I brought you back my paper. As you can see, I fixed it up."

"Oh, a bit more paraphrasing?"

"Yeah, some. Mostly, I just gave you credit for what I'm now calling 'quotes.'"

Wincing—"Well, thank you for the citations, I guess. Certainly, it was the right thing to do."

Whitney unwraps a moderately-sized canvas, then pauses. "You know—I'm really not sure why I'm doing this. Of course, you asked—"

"I truly appreciate this chance to see some of your work."

"Okay, well—I hope you're ready."

Taking the painting up in two hands, Whitney places it on the professor's desk—slides it over to her right. Alex immediately reacts to the strong swatches of bright magenta slashing across what looks like a young woman's face.

"This one's titled, *Rachel*—an obvious alias," Whitney smirks.

"Oh wow," says Alex, unable to stifle his gut reaction.

Somehow this image circumvents the pure critic in him. Then, a rush of thoughts escapes his mouth.

"On a spruce green ground, you've painted a highly nu- anced portrait. You use mostly ochres and oranges—hot col- ors. But the face is sensitively rendered—look at her eyes, her lips. Your level of skill is quite high. You must have taken many years of painting classes."

"Not really."

"That's amazing. But you've painted for a long time—"

"That's true."

"Now, over this exquisite face, your magenta strokes powerfully cover—actually attack the image—almost brutalize her face. I feel the energy of some incredible what? Anger, I'm afraid."

"Well, don't be afraid. She deserved it."

"This is someone you know, someone more than just a model."

"You could say so."

"Some history behind this image?"

"Definitely."

"It's an interesting process you have here. Formally, you do a wonderful job in a realistic style—even as you utilize a Fauvist palette."

"Please, Dr. Arai. If you could hold off on the references—"

"I'm sorry." Alex leans closer to the canvas. "After painting the face, displaying a high degree of skill, you basically *vandalize* the image. And while doing so—you erase the record of your own considerable talent."

Starting to fidget—"Skill is overrated," Whitney asserts. "There's a lot of artists out there who can't even draw. These days, you don't have to attend an academy before claiming your style."

"Sad, but true. But I, for one, believe skill should be a part of any evaluation of art. Take Picasso," he says—in spite of Whitney's request. "He was a great draftsman, as skilled as any previous master in his ability to faithfully render nature. When I view *Les Desmoiselles d'Avignon*, or his later Cubist masterpieces, I always appreciate the skill behind his revolutionary images."

"You mean," asks Whitney, an edge to her voice, "if you take two Cubist paintings—one by Picasso and the other by an artist who can't really draw—you would seriously judge the Picasso as better?"

"Why, yes."

"Even if they looked essentially the same?"

"Yes, and furthermore, it's not as easy as you might think. In fact, it's virtually impossible to duplicate a Picasso, Cubist or otherwise."

"I really don't get it. It's just the same picture, you know? But of course, you're the art historian." Seizing her painting, Whitney places it squarely on her lap. "You and the critics, the agents, gallery owners, museum curators—you've got all the power to decide who makes it big and who doesn't in the so-called 'art world.' That's always been the case—kind of ironic. We're the ones who create the art—you're the guys who control it."

"Well, putting the issue of skill aside, that's a whole other topic." Collecting himself—"Whitney, your work is very powerful. I obviously get a lot out of it—the experience of it. Forget for a moment I'm an art historian. I really like your painting."

"Thanks—" Whitney eases *Rachel* onto the floor and starts to wrap her up. "You know—Mark Rothko didn't think much of the artist's skill level either. He might have been great with the big brushes, but apparently he was not much of a draftsman."

"So, you did read the chapters from Rothko's *The Artist's Reality.*"

Standing up to leave—"I admit, I did. And to think how hard his son worked to get that manuscript printed."

"That's a moving tale in itself, the family and all—especially after his tragic demise."

"And I was there when you talked about Rothko—showed us his paintings. Actually, I thought your lecture was kind of interesting."

5

Bill's Wheels

Joey looks up from the trunk of his car—"Say man, your shooting was crap the other night."

"Yeah, I know," says Alex.

"Something like 'oh' for what?"

"I managed to make a layup—didn't you notice?"

"Oh yeah, but your free throws—"

"My arm was sore. Remember, I was helping you buff the wall earlier that day."

"Oh, right. Well—here we are again." Joey examines Alex's gray sweats and dilapidated running shoes. "Don't worry about messin' your clothes—I'll be handlin' the paint today."

Alex takes a peek into the crowded trunk—a boom box and two large crates of spray cans. Atop a duffle bag lies a black sketchbook, or album of some kind.

"It's my piece book," says Joey, noticing Alex's interest. "Wanna see the insides?" Joey opens to the beginning pages. "Here's some work I done in the late '80s. Wished I'd taken more pictures back then—especially the stuff from *Psycho City* and all. Of course, none of them pieces are around today."

Alex watches as Joey flips through the pages explaining the location of each work. "So," he asks, "you call these 'pieces'?"

"Yeah, that's what we call 'em—short for *masterpieces*. Mostly, there's three kinds of graffiti cats can do. There's the basic *tag*, when you want to get your name up fast. You know, the one color—quick. That's the kind of graffiti people have the most trouble with. But you know, it's not just gettin' your name up all over town—it's the style that counts." Pointing—"The second type of graffiti we call a *throw-up*. It's meant to go up fast too, but in two dimensions. Usually only a couple colors. Here, I put up some simple *bubble letters*—a black outline with a white fill-in. But it's the pieces that take the most skill, if you catch my drift. They got all kinds of colors, designs, and effects. Characters, too."

Alex's eyes pursue each image as Joey quickly flips through the pages. Incredible, complex, beautiful creations strobe past.

"Slow down a little," he implores. "I see the letters—but they're so stylized, I can't always make them out."

"Cats are always rockin' new directions. It's not about people readin' it, man. It's all about the respect we get from other writers."

"So, Joey—what name do you use?"

"My name is *DRAZ*—sounds like what you do with a pencil, 'cept I use a *Z*. My pop was Croatian, you know. When he seen me play basketball as a kid, he said I was good enough to be the next Drazen Petrovic. Big NBA star—big world star. So he called me *Draz*. I liked it 'cause the letters are good to work with. You know, some letters just suck."

"Is that what you're going to put up here?"

"Yeah, man—check out this page."

"Say, you've got some interesting depth going on. It's kind of like—your name is disappearing into the wall."

"Glad you see it." Joey puts his book to the side, then removes his crates. He shows Alex a plastic bag with various nozzle tips for different effects. "I took a lot of years off from writing. Thought I retired—thought I was gettin' too old. Then I started seein' some crazy-ass shit out there. The new styles. I thought, *I got to get back into this*. It was all about the new paint—the new Euro paint."

Alex examines the various choices. "So—what's the difference?"

Joey displays a spray can with the number *94* on the label. "With the new stuff, everything comes out better—colors, effects. The possibilities are endless, man. The paint covers over real good—dries just like that. The Montana 94 is a flat paint, so there's no glare when you take pictures. It's also got lower pressure, so you can get finer detail." Joey hands Alex the can. "If you wanna catch a *Hard Core*, it's semi-gloss and comes out a little faster. Then you got your *Nitro*, which is really gonna shoot out. That's great for *bombing*—when you're gettin' up fast, when you're taggin' as many places as possible."

Alex hands the spray can back to Joey. "When did they come out with paint like this?"

"Somewhere around the mid-'90s. Hard to get at first. Them Euros knew that writers was their biggest market, so they asked the right questions—made paints that was better and easier to use. Not like that old Krylon shit—Rust-Oleum. Those guys never wanted to admit that graffiti cats was usin' their stuff. So now they're hurtin' man."

Joey pulls his boom box from the trunk, dials up some Ice T. "Hey—I'm on the comeback trail. I'm gettin' back up again, startin' right here at Bill's."

Alex watches as Joey approaches the fearsome *blank canvas* of the wall—a dark gray rectangle, twelve feet high and twenty feet across. It's a heroic image for him—a man facing that moment of artistic truth. He almost expects to hear something profound.

Instead, with piece book in one hand, a can of spray paint in the other, Joey announces—"This is just the cheap shit, man—just for outlinin'."

As the can rattles to life, he extends his hand off to the side—releases a fine mist of white paint with a soft *pssst*. Now he stations himself within an arm's length of the wall—moves his head back and forth for orientation. Starting in the middle, he makes several clockwise sweeping movements for practice. With his whole body, he defines a semi-circle from the top of his head to mid-thigh. In one graceful motion, he retraces the path—this time spraying the entire arc of the curve. Next, he completes the rest of the circle with a confident whirl to the left.

From this focal point, he combines longer strokes with short bursts. If unhappy with a line, he simply goes over it with another. Having seen the sketch, Alex identifies the head of a comet shaped like a blazing basketball. Exploding through a cosmic hoop, sinewy figures comprising *DRAZ* form the tail.

For over an hour, it goes like this—Joey consumed by an elaborate dance between self and wall. Sometimes the movements are bold—grand. Sometimes, they're small, gentle—intimate. He leans in close then pulls back, but never loses contact with his companion surface.

Alex knows he's in the presence of something remarkable—imagines the great painted cave walls of France and northern Spain. What a reenactment of a rite so primal, so human. All the mysterious power of the man-made image—that natural instinct to create art. He feels truly blessed to watch Joey perform. And all the magic of those distant, prehistoric times comes clear to Alex, strikes him hard, makes him want to cry.

And so, for the next few days, the rhythm continues. Alex follows the flow of creation. When Joey finishes, he goes to his trunk to grab a soda. Upon return, he exalts to the music. Alex, himself, feels exhausted. He's completely drained, and he can't even explain why.

Joey's piece proves spectacular. For once, Alex doesn't try to articulate his thoughts and feelings about art. In a day or two, he'll write down his impressions while sitting alone at his computer. In the meantime, he congratulates Joey, congratulates the artist—the grown man. Alex congratulates the young basketball player his father once called *Draz*.

* * *

The house on Escalona Drive

It's just past noon and Alex scrambles to his loft—enters the small space hidden behind the tall *shoji* screen. Whenever he does this, he feels like a young child. Even back in the early days, he had a special place to draw. Of course, he never had a drafting table like this—birds-eye maple—its canted surface reminiscent of a Cezanne tabletop. Ever helpful, his mother used to cut him sheets of butcher paper from a large roll in the corner of his room. The shallow space between his face and desktop constantly swirled with the smells of crayons, markers—graphite pencils.

Alex eases into a slim leather chair—perfectly pliant for whatever his mood. Hands folded, he indulges himself in the history of his personal art. For starters, it would have been nice if his father had appreciated his childhood creations. Something about Alex's offerings seemed so coarse and *uninspired* to Kazuo Arai. They lacked the symbolism and precocious sensibility that characterized his own early works.

Kaz had a separate studio behind the house in San Jose. A high school art teacher, he spent most of his free hours perfecting his own designs. The only family allowed in his space were his wife, Sumi, and Alex's older brother, Henry. Kaz had named his boys after famous Modern sculptors— Henry for the Englishman, Sir Henry Moore, and Alex for the American, Alexander Calder. A future engineer, Henry was always welcome to visit—could discuss matters of structure and fabrication. In contrast, Alex was banished from Kaz's studio, ever since he *broke in* one day at the age of five and added his own ideas to a draft of his father's latest commission proposal.

Alex extracts a heavy portfolio from a set of drawers beside his table. Opening his cache of artwork always feels a bit precarious. Collected over the years, the hefty contents seem to waffle in his hands. It's as if the individual works were trying to escape—trying to get back into the light in which they were created.

First up—a drawing of his boyhood bicycle. Next, a charcoal drawing of the family's beloved chow. It's still a surprise how well the thick black coat reveals itself in all its glorious texture. Two drawings later, he liberates a pastel study of his old backyard. With his father's studio as a hazy backdrop, his mother's roses glow red and yellow, right beside her prized Japanese maple tree.

For a half an hour, it goes like this—discoveries— rediscoveries. Alex finally reaches a layer of portfolio that contains the bulk of his caricatures. Rendered in various *New*

Yorker styles, the drawings have a quick and easy quality about them. He recalls how much diligent practice it took to capture that effortless look. Of course, not that his father ever appreciated the work—*cartoonish* work, of all things. And among the clever renditions of former teachers, coaches, family members—the face of Kazuo Arai figures prominently. Alex shakes his head at the deliberate distortions, the exaggeration of his father's already prominent features. Here he is—the renowned sculptor and maker of memorials—Elvis-like pompadour, beetle-browed, busy mustache—a veritable stick-figured, mock-up of a man. So many of these caricatures feel mean-spirited. Surfacing now—a final suite of drawings, one involving a select group of faculty members Alex had clashed with over the years. An instructor here, a fellow professor there—certainly a department chair or two.

Although reassured by all he's done, Alex has decided to take his art into fresh territory. He wants to change directions, determine a new course—reclaim his own artistic freedom. Pondering all the possibilities, he craves a way to make his art more *real*. Whether it's altering his satirical portraits, or finding a method to create art *in the moment*, he can't tell. Whichever way he decides, all he knows is that the work will involve the act of drawing. Alex can't help but follow his own hand and the unique line with which he was born—even as he continues sitting in his loft, hiding.

* * *

From memory

Lisa—

It was that very first quarter at school. The first time I'd been so far away from my family. Hard to leave home with Mom, Dad, sibs, and all.

But it wasn't a bed of roses either. For quite some time, my parents would fight over how much longer their money would last. It all had to do with Grandpa Keller and the family hardware business. Ended up selling the stores to a big chain. So much money, and Dad—the last of three sons—certainly got his. Right away, he stopped working—jumped at the chance to put all his ideas and weird inventions into reality. Problem was, nobody was interested in what he designed. So, as he pursued his own dreams, the family accounts kept dwindling. Mom was anxious, fearful—really laid into him. I was usually the peacekeeper—knew I needed to get away. Fortunately, after one year at Penn State, I got a scholarship to come out west.

When I met Alex, I was just getting used to the Stanford campus—so spread out. I got myself an old bike. And that Central Coast, California weather—those constantly blue, cloudless skies. That completely got to me. Even in the fall— nothing but beautiful, vacant weather, no change in the leaves— that oppressively blue sky.

And, yes, Alex was really cute—something always going on behind those bright eyes. The first time I noticed him was during a basketball game in front of Flo-Mo. I especially liked the way he moved on the court. After meeting, we found ourselves talking at mealtime. Alex couldn't believe I'd never seen the Pacific Ocean. But as I quickly found out—he'd never seen the Atlantic. So, a week or two before Halloween, he asked me if I wanted to go for a ride. I guess that was our first real date.

Alex scrounged up a car from a friend of his, and it was a total crack-up. It was an old Rambler station wagon with no paint—just the gray undercoat. I'd never been in a car that loud—spewed exhaust all over the place. The friend named the car *Rhoda—Rhoda Rambler*.

That Saturday, I think—we got off to a late start. We must have packed some sandwiches and chips and pop. Heading west from campus, I got to see up close those rolling yellow hills beside the linear accelerator. Alex drove us up a long, winding road through wooded foothills all the way up to Skyline Boulevard at the summit. Somewhere up there, we passed Alice's Restaurant before taking that beautiful plunge toward the ocean. It really was like that big drop you get after making it to the top of a roller coaster. Just like the "Leap the Dips" ride back in Altoona. Such a rush—the light just made everything sparkle.

Then in the distance, I spotted farmland—and just beyond, the bright blue edge of the Pacific. I must have let out a holler—

would have jumped up and down if I could have. Alex let Rhoda coast down that last straight stretch approaching the intersection with Highway 1. Crossing over, we parked in a sandy lot by a dune. I think I must have sprung out—climbed to the top of the dune and just stared. The sun was bright, and it was windy. It's hard to describe, but the big blue ocean looked so healthy. I think Alex came scrambling after me—said that Rhoda was overheating and needed a rest. So, we just spent the afternoon running around, splashing, sitting between grassy clumps on the dune—ate lunch.

Eventually, we realized it was getting late. Alex wanted to head up the coast to the pumpkin festival. But I wouldn't leave at first. I made him stay to watch the sunset—our first sunset. After that, it was a dicey ride until we sputtered into Half Moon Bay. Off to the side of the highway, fields of pumpkins stretched out as far as I could see. We parked the car, then started walking through the fields. Young families were all about. Little children scrambling around, excited to find just the perfect choices for jack-o'-lanterns. Little children, little ghostly faces floating in the dusk. I think, walking around—that was the first time I took Alex's hand.

After choosing our own pumpkin—not as easy a task as one might think—we climbed into Rhoda and probably finished off our chips. We headed back south on Highway 1 to San Gregorio. Of course, it was totally dark back at the beach. Yes, that's right—it was incredibly black, and the sky was huge and vast—just like the ocean. We must have stood a while on the dune. It was still windy and chilly, and he gently pulled me toward him. He opened his jacket and kind of enclosed me. Then I looked across at his face. I'm sure I appeared as vague as he did to me. But, it had been such a perfect day, and here it was—the start of a perfect night. And Alex went ahead and kissed me for the first time.

After a long while, it seems, we walked back to the car. He opened and closed my door for me. We sat—scooted across the bench seat and kissed some more. In the dark, we both agreed it would be best not to drive back to campus. No telling what Rhoda was capable of doing. So, we climbed into the back cargo area. I guess you could say I was all excited—more like a teen. I may have felt tingles and all, but mostly I was just feeling amazed. Alex, as always, was a gentleman. Sure we made out—made out *lightly* is the best way to put it. And then—after a little bit, I got so completely sleepy. I felt totally comfortable, totally safe. I went to sleep beside Alex—went to sleep for a long time."

* * *

Whitney's place, downtown Santa Cruz

Just west of Pacific Garden Mall lies a ten-block area designated the Downtown Neighborhood Historic District. Along tree-lined streets, landmark Victorians squeeze together with Craftsman-style bungalows and houses and cottages of more recent vintage. Many of the tiny front yards overflow with dazzling arrays of seasonal blooms. With housing at a premium, granny units and add-ons give the neighborhood an improvised, cluttered look.

Whitney lives in the second-floor addition to a formerly modest canary yellow cottage. To get to her perch, she climbs a long outdoor flight of stairs, charcoal in color, the same as the rest of the trim. Today she returns from a trip to the local farmers market. In her canvas bag, she totes a load of strictly organic shucking peas, carrots, and potatoes. As she eases into her crowded room, she hears her cell phone go off. Checking—*It's Mario.* Whitney decides to call back later.

After stashing the vegetables in the miniature fridge, she kicks off her sandals and pulls off her sweatshirt. She adjusts the hem of a cropped white T-shirt until it comes to rest a hand's width above her jeans. Afternoon light—warmer and somehow deeper than morning light. Without a doubt, the two opposing windows form the best features of her little studio. The *morning window* faces east. The *afternoon window*—west. She scrunches her toes in the paint-splattered tarp that covers the floor.

Whitney likes to view her space in four quadrants. A small bed takes up the entire *northwest* section of the room. A step east gains entry to a snug, closet-like half bath. Just below the morning window runs a counter top with sink. The multiuse surface supports a hot plate, microwave, fridge, and laptop. In the *southwest* quadrant stands a battered dresser of indeterminate wood. On top, stacks of sketchbooks obliterate a small mirror. The irregular space in the middle belongs to Whitney's art. A tall metal easel serves as the centerpiece, easily rotated for the best light. A red crash cart from her father's medical practice holds all her paints and brushes. Depending on her mood, finished canvases travel about—some larger works covering the meager wall space.

Geographic terms fit Whitney's room, even with its limited dimensions. After all, it's a matter of orientation. This is her world—this is where she creates. Somehow, with the help of friends, she's managed to incorporate everything she needs. Her parents would have loved to have done more, but their daughter wouldn't let them. It's enough that they pay for her education, pay for this place. At the top of her agenda is to find a way to earn some extra money.

Whitney hears her phone go off. This time, a text message—Mario again. He wants to confirm dinner plans for tonight. Smiling to herself, she tries to gauge the strengths of her various needs. Sprawling back on her bed, she rests in a pool of golden light. Taking stock of her body, she gazes across at the easel. With its russet hair and azure eyes, Mario's face beckons to her. It's times like these that truly confuse her, even though she enjoys the mixing and merging of whatever's tugging inside. Drawn to this beautiful young man, Whitney feels a quick stirring in the area where the warm light touches her. But she can't quite fathom—can't quite decide if it's the man, himself, she wants to engage—or the image she's creating in her room.

Media Theater, picnic table

"That's right, Carter. No more Rodin—no more Brancusi, Calder—no more Noguchi, for that matter. No more Modern Sculpture."

Carter can barely swallow—sets his sandwich down on his lap. "You've got to be kidding," he sputters.

"It wasn't exactly a surprise, really. The big area meeting—a huge discussion comparing the importance of Modern versus Postmodern, or Contemporary Art."

"But the study of Modern Western Art—that's a college staple. Your classes have always gotten good reviews."

"Well, it's not what's happening *now*," says Alex. "Modernism is becoming irrelevant. It's like—*I'm* becoming irrelevant. What used to be exciting and new is just as dead to a lot of these kids as all the previous eras. And the chair of the department follows suit. 'Give them something they can identify with, something that will *turn 'em on*. Teach them about street art, performance art—installations.'"

"Oh, screw the chair."

"Preaching to the choir. I've spent most of my academic life on an era that ended some fifty years ago. The one exception is my work in memorialization—the only subject that keeps me current."

"You've got three well-received books, for godsake."

"But as for teaching—kids don't want to spend their time studying the past." Shaking his head—"I've got this one student now, quite an excellent portrait painter. She couldn't care less about the historical context of her work."

"Well, that's bound to happen."

"I even caught her plagiarizing an old paper of mine."

"So, did you doc her grade—report her to the provost?"

"Not really."

"Of course, that's your prerogative—"

"She makes me feel like a stale academic. Maybe she's right. Or—at the very least, she's got a point. Checking out her work, I really like how she commits to the *now*—even as she just about destroys her painting. I spend a lot of my life thinking about the past. Maybe I should quit my obsession—commit to something more current, more immediate—more alive."

Carter resumes eating his sandwich. A couple bites later—"You're a thoughtful guy—that's just who you are. That's how you can write such deep stuff. About the only time I see you *go for it* is when we're playing hoops. And even then, you've got some kind of strategy in mind."

"I'm just losing my place, that's all—losing my position in academia. And all I can do is what I'm told—just put a new class together for the fall."

Carter scans the sweeping view in front of them—a hundred eighty degrees of fields, trees, ocean, and light. "Al—at the risk of sounding like a psychologist, a therapist—I always thought there was some kind of extra charge to your love of art. Your father really did well—benefited a lot from making memorials to the Japanese internment. He's got what—four major works around the country, honoring the sacrifices of your people during the war?"

"He's got five, actually, when you count the one in L.A. It's really his least known—kind of in the shadow of the *Go For Broke Memorial* nearby. That's the big one for the *Nisei* soldiers of my parents' generation. You know, my mother's cousin was killed in France trying to save the so-called 'lost battalion' from Texas."

"You see? That's all an important part of your ethnic narrative. Somebody has to tell that story, or it's gone forever."

"Yeah, I know. But the way my father does it is so counter to Japanese aesthetics—so *in your face,* if you will. There's a Japanese term for that style—*hade.* Roughly translated, it means *garish.* And that idea he got from me—that through his sculptures, he's encompassed the entire stylistic span of Modern Art—it makes me violently ill. I'm sorry I ever suggested that."

"I really get it, this stylistic war," says Carter. "It's just that—being a historian and critic, you've got the ability to contain and control him by how you define his work. So, congrats—you've managed to rise above your father in the pecking order. In the world of art, who's ultimately got the power—the one who creates the work, or the one who judges it?"

* * *

San Jose—Autumn, 1969
Phone call from Kazuo Arai to George Tsutakawa

"Thanks for sending me the catalogue from the exhibition. Strange idea, though—everything's printed on a stack of index cards. Of course, Lucy Lippard is a big art critic—put together an interesting show on the latest trends. But, golly George—it sounds really kooky to me. All this stuff about Land Art, Process Art, Performance Art—Conceptual Art. It's all just a reaction to Modernism. I don't really know about all this. What do you think?"

From the ninety-five 4x6 inch index cards of the catalogue:
Title of exhibition: "557,087"
> "...organized by lucy r. lippard for the contemporary art council of the seattle art museum at the seattle art museum pavilion from September 5 to October 5 1969..."

Foreword—
> "The Contemporary Art Council of the Seattle Art Museum is proud to present '557,087.' The title '557,087' is roughly the population of Seattle, and it is hoped that all of Seattle will be stimulated and involved with the

exhibition. Consistent with the theory that '557,087' will not deal with the conventional stylized art forms and frameworks is the fact that the show is not confined to the Pavilion at the Seattle Art Center, but extends to other locations in the Seattle Center and areas outside the city..."

Examples of submissions—

1. Joseph Kosuth

    "The work in this exhibition is related to four concerns:
    a. Concept as art [as idea]
    b. Information as art [as idea]
    c. Visual experience as art [as idea]
    d. Investigation of chance for non-compositional
       presentation"

2. Robert Barry

    "All the things I know but of which I am not at the moment thinking 1:36 PM; 15 June 1969."

3. William Bollinger

    "Large log [to be selected in Seattle], floating in a lake or bay."

4. Vito Acconci

    "A postcard sent, for the duration of the exhibition, at the same time each day, from the same mailbox in New York City, to the exhibition site; the postcard, when received placed on a calendar, on the date-rectangle of the day it is received."

5. Jeffrey Wall

    "Materials: turf/sod
    Dimensions: Unlimited
    Procedure: 1. Predetermined number of markers [75] are

distributed over area the size and shape of which is indeterminate & which is established in accordance with conditions of practical availability. 2. At each marker a 10-inch square of turf is removed. 3. All squares are collected, then all are replaced. Note: Step 3 is entirely indeterminate."

6. Rick Barthelme

    "Instead of making any art I bought this television set. The Rubens A6507W Space Command© 600 Remote Control" [complete description of model]

✳ ✳ ✳

Soquel hills

Three miles up a twisty road, Mario Patino lives in a converted storage shed on a five-acre parcel of former ranchland. On a Friday afternoon, he settles into his Corolla and heads down the gulch toward Highway 1. The *Courier* staff has asked him to write an article on the Watsonville Farmers Market. The last assignment he had with a *Spanish* flair was to cover a fundraiser for Mexican children orphaned by the recent drug wars.

Mario recalls that visit to the university—art students auctioning Mexican-themed works. Walking about, he spotted a pretty auburn-haired girl in a long white summer dress. The straps of her outfit hung loosely over nicely tanned shoulders. Judging from her build—*Could be a swimmer or one of those local surfers.*

After eyeing her paintings, he hesitantly approached. Wanting to impress—*Looks like something Diego Rivera would do.* Put off, the girl insisted she had no intent on mimicking the work of others. So much for a pick-up line. Somehow, he still managed to persuade the girl, Whitney B, to do an interview. For starters, he asked if she had any personal experience with drug war victims. *No*, she replied, but one photo of an orphaned child was all she needed to see.

Smiling at the memory, Mario follows the curve of Monterey Bay the thirteen miles to his old hometown. About once a week, he visits his mother and sibs in a crowded rental close by the river levee. Today, he parks near the city plaza, or *La Placita*, just a few blocks from the high school where he was once a baseball star. Back then, he was known as "Super Mario" to most. But he was also called "The Big Wopper," and "Stallion" by some old-time Italians, when they came by to watch one of their own.

Crossing the street toward a hot dog stand, Mario spots a utility box with the number *13* written in blue marker. He notes how gracefully someone has rendered the Sureño gang sign. A few steps over, the Watsonville Farmers Market begins, claiming two sides of the large rectangular plaza.

Mario hasn't been here since he was a kid—just before his father was killed in a car accident. Today, he decides to cruise the vendors to gain a kind of overview. What strikes him at first is the proliferation of color. Blazing red dahlias vie with purple eggplant, magenta onions, green and yellow chilies, lush strawberries, and baskets of buff-colored raspberries. Mario observes the meandering crowd—almost exclusively Hispanic. The pace of the patrons flows with a casual busyness that feels familiar.

Just past the entrance, a set of tables provides information on free street art classes. From the Pajaro Valley Art Museum, a pretty Latina displays stickers, airbrush, and stencil designs. She courts the attention of two adolescent boys in T-shirts and oversized Dickey pants.

As Mario continues his trek, the colorful signage beckons him on. He's struck by the fluid transition from English signs to Spanish.

Over to his right—
White letters on a blue background:
Fruit Factory
Ask For Organic
Fresh Picked Daily Since 1991

After buying a chewy cinnamon-covered churro—
Black letters on a yellow sign:
Order here/Ordenar aqui

Farther along, a woman stands behind a portable grill—
    Red letters on a yellow sign:
        Ricos Huaraches, of tinga/Sopes
        Quesadillas of chicken, Posole Verde and more.

Nearing the end of the market, he finds an old man in a cowboy hat, playing Mexican music with his blonde guitar. Peering into the plaza's center, Mario finds the Spanish signs reverting back to English.

    A bronze bust of George Washington:
        Father of his country. First in war, first in peace...

    Black letters on a yellow background:
        Earthquake warning
        This is an unreinforced masonry building

    Red letters on a white background:
        Hold it! Unauthorized or illegally parked vehicles
        will be towed away immediately at owner's expense.

As Mario begins a second tour of the market, his focus has clearly broadened. He studies the people of La Placita—the mostly Spanish speakers, some documented, others not. He looks for any furtive behavior, the presence of vigilance or worry. Beyond his assignment, he decides to gather their stories—explore the impact of their legal status. Here in the Watsonville Farmers Market, he will compare the lives of U.S. citizens with those of *illegal aliens.* If necessary, Mario will use his best Spanish to ask how they manage, how they all fare in the greater marketplace that is America.

* * *

Torrance, California, 1995

Shauna Gibson moved from the East Coast to Southern California when her daughter, Whitney, was four years old. Shauna found work as a receptionist in the family medical practice of Dr.

Charles Willis. Soon enough, she became notorious for her wild red hair and quirkiness. The latter evolved into an alarming unpredictability and even a bent toward paranoia.

One day, she cornered Evelyn, the doctor's Japanese American wife. Saying her former husband was Japanese, Shauna insisted that Evelyn provide some special insight into the man's mind. Shauna feared that her ex would one day track her down—kill her and abduct Whitney. It was Shauna's *scent* that gave her away, she said—a kind of olfactory beacon that inevitably revealed her location to him. Despite obsessive washing, she could never totally remove that provocative extension of herself. Because of this problem, she and her daughter were forced into frequent moves.

On another occasion, a nurse overheard a stricken Shauna talking to herself about how she'd rescued Whitney from a pond near New Haven, Connecticut. Something about how the pond was a good place to bathe until it was contaminated by the girl's father. Shauna continued to decompensate until the staff called Child Protective Services. Before anyone could arrive for an evaluation, she inexplicably vanished. She left behind a note asking the childless doctor and wife to care for Whitney and to provide her the kind of life she could not. Upon leaving, Shauna managed to abscond with two dozen bottles of the surgical prep soap, Phisohex.

Chuck and Evie Willis gladly took in the young girl, and in time—Whitney was legally theirs. From the start, the new parents realized the importance of art to their daughter. When left to herself, she drew constantly—drew compulsively. The activity of her hands contrasted sharply with the firm and silent set of her mouth. Drawing was Whitney's language of choice. Nearly mute, she channeled herself onto reams of paper. Each time she finished a sketchbook, she simply placed it atop a pile of all her previous work. In a dark closet stood layer upon layer of drawings, chronologically stacked—a kind of archeological dig in the waiting.

* * *

UCSC campus

The Sessions' Prius shimmers the color of light green glass. On this crisp Saturday morning, Alex and Lisa join Carter and Nita on an off-duty trip to campus. The university's end-of-year Print Sale enjoys a fine reputation. Art lovers looking for fresh talent know this show to be a gem.

Fortunately for all, the dark bell jar of recent rain has lifted. This is a day for big inhalations, for breathing freely. Upon parking, Alex's group ascends a meandering rise. Atop a knoll, the Baskin Visual Art Center forms an angular "C" as it wraps about a tree-studded, grassy courtyard. Joining a pool of recent arrivals, the group funnels through an open door to the right. Inside—the initial print room teems with animated viewers. Stacks of prints cover the central tables with more work lining the walls. At times, only Carter stands tall enough to see over the heads of fellow patrons. Motioning to Lisa, Nita departs for the adjoining studio.

After peeking at several offerings, Alex follows the women's lead. The adjacent room, much larger than the first, pulses with a scintillating light from a raised bank of north-facing windows. Immediately, he feels a lifting of spirits. The space provides a stunning vessel of luminescence. Everything looks good—every-*one* looks good. Probably two-thirds of the viewers are college students, classmates of the youthful printmakers.

Drawn to provocative, quirky imagery, he pauses at an etching whose abstract lines coalesce at nodal points to form faces. As he studies the print, he detects the subtle, yet *physical* impact of a conversation occurring nearby. As the voices disentangle, he strains for recognition. Something a little caustic in the tone—something sardonic about the laugh.

He startles to find his student, Whitney B, standing right behind him. With her back turned, he's about eye level to the top of her red tresses. She's talking to someone named Julie, a friend of hers—the maker of the print he finds so fascinating. Stepping away, he attempts to slip past a fellow patron—wonders what he's trying to avoid.

Turning—Alex pauses. Fighting his bent for rumination, he moves decisively back in Whitney's direction. At her friend's table, all the people have shifted. Looking about, he struggles with sightlines. All he perceives is a maze of human walls. Just then—

"Hi Professor Arai."

Full-facial—Whitney appears too close for comfort. That same light—*this* same light makes all her features glow. "So, what are you doing here?" she asks. "This is sort of *my* territory."

Alex takes a step backward. The vertical equivalent to peripheral vision captures a pink halter top and hip-hugging jeans that lead to *wherever*. Recovering—"It's something I attend yearly. My partner—my partner and friends. We always find things we like."

"I think that's great. My girlfriend, Julie, is part of the show. She does some really interesting stuff. Have you checked these out?"

"Yes, I have."

"But before you give me the historical rundown, you can see right here—she's almost sold out."

Happy for her friend's success, Whitney appears expansive—giddy, even.

From directly behind, Alex hears another familiar voice. "Al," says Carter, "we're going to meet up with the gals in half an hour...." Voice trailing, he discovers Julie's print with the strange faces emerging from a matrix of complex lines.

"Let me do the introductions," says Alex. "Carter—this is one of my students, Whitney B. She's quite an interesting painter. Whitney—this is my friend Carter—Professor Sessions."

After exchanging pleasantries, Carter decides to buy Julie's print. Looking even happier, Whitney thanks him for his patronage.

"Your friend has really good taste, Professor. I bet he'd like some of my *twisted* paintings, too."

Carter shrugs, then turns to Alex. "So—is this the young lady you were telling me about—the one with the rather unusual treatment of portraits?"

"Well, yes—"

"Oh," interjects Whitney, "did he tell you that?" Looking pleased—"If you want, I can show you one of my canvases. It's over at the figure painting studio around the corner."

"I suppose—" says Alex.

"We have the time," says Carter.

After making the purchase, the two men follow Whitney outside. The trio circles behind the complex to a separate building. Once inside, it's like magically discovering a small, hidden harbor of sorts. A dozen tall, mast-like easels jut through the air at various angles—their square canvases raised like sails. All float about a small wooden barge, upon which rests a single chair draped in blue gauze. Whitney explains that the platform is where the models pose. Eyes wandering, the visitors drift slowly out onto the concrete, paint-speckled floors.

Calling to her guests, Whitney leads them to her own station. There, they find a large canvas with the painting of a middle-aged woman sitting on a chair. Unlike the other studies, the woman in her version has wild red hair.

Alex deems it remarkable—the fine, realistic detail in her treatment of the subject. Carter nods in agreement.

"Are you pretty close to finishing?" he asks.

"Not yet," replies Whitney.

Knowing her process, Alex asks—"What do you plan to do with it?"

"You mean what do I plan to do with *her?*"

Whitney shifts to the side of her easel. As she reaches up to adjust the canvas, the hem of her pink halter rises. Alex observes some kind of marking, or partial *tattoo*—just below the crest of her left hip. Distracted, he doesn't register her plans to deform the image on her canvas. However, Carter does.

"That's pretty heavy," he says. "I kind of wonder what all that means."

Whitney continues without missing a beat. "So, I hope you all enjoyed the tour."

After a round of appreciation, they head in the direction of the door. With a lilt to her step, she walks side-by-side with Alex.

"Professor Arai, I really do get it—how good it feels to be the expert, even if it's about my own paintings. I'd like you to know that I really understand—why you like to teach so much."

"Thank you," he replies.

"Well," says Whitney, as they approach the threshold of the door—"I had a nice time, too."

Media Theater

*A*lex always feels sad before delivering the final lecture of the year. Quite a number of those young faces have names attached, as well as stories he's had the privilege of hearing. And he's pleased this morning that the size of his audience is about the same as it was at the start of the quarter.

Turning to his audience, he begins with a joke—

"How many artists does it take to use a urinal?" A few titters follow.

"The answer? Just one, if he happens to be part of the Western canon." Smiling at his student's faces— "Now, you might ask—why did he start off with a tiny bit of humor? After all, this morning's lecture is titled, 'What Is Art?' And what could be more serious than that? You've been listening to me for ten whole weeks, and only now do I define the concept central to the subject matter. By the way, tell me—did anyone find that joke funny?"

"I did," comes a tentative response—a young woman with pink-dyed bangs beneath her plaid beret. "Kinda— I mean I think you might be referring to Marcel Duchamp—the artist who did all the 'readymades.'"

"Very good," says Alex. "Usually that joke is met by a sea of blank stares." As he dims the auditorium, the image of a giant white urinal explodes onto the front screen. "By 'Western canon,' I am referring to the predominantly male, Euro-American tradition under which Modern Art is subsumed. That being the case—a porcelain urinal is an appropriate fixture for contemplation. But as you've already anticipated—the dialogue and controversy surrounding the definition of 'art' owes much to the French-born artist, Marcel Duchamp." Sweeping a hand up toward the screen—"I hereby present to you—the piece titled, *Fountain*—the single most notorious and influential work in all of Modern Western Art. What you see here is a photo of a subsequent version of the piece. Why a need for a re-creation? One of the artist's sisters dumped the original work in a junk heap."

Pausing for effect—"Duchamp and his peers bore witness as the Western world descended into the bloody abyss of World War I. Between 1914 and 1918, trench warfare claimed over thirteen million lives and fifty-nine million total casualties. To many Europeans, the world had indeed gone terribly mad.

"Meeting in Zurich, Switzerland, in 1916—a group of young intellectuals and artists gave birth to a movement that reacted not only against the war and the society from which it sprang, but against all conventional, hallowed institutions including government, literature, and art. They named their movement 'Dada,' a word found at random in a French-German dictionary, a child's word for 'hobby horse,' also taken to represent the first sounds uttered by an infant. At the time, Duchamp was already an important Modern artist in New York, where he created a number of works in the Dadaist spirit.

Alex steps to center stage. "So, what is he trying to do with his readymades—those 'ordinary articles of life,' he's chosen for reassignment? In what ways does he attack the whole tradition of Western art?"

A young woman speaks up. "All the qualities used to define art are not meaningful if *Fountain* is accepted as art."

A young man follows. "He's taking an object that's clearly not art, and by just declaring it—transforms it into art."

"Correct on both counts," says Alex. "If *Fountain* becomes art, then anything can be art, so long as someone says it is. It makes no difference if the work is aesthetically pleasing, involves skill, or adheres to a particular, traditional art form. The making of art is now in the *naming*."

A student up front—"So someone could say that 'everything is art' and then—everything *is* art."

"Or what if I say that *nothing* is art?" asks a student in back.

"You would both be right, and simultaneously so. 'Art' is a word in the English language that—like all words—denotes a particular concept. When *Fountain* was accepted as a work of art, the word 'art' lost that specificity. So when 'art' can mean 'anything,' it simultaneously means 'nothing.'

"Furthermore—what Duchamp has done to the word 'art' can be done to any other word. Therefore, it could be said that when *Fountain* was allowed to be a work of art, it opened the door for *all* words to lose their specificity."

"But Professor—that's totally warped. We all use language, and it works for us. Practically speaking."

"That's correct. In terms of language, we assume there are standard meanings attached to words, and we proceed to communicate. In the world of art, however, Duchamp has been allowed to play this clever, semantic trick on us. He was able to attack language itself, then forced this truly alien object upon our 'common sense' understanding of art. Duchamp made 'idea' or 'concept' the central quality of art. It's as if he vaulted over the subsequent fifty years—the remaining span of Modern Art—and arrived directly at Postmodernism, as manifested by Conceptual Art and other practices.

"So, today—let's make a concerted effort to respond to Marcel Duchamp's challenge. Do we as a group define art as 'everything' and 'nothing?' Or is there a definition that describes a special subset of 'everything' that we can agree to call 'art?'"

Alex addresses the chalkboard panels beneath the giant central screen. "As for reclaiming a pragmatic, 'common sense' definition of art, one approach is to make a list of qualities most people would associate with a work of art. People who take this approach refer to 'cluster criteria,' whereby an agreed upon number of characteristics must 'cluster' together in order to qualify for inclusion in the category."

Over the next half hour, the class assembles a list of cluster criteria to define for themselves the definition of "art." Although there is heated discussion, thanks to some Neo-Dadaists who object to any definition at all, the class arrives at the following seven criteria—requiring at least four to be present to allow inclusion.

Today's definition of art:
    "Art" refers to an object, or a process [including performances], that has at least four of the following characteristics:
1. Artist's intentionality— The artist intended to create art.
2. Aesthetic interactivity— It doesn't have to be pretty. It can be ugly, as long as it registers somewhere on the aesthetic scale.
3. Skill and virtuosity— Also, refers to a matter of degree. The more present, the better the art.
4. Individuality of expression— A sense of authenticity.
5. Novelty and creativity— A matter of "creative chops."
6. Intellectual challenge— Where the pleasure of aesthetic contemplation blends with the pleasure of intellectual contemplation.
7. Contributing to an altered state— In the experience of art, the viewer/participant undergoes a distinctly different state of mind.

Alex steps away from the chalkboard upon which he has finalized the list. "Now," he asks— "by these cluster criteria, does Marcel Duchamp's *Fountain* qualify as a work of art?"
    A spirited discussion ensues— Finally, by show of hands, the following responses are tallied:
1. No and Yes. Some students believe that Duchamp himself did not consider *Fountain* to be a work of art—that he enjoyed the absurdity of the art world's inclusion of it—that this constituted a "Dada moment."
2. Yes. But some students say that Duchamp's intent must have been to eliminate aesthetics completely—to leave the viewer with a sense of aesthetic indifference.
3. No.
4. Yes. The concept behind *Fountain* was an expression of authentic beliefs.

5. Yes. Duchamp had "major chops."
6. Yes. Definitely.
7. Yes. But, in a different way than ever before. Only because of works like *Fountain* does the cognitive experience explicitly add to the altered state.

Alex returns to center stage. "So, by virtue of our exercise, most of you would consider *Fountain* to be a work of art." After a smatter of applause—"It's interesting to note, of course, that without Duchamp, some of our criteria would not even have been included here. He's managed to change the traditional 'common sense' principles."

"One last thing. Through his manipulation of language, Duchamp provided Western civilization a powerful metaphor for what many experienced to be the meaninglessness of culture, the meaninglessness of life itself. He was deviously successful at forcing people to share the central Dadaist experience of absurdity, chaos, and the potential loss of all meaning. But although he probably enjoyed his little joke on the art world, he ultimately failed in his attempt at a kind of cultural destruction."

Alex opens his arms. "It is my personal belief that human beings strive for a sense of meaningfulness—a kind of an instinct, if you will—one shaped by Darwinian principles. The pursuit of meaningfulness in our lives must surely provide the human species a survival benefit. The art world triumphed over Duchamp and Dada by being adaptive—by changing its sacrosanct beliefs on the nature of its own being. When confronted with Duchamp's brand of nihilism, it opened itself up to the inclusion of this 'non-art.' After much gnashing of teeth, it consumed *Fountain*—wholly digested it, and moved on. So, one might ask—who ultimately bore the brunt of Duchamp's Dadaist joke? Who was afforded the last laugh?"

Stepping forward to the edge of the stage, Alex makes eye contact with as many students as he can. "As we've seen these past ten weeks, Modern Western Art continually evolved, motivated by a desire for creative novelty and change. In this current day, given the nature of the world around us, it would be easy to fall prey to destabilization, fragmentation, the loss of belief—the loss of meaning in our lives. But I believe that art will always be here to comfort us, just as it intrigues us. Art is a human activity that, even when it tries to deny it, consistently finds something of value. So yes, it only takes one artist to use a urinal. But since that artist was Marcel Duchamp, we can all be grateful for how he enhanced our experience.

"As we conclude our time together, I urge you all to appreciate and to enjoy your youth. Consider living with the same zest and creative spirit of the many great artists we have studied together. I wish you all good fortune in the grand unfolding of your lives. My best to you."

Latest news on Japan earthquake—breakingnews.com

5/9   Evacuees from the no-entry zone around the Fukushima nuclear plant begin home visits today to collect belongings— @Daily Yomiuri

5/29 Stabilizing reactors at Fukushima by year's end may be impossible, TEPCO says— Kyodo

5/29 MT @Daily Yomiuri: Radiation fears prompt Ibaraki-shi to stop using prefectures food in school lunches. Farmers upset— @W7VOA

5/31 Japanese non-profit says more than 1,100 children lost parents in the March 11 earthquake, tsunami— NHK

5/31 New York Met opera stars cancel Japan tour over concerns about radiation— Reuters

5/31 Embattled Japanese Prime Minister Naoto Kan set to resign in autumn or later— Reuters

* * *

Soquel hills

The sound of rain in the middle of the night. Rain pelting the moss-covered, shake roof—occasional splatter against the windows. The moan of wind through stands of eucalyptus, creaking of oak. A draft from under a door. The squeaking springs of a cast-off bed, shudders wracking the worn mattress. All night long, the storm wreaks havoc outside, rages outside. And then the storm comes inside, comes in and invades an empty space in Whitney's dreams.

Another nightmare and she startles awake—a mixture of fear and relief, like breaking the surface after holding her breath underwater. But the images, the video—that horrible feed— keep replaying. She cries in silence so as not to disturb the man beside her. Then again, her shaking body gives her away.

Even in sleep, Mario remains attentive, vigilant—his own body shifting closer now.

"Whit—are you okay?"

A strong arm wraps about her waist, even though she's turned away—turned on her side, locked in a position meant for taking care of herself. The arm is large, feels heavy—feels possessive. But now the warm, feathery breath down her neck reassures her, makes her shiver. She feels better, and then— worse.

"Tell me Babe, what happened?"

Normally, she keeps her dreams to herself, keeps them closed—filed away, like the piles of sketchbooks that contain the record of her disordered life. But tonight, she finds herself wanting—wanting for someone to soothe her, wanting someone to make everything okay. Loosening her arms from around her pillow, she turns to Mario, reveals herself—even knowing she can never fully trust what comfort she receives. Nothing in her life, nothing of stability ever lasts. But out of weariness, she decides to speak—yields to Mario, nuzzles a cheek against his chest.

"It started on a beach," she says—"and I was by myself. I was a little girl sitting in the sand, and the sand was like—like the color of a nice, new canvas. So, I was playing," she says, "and the sky was beautiful—all these palm trees just sticking up in the blue sky. The water was completely calm," she says, "and I thought I could stay there for a long time. But then, that's when the storm came in. It hit really hard," she says. "It was like the wind was really strong, like a hurricane—palm trees swaying all over the place. The trees were like giant paint brushes," she says, "and they were painting the sky and making it all dark.

And then, the sky began pouring water. I started crying for my mom," she says—"but my mom wasn't anywhere I could see. The rain kept getting heavier and heavier. I started running—crying and running—but I couldn't find a way off the beach. For some reason, I had to stay on the beach," she says. "I thought maybe I could swim to safety somehow—my mother always said I should learn to swim. But just as I stuck my foot in the water—it was like the whole sky opened up on me—like the water in the sky and the water in the ocean were going to slam together. I was screaming," she says—"I knew I was going to die. No way to survive it. In that last second—I didn't know if I was going to drown in the ocean, or maybe I was going to drown in the sky—"

She's shaking again, as the rain surrounding the house persists—the rain that continues to besiege her, the rain that wants to suffocate her. Mario rubs her shoulders, rubs her back. It's the touch, the physical contact that keeps her in the center of his harboring embrace.

Carefully, he strokes her hair. "It's all right now—it's okay. You're here, Babe, you're here with me. I'll keep you safe. All you have to do is let me…."

Inhaling his words, she breathes them in as if they offered her life. By these gentle words, she lets this man resuscitate her. Mario is tender, Mario is good. It doesn't matter that he has a hard-on—she won't be pressured to make love again tonight.

✳ ✳ ✳

Lisa—

I recall that first Christmas back in Altoona—the cold, the snow. And, of course, the Christmas Eve dinner at Grandma and Grandpa Keller's. I just loved that house in Mansion Park. It was big and made of brick—beautiful mahogany doors separating the parlor from the dining room.

Even though Mom and Dad had their usual arguments, I just didn't care anymore. What really made me happy was thinking about the letter I'd be writing to Alex, after the presents had been opened—after certain uncles got carted back to their own houses, drunk.

Growing up in Altoona, I'd gone to the local Catholic girls schools. Of course, the nuns were strict—thought of me as a *live wire* of sorts. Academically challenging—curious about everything. Sure, we had dances and mixers with the boys schools, but there really wasn't any way to carry on with guys the way I thought I would like. Dad was all over the place with his inventions—and his drinking. My mom being Italian was devout and terminally overprotective. I thought I could get on with my social life when I went to Penn State for college. But an hour away from home wasn't enough to make a real difference. Being the oldest sib—I got regular phone calls from my younger sisters. I drove home pretty nearly every weekend to help maintain the peace.

With everything going on, it was hard to date. The couple guys who asked me out—they probably didn't believe I was so tied up. And as for sex—well, there wasn't any. I think I was physically ready, but it never felt like the right time to do anything. There were a couple guys I let grope me during make-out sessions, but that was about it.

So, during that first quarter at Florence Moore, I really enjoyed the coed atmosphere—made a lot of friends. Alex was definitely on the elusive side, though. I think he had another girlfriend at Wilbur Hall. He just seemed busy a lot. But we got to talking some, and then we started doing things together. I think we just liked each other—liked each other's company.

We would go out on study dates, then come back to the dorm. We would often end up in his room, because he and his roommate had a system when it came to *entertaining* girls. They had this tag cut from an index card stuck to the door with a thumbtack. If the tag pointed up, it meant the other guy had to stay in the lounge downstairs. I never spent the whole night there. That actually would have looked bad to the other kids. Back in those days, it was still a disgrace to act like a *slut*. In any case, I never stayed too long in Alex's room.

But naturally, those nighttime sessions started getting heavier. It was such a great feeling to be in my body that way. At first, I never tried taking off Alex's clothes. He just matched me in whatever degree of disarray. But I touched him a lot—I was fascinated by his body, a man's body. It was a long time before we had intercourse—long after that first Christmas break. Looking back, I was just happy to be exploring this new, this special kind of relationship with him.

But then, just before I left for home that winter, something really different did happen to me. One night, my top was open, and Alex reached down and slid everything else off. It was dark, but the curtains were apart, so some kind of light—moonlight— was coming in. With his hand he gently opened me up—then touched me differently than he had before. And it was all in the way he was making me *feel*. For the first time, I wasn't going to hold myself back. I turned myself loose with that intense surge that started in the center of my body. And so I came—I shared an orgasm with a man for the first time in my life. And as it began to subside, when it was finally over—I felt elated. And when Alex held me, it was like he'd staked a claim on me—not that he was trying to. But somehow, I was now his—like some small bird getting imprinted on something. Something like that. It took me such a long time to understand."

* * *

Whitney's place

After a less turbulent night, Whitney ties her hair back. Wearing only an oversized T, she gathers the loose hem into a knot. A fine gray light streams in from her morning window. About an hour has passed—an hour since Mario left her tiny loft. She can still hear his shoes padding down the outside stairs as she lay in bed. She contemplates opening a window, but enjoys the feel of last night's humid air, the nocturnal atmosphere that enveloped them both. But now he's gone. In a few hours, he'll give her a call—will give her another one later this evening.

Approaching her easel, she selects her longest brush, and as if forcing herself to maintain a distance—reaches out until it barely touches the painted surface of Mario's chiseled face. *It always ends like this.* To be alone, high up in a room—a room made taller by her big imagination.

Mario had to leave for work, leave for school—leave for whatever reason. It doesn't matter—that's what men eventually do. And over time, she's come to appreciate the fact—the fact that they leave, the fact that they vacate her private space. *Go ahead and go,* she would like to tell the men in her life. She doesn't need them—needs them only to the point where some brief satisfaction happens to overtake her. She absorbs their residue—their scent hovering in the post-coital morning—a marine layer of spent lust, dissipating well before noon. What she doesn't need is for a man to hang around, to be underfoot, to keep bumping into her for certain favors. She also hates the matter of long-distance hovering—the cell phone check-in, the constant self-accounting that keeps her electronically contained.

Whitney has grown expert at providing men with plausible reasons to leave her. And all the while, she continues to vent her harshest emotions on canvas. The most recent example is a series of portraits of Mario—painted images of the most gorgeous man she's ever had. After all the hours of steady refinement, they can't be any more real.

Now, the time has come for a definitive change. With the tip of her brush, she caresses the faultless face of her lover. She has him in her sights—dead to rites. She draws a bead—takes deadly aim on the eyes that pursue her, the mouth that's always eager to explore her. Now she empties a tube of bright yellow paint on her palette—dips the head of the brush into the thick rich pigment. Standing clear of the easel, she reaches once more for the flawless image. She scrubs the upper corners of the canvas with the yellow paint, churning it into a cloud, a gathering turmoil, something of great threat. And then it rains, a sulfurous rain that streaks across Mario's visage. The paint infiltrates his tussled hair, turns the strands into a color so at odds with his skin. And then the bristles descend—close each of his blue eyes with a drooping, yellow lid. And then they pursue his lips—turn them the color of something expelled from deep within, something curdled, half-digested. And the color comes from her, but she doesn't know exactly why—and as always, she doesn't bother to wonder. The twisted color pours from her, attacks Mario—*de*-faces him.

Coming to a finish, she backs her way to the countertop. She doesn't need a tool anymore to keep her at arm's length from the subject at hand. Who would want to get close to a man who looks like this? Whitney's managed to brush away his rugged beauty, just as she'd quietly brushed him away this morning. Feeling tired, she sprawls back on her bed, still wrapped in the shirt that hints of Mario's body. For the moment, that's all she needs.

"When the artist produces something which is intelligible only to himself, then he has contributed to himself as an individual, and with this effect has already contributed to the social world...."

—Mark Rothko

"You don't really choose the arts—the arts choose you. You don't pick the clarinet...the clarinet picks you. You don't choose to paint water colors or oils...your medium picks you."

—NEON

"...At this point, [graffiti] is kind of like a religion to me. I know it may sound strange, but it's my way of prayer. It's kind of a meditation, in a way...a release. It's a praise to the good and a sacrifice to the bad. It's creative destruction really."

—SENOR ONE

***

Whitney's place

Stepping from the bath, she wraps her body in a thin white towel. Propping a mirror atop the sink, she grabs a brush and attacks the tangles in her hair. Normally, she doesn't examine her face, an object of keen indifference to her. But tonight, she pitches her hair forward—distorts the image. Behind the curls, her eyes evade her, even as she tries to tease them out. Feeling silly, she tosses her hair back—clears her face. Her eyes look so wide, it's as if she were caught by surprise—completely naked. Shedding the towel, she slips into a pair of panties and a light green summer shift. Anticipating her new job, her mouth feels dry. Reaching for the fridge, she pulls out a carton of orange juice.

Self-portraits have always been intrusive to her. The thought of posing for herself makes her fidget. She's handled her share of class assignments—official studies she routinely tosses upon completion and grading. For all the mandatory effort, she hasn't saved a single copy of herself. But somewhere inside, some growing part—she wonders how it would feel to be the focus of another person's eye. How would it be for some other artist to study her, capture her—make her the center of such keen interest?

Donning sweatshirt and sandals, she grabs her backpack—exits her apartment. Hopping on her bicycle, she soon establishes a comfortable, loping rhythm. Her trip takes her through the downtown mall and across the bridge over a resurgent San Lorenzo River. Avoiding the drug-addled Beach Flats area, she finally pulls her bike into the parking lot of the Santa Cruz Art League.

By now, Whitney's heart hammers away, but not from the physical exertion.

"Oh my God," she mouths, as she approaches the steps to the front door.

Cecil, the coordinator, smiles in greeting—thanks her for being punctual. A big, pot-bellied man, his hair would be called *salt and pepper* if it weren't so stringy and tied in a ponytail. Fortunately, he has a gentle voice, and she chooses to follow that voice, even as part of her wants to run.

Passing through a second door, her chest begins to heave. She scans the room before dropping her gaze to the floor. The brief, vertiginous view reveals a large space centered about a small platform—an orbit of tables, behind which *lots* of people sit.

Cecil ushers her to a nearby corner walled off by a tall translucent *shoji* screen. Within the enclosure, a surge of panic ensues. "I can't do this," she mumbles to herself—summons Cecil to negotiate a bit more time.

Struggling for composure, she hears him humor the group, saying that their new model has mistakenly worn "complicated clothes." Motionless, she absorbs their laughter. Certainly, there's a number of men in attendance. Maybe more men than women.

Sternly, she tells herself—*I've taken these stupid classes before.* With figure drawing sessions, drawing from the nude—adult students are normally middle-aged women and the sporadic older man. But, tonight, she detects the occasional tones of younger people. *They're all artists,* she reminds herself. *Fellow artists.* As another minute passes, she regains some semblance of control. Most significantly, she reasserts the importance of this experience for herself. *Come on,* she thinks—*this is for me. I want to know what it's like.* Committing to the moment, she peels off her sweatshirt—strips off the rest of her clothes. Donning the terry cloth robe provided for her, she sighs deeply—reenters the studio.

Somehow, Whitney makes her way to the wooden platform in the middle of the room. A scatter of tables surrounds her on all four sides. Although her lungs are settling, her fingers and toes—her lips—go numb. She can't feel her grip when she attempts to uncloak. It's as if someone else's hands were about to expose her. But she doesn't want to appear frightened, weak, or small. So she manages to doff the robe, and in a show of false bravado, steps smartly onto the stage.

Atop a swatch of carpet, she feels terribly cold. Fully exposed, all alone—she finds the glare of the overhead lamps overwhelming. She notes a prickly heat across her skin—wonders how much of it comes from all the eyes that now clamber about her body. She feels the probe of the collective gaze, as it traces every contour—enters every crease and hollow. Her mind starts to drift away—as if she were about to abandon herself. But she *can't* leave her body endangered like this, can she? She tries to focus on physical sensations—her tightened stomach muscles, the trickle of sweat down each of her flanks. On the verge of trembling, she keeps her eyes fixed above the level of the students' heads.

Quietly but firmly, Cecil gives Whitney her first instructions—starts with a five-minute pose. He directs her to raise her left arm and to place her hand atop her head. Then he asks her to lift her right knee so that the leg stays balanced on the ball of her right foot. The need to concentrate definitely helps, but it's only after the first half hour that she experiences anything close to relief. *I'm doing it now. I'm doing this thing.* With the longer poses of twenty minutes, she attains a level of tentative comfort. From this perspective, she actually welcomes the scrutiny, the attention—silently revels in the experience of an incredible *freedom.* She delights in an amazing combination of an internal stillness and a pleasurably electric aura. *This is good,* she allows herself to think. But what she only now begins to formulate—*I am beautiful. My body is beautiful. I'm so perfect in my body—I'm perfectly me....*

Approaching her now with two oversized pillows, Cecil asks her to recline on the stage. For the first time, she sneaks a peek at the students—catches the flickering eye of a shy young man in a green sweater. As she settles into a classic *odalisque,* body outstretched, arms cradling the back of her head—she wonders how he might be responding to her. When she shifts herself ever so slightly, is it a matter of comfort, or is she really posing for him?

At the first break, she gathers her robe—lets herself drift in the direction of the young man's table. Before she arrives, another male student—much bolder than the first—introduces himself, asks Whitney her name. All around, people rise and stretch to the sound of metal stools grating against the concrete floor. A pair of middle-aged women critique the display of oils in the gallery next door. An older man named Ari impresses Cecil with his drawings—all rendered in gorgeous red Conte crayon. Another man says "hi" to a friend named Ellen from across the room. What Whitney doesn't see, sitting behind in a distant corner—is the furtive figure of Professor Alex Arai.

***

Phone call from Mario—

"So Whit, where were you the other night?"

"I was at my new job, remember?"

"But we were supposed to get together—"

Andrew Kumasaka

"Well, I told you something came up. I must've texted you."
"Is that right? I guess I didn't get it."
"I'm sorry."
"Look—I was there at that place you wanted to try."
"Oh no, I hope you weren't."
"Yeah, I was. I got there—seven o'clock like we planned."
"I feel so bad—that's terrible. So, what did you do?"
"I got kind of worried—tried calling you, texted you."
"Yeah, I turned it off—couldn't have it on at work."
"Well, I'm not sure that's a good idea—you working so late at night."
"It's okay, really."
"So—are you going to tell me what kind of job you got?"
"Oh, sure I will—"
"Well?"
"Okay—I got a job at the Santa Cruz Art League. You know that place on Broadway? They got a nice gallery there. A lot of local artists get to show their work in a really cool venue. I've gone to a couple shows."
"So, you help at the gallery? Are you some kind of what—a guide? Does a place like that really need a docent?"
"Well, actually—I'm helping out with the art students."
"And, how's that?"
"Well, there's a class."
"Sounds good. What are you teaching?"
"It's not like I'm actually teaching, but in a way—I guess I am."
"Okay, enough with the riddles. Come on—what are you supposed to do down there?"
"All right, well—I'm a model."
"A model? What kind of a model?"
"It's a class on figure drawing—drawing from the nude."
"Which means?"
"It means I get to pose in the nude."
"Whitney—you think that's smart—taking your clothes off for a bunch of strangers? What kind of people take that class? You don't know all the crazies out there—"
"Look—it's all fine. Cecil, the guy who organizes it, is a well-respected painter in town."

"Is that right? Well-respected? So, how old of a guy is Cecil?"

"Oh, he's an old guy—probably in his sixties."

"I bet he enjoys having cute young girls exposing themselves."

"It's not like that."

"Oh really? What about the other people? Is it mostly guys who can't get any other kind of action?"

"No, there's a number of women there, too. Actually, I didn't exactly look around that much. I was trying to focus on my poses."

"Your poses? I'm sorry, Whit—I mean, what were you doing? I guess you just showed them *everything*. Didn't it feel weird to be naked in front of all those people?"

"Well, it did—at first. Then, I kind of got into it. I started getting into that space—that special space I wanted to experience."

"Like what?"

"Like being the subject of artwork. Like being the object of someone else's artistic eye."

"Oh, well—that should make me feel better. I mean—don't I make you feel special?"

"Of course you do. But this is different."

"Any younger guys?"

"No, not really."

"Well, maybe you should pay more attention next time."

"Mario, look—I'm sorry this is bothering you. It's really a good job for me right now. I need to help out with expenses. I hate calling up my folks to pay for extra things."

"But you're making a great big mess for us. I mean, this is crazy—don't you get it? Whitney—you're a beautiful girl. Guys like beautiful girls. You can't trust a bunch of guys who get off on drawing naked girls. You know, there're some real creeps out there. Somebody really dangerous could be in that class."

"I know you get worried for me, and I appreciate it. But you don't have to. I can take care of myself."

"But I'm telling you Whit—I'm not used to this kind of thing—not in a relationship. I'm not going to share you with other guys. You and I are together—there's no need for anyone else."

"Sorry you feel that way, Mario. You just got to try and get used to it. It's what I'm going to do."

"I guess—"

"So, it's still early. Would you like to come over and visit?"

"I don't know now. I need to think about things—need to think things over."

"We could go somewhere quick for dinner."

"Yeah, I suppose."

"Well, I'm going to be here all night."

"Okay, Whit. Just let me get myself together."

"Hope you don't take too long."

* * *

The house on Escalona Drive

With a *whoosh* of the shower door, a tide of white vapor filled the room—dimmed the harshness of the halogen lamps. Alex stepped through the softened light to one of two matching sinks in the handpicked marble counter. With a face of primordial clam shells, the slab of stone formed a monument to life as it existed two hundred million years ago. A triptych of glimmering mirrors hovered above this piece of prehistory. With its panels flared open, he could see not only his face, but both profiles as well. If adjusted just so, he could create an infinite stream of his own image arcing in either direction.

For now, he peered into his eyes and found a kind of weary recognition. His hair shown nearly all black, the hint of five o'clock stubble, increasingly silver. And caught between— the face that looked far wiser than he felt inside. Thinking of tonight, he wondered if he was truly prepared for something new.

Toweling off, Alex exited the master bath and headed for the closet. *Got to find something relaxed, comfortable.* He didn't want to look like a slob, but mostly, he didn't want to look like an *idiot*. Such a terrible assessment, one that affirmed his father's opinion of his earliest drawings. And as much as he tried, he couldn't help but continue the harsh judgement of that child—never allowing him to make mistakes, never allowing him to experiment with his art, never granting him the room for artistic play.

But that night, Alex chose to indulge himself—child and all. In a strange studio, surrounded by people with talent and expertise, he would lay himself bare to their eyes, their judgments, their snickers—their dismissals. He promised himself to do the best he could. He would try his hardest to learn, *relearn* the tools and techniques needed to improve his art—to reinvent his art for relevance in these contemporary times.

Upstairs, he gathered his materials—a sketchbook of vacant newsprint, two German pencils, a small red pencil sharpener, three yellow boxes of vine charcoal—a crumbly eraser and a kneaded eraser. *Feels kind of juvenile,* he mused. Placing his utensils in a blue plastic box, it looked like he was heading off to grammar school. Only, it was fast approaching seven p.m. and he was about to climb into his car.

The subsequent drive to the Santa Cruz Art League took about five minutes. As he pulled into the parking lot, his neck felt tight and his hands, cold.

Shuffling up to the front door, he exchanged greetings with the coordinator. *Thanks, Cecil. Yeah, I haven't done a class like this in a very long time.* Next, he passed through a second door—entered the spacious studio. A raised wooden platform stood at the center, with concentric zones of concrete floor and wooden tables spreading to the walls. About seven people sat quietly, most of them intently sketching.

Politely, he made his way through fellow students to a table at the opposite corner from the door. Clutching his materials, he smiled at the fellow sitting to his right. Old and grumpy, the man glared back over rimless glasses—remained silent. Glancing at his work, Alex spied an incredibly detailed portrait of a nude woman in beautiful red Conte crayon. *Oh, God,* he thought to himself—*what a horrible mistake to be here.* After opening his box, he placed his sketchbook atop a portable rectangle of paint-splattered wood. Taking a peek at the woman to his left, he found another alarming example of native talent and hard work.

Approaching the top of the hour, a gaggle of younger students arrived, filling up the rest of the tables. One strapping fellow looking full of himself—opened his sketchbook with an audible flourish. His exaggerated movements seemed to bother a second young man, sitting beside him in a green sweater.

Cecil peeked in, disappeared—returned in a few minutes to announce the arrival of the new model. At first, no one could see past his considerable girth. Then, as with the passing of an eclipse—he stepped aside to reveal the comely shape of a young woman. Head drooped, long reddish hair obscured her face. He ushered her into the adjacent corner behind a tall screen.

Kind of a pleasant surprise, I guess. As Alex recalled, models came in every size and shape, gender, age—what have you. Selecting his 4B pencil, he reminded himself to hold his instrument as he would a spatula or a knife. He began to draw in circular motions, careful to allow his entire arm to move freely.

As the seconds passed, there seemed to be a glitch with the model. Cecil said she needed more time to prepare. Watching his circles accumulate, Alex labored to establish a steady rhythm. When the young woman finally appeared, he was consumed with self-castigation. By the time he looked up, the young woman had already taken her place on the platform—

The concussive shock of what he saw froze Alex. For the moment, he was unable to turn his eyes away—couldn't drop his gaze, hide his face as he thought he should—*knew* he should. Actually, he was simply beyond coherent thought. *Oh my gosh*—he mouthed to himself. Just a few feet away, his student, Whitney B, stood completely naked. What he perceived must be a total apparition. He wondered if such a thing could exist—a *flesh and blood* apparition. Her luxuriant hair glowed red under the lights, her brave face upturned. Faint glimmers emanated from her eyes—her often fretful mouth, forced to be still. And her body—Alex had seen such bodies before, but not completely disrobed. Bodies associated with water—at poolside, by the beach—competitive swimmers, surfers, divers. As she turned his way, he observed a set of tempered shoulders—her chest tapering to the flare of slender hips. He noted the supple legs meant for fierce churning, the neatly defined toes and feet.

Now, Cecil began to speak. In response, Whitney raised her left arm and placed her hand atop her head. She lifted her right knee, balancing her leg on the ball of her right foot. Such natural elegance—she looked sheathed in skin so sheer as to slide over the dips and curves, the planes of her body. With this initial pose, one half moon of a breast ascended, the other slung in gentle repose.

Alex followed the elegant line bisecting her—from chin to sternum to navel to the perfect triangle of her sex. And what he saw, what he regarded went far beyond a man's primal needs and his response to biological allure. For the time being, he celebrated the magnificence of a young woman's beauty.

While he stared, everyone else began to draw, even the young guys on the other side of the room. Returning to a blank sheet of paper, he contemplated the uncanny nature of his predicament. Leaving would only attract attention—might even cause Whitney to discover him. He didn't want to embarrass her, embarrass himself. But *already,* he felt embarrassed—felt like a complete *idiot.*

Grabbing his pencil, he took up the challenge. Having lost valuable time, he still hoped to capture the essence of her pose. Telling himself he was *sanctioned* to look, he strove to convey the movement, the rhythm—the flow of what he saw. But it had been too many years since he took on an exercise like this. Annoyed, he couldn't make his hand perform the way he wanted. Part of the problem stemmed from the jamming effect that Whitney's presence had on his brain. Another part was simply a matter of forgetting. *Is it five, or is it seven? The number of heads to the length of the whole?* The man to his right used his thumb as a reference—maybe that's what he should be doing.

As time passed, Whitney ironically became less of a distraction—even as she remained the focus. Then again, during longer poses, he sometimes indulged in what he saw— lapsing into a kind of art *appreciation* as opposed to practice.

Cecil asked Whitney to recline on a pair of pillows. Alex welcomed the new perspective. He noted the two-tiered structure of her nipples, and as he did—admonished himself to get back to his drawing. He couldn't help but notice how the shade of various garments had leant subtly different hues to her skin. And for the first time, he visualized three tattoos

starting near the crest of her left hip and descending the cheek of her left buttock.

In a rush, he attempted to include too many details much too soon. As his focus constricted, his hand tightened, and the drawing ended up looking constricted and tight as well. He needed to relax, try to stay fluid. Beginning each pose as a loose sketch, he was finally able to hone the image into something both realistic and alive.

Cecil announced a break. Remaining seated, Alex watched as people got up from their tables. The man on his right scurried to show Cecil his work. The woman to his left engaged a friend—commented on the paintings in the adjacent gallery. Shielding his face with a hand, Alex returned his tools to their container. He glanced across at a draped Whitney talking to one of the young students—the guy who had entered class with a flourish. Too close to the door, she made it impossible for Alex to leave without detection. With more than a little ambivalence, and a surprisingly pleasant sense of resignation, he settled back in his chair.

When the class resumed, he reached again for his box of materials. Sharpening his pencil, Alex reopened his sketchbook—returned once more to work on Whitney's body.

10

Alex—

I remember how we spent a lot of evenings on study dates. Sometimes we'd go over to *Ugli*, the undergraduate library. At other times we'd go to the art library, which was pretty convenient for me. It had a sculpture by Henry Moore out front, and inside—a bronze by Aristide Maillol. What a beautiful torso of a woman—her chest proudly extended.

But our favorite place to go—and it seems strange, since no one else seemed to do this—was the campus Main Quad. That's where *Mem-Chu*, or Memorial Church, stood—and still does, of course. Just to describe it—the Quad is made up of a big rectangular plaza, the size of a football field. It has six circular gardens with palm trees and oaks and is enclosed by the church and other buildings used for classrooms and offices. The entire complex is Romanesque in style and built of beige sandstone topped by red tile roofs. The face of the church features a beautiful mosaic that flickers gold in the sun, or in the flood lamps at night.

All this description is just to say—that this incredible site forms a hub of activity during the day, but at night stands virtually empty. After normal hours, I never saw a single security person—maybe just a maintenance worker or two. And at most, Lisa and I—we might have spotted a small seminar letting out, or some professor leaving late. Otherwise, she and I would be all alone in this vast space.

So this one evening after dinner, we grabbed our books and walked the five or so minutes to the Quad. It was dark when we got there, but the walkway and the face of the church were lit. We headed for one of the corner classrooms just down a ways from the church. Like everything else, the room was unlocked. We stepped inside, turned on the lights—spread out our things on one of the tables facing the blackboard. I don't know what we were studying, but it was pretty relaxed. We mostly sat around talking, not getting very much done.

After a while, Lisa hinted she was ready to go back to the dorm. When I asked why, she said she wanted to spend some time with me in my room. So, I teased her—said my roommate had dibs for the evening. She got quiet—looked disappointed.

"What's wrong—do you really need to get naked tonight?"

She scolded me for asking her that—said it was embarrassing to her. But just a bit later, I pressed things further.

"You know, I can tell by the way you're sitting. How does it feel when you get all *restless* like that?"

"Oh, Alex—" she must have said, indignantly. But a few minutes later, she put her pencil down. "Well," she said, "I guess, when I'm feeling that way, it's certainly in the obvious place, or places. Actually," she continued—"I kind of get that funny feeling all over."

"Oh really?" I asked. "When you get horny, you feel it all over?"

"Alex," she said in a hushed tone—"what if someone can hear?" And with that, I walked over to the blackboard, picked up a piece of yellow chalk and wrote, *LISA KELLER GETS HORNY ALL OVER.* And I told her, since I'd been so bad for asking—I should be punished by writing it a hundred times.

Lisa was half screaming at me and laughing. Before I could finish a second line, she tried to tackle me—tried to get the chalk out of my hand.

"Stop it Leese—I need to document the truth!"

"Give me that chalk!" she yelled.

Then I scrambled to the door, and as I bolted outside—I shouted back something like, "The whole school's dying to know!"

I was running as fast as I could now across the dark expanse. After sitting around, it felt really exhilarating. Back then, I could run really fast. But Lisa was running fast too, being so long-legged.

I still got to the other side way before she did—broke into another classroom. I flipped on the lights, rushed to the blackboard, and wrote out the six revealing words. I got out of the room just in time—headed off for another door that was kitty-corner in the distance. This time, I just turned on the lights and hid behind the lectern.

Lisa came bursting through, breathing hard—wasn't laughing anymore. So, I popped up and told her I was sorry. I was kind of smirking, so I guess I wasn't *that* sorry.

She said something like—"You think you're such a funny guy, Alex—*too* funny."

I saw she was a little upset, so I tried to apologize for real. "I promise never to do that again—never, ever."

After that, we erased everything and walked back to where our books were waiting. By the time we got there, Lisa had pretty much settled down. Actually, she said it felt really fun and "freeing" when she ran so fast across the Quad. I admitted to her I was only joking about my roommate having reserved our room—asked her if she still wanted to come by for a visit. She said she did, and so we gathered our things and left.

That night, we went as far as we normally did, but it felt different, more passionate in a way. I was really liking Lisa— liking her a lot, and more. After getting dressed, I walked her over to the door but kept the lights dim.

We kissed a little longer, and now it was her turn to catch me off guard. She probably smoothed her hair back— straightened her blouse. Then she said, "I think it's time we talk about something."

I watched, as she took in a quick breath.

"Alex," she said, "I think we should discuss the possibility of—consummating our relationship."

I thought to myself—*No one's ever said that to me before, not like that.* I resisted asking her what she meant by the term—like, was it going to feel good or what? But really, she was so sweet—the formal tone and delivery. The choice of words, definitely endearing.

"Yes," I said—and I know I drew her close to me. "Yes," I told Lisa, "I would be happy to discuss it."

I promised her that we would talk about "it" for sure.

∗ ∗ ∗

Charlie Hong Kong's, Eastside Santa Cruz

Fast food—noodles and rice bowls, vegans welcomed. The place fills with geriatric hippies, college students—contemporary moms with children on perfect organic diets. Joey and Alex order lunch—grab two stools at the counter overlooking Soquel Avenue. Just down the street from Bill's Wheels, Joey wants to share his ideas for a new legal wall that just opened there. But first—

"You know, man, the other night, you was open for that last shot. Right in your range. Sagged off on you, like they was darin' you to shoot."

"Well, I wasn't feeling it—didn't have any rhythm that night. Besides, Carter was open underneath."

"Yeah, I know Silk's money, but that wasn't easy—him goin' up and under the big guy inside. Your shot was made to order—fifteen-footer, no one guardin' you. Seen you make plenty of 'em over the years."

"But we still won the game, and I got the final dime off Carter's shot."

"True, true—"

"You two should get together sometime—compare notes."

"Sure, why not? Basketball and hip hop—they're connected, you know? This Bay Area guy—Jim Prigoff—used to study writers big-time. Put films and books together, has the biggest collection of graffiti photos in the world. Says hip hop has *four legs* to it. Like, there's rappin' for the word part of it—break dancin' for the movement part—DJ-in' for makin' up live music, and graffiti writin' for the visual side of things."

"Is Mr. Prigoff still around?"

"Oh yeah. In fact, I seen him a couple months ago. Had a barbeque over at his place. He's a good guy, you know—been takin' care of his wife. Anyways, graffiti's been around a lot longer than hip hop itself. That scene started in New York City, early '70s. But writers was already there, and they was all different colors, bro. Race and such—it didn't make no difference. They was all just writers, and cats could be listenin' to rock, punk, soul—what have you. But the whole graffiti thing was up from the streets, so it fit hip hop when it came around."

"So, what about the basketball connection?"

"Yeah, the point I was tryin' to make. You know—I'd say there's more than just four legs to the hip hop scene. I'd say there's actually five, and schoolyard basketball is what's number five—the athletic, sports part of it all."

"Ever talk to Prigoff about that?"

"Nah, but I should. You know how basketball's got so many rules—drives me nuts? They play like that from rec to high school, college—the pros. And for a long time, let's face it—this was a white man's game. Real team-oriented—kind of like you, Alex—pass the ball first."

"Well, that's how you're coached. You've got to learn to play *the right way.*"

"But you know, bro—when you go to the schoolyard, it's more of a man-on-man kind of thing. It's a game where the player hisself is what it's all about. Like what he creates to beat the guy in front of him. And there's so much style happenin'. Just like graffiti, man. It's individual—it's got to do with your name. And that style was brought to basketball by black players—guys so good they had to let 'em in. College, pros. And people love that style of play. Sure, teamwork's important. But folks pay to see the big names do crazy-ass things they never seen before. So, like I'm sayin' to you—schoolyard basketball is the fifth leg of hip hop—comes from the same source."

"Oh yeah, Joey, that's a terrific idea. Once when I was younger, I visited New York City—actually played ball on the courts near Greenwich Village...."

Interrupting him, the counter guy calls out their names. Alex and Joey grab steaming bowls of stir-fried *Gado Gado*, pork added. Joey eats as fast as he can, while Alex struggles to keep up. Soon enough, they're walking down the street to Bill's.

The virgin wall stands opposite of Joey's original piece—stretches some fifty feet across. This time, Alex welcomes the chance to help with the buffing. With the boom box blaring

Snoop Dogg, they grab their rollers and start applying the gray latex house paint. Talking over the music, Joey shares his vision for the upcoming work.

"Oh yeah, I got this cool idea, man. This piece—it's gonna be a tribute wall. I'm gonna get up the names of some really great cats that was instrumental in Bay Area writing."

A half-hour in, Joey borrows a ladder from Bill's—finishes buffing the top of the wall. Jogging to his car, he yanks out one of his crates of spray cans.

"Gonna bust up the space—gotta mark out the areas I need—"

Alex studies the colorful plastic tops. He feels like a kid wanting to break into a new box of crayons or colored pencils. As Joey finishes dividing up the wall, he catches Alex staring into the crate.

"I know what you're thinkin', Professor. Why don't you grab a can—come over to the wall. Let's have you tag this thing. It'll be a first for you."

Alex can hardly believe this opportunity—a chance to explore a new medium. He chooses a can of silver paint. Tilting it about, he guesses it to be about half full. Placing his index finger where the cap should be, he stops....

"Oh, sorry," says Joey—"let me get you somethin'." From a plastic bag, he selects a *skinny cap*—inserts it into the top of the silver can. "There now—go ahead and shake it up."

Following instructions, Alex notes the sound and feel of the rattle.

"Now, check out the flow—make sure the nozzle's okay."

Hand out—Alex releases a spray of silver with a satisfying *pssst*, catches a hit of aerosol vapors. Like a young student, he waits for permission before approaching the wall.

"Go ahead and practice a couple lines," says Joey. "After that, you can try doin' a square."

As Alex raises his arm, Joey makes an adjustment to his wrist. "Here—get closer and hold your can upright. Make the first line straight across."

Concentrating hard, Alex steels himself for the task at hand. Clutching his can, he's bombarded with thoughts. *Okay—press the cap. Come on now—press the cap—you can do it.* Cap engaged—a rush of bright silver paint suddenly strikes the wall. *Oh no! Too much paint—look at the drips! Move the hand—move the hand! Keep going—don't stop.* A couple feet later, Alex struggles with the erratic results. *What a total mess!* Appalled—he ponders the thick application, the spray of speckles all around. *Must be something wrong with the nozzle.* Standing back, he feels confused.

"Not too bad," says Joey—"try it again. This time, keep the can about an inch from the surface. That'll get you a cleaner line, without all that spread."

Regaining focus, Alex extends the can once more. Holding his breath, his entire body tightens to match his hand. Cap engaged, he produces another clumsy line replete with drips—a line that looks straighter, but angles upward. Acutely embarrassed—he isn't used to struggling with artistic tools.

"God, Joey—I don't know what's wrong. I'm actually a fairly good draftsman."

"No worries, man. Here, let me show you." Grabbing the can, Joey smartly approaches the wall. *Pssst, pssst, pssst, pssst—* Effortlessly, he renders the four sides of what looks to Alex like a perfect square. "You're thinkin' too much, bro. Just let it flow—just *feel* it. Try movin' the can a little faster. It's important to find your right speed."

For the next ten minutes, Alex struggles—his head numbing with paint fumes.

Joey offers helpful comments. "I see it's better when you go from left to right. Now try it again." Later—"Just for fun—why don't you do a vertical line. Actually—just go ahead and make yourself a whole square."

Soaked in sweat, Alex steps back—wipes his face. Mulling his return, it's truly a matter of approach/avoidance. Gamely, he goes to a fresh section of wall—shakes his can, then places it upright an inch from the surface. Straining, he starts from the top, proceeds downward.

Too slow, he thinks—*you've got to go faster!* Editing himself the entire way, his line looks pathetically irregular. Alex persists until he finishes the square—feels totally at a loss, ineffectual— truly miserable.

"Well, I think that's enough for today," says Joey. "It just takes a lot of practice. You know them artists you teach about in school? They all worked their asses off to get to where they got."

"Yeah, thanks," says a befuddled Alex.

"It's gonna get better"—Joey says, retrieving his can. "You know why I can say that, Professor? It's 'cause I seen the way you play basketball. Kind of a head trip thing for you. Once you stop thinkin' so much and get into the flow, you can still do some great things."

* * *

"Hi Professor A. U can catch my work this month at Stripe, a really cool store downtown. Nice stuff, vintage and contemporary. Whitney B"

First Friday Art Tour Galleries/July 7
  Annieglass
  Artisans Gallery
  Pure Pleasure
  Santa Cruz Art League
  Stripe

Surprised and delighted by Whitney's email, Alex accepts the invitation. Lisa's been home a week now, and it's time to try something fun.

It's seven p.m. when they enter the small, downtown boutique. Lisa delights in the rustic mirrors crafted from salvaged window frames—smiles at the novelty wigs made of rubber spaghetti. Alex favors a set of plates reminiscent of *The Dinner Party*—Judy Chicago's controversial, feminist masterpiece. The boutique is just as Whitney wrote—an eccentric, *cool* place, a quirky combination of the refurbished past and the present.

Alex studies the eclectic patrons, half of whom look college-aged. Searching for Whitney, he weaves his way to the end of the room. At the reception table, he asks for a glass of Pinot. Lisa follows with some Chardonnay, and together they approach the art. For the city-wide exhibit, the boutique features two local artists. Whitney's paintings command half of the back wall and parts of the wall to the right. The second installation, involving prints, creates a mirror effect on the left. Posted in the right hand corner, a white placard bears Whitney's artistic statement—

My paintings start with a subject, usually a human model. It may be from a sitting, a picture, or from my own memory. I paint exactly what I see with my eyes or my mind. I never spare the subject this honest witnessing. When people see my paintings at this stage, they often remark how pretty or beautiful they are. It's almost like they would want to get to know some of these people on my canvases. But I'm not finished just yet. There's still another stage to my creation, one that involves things I know inside. These are things that no one else knows, or maybe no one else admits to. I trust my art, this second wave of expression that washes over and sometimes even attacks the person in the painting.

I don't want to know what this process is about, although I might have ideas. I prefer to keep my process out of the domain of words, because words encode things and ideas in a way that's harder to ignore or take back. I just let myself, my insides, come out. And what comes out is mostly me but can have a lot to do with you, the viewer. As you can see, the results are not often pretty or beautiful anymore. It's fine with me. Actually, it's mostly a relief. I get it "out there," get it outside of myself. And then it's easier to go about my daily life.

—Whitney B Willis

Lisa waits for Alex to finish, then each turns to look at the other. Alex shrugs. Slowly, they work their way down the main wall displaying Whitney's work. Immediately, he recognizes two of the paintings—the one titled *Rachael*, and the one with the red-haired woman. The latter canvas now bears the title, *Missing*. Coming to a halt, Lisa stares at what appears to be a man's face—a portrait absolutely brutalized by yellow paint. Again, Lisa and Alex exchange looks.

From the shop's entrance come the sounds of a disturbance, but it quickly settles. Whitney strides up the central aisle, pursued by an athletically built young man. She wears a slinky black dress that clings to her body just before vaporizing mid-thigh. Keeping pace, the man wears a light blue work shirt and dark jeans. His face—rigid with concern—can't hide the fact that he's ruggedly handsome. Whitney refers to her companion as *Mario*—as in, *Mario, stop it already.*

When Whitney sees Alex, her face lights up. "I'm so glad you're here," she says.

Returning the smile—"This is my partner, Lisa. Leese, this is Whitney, a student of mine—a *former* student. I'm not sure if you met at the print sale."

The two women shake hands, with Lisa scrutinizing Mario. Noting this, Whitney completes the introductions.

"Well, I hope you enjoy the show," she continues. "My friend, Julie, is the other artist featured tonight. I think it was that tall friend of yours who bought one of her prints at the sale."

"Of course," says Alex—glancing at the lithos on the opposite wall. "Carter hung it in his office across from his desk."

"Well, maybe we can talk more later on. Right now, I'm just making the rounds."

Whitney departs—Mario following close behind. It doesn't take long before they start to argue, drifting into a distant corner of the room.

Lisa leans close to Alex's ear. "You know, it's that dress"— she whispers. "Her boyfriend doesn't like her in that dress."

"How do you know?"

"Oh, come on—she's darling. All the guys here are either looking at her—or trying hard *not* to."

"I suppose you're right. She's certainly very nice looking. In fact, they really make a beautiful pair."

"But I think they've got some serious issues."

Alex can't help but worry for Whitney. Awaiting her return, he notices another young man enter the store. The guy looks familiar, possibly a recent student of his. But as the man returns his gaze, Alex identifies him as the loud-mouthed artist from the aborted figure drawing class. *For godsakes—* When Whitney reappears, Alex has abruptly crossed the room, presumably to look at Julie's prints.

"What's happening?" Lisa asks, as she comes to join him.

"A long story. I'll tell you later."

Of course, she knows about his drawing class, but not *all* the details.

The young man approaches Whitney.

"I think this could be trouble," says Lisa.

Both turn to watch Mario coming up from behind.

"Say Whit—" he asks—"would you like a glass of wine?"

"No, thanks."

"Okay then—are you going to introduce me to your friend?"

"Well, he's not really my friend."

The young man fills out his denim overalls. A plaid shirt drapes the contours of his barrel chest. If not in height, he's bigger than Mario—outweighs him.

"Oh Whitney," he says, "you hurt my feelings." Then he laughs, nodding at Mario. "Is this your boyfriend?"

"Yes, he is— Mario, this is Tom. Tom—Mario."

"We know each other from the same class," says Tom.

Glaring—Mario takes a step closer. "So, you're one of those pervs from the drawing class. What the hell are you doing here?"

"Well, I saw her name in the *Good Times* ad, like—is there a problem?"

Another step closer, Mario squares up—"As if you didn't know—"

Tom starts to back away. "Say, man—I didn't mean anything, I swear. I'm just an art guy. I wanted to check out her art."

"That's bull—" Turning to Whitney—"Don't tell me you pose for losers like this."

"Ah, come on, man," says Tom—a shaky grin creasing his face. "I just like talking with her. I mean, you gotta admit she's cute."

In one quick move, Mario thrusts his left hand into Tom's chest—his right hand raised in a fist.

"Okay—" Tom spouts, "I'm outta here!" Tearing away, he clips a table, knocks over a sign—scrambles to exit the store.

Grabbing Whitney by her wrist—Mario pulls her past the merchandise toward a fitting booth.

"Let go—" she whispers harshly. "You're acting like a jerk!"

Struggling free, she heads in the direction of Alex and Lisa—hands smoothing the contours of her dress.

Fuming, Mario can only watch. A split second later, his face startles as if snapping out of a trance. Glancing at the others—a look of embarrassment, maybe—but more a look of having been *discovered*. He goes to his girlfriend, says something in her ear—gives her a prolonged kiss, then leaves.

Alex and Lisa receive Whitney. "Are you okay?" asks Lisa.

"Oh yeah, I'm fine."

The upset look in her face dissipates, replaced by a hint of a smile. Leaving the reception table, Julie hurries to her friend—wraps her in a comforting hug. Alex notes that one of Julie's slender arms bears a small tattoo of a starburst and letters.

"I'm sorry that happened," says Alex. "Is there anything I can do?"

"No, not really. I'll be just fine."

"Has that stuff ever gotten out of hand?" asks Lisa.

"Oh no—never—"

"Well, I just hope you guys are good for each other."

"Seriously, it's okay—no big deal. Anyway, I know what it's about—I totally get it."

Julie gives her a quick kiss on the cheek, slides her arms off—returns to the table to retrieve a glass of wine. Turning, Lisa walks off to re-read Whitney's artistic statement.

"All right—enough with the drama," says Whitney. "Hey, everybody, I really appreciate it." Smiling again—"Let's get back to enjoying the show. I mean, I *hope* you're enjoying it."

Alex would like to give her a hug of his own, but decides against it. Changing the subject—"I notice your friend, Julie, has a rather artful tattoo—"

"Oh yeah, she does—a really cool one." Then—"I bet you didn't know—I've got some tats of my own."

"Really?"

"In fact, I've got them right here on my butt." Whitney

smiles—laughs. "But you can't see them unless I take off my dress."

"I guess you better not do that." Alex wants to ask—knows he shouldn't, but finds himself asking anyway. "So—what are your tattoos about?"

"Well," she says, brightening further, "I've got three of them—one for every guy I've been seriously involved with."

"Now," asks Alex, "don't you think that's kind of impulsive? I mean, getting tattooed every time you—fall in love?"

"Oh," says Whitney, her green eyes flashing, "I don't do it when I fall in love. The only time I get a tat is when I finally get rid of the guy—"

11

San Jose

Kazuo Arai—
"Put it over there, Sumi—I don't want anything to spill on my slides. It's fun though, reviewing my work. One thing about a big retrospective, I've really made it—I've done good for myself. And gosh—I sure wish George Tsutakawa were still alive. Died back in what—'96, '97? For sure, he would have been proud of me."

"...Yeah, he was a soft-spoken guy, right? Not one for making big statements. I remember his studio up in Seattle—one room in a nice house overlooking that lake and the mountains. Really cluttered, with little mock-ups of his fountains on a table. So he's rummaging through papers, and he finds a small painted canvas—tosses it off to the side. Actually mumbles something about 'Oh, here—it's a Mark Tobey.' I couldn't believe it. One of those mysterious paintings—the 'white writing' he was famous for, and George just casts it aside."

"...You know, people will ask how I fit in the last half of the twentieth century world of art. And when they do, I'm sure they'll bring up Isamu Noguchi. Famous Japanese American sculptor—a *hapa* really. Mother was white— And you know, I think he had quite an ego—wanted to make the grand statement. He goes bigger and bigger the older he gets. Big environmental stuff—playgrounds and parks and other environmental sites. I think he declared the whole world to be a piece of sculpture at one point. Some critic called him 'the greatest living American sculptor' before he died. I bet he probably believed it."

"...So, I'm looking forward to my birthday dinner at Alex's in a couple weeks. He and I can go over a lot of this material. He's got to come up with an introduction for my catalogue. I want him to highlight my best works, of course. But I also want a clear statement about my contributions to Modern Art. I'd like Alex to get it all—get it right. I want my place in art captured in a way that we can all be proud. And that inevitable thing about Noguchi and me—whatever comparisons? I know I can count on Alex to set things straight."

* * *

KRUZ— FM 88.5

Musical strains—Seal covers Nat King Cole
    "Mona Lisa, Mona Lisa
    You're so like the lady with the mystic smile..."

"KRUZ thanks Cruzio for its support, celebrating twenty years of service. Located on Pacific Avenue across from the Metro Center.

    "Hi folks, this is Molly Mendez, the girl in the floppy yellow dress and skinny black sweater. Let me start with a shout out to Wild Flag—a great new group coming to the Rio next Thursday. Featuring gals from Sleater-Kinney, one of my faves—part of that *riot girrrrl* scene back in the nineties. Tickets available at Logos bookstore downtown, or at the door.

    "All right—you're listening to 'The Art of the Matter,' a show that features local artists and other experts from the Santa Cruz art scene. It's my pleasure today to be talking to Dr. Alexander Arai, an art history professor at UCSC in the Department of History of Art and Visual Culture. Wow, that was a mouthful— Welcome, Professor. You're looking sharp today—blue blazer and all—"

"Thank you, Ms. Mendez, it's great to be here."

"Beyond your classes on Modern art, I believe you specialize in contemporary memorials, am I right?"

"Yes. That's an area of concentration for me. I teach graduate-level seminars on the subject."

"Very good. I see from my screen here, you've written three books on the subject. Now, Dr. Arai—how did you get started with the study of memorials?"

"Well, Ms. Mendez—"

"Please, Dr. Arai—everyone on the show calls me Molly."

"All right, Molly— My interest in memorials began as an art history student. In college, I focused on the French sculptor, Auguste Rodin, whose work spanned the late 1800s to the early 1900s...."

"Of course—the creator of such well-known sculptures as *The Thinker* and *The Kiss*."

"Why yes—and even beyond those iconic sculptures, Rodin's monuments proved truly groundbreaking. Two examples are *The Burghers of Calais* and the *Monument to Balzac*.

"And how so? What was so groundbreaking about those two works?"

"Well, for a little background on the first— The French town of Calais was besieged during the Hundred Years' War by England. Edward III agreed to spare the citizens of slaughter if six of their most prominent townsmen offered themselves up for sacrifice—barefooted, with ropes around their necks. Upon fulfilling the terms, the town was saved, and the men were actually pardoned.

"To honor the six, the citizens of Calais commissioned Rodin to design a monument. They expected a statue depicting the men in heroic pose—mounted atop the traditional, imposing pedestal. Instead, Rodin proposed six separate figures, each struggling with deeply conflicted emotions—the men strung together like beads on a string of fate. He also wanted the figures to be placed at street level to express their kinship to current citizens. Rodin designed *The Burghers of Calais* to be interactive—and therefore presaged important Modern and even Postmodern developments. He encouraged people to enter the work and to engage directly with their history."

"That was pretty radical for the times. What was the initial reaction?"

"The planning committee was outraged by Rodin's proposal—insisted on clumping the figures together, and of course—demanded a pedestal. Only many years after Rodin's death was the monument displayed at the level of the people."

"Quite an interesting story, Dr. Arai. Many say that Rodin's work signals the beginning of Modern sculpture."

"Yes, that's true—a clear break from the French Academy."

"Now, what about the second example? Honore de Balzac was a novelist—"

"Yes, and the design for his monument was also controversial. Balzac was overweight—rotund. Rodin struggled for seven years to turn him into a more inspiring figure. One version had a nude Balzac proudly displaying his protruding belly—the hand placement suggesting the grasping of his erect penis."

"Wow—I hadn't heard that story. I knew that Rodin distorted anatomy to express things. But that study of Balzac—that's totally wild."

"Rodin eventually dropped the idea—dressed Balzac in a loose robe and presented him standing in the middle of the night, captured at the moment of inspiration. The head and face were vaguely modeled, the whole body tilted toward the moonlight. One critic charged Rodin with having taken Balzac's brains and smearing them all over his face. But in the end, Rodin reconciled the author's powerful intellect and corpulent body. The final version—the robe having smoothed and appearing to lengthen Balzac's torso—surely constitutes the finest phallic symbol in the history of Modern Western Art."

"Without a doubt, Rodin was an artist who was way ahead of his time. Thank you Dr. Arai—what an entertaining story."

"Glad you liked it."

"Moving on, now—you wrote a recent article for the *San Francisco Guardian*. In it, you say that this is a special year for memorials. Would you care to elaborate?"

"Why yes, Molly. In the United States—in this year alone, hundreds of new works will be dedicated. And the two most important will be the *Martin Luther King Jr. National Memorial* in Washington, D.C. and the *National September 11 Memorial* in New York City."

"As you point out in your article, there's been a great acceleration in the building of memorials in the past thirty years or so. They seem to be everywhere—dedicated to just about anything you can imagine."

"That's right—a tremendous surge in memorialization. There's actually quite an industry if you will—one involving artists, designers, architects, and their corporate, civic, governmental clients."

"And what are the reasons for the surge?"

"There are a lot of factors. Memorials deal with memory, and memory has everything to do with identity. Defining oneself has become increasingly important in society. Memory tells us who and what we are—as individuals, ethnic groups, nations, cultures. The memorial is a powerful medium for affecting memory. It instructs, informs, reinforces—even alters our perception of self and others.

"So, what can you tell us about our national narrative? For example, you've mentioned the memorial to Martin Luther King Jr. What does this memorial say about our nation?"

"For Dr. King, the road to memorialization has been a long one. Such a memorial would naturally affect the American narrative of the Civil Rights movement. The project began in the 1980s and caused significant conflict. At stake—*whose vision ultimately determines the historical memory of Dr. King and the struggle he represents?* The U.S. Commission of Fine Arts argued that the proposed granite sculpture looked too *confrontational.* The figure, titled the *Stone of Hope,* appeared to deviate from the original inspiration—a 1966 portrait by professional photographer, Bob Fitch—"

"Let me interrupt a second, doctor— You know, Mr. Fitch currently lives in Pajaro—just down the road from Santa Cruz."

"Yes, Molly—a fine local connection. As you can see, the man in the historic photo looks less robust than the one in stone. The folding of King's arms is not confrontational, but looks more like he's bracing himself for what lies ahead. For me, his eyes display a strong resolve in the presence of understandable fear and uncertainty. The man in the photo looks much more complex than the man of the sculpture—reveals himself as profoundly human.

"To the commission, the proposal mimicked the gross monumentality favored by past and present totalitarian states. But unlike the commission's vision of King as a man of peace, the consulting artists saw him as a man of power—a *warrior for peace*. In the end, the design was modified slightly to include the beginnings of a smile."

"Wasn't there also some controversy regarding the sculptor chosen for the work?"

"Yes, the memorial foundation selected the Chinese sculptor, Lei Yixin. Among other works, his portfolio includes numerous monumental sculptures of Mao Zedong. Also, the stone chosen for the memorial is a pink-hued granite, which some people think would make Dr. King look white."

"Dr. Arai, I've got to ask. Would you agree—these are two examples of Postmodern irony?"

"Possibly so, but I don't think I would laugh about it. That choice of material had a lot to do with being able to *read* the sculpture's features at night. And it should be noted, I suppose—that ten of the twelve members of the foundation were African American. Still and all—"

"So, do you consider the national memorial to Dr. King to be compromised?"

"Definitely not. Judging from what I've seen of the design, the overall impact will be very positive. I plan to attend the official opening in August. While I'm back east, I'll visit the 9/11 memorial as well."

"Thank you for all your insights, Dr. Arai. I really appreciate our discussion today. You certainly help us to understand the cultural importance memorials have. I hate to cut things short— half an hour just isn't enough time for a topic like this. Dr. Arai, I hope you'll return for a visit after your trip back east. I'm sure the audience would love to hear your firsthand impressions on both of those exciting new memorials. It also occurs to me now, and I'd really planned to mention it earlier— You're the son of Kazuo Arai, the famous sculptor. He's got a big memorial right here on campus. I'm sure your father had a lot to do with you going into your field— Well, to my audience—if you just tuned in, you've missed a thought-provoking program with Dr. Alexander Arai, an art history professor here at UCSC. You can catch the whole interview later online at kruz.org. Thank you so much for being with us, Professor Arai."

"Thank you, Molly, for having me."

* * *

Whitney's place

So much for higher thought processes—top-minded ideas. It was nice that Professor A. had emailed her about his radio interview. In fact, she had tuned in briefly for a listen. Then it was back to work—back to her private world of paint.

But Mario still presents a problem, seeking her out whenever he can. She can just about *feel* his presence, as if a chip in the scruff of his neck alerted her to his skulking intentions. Distractions—she hates distractions. She's bothered by the disgust, the spite—the *lust*—and all of the other mismatched feelings churning inside her body. What to do with that squirming, physical ambivalence?

So, it all comes down to this. Mario at the front door, Mario that dog. Begging, baying to be let in, to be let in out of the cold. And so, Whitney relents. Actually, she only pretends to relent since she really *wants* him in. And soon, the whole place fills with the scent of dog—just as he goes about sniffing her out.

She's pissed at this latest infringement on her autonomy— or is it her anatomy? This latest expression of his dog-like love through cloying attention, his pathetic attempts to protect her, *control* her. And she just can't stand the treatment, can't stand him—really she can't. In fact, she hates him so much she just wants to *fuck* him tonight. No making love, no talking—she just wants to do it—do it *now*.

Peeling off his coat and her own scanty clothes, she lets him nuzzle her, lets him lap at her skin. Such a change from the way it all started—her body usually so coy in matters of accommodation.

But once it begins, she likes to engulf her men—likes to tighten her grip, tighten over and over, rhythmically making them go *uh...uh...*that sound she orchestrates to a loud, guttural climax. But Mario's been cursed with that *big* thing—Mario, all about being big and beautiful. And lately, it seems, the guy's gotten even bigger. Maybe it's because he's angry too—certainly Mario must hate her too. Lately when they do it, it feels like it's all in the service of penetration.

If Whitney could, she'd be a dominatrix—demand what she wants and when she wants it. If she'd like her man on a chain, a leash, in a leather choker—she'd make him heel for the opportunity. Top, bottom, boot, or whip—whatever kind of degradation. But now it's beyond simple resentment. The anger's gone too far this time—results in too much heat. Tonight, she feels so hot and bothered, she's a total mess down there.

Mario does his thing with her—turns her around and humps her to the point she buckles at the waist. Furious—she responds by shoving him back, shoves him back harder than he can—inhales/exhales harsher than he can. When the time comes—she howls even louder than he can. And Mario is crazy and Mario is grateful, and Mario doesn't know what this all means. When finished, he simply rolls over, panting away—just as dumb as a smart dog.

12

The house on Escalona Drive

*A*lex normally follows the line—the party line. But lately, he returns to his *personal* line—the one that naturally flows from his hand. He's okay when it comes to fine muscle movement—no sweeping statements, no big body language from outstretched arms. No tossing around of hyperbole. In his artistic nook, he practices drawing small letters on sheets of paper.

"ALEX, ALEXANDER—ARAI." "DR—PROFESSOR...." These are the letters that define him. But a fresh, subversive version is what he needs now. How appropriate—launching a Postmodern assault on his formerly Modern self. Striving to be *Contemporary*, his imagination creates wild permutations of his name. "ALEX" written in print, in cursive— "ALECKS," "A-LICKS," "ALIXER—" Lacking the ability to create pieces and throw-ups, he'll design tags instead.

Joey's just returned from the City—has brought back several cans of Montana paint and a set of caps for him. All this, he carries to his backyard wall, safely hidden from public view. He pours out a can of cheap house paint into a metal pan. Roller in hand, he slathers on layers of thick gray latex.

Scanning the stretch of cinderblock, he's reminded of a number of barriers he's dealt with in the past. He thinks of the university, the tenure track—that initial attempt to pigeonhole his identity. And he ponders the recent edict to change the focus of his teaching. He thinks of his father, the original wall—the one who withheld approval, blocked entry into the artist's world—until Alex climbed the academic ladder to peer into that sanctum himself.

As an authority, he critiqued what he saw inside. And when it came to his father, Alex's publications only served to champion his work, even while constituting a stylistic affront. And to be fair, he admits to his own hand in creating impediments. Alex, forever ensconced in glorious history, forever looking back—an expert at the rearview mirror, the wake trailing the prow of a boat. He can never seem to commit to the present until it's safely in the past—harmless and open to endless scrutiny and interpretation.

The wall receives a thorough buffing. The gray paint reminds him of his mood most mornings—of the marine layer that engulfs the coast at daybreak. Gray emerges as the great neutralizer. Neither black nor white—just the color of equivocation, of endless cognitive obsession.

So, Alex stands before a symbol of his lack of resolve—his capitulation to his father's persona. Kazuo Arai, the Japanese American Moses—the man who would lead his people out of bondage to the promised land of ethnic acceptance. Kazuo, who dares to be the voice of a decimated generation when he barely remembers those terrible times—spared of the trauma as a child. And Alex must declare his *self* in order to make his mark on the wall before him. He searches his head for a design—a design that *is* his name. In the fierce, anarchist spirit of graffiti—a spirit which now consumes him. For that unexpected twist, the surging anger—Alex chooses the name "AWRY."

Calming his breath, he positions his can the way he's been taught. He visualizes his name in his head—feels it in his hand, and this time—*moves* with the feeling. Paint meets surface—a revelation. It takes just seconds, and Alex is done. It's over—the sinewy, continuous line complete. He marvels at the effect—the clean rendition, the letters looping to fulfillment. Ecstatic, he continues with myriad iterations—dances with the wall—bending and swooping, now standing tall. He doesn't stop until he's tagged the entire length of cinderblock—and the gray expanse sparkles with his declarations of self.

✱ ✱ ✱

Alex—

I remember taking this set of pictures. It was with an old Nikon from the early '50s. Pretty hefty, but a great camera, and I used it a lot for my studies. It was the summer before starting grad school, and I was thinking about heading back east to check out a museum or two. That's when Lisa surprised me with an invitation to visit her in Pennsylvania.

It turned out to be a nice stay in Altoona. The Keller's house was on a shady street lined with chestnut trees. Two stories tall—and the kids' rooms were all on the second floor. Lisa's bedroom now belonged to a younger sister. Still—she said, it looked a lot like when it was hers. The small bed was topped with a flowered coverlet—had a rosy dust ruffle.

During those hot summer days, we spent a lot of time playing horseshoes in the back, then cooling off in a screened-in porch. We visited several local spots like The Horseshoe Curve—the place where the railroad tracks cross the mountains in a curve so big you can see the front and the back of the train at the same time.

Lisa's parents were welcoming—seemed just fine with the both of us. I thought they might be a little shocked or upset with the adult nature of their daughter's relationship with me. Lisa's father was pretty ill but was still quite the entertaining character. Her mom tended to hover a lot, and I'd say she was more deferential to me than warm. She always had a pitcher of lemonade or ice tea on hand, coffee brewing in the background. And the food—cold cuts, bread, cheeses from the local Italian deli— If anyone stopped by, and they often did, there was always food served.

After each delicious dinner, the family would watch TV together. Following dessert, Lisa would go upstairs to her former bedroom. As for me, the accommodations in the first floor den were quite comfortable. I remember lying on the couch that first night, sheets kicked off—just wondering if Lisa would appear. After a while, I dozed off—and it wasn't until later—a good deal later—I woke up to the feel of her kissing me....

Eventually, we packed our things and drove to Philadelphia. Beyond the normal tourist stops, we spent an entire day at the Rodin Museum, viewing the largest collection of the artist's work outside of Paris. I was so excited that I started talking way too much—telling Lisa everything that I knew about the sculptures. Although she was patient with me, I know I was being way too pedantic.

And so, getting back to this stack of pictures here. That day, Lisa was wearing these black denim shorts and one of my white dress shirts. She had fun rolling up the sleeves—opened up the collar an extra button. I told her that I liked her hair looking all tussled like that. Of course, the light in any museum is crucial, whether inside or out. And that afternoon, it was vibrant. And as these pictures show, it shone beautifully off Lisa as well. And it was the *light* that holds these compositions together—a shimmering bronze by Rodin, right beside a lanky, flesh and blood Lisa.

Here she is, taking her place beside the *Burghers of Calais*. And here—a side view of her, looking pensive before the hulking presence of *The Thinker*. This is one that she likes a lot—her gazing at the smooth white marble figures of *The Kiss*. In this one here, she's clearly having fun—blowing her own kiss into the ear of *The Colossal Head of Balzac*. Then there's this last photo—the one I thought was almost comical, but I'm not so sure I do now. It's this image of her standing in front of *The Age of Bronze*—Rodin's rendering of a young Belgian soldier—so accurately done, he was charged with casting from a living model. A gorgeous male nude—Lisa caught staring at his crotch. I look at her face—study the expression. She looks quizzical—or is she really enthralled? Her mouth open— lips parted just so. She appears transfixed. Her eyes—while focused on his member—have a faraway look, as if she were lost in fantasy.

And I remember, too—some of the other thoughts I was having that day, when I stopped talking and just observed. And it makes me sad, really, how I could possibly judge her—the lovely Lisa—her face, her body—by the standards of some artistic ideal.

She enjoyed the sculptures very much, listened to my words, but I know she just didn't have that special passion inside. And it hurt my feelings that the experience didn't mean more to her—although I know that was silly. I felt bad that she would never be able to fully understand how much art meant to me. But after all, that's the way it should have been. I was the future professor—she was the future business woman.

And this collection of photos—it's not a static proposition. It's really a matter of what *stays* and what *goes* in life. It's about the shininess of a smile, the slenderness of those long legs—the brightness of her eyes and the gleam in her dark brown hair. So many years later, I look at these pictures. It's not the *art* that's captured here, but rather—certain ephemeral human features, now lost and gone. Rodin persists and always will. His sculptures retain their remarkable beauty. But that young woman in the photo no longer exists, and neither does the young man with the camera.

* * *

Mario's place, Soquel

Before his shift at the Capitola Book Café, Mario prints out a Santa Cruz County press release about the arrest of a major graffiti vandal. The *Santa Cruz Courier* has asked him to write a story about the local urban art scene. For starters, he ponders the chasm between commissioned murals and common graffiti. *Better start with an overview,* he tells himself—*check out the legal issues first.*

> Press Release
> From the County of Santa Cruz
> Office of the Sheriff-Coroner
>
> On 7/15/11, the Santa Cruz County Sheriff's Office Community Policing Team arrested 18-year-old Robert Guidry for felony graffiti vandalism. The arrest resulted after an 11-month-long investigation in which Guidry was identified as being the graffiti vandal known as "DINGO."

Guidry is described as a "prolific graffiti vandal." In addition to 'tags,' he is known to have done large murals known as 'pieces' and 'burners,' as well as etchings on glass and plastic surfaces. He was reported via the graffiti hotline by a private citizen on 5/13/11. Guidry was spotted 'tagging' a convenience store in the Live Oak area around 1 a.m. that morning.

Guidry was booked into the Santa Cruz County Jail on a bail of $35,000. A photo of Guidry is available and attached to the electronic version of the press release.

As Mario continues his online search, his cell goes off. Halfway through the ringtone, he grabs the phone hoping it's Whitney. Considering it's only eight in the morning, he ought to know better. Instantly—the strident voice of his mother floods his ear. Mario asks her to slow down, but she can't help herself. He asks her to start at the beginning, but that's never been her style. It appears that one of his younger brothers is in trouble again—Fredo, a sophomore at Watsonville High. Something about staying out late last night—maybe drugs involved. And it sounds like someone's called from school today—maybe something bad has happened there. Mario's mother gives him a number—a number of a woman who works with students, possibly a counselor. Trying to calm his mother down, he agrees to contact the school as soon as they finish.

Calls like these have been a part of his life for as long as he's had a phone—frantic, tearful calls—a kind of off-loading, a visceral purging. And Mario's left cleaning up all the emotional vomit—has to remind himself how much better his mother will feel after making *her* problem *his*. Of course, his mother doesn't mean to cause him distress. And she appreciates the support, the extra money he provides the family. It's just that, at the moment—she's not really thinking of him.

Certainly, he feels frustrated at times—not quite angry, but frustrated over his mother's dependency, neediness—her ineffectual ways, her incompetence, her— He needs to stop himself from this line of thinking, this line of feeling. With a lengthening set of promises, he gets his mother to stop talking. It's only then that she abruptly hangs up the phone.

Mario places a call to Ms. Judy Morrison, the school psychologist. She informs him that Fredo has been truant on two occasions, but that communication with his mother has been virtually impossible. Fredo was pulled aside this morning for wearing red socks—a clear violation of the dress code. Because of gang problems, students are not allowed to wear red, the color of the Norteños—or blue, the color of the rival Sureños. Fredo denied any gang affiliation—gave the weak explanation that he was a fan of the San Francisco 49ers.

Mario wants to assure Ms. Morrison that the Patino family is *Italian*, not Hispanic, but immediately realizes the absurdity of that. He says he will talk with his brother—agrees to family counseling. He and Ms. Morrison exchange their mutual appreciation. Snapping his cell phone shut, he tosses it onto his bed.

* * *

San Francisco, Holly Park Court Projects—Summer, 1985
   Early evening—

"Hey Joey—gimme the ball. We need you man!"
   "Ahh shit—what's goin' down?"
   "Somethin' bad if I can't be findin' you—"
   "But I'm always here at the park playin' hoops."
   "Yeah, shoulda knowed. But you better come quick. There's a war goin' on!"
   Joey follows his buddy down Appleton Ave. toward Patton Street. So, how long has it been since he's lived in the projects? How long since his dad cleaned himself up and brought them both to Holly Park? *Crazy ol' fool,* some would say—messed up in the head on account of his *own* dad being messed up. Something about the war—back in the old days. Joey's "Gramps" was a POW—tortured by the *Japs* in the Pacific somewhere. Joey flashes on his father's stories as he heads for another battle, another war. Living here was better than foster care, but still—it was tough for him coming to the projects as a kid. When he first arrived, there were a lot of old guys just *sittin' around drinkin' forties.* Everybody here looked *war-torn.*

Joey remembers asking people why. *It's them drugs* came the answer—each new wave brought violence. He could tell people were afraid, as he watched them *standin' against walls just shakin'*—

And then, there were all the gangs that seemed to come from everywhere. So, who's it going to be tonight? *Excelsior, Mission, Daly City?* Gangs from other projects—*Hunter's Point, Valencia Gardens...Potrero Hills, Army Street? Oh fuck it man.* At sixteen-years-old, Joey's a soldier too—his father taught him how to fight, how to take care of himself. But somehow, he ended up protecting the entire neighborhood, it appears. *Protectin' the civilians,* as he would say. Ever since Bull Dog got blown away. *Ahh, that man—a big black guy—served in the army, too.* He kept the peace until somebody gunned him down. *But*—people say, *you fight like Bull Dog. That's why we need you.* That's why Joey's buddy needs him today.

So, the sun's setting—been setting for a while, it seems. And something bad's happening at the concrete buildings of the project. Some *fuckin' punks* came by, but most of them have already run away. Approaching the courtyard, Joey hears something—spots an *ugly-ass guy* beating up on one of the neighbors. The man's face-down and defenseless, but the thug keeps kicking him in the side—*stompin'* his head. Joey runs fast—*real quiet-like.* Then *boom*—he grabs the bad guy from behind. Whirling him around, Joey punches him in the face, knocks him down. The guy pulls out a knife, but Joey mashes his wrist into the ground.

"Get the fuck outta here—fuckin' piece o' shit!"

The man wonders why this lanky kid has the balls to fight him. Doesn't wait for the answer. Scrambles up—takes off running.

"Ah man, Joey—that was too easy. If you was here early, there was like a dozen guys. From Double Rock, I think."

Joey's body feels completely charged—ready to fight them all. Helping his neighbor to his feet, he recognizes the face, recognizes the effects of all that powder cocaine. *Man, where's he get the money for that?* But Joey knows.

Back at his own place, his dad's been home all day since the Methadone clinic. He's sleeping on the couch, passed out in front of the TV. Joey would like to talk, but most of all—he would like to cry. He wants to cry because all this fighting is destroying him. It *messes* with school, *messes* with his game. Sometimes the skirmishes go on for two or three nights in a row. Joey feels like hiding sometimes. He thinks maybe, he should just run away.

But his dad did something good for him a little while back. He took his son to the York Theater on 24th. Joey watched this movie, *Style Wars,* and it was *crazy-ass good.* All about some *cool cats* in New York City, and *they was gettin' up with spray cans—and was gettin' lots of fame.* And so he *racked* some paint at the local hardware store. He'd already tried that *Cholo* writing he'd seen around. But now, Joey was creating his own tags and it turned out to be a real eye-opener. *Yeah—*it was something he was good at—*somethin' I can control.* He told his dad he wanted to go to New York City and write on trains. His father said something like, *Son, you got enough problems right here.* But Joey's had enough of it all—enough of the projects, enough of all this fighting. Later tonight he's going to rack some more paint, take his newfound talent—head down the hill for the Mission.

* * *

Bill's Wheels

Joey and Alex board a #71 bus headed for Watsonville. Along the route, they'll pass through Soquel Village before exiting at the next town of Aptos. In the back of the bus, Joey grabs a seat while Alex frets.

"Don't worry," says Joey. "It's an illegal wall, but nobody cares. Same shit's been up for what—six months?"

"I really shouldn't be doing this—"

"Look—I'll be the cat gettin' up tonight. You're just a bystander, an interested passerby. Deputies show up, I'll swear—I never laid eyes on you before."

"Yeah, except I'm dressed like a—cat burglar."

The next few miles, Joey recounts his days as a *bus hopper.* Back in The City—when kids invaded buses and plastered the insides with tags. As they pass the recent additions to Cabrillo College, he stops talking—strains for a closer look.

Several stops later, the two exit at the shopping center—take the winding sidewalk to the concrete bridge over Aptos Creek. About fifty yards long, the curved span marks the entry point to the dusty center of town.

Alex knows he's entering dangerous territory, mincing across in the evening light—random cars hurtling past. Peering over the side, he finds a gaping ravine that plunges over a hundred feet. Farther to the left, a massive railroad trestle bisects the same dark space.

In time, they enter the parking lot of the Britannia Arms pub and restaurant. From there, they circle back to the ravine. As Alex follows Joey beneath the trestle, his footing suddenly gives. Overcorrecting—he grazes the concrete wall to his right.

The trestle itself looms overhead like an evil starship—thrusting out across the gap, dark and ominous. Multiple graffiti tags form colorful battle scars on the beams and struts. Alex gazes into the depths—realizes he's standing on a dirt ledge overlooking a cliff. All the way down—a tangle of trees and shrubs, just a small patch of standing water shimmering in leftover light.

At the absolute base of the trestle's piers—several two-tone throw-ups glimmer. He even spots some artful pieces—like *KAVI* written in gold and black, *CRAZE*, in a beautiful blue to green fade. Skirting the precipice, he feels dizzy. Joey directs him to a wider, more sheltered spot just beyond. Cluttered with trash, the dirt pad features a shopping cart filled with clothes and cardboard pieces. Empty wine bottles lie scattered about, plus a love seat covered in tattered fabric.

"So what do you think, Professor? It's been quite a while since I got up here last. A good spot though—shouldn't be no one botherin' us tonight, 'cept maybe some homeless folks."

"Yeah, it's amazing—beyond anything I could've imagined. Where do you plan to work?"

"This section here at the front of the base—the part overlookin' the plunge. It's catchin' some light from the street lamp by the road. This here wall—that's what people be seein' when they cross the bridge durin' the day."

Approaching the spot, Joey deposits his backpack—unloads his tools. He lines up four cans of spray paint, then selects the appropriate cap from a baggie.

"Gotta buff this other shit first." Krylon in hand, he outlines a rectangle, six feet by twelve—fills it in with gray primer. "You know—there's certain kinda rules about goin' over other people's work. It's sorta understood, man—you gotta go bigger and better. Like—to go over tags, you gotta use a throw-up. To go over a throw-up, you gotta do a piece."

Buffing complete, Joey opens his piece book—studies his latest creation. Beginning with a white outline, he engages the wall—surrenders completely to a rhythmic, trance-like state. His design emerges, punctuated by a *pssst, pssst* and the intoxicating smell of paint fumes.

Immersed in a sensory haze, Alex's mind starts to drift to other matters—other parts of his life. He meanders through changes that have come about, some impacting his work, some affecting his passions, even.

With a good flow going, Joey lays out a piece that looks like a stylized atom. His blue-and-white *D* orbits a hot orange nucleus that makes up the rest of his name. Multiple images of the *D* give a sense of movement—the electrons set to flee the composition.

As Joey adds highlights to one of his letters, a gruff male voice enters from the periphery. A sloppy, sing-song voice—one that only Alex seems to hear. As Joey continues, the voice gets louder—erupts from around the corner. A haggard old man stumbles in—dressed in a filthy overcoat. Smelling of alcohol, the toothless man flings his body around to see who's infested his erstwhile living room.

He mumbles, then spits out the words—"If you don't get the fuck out, I'm gonna call the sheriff!"

As annoyed as he is alarmed, Alex would remind the fellow that the authorities would likely remove all three of them.

Concentration broken, Joey examines the disheveled figure. "Hey man—it's okay. We just wanna spruce things up." Reaching into his pocket, he produces a couple dollar bills. "Just sleep it off, man. You'll be surprised when you get up in the morning. I think you're gonna like what we done."

"Yeah, whatever," says the man crumpling the bills, then trying to locate a pocket. "I know what you guys are doin,'" he says—heading off for the couch. "You gotta nice piece goin' on.

You make a nice piece, man." Stumbling—"Make piece, bro," and the man disappears around the corner.

When Joey finishes, it's way past midnight. Beneath the atomic rendition of *DRAZ*, he writes *J-Boy* and *#3*.

Turning to Alex—"Come on over, man—I saved a spot for you."

"What are you talking about?"

"Like I said—get yourself some paint. I want you to put your name right here by mine. I figure we're a crew now." Joey laughs—"I ain't feelin' like an *indie* no more."

"That's flattering, Joey. Really, but—"

"Come on, Professor—hurry up before the deputies show up."

Alex grabs a can of purple paint. His hand tightens as he contemplates his first illegal tag—his first real act of graffiti vandalism. After glancing all about, he faces the wall. Needing a solid commitment, he pauses and then—throws himself into the act. So practiced by now, his hand flows more smoothly than he might have expected. A few seconds later, he and Joey admire a looping, soaring rendition of *AWRY*.

Now, Joey wants him to add something else to their names, something besides a tag—some kind of finishing flourish. After scanning his mind, Alex reaches into his *heart*. Haltingly, he makes a vertical line—dots the top with a small circle, then surrounds it with four dashes—a fifth one separated by a small gap. The effect is that of a stylized, but drippy, palm tree.

"That's what I'm talkin' about," says Joey—"now you rockin' some *real* style! Go ahead, man—put another one on the other side of your name."

Quickly, Alex complies. How amazing—this strange world of Joey's art—as if there were enough room for someone like himself.

Collecting his supplies, Joey takes one last look at the piece. "I'll come back when it's light out—take me some pictures—somethin' for the record. Good job, bro."

Several minutes later, at a Chevron station, the two writers catch the #71 heading back to Santa Cruz. Alex loves having gotten away with something illegal—an affront to society and all the authorities. As his mind dissolves into a pleasant revelry, he's jolted by an urgent nudge to his shoulder.

"We need to be gettin' off," says Joey. "I noticed somethin' when we was headin' over here."

"What are you talking about? I think the next stop's Cabrillo College."

"I know, man—now let's go." Just past the campus's main entrance, the bus lets the two men off.

"So, what are we doing here?"

"Let me show you." Joey leads Alex down the block to a retaining wall just below the parking structure. "See that? A couple bad throw-ups by someone usin' JINX."

"There's not a whole lot to look at," says Alex, glancing furtively up and down the street. "Did we really have to get off?"

Without warning, Joey drops his backpack—reaches inside for a can of paint.

"Hey, wait a minute," Alex whispers—"you can't do that here. It's the middle of Soquel Drive, for godsakes."

Not listening, Joey shakes up some white paint—starts buffing the crude, uneven letters before him. A car approaches. Alex ducks behind a nearby concrete planter. For the moment, Joey ducks too.

"You've got to stop—we're going to get busted!"

"But the guy who did this was just a *toy*—did a crappy-ass job—didn't know what he was doin'."

"Oh, come on, just leave it alone—that's not your problem."

"I'll do it fast—just a few minutes at most, bro."

Pumped and inspired, Joey works at an amazing clip, but still maintains control. His pace far outstrips what he did back at the trestle. In seconds, it seems, *DRAZ* appears in perfect bubble letters outlined in black.

Two more cars appear—the edges of their headlights just skimming the two crouched figures. Alex's heart reverberates—his hands go stiff again.

"You're crazy, Joey! That's what I've always said. Something wrong in that head of yours." Alex stands. "I'm out of here," he says, jogging away.

"Come on, man—it's just about done. Lookit—we just gotta list our names here. I got you a space. Tag this thing and you can go home!"

Turning his head, Alex slows—slows further, then finally stops. He knows he should keep on running, but then again— here's his chance to do something really rebellious, really criminal. Scared and excited, he returns to Joey, grabs the can—writes *A-W-R-Y*, then tosses it back. Running again, he feels euphoric—starts to sprint.

"Thanks, bro—" Joey calls out. "Got me an idea 'bout our new crew—meet you at the next bus stop." Joey reaches for another color. "Hey—if I don't make it, you don't hafta worry. I'll catch you at your next game."

By now, Alex is too far away to hear the last of Joey's words. With the approach of an oncoming car, the writer named AWRY forces himself to slow down. With great effort and trepidation, Professor Arai effects a brisk, but otherwise unremarkable walk.

13

From the San Jose Mercury News:
San Jose officials say annual surveys done each January noted 44,405 graffiti tags citywide this year, up from 29,285 in January 2010. This was the highest figure since the city first started tracking graffiti tags in 1999...

From Time magazine:
35.4 million—
Area, in square feet, of graffiti removed in FY 2010 by the city of Los Angeles; tagging incidents rose 8.2% from FY 2009 amid cuts in the city's graffiti-eradication budget.

From the Associated Press:
"Street Art Exhibition at Museum of Contemporary Art Prompts Praise and Concern"
By John Rogers
Los Angeles, CA

It's art from the streets that's been moved into the museum, and critics are going gaga over it. Words like stunning and near-overwhelming have been used to describe the colorful, esoteric works of Futura, Smear, Chaz Bojorquez and dozens of other street scribblers covering the walls of the Museum of Contemporary Art's Little Tokyo campus.

But take the art back to the streets, as some over-enthusiastic artists, or perhaps just wannabe

Banksys, have been doing since the exhibition opened at the MOCA's Geffen Contemporary campus earlier this month, and the reception hasn't been quite as enthusiastic.

"Art really is all about taste," says Mr. Cartoon. That was perhaps best demonstrated when MOCA Director Jeffrey Deitch commissioned the prominent Italian artist Blu to paint a huge mural on the side of the Geffen ahead of the show's opening, then ordered it whitewashed almost immediately. It was feared the mural's anti-war sentiments [it showed coffins draped in dollar bills] might be offensive to people visiting a nearby memorial honoring Japanese Americans who fought in World War II.

* * *

Little Shanghai restaurant
downtown Santa Cruz

By the unadorned windows of the small eatery, Whitney and Mario await their order. They've spent the evening at the Del Mar Theater watching the film, *The Cave of Forgotten Dreams*. The food arrives, interrupting a discussion on the director's portrayal of cave art and artists. At stake—to what extent were the scenes repetitive, due to the film crew simply running out of material?

Whitney spoons chili oil on her poached chicken and rice bowl. Ignoring his noodles, Mario needs to talk about something else.

"I tried calling you Friday night. Were you out with some friends, or what?"

Whitney snaps her chopsticks apart. She *hates* questions like that, even as he tries to cut the accusatory tone in his voice.

"I thought you'd be someplace you could answer. The last time I called was around midnight."

Chewing her food as if grinding her teeth—"I must have been working on one my paintings. Sometimes, I just turn off my phone."

"But you never did that before."

"Oh, sure I have."

"Well, anyway—you remember that new assignment they gave me at the paper?"

"Yeah, I think you told me about it last week."

"That's right. I've been doing some research on the topic—you know, it's about street art here in the community."

"Sounds interesting. How's it going?"

"I met some really cool people who happen to be a part of an art collective. They're also into social consciousness. They give street art classes to help youth stay out of trouble—develop their talent."

"So, were they able to help you?"

"Yeah, they promised to take me to some graffiti sites around town. But you know, I saw something interesting when I went to park my car at Cabrillo. There's this wall just below the lot that had some of the most complex graffiti I'd ever seen. I went down to the sidewalk for a better look. You haven't been there, have you?"

"I hardly ever go that way," she says. "Oh maybe, once—yeah, when Julie drove us there for the farmers market on a Saturday."

Leaning forward—"Then let me tell you what I saw. There was what graffiti writers call bubble letters. I clearly made out a *D*, an *R*, an *A*, and a *Z*. That was the main part of the design. Then just below was this fancy, Old English script—like *cholo* writing going back to the 1930s. It read *Make Piece Bro.* Then, just below that was a small *MPB crew*. Then a *J-Boy*, the number *3* and something else that looked like a tag." Gazing intently at Whitney's face—"By the way—does any of this sound familiar?"

"No, not really."

"Then I guess you don't know what symbol he used to frame the piece—right?"

"No, I don't."

Mario looks deep into his girlfriend's eyes—"It was one of your tattoos, Whit."

"What do you mean, it was one of my tattoos?"

"It was the one on top—near the crest of your hip. Looked pretty close. That stalk that goes up to a circle—the four wiggly fingers and a thumb. Looks like a weird palm tree or something. The only thing—the circle didn't have a face inside."

Wrinkling her brow, Whitney stares at Mario, then stares *through* him into some vague territory beyond. "That's amazing," she says. "It does sound like one of my tats. I got that about three years ago—right after I moved to Santa Cruz."

"So, why's some guy tagging my school with your tattoo?"

"I don't know. It sounds totally weird—kind of creepy."

"Really, now?" Mario's eyes narrow to a glare—one he rigidly brackets with the rest of his face. "Who's gotten that close to your body? Some old boyfriend—or maybe someone at the art class—someone you pose nude for?"

Struggling to contain his voice, he shoves it into a deeper register. "Come on—you've got to have *some* idea—unless you're trying to hide something."

Whitney shrugs—places both hands on the table.

Needing to back off, Mario can't. "I don't know who *DRAZ* is, but part of the design uses gang lettering. He's got the name of the gang, or *crew*—the *MPB crew* he writes below. The *Make Piece Bro* crew. Then he lists the members under that. You still listening?"

"Yeah, I am."

"This kind of graffiti—it uses different styles. It's got a throw-up on top, but comes off like a *placa* done by some gang-banging Mexican. It's all about marking territory. The word *piece* has to do with something big. But it makes me mad—this guy's staking a claim on you by using your tat and pointing to another kind of *piece*."

"But I don't know anybody who could do something like that. Not that I can think of."

At best, Mario feels like an investigative reporter—at worst, a police interrogator. "This guy who has the hots for you—he's got some Latino connection or background. He also knows the hip hop style of graffiti. He's got to be someone in that class of yours—"

"I don't think, I mean—I'm not sure anyone there fits your description."

"Then, what about an old boyfriend? I know you've had other guys in your life."

"That's interesting. At first I thought—maybe it had to do

with my first boyfriend—my first real lover. The way he was and all, except he wasn't an artist. But the main thing—he would've never seen that tat. I got it right after I dumped him—and he was still back in Torrance."

Intrigued—"So, did the tattoo have something to do with him?"

"Oh yeah, it did—" Whitney smirks. "That design is something I made up. I did it to look like a hand. The guy was a body worker. I thought maybe he could teach me something I didn't know about myself—about my body, you know? And I guess he did with those hands of his—those great big hands. The wiggly fingers around the circle—that's because I turned the hand into a sea anemone. Turns out that guy wanted to hurt me. He liked to hurt me and got off on that. On my tattoo, the circle has a woman's face inside, and she looks peaceful. That's because she's really Medusa and in control. Those fingers are now her snakes. And that's what I did to him—turned him into stone. Then, I got the fuck out of there."

Hearing all this, Mario feels both stunned and strangely aroused. "So, what about the other tattoos? Do they stand for other guys—other lovers?"

"I don't know—what do you think?"

Simultaneously, Mario feels both large and small. He doesn't understand how his crotch can swell, while his sense of self feels so diminished. "So, the guys—what's the stories about those other two guys?"

"Oh—you're curious about my other lovers? Well, you've been such a jerk—I'm not going to tell you any more stories." Picking up her chopsticks, she sticks them back into the luke-warm rice. "Maybe you should think through your questions more. You might not be happy with the answers."

Mario has no appetite now. He ignores his plate of tepid noodles. For the rest of dinner, he sits by the window, watching Whitney eat. From time to time, Mario swallows, but he only swallows his words. He would still like answers from his girlfriend, answers to all his many questions.

But the ones he focuses on—the practical ones he can't stop thinking about—"Are we still going back to your place?" And—"do I still get to spend the night?"

* * *

The house on Escalona Drive

Kaz—the guest of honor—sits at the head of the dining room table, once more celebrating his "69th" birthday. Sumi occupies the next seat over, while Alex and Lisa, Carter and Nita fill the remaining chairs.

"That was a delicious meal," Sumi says, as if prompting her husband.

"Yes," he adds—"a nice meal, Lisa. The chicken marsala was really tasty. Just right for our special get-together."

"Thank you, Kaz—you know I had help."

"Of course—credit to you as well, Alex." Rising from his chair—"I think I'll head upstairs to set up my slides. Sumi—you can stay here and help clean up."

Quickly, Nita volunteers to lend a hand, as does Carter.

"Oh come on," says Lisa. "You know how it goes with us. We don't help you out at *your* house, and you don't need to lift a finger at *ours*. Go on now, all of you. I'll just clear the table. Alex and I can take care of the rest later."

"Now, Dad—" says Alex, trailing. "Let's hold off on the slides until another time. Just relax—enjoy the company."

"But, why should we have to wait?" asks Kaz, continuing up the stairs. "I'll just put together a quick review."

"Let me help," says Carter. "I'd like to see what you were talking about—your new ideas for glass."

As Nita joins Sumi on the suede-covered sofa, Alex sneaks his friend a frustrated look. Reserving the leather chair for his father, he claims one end of the matching love seat.

"This has always been such a nice, airy space," says Nita. "Here we are, just above that old oak tree by the window, enjoying the sunset across the bay." A liquid, tangerine light infuses the room—amply illustrates Nita's point.

Kaz hands Carter the portable screen. "Old-time equipment," Carter notes. Finding a spot across the room, he chuckles as he splays the legs—raises the granulated face by its skinny neck. "Well, beyond the artistry, you've done a lot to shape the Japanese American narrative." Settling between Nita and Sumi on the sofa—"And that enriches the national narrative as well."

"I really like the way you put things," says Kaz. "I truly believe I speak for my people, about their struggles against injustice, their heroism. I've created memorials so that we as a people know our identity—who we are—what we've gone through."

Lisa enters with a tray of coffee mugs with the usual distribution of caffeine. Finished serving, she takes a seat next to Alex. "Well, what have I missed?" she asks.

"Carter's been giving Dad credit for his work. You know, the social impact—the collective memory part of it all."

"Of course," she says—"Carter always has something interesting to say."

Kaz selects another slide. "Run that by me again, Carter— all that *collective memory* stuff."

"Well, as they say, it's a long story—enough for a whole class or two," he smiles. "I mean, a lot of people study memory in academics. Kind of messy with all the different disciplines. When it comes to individuals, you should ask Nita about the psychology part—"

"Just take it from a therapist," she smiles. "We all use memory to make stories about who we are. Trouble is— sometimes the stories are destructive, negative. A lot of my work has to do with rehabbing faulty self-narratives."

Carter clears his throat. "To put it simply, the way I teach collective memory would go something like this— Memory takes place on the level of the individual—memory takes place inside a person's head. But powerful social influences are also at work. Group dynamics can actually determine how and what a person remembers. Collective memory is about a kind of consensus—one that serves the group's agenda. Like when a political party chooses a candidate from a slate of contenders— *We're the party of So-and-So....*"

Carter glances at Kaz to see if he's following. "Take a family, an ethnic group, or an entire nation. They all define themselves through collective memory. They put together narratives that tell their members who they are and why they're unique."

"So, give me an example. Maybe use something like America—the American story."

"Certainly," says Carter. "The main narrative is that a band of upstart English colonies joined together to fight tyranny and to win their independence. They subsequently formed a democratic union that featured the most enlightened governing principles the world had ever seen."

"Terrific stuff," says Kaz. "I think our identity is also about being the best and most powerful country in the world. It's because of America that we won the two world wars. Too bad that serious injustices happened—like civil liberties violated when Japanese Americans were illegally interned during World War II. Is that a part of the national narrative?"

"It is now," says Carter. "The redress movement, a formal apology, financial reparations. All that, plus books, oral histories, and memorials like yours have changed the narrative to include a group of people who didn't belong in American history before."

Collecting Nita's mug, Lisa ambles toward the stairs. "Why don't you talk about the *memory boom*—the whys of it all. It's as if we've all become hoarders of memory."

"Why sure," he says. "There's been a huge focus on memory since the late 1970s. You've probably seen it—a big interest in genealogy, memoir writing, scrapbooking, photos and videos, heritage trips—doing the *Roots* thing." Glancing at Nita—"Of course, a lot has to do with self-definition, asserting the sense of self."

"Well then," says Alex—"why don't you tell my father about your thoughts on the so-called *trauma narrative*?"

"Ah, I don't know about that," he says, as Lisa reenters with Nita's freshened brew. A quick aside—"I'm not sure it's a good idea with what we've been talking about—your father's art and all."

"Oh, come on, now. We're all open to new perspectives."

Abandoning his slides, Kaz marches over to the leather chair.

"Well, I suppose," relents Carter. "Obviously, everyone likes a positive story. What we call *progressive narratives* are positive in nature. Like—how the allies triumphed during World War II."

"And, how's that?" asks Kaz.

"World War II is seen as a *good* war in which the noble allied forces defeated the wicked axis powers. In particular— Hitler and the Nazis will forever be seen as icons of human evil. And likewise—nothing will ever top the Holocaust as an example of the absolute worst in humankind. In the progressive version, the allies brought freedom and economic well-being to the West, while Jews were given the opportunity to return to their homeland to rightfully establish their own state."

"So, isn't that correct?" asks Kaz.

"Well, to be fair—the collective memory of Palestinians and other Muslims runs counter to that. But the point is, that since the '60s, things have shifted away from the progressive narrative to what's been called the trauma narrative. In addition to the Holocaust, there's the history of slavery and racial discrimination in America—the civil rights struggles of the LGBTQ community—"

"And the rise of feminism also plays an important part," adds Lisa. "Women have certainly suffered oppression. Our narrative clearly has a traumatic component."

"That would be right," says Nita.

"Of course," says Carter.

Alex shifts positions in the love seat. "I've talked to Carter a lot about this. You know, Dad—this inclusion of minority narratives is just one part of the memory boom. It's as if we're all standing in line, demanding our fair share of validation and compensation. But let's face it—in our efforts to be seen and heard—to have past wrongs acknowledged—we end up cultivating that identity of the *victim.*"

Alex notes a surge in his voice—"I've studied all the resulting memorials. Heroic renderings are getting harder to come by. Apart from MLK, we've got a maze of concrete blocks in Berlin, bronze and glass chairs in Oklahoma City—a huge void and inverted fountains in New York City." Stronger, still— "And if you think about the greatest contemporary memorial of all—Maya Lin's Viet Nam *wall*—how gloriously ambiguous it is in naming the fallen. Are they heroes—or victims? That black granite chevron wedged into the ground—serves as the great national Rorschach for an American trauma."

"So," snaps Kaz, "what are you trying to say?"

"Oh, I don't know—I guess I got off on a little rant, that's all." Alex hesitates—hates to capitulate to his father. But still— "I mean, you've done some really good work. You've created symbols the community can be proud of—even though we've become steeped in victimhood."

"Is that so?"

"Well—maybe you could move beyond your usual, basic design. Define a new dimension to the Japanese American narrative—add further to our identity, beyond the war."

"What do you mean? I'm well-known for my so-called *basic design*. The things I create really speak for our community. Remember, I was there—I was there in camp with everyone." Voice rising—"The story is not just about being victims, but how we finally triumphed on the battlefield. Just think about it—you don't put up memorials for the average, common man. I mean—what would you think about a statue of a shop owner, a mechanic, a pharmacist—a teacher?"

"But, your ongoing use of figurative bronze sculptures—I wouldn't say they're dated but...."

"What are you talking about?" Standing now—"You've written positive critiques about how I handle bronze surfaces. How did you put it? *Kazuo Arai is one in the tradition that stretches back to the great Auguste Rodin.*"

"Well, you've also done interesting things with glass— absolutely unique, quite dramatic. But some critics think the industrial bases look out of place."

"For cryin' out loud—since when have you paid attention to other critics? Your opinion is the only one that counts. People believe you have some inside knowledge—an appreciation for the man I am. It gives your judgments extra punch. You were the one who wrote—*Kazuo Arai spans all of Modernism by placing his magnificent sculptures triumphantly atop their spare, Modernist platforms.* Didn't you write that? Didn't you mean that?"

"Oh Kaz—" interrupts Lisa, "I definitely recall reading that essay. It was from a group exhibition in Los Angeles. The catalogue. Of course, Alex wrote that."

Alex catches himself slumping. "You're correct, Dad. I wrote it—and so I need to stand by it."

"So what's this big turnaround? What's all this negativity about?"

"It's just that—maybe I thought you could take a bold evolutionary step. You know—go Postmodern and give the viewer a more interactive experience with your pieces."

"Postmodern? That's all a bunch of garbage." Starting to pace, Kaz turns—"If you want to know—I've got big plans for taking a jump into the future. You know how Sendai, Japan, was devastated by the earthquake and tsunami? I want to find out if the fountain by my friend, George Tsutakawa, was destroyed in all that. I want to build a memorial to the Japanese people who survived that catastrophe—the people who will rebuild that country and make it strong again. I'm going to create a giant wave of concrete and glass—towering over my bronze figures."

"That should be quite effective—"

"And you—it's just like when you were a kid that one time. Remember? You got into my studio and actually marked up one of my designs. And you had the nerve to say you were trying to help me make it better. Well, I haven't forgotten."

"Neither have I."

"So, I'm not going to harp on it now—but *I'm* the sculptor, for gosh sakes—*I* do the art. That's where the talent is. You're the student—and a good one at that. You're an excellent writer. And that's all I'm asking you to do. Just write. And please do justice to my work."

"Yeah, I get it Dad."

"And you should know—I was poking around your little table behind the *shoji* screen before dinner. And I can tell you, my judgment of you hasn't changed. Those drawings of yours—those drawings of a young woman, I think. They're so unbalanced—so overdone. The only thing they show is your big struggle with technique."

"Say you two—" interrupts Nita, "you're both very talented in your respective ways. It's just that—sometimes it's hard to have empathy for each other when you butt heads. I know you respect your father, Alex. And I know you'd like to feel that coming from him, as well."

Kaz reclaims his chair—continues to fume.

Alex turns to Nita—"Thanks, I do appreciate your words.

But don't worry—you don't have to do family therapy tonight." Nodding to his friends—"It's just great having you and Carter here." Steeling himself—"Now, where exactly were we?" As he reaches for his mug, his eyes look blank. "I think we were talking about trauma narratives and such." Mug to his lips—he discovers it empty.

Lisa unfolds herself from the love seat. "You know, Kaz— it wouldn't hurt for you to be a little more understanding. Birthday aside—it always ends up being about you, doesn't it? Kazuo Arai, the great sculptor. In fact—" she says, "maybe it's time for you to be going home. Sumi—I'm sorry. But as for you, Kaz," she says sternly, "it feels like it's getting late."

Surprised—Kaz attempts a warped version of a smile. "But my slides—"

"That'll be for another time," says Lisa, walking towards the projector. "I'll help you take the equipment down to your car."

"But, wait. You can't do this to me—"

"Oh, yes, I can."

Alex's mother has been silent throughout. As her husband reaches the stairwell, she finally stands. Passing Alex, she utters a single word to him—the Japanese word, *gaman*, for "buck up," or "bear it with dignity." Her face looks stiff behind her intent not to cry.

Carter walks over to his friend—puts a hand on his shoulder. Nita insists that they stay a bit longer—to help in the kitchen, even though that's not the routine.

Alex remains in the loft as everyone else goes downstairs. The sense of humiliation scours his stomach—hollows him out. He waits until he hears his parents' car depart. Glancing at the *shoji* screen that hides his artwork, a searing shame consumes him—a shame he can't quite remember feeling before. Or, actually maybe he *can* remember. Maybe it's an old shame, one that's still a part of his story.

14

Lisa—

I recall it wasn't all that easy with Alex when school started up in the fall. After his visit back east, I thought we'd be spending more time together. Well, at least we did at first. Then he got a room to rent off Mayfield Avenue, just down the road from Flo-Mo. It really felt strange being left behind— like someone in my family had moved out of the house.

It was at the start of the new year. That's right, because we'd spent the night at Alex's parents' house in San Jose. To them, it didn't seem like a big deal, but Alex insisted I use his bed, while he slept on the living room sofa.

That New Year's Eve, they had a small party. His brother Henry came by, along with a few family friends. Sumi made the traditional buckwheat noodles—explained that they were for good luck. It was a lot of fun that night, playing cards and watching TV—counting down as the big crystal ball fell in Times Square. That was the signal to eat the noodles—then came a big round of "Happy New Year!"

The next morning I woke up to a wonderful aroma coming from the kitchen. Sumi was up early making a special soup called *ozoni*. The broth consisted of bonito stock and was filled with Japanese mountain potatoes, carrots, kelp—and some kind of earthy root. That was the first time I had eaten *mochi*, the special rice cakes that their friends had made by hand.

Anyway, before we could eat the *ozoni*, we all took part in a traditional ceremony by drinking *sake* from this tiny lacquered cup. When Kaz was ready, he summoned us all to the living room. He explained to me that we'd be following Japanese custom regarding the order of things. Kaz, as the oldest male, entered the dining room first. Then came the other two males, starting with the older brother, Henry. After Alex went in, Sumi, the oldest female, was allowed to follow. That left me to bring up the rear. Our seating was also determined by tradition, as was the order for drinking *sake*.

Sumi served from a spouted porcelain pot. When it was her turn to sip, Henry did the honors. I just kind of sat back—took it all in. I liked the little bit of drink and especially the marinated fish eggs I was told to receive in my upturned hand. I thought it was quite an honor just to be there. Following the *sake*, Sumi served us some green tea and pickled delicacies.

After finishing the delicious soup, it felt good heading back to campus. By now, Alex had his own car—a well-worn Camaro of all things. He said he liked the white stripes on the blue hood, but I knew he was kidding. Bought it from a classmate—just a source of transportation to him. It was raining lightly as we drove up Highway 280, singing along to Abba on the cassette player. We got off at Sand Hill Road then hung a right onto Junipero Serra—passed through that wooded section—Lake Lagunita on the left, all misty looking.

As Alex drove up to his place, he joked how happy he was, now that he lived in the *high-rent district*. By then, I'd been to his *pad* several times. It was a house he shared with a couple other grad students. I liked seeing how he arranged things in his little room with its side bath. He had posters on his wall from different museums he'd been to all across the country. I'd given him a poster of Rodin's *Prodigal Son* and liked seeing it featured above his bed.

You know—I never planned to say what I said that day. That afternoon, in fact— There was this pitter-patter from the rain, and I remember thinking how the insulation wasn't all that great. I guess maybe because I remember feeling kind of cold at the start. Of course, Alex did everything he could to warm me up—was always good about that. So, pretty soon, our clothes were off, and we were huddling under this big, soft comforter. I only thought about it later—that when we had fun—when we laughed a lot—making love was just a different experience. It was comfortable and easy—not so passion-driven. That gentle way of being together was so comforting to me. And it's really such a caring, considerate, tender thing to do—to bring one's partner to completion like that.

So afterward, I was in his arms, and we were still a little tangled and on our sides. And I was facing him, and I just reached across that small gap. I reached with my hand and pushed the pillow down just a bit, so I could see his full face. And then I touched his cheek, brushed it with the back of my fingers—and I told Alex I loved him.

* * *

Art League of Santa Cruz

Having toured a number of graffiti sites, Mario's obsessed with the identity of the graf writer named DRAZ. As a journalist, he always seeks the truth—but this time, it's personal. Helped by an art collective member, he saw nothing suspicious at the Aptos ditch, the Soquel arches, or the tunnels off Old San Jose Road. But beneath the Aptos trestle, he discovered a full-blown piece by DRAZ and his MPB crew.

Mario was incensed when he saw Whitney's tattoo attached to the list of names. Some *dick-head guy* has been sneaking around, vandalizing walls with an intimate image of the only girl he's ever wanted. Some guy—flaunting his relationship with her, claiming her as personal property. Mario resolves to find and punish the criminal who disrespects him so.

Fidgeting in his car, he monitors the façade of the Art League building. In just a few minutes, class will adjourn, allowing him to observe the departing students. With the unseasonable cold, he's brought an extra wrap should Whitney need one.

Time passes, and the class is definitely running late. It just *kills* Mario to imagine his girlfriend inside, her nude body on display for a group of men and women. *Posing* for them all at this very moment—all those eyes taking advantage of her. At least that's what's going on with the guys, he thinks.

And it's not just Whitney's body, her face—not just the sweet proportions of all her parts. It's something that wells up from deep inside her, something she projects—a strange kind of *devious* soulfulness. Mario tries to invoke the look— can't decide if she's being purposeful or merely careless. He's haunted by that flickering visage—the one that wavers between disdain and *come hither*. A look that rejects, dismisses—while still conveying to a man that he might just have the slightest chance.

The front door opens. Mario scrambles out of his car. An older fellow in a maroon jacket descends the stairs, followed by two middle-aged women. Quickly, he discounts the man as being too old for a viable suspect. Next emerges a college-aged guy in skinny jeans and a dark hoodie. Trotting over, Mario looks for a certain vibe. The guy's build looks unremarkable— certainly, not a stud.

"Hey," calls Mario, "I was wondering what you thought of the class."

"It's been really cool. We've got a good instructor."

"And the models?"

"Yeah, they're great. And the girl that comes on Tuesdays, like tonight—well, she's really hot. But still—she does a nice job with the poses."

"What's her name?"

"Oh, I don't know—can't remember. You could ask Cecil, though."

"Thanks," says Mario, crossing him off his list. Looking around, he spots a college coed in a long peasant dress and sandals. Next comes a middle-aged man in the company of an older woman. Then, a slightly-built younger fellow in a green sweater appears. Mario wants to believe he's not Whitney's type—but apparently, he doesn't really know her type. In any case, the guy looks Latino and therefore fits one of his profiles.

"Hey man," he begins, "I was wondering what you thought of the class."

The young guy appears awkward and shy—kind of hard to hear. Beneath his carefully combed hair, his dark face consists of a finely shaped nose and a smallish chin. Mario acknowledges a kind of cuteness factor.

"The class is good," the young man says.

"What do you like about it?"

Pausing a moment—"It's a good opportunity. It doesn't cost much."

"And what about the models?"

Shoving both hands into his pockets—"I like the models."

"So—tonight's model—do you happen to know her name?"

Eying Mario suspiciously—"Yeah, her name's Whitney."

"So what do you like about her—as a model?"

Pausing again—"She's on time. She does good work."

"Anything else?"

"Well—she's a nice person."

Mario feels okay about the current interview, but has one more question to ask.

Looking directly into the young man's eyes—"As an artist, what do you think about graffiti?"

Looking more annoyed than frightened, the guy shakes his head. "You know, it's bad for businesses. It's a crime."

Mario offers a quick thanks—returns his gaze to the front door. Straining, he can hear laughter—male laughter—coming from just inside. He spots Whitney in a white shift emerging through the door. Smiling brightly, she turns to the person who's cleared the way. Big belly laugh—male. It's the same guy who showed up at Stripe for her art show. At the top of the stairs, her gaze plummets to find her boyfriend standing on the sidewalk.

An immediate frown—"So, what are you doing here, Mario?"

Upset at the sight of Whitney and her friend—"I just wanted to check out your workplace—your job." Mario glares at the big guy on the staircase.

"Oh, hey man," says the guy—looking alarmed. "We just got out of class." Lifting his sketchbook into the air, he gives it a shake. "Just practicing, you know—always practicing."

Whitney's hand flies up to her mouth, as she tries to cover a smile.

Mario doesn't think it's funny.

Recovering—"I'm pretty sure you remember Tom."

"No kidding," says Mario, pointedly. "I knew you two were close—"

"Ah nah," says Tom, stepping fitfully down the stairs. "It's not like that. We're just joking around—I swear."

Whitney glares at Mario—"You didn't tell me you were coming by."

Holding his ground—"It was cold tonight, colder than expected. Thought you might need a jacket or something. I know you ride your bike."

"You've got to stop it—"

Mario waits for Tom to reach the pavement. "Hey listen," he says, "I want to ask you something. I'm doing some research for an article I'm writing. Tell me—what do you think about graffiti?"

Whitney interrupts, "Don't ask him that—"

"It's okay," says Tom—relieved to be changing topics. "Well, you know—actually I think a lot of graffiti is pretty cool." Tom searches Mario's face for a reaction—"Not the tags so much but the other stuff—the throw-ups and pieces and all."

"Sounds like you know something about graffiti."

"Yeah, well—we've all done it at some point in our lives, right?" Venturing a smile—"I got up a little in Sacramento when I was younger. You know—skipping school, skating around—listening to the Deftones. But that was a while ago. Takes a shit-load of skill to do it right. I give those guys major props—the ones who get known in the writing community."

"Were you ever a member of a crew?"

"Oh hell no—I really wasn't all that good. Nobody wanted me within a mile of their crew," he says, laughing. "I'm afraid I had to settle for a career in the fine arts—"

Mario wants to hate the guy—wants to believe he's the one who's been getting up and *off* on Whitney's tattoos. And it makes him mad the way the two of them carry on like that after the weekly *show*. Even if Tom isn't the writer named DRAZ, Mario still wants to *crush* him. He knows men—knows that Tom likes jerking-off over the drawings he makes each week at the Art League.

Whitney's good-byes trail a rapidly retreating Tom.

Glad to be rid of that hulking presence, Mario tries to be conciliatory. "Look, I'm sorry I upset you. It's just that—"

Whitney shoves him—"You're so annoying, Mario—you fucking piss me off!" Under the street light, her eyes glow big and white. "I'm sick and tired of you monitoring me, following me—stalking me!"

"Look, I'm just trying to find out what's happening, that's all."

Wanting to comfort her, he extends his arms. Whitney responds by slapping them down.

"Just get out of here—get out of my life, why don't you? Go find someone else you can freak out on!"

Mario expects her to cry, but she doesn't.

"Come on over to the car," he says. "We'll put your bike in the back. I'll drive you home—it'll be safer that way. You're way too upset—"

"Quit trying to protect me! Besides—I didn't ride my bike tonight!"

Mario steps forward—steps too close. "Don't tell me you walked all the way from downtown."

Finally, Whitney begins to cry, and it makes her angry. She points down the sidewalk to the young man in the green sweater. "I got a ride here from Carlos—Carlos drove me here."

Mario turns to find the slender young man who looks to be drifting in and out of the shadows. "That guy drove you? What's that all about?"

"He's a nice guy—really talented. We talk about art. I showed him some of my paintings."

As confused as he's angry—"What do you mean—you took him back to your place?"

"No, I just had him stop by when he picked me up."

Mario marches over to where Carlos is standing. "Okay—you've done your good deed for tonight. In case you don't get it—I'm driving my girlfriend home—*comprende*?"

Carlos appears calmer than Mario would have expected or wanted. The man in the green sweater nods, then walks away.

On the ride home, the car fills with recriminations. Mario's cell goes off, but he decides to answer it later. The heated talk continues as the two climb up the external stairs to Whitney's apartment. Barging in, he tells her he just wants to know the *truth* behind the strange graffiti he's seen.

"It's not about the graffiti," she insists. "You're so insecure—it's like you had a bad life or something. Just imagine—a guy who looks like you, a guy with a good future—a good future with writing. You of all people!"

"But the truth matters! I've been wondering if there's someone else in your life—some other guy. I get that feeling, because you've been pulling away. We haven't been close in what—two weeks?"

"I'm telling you the truth Mario. I've been doing my art. After you—what would I want with another guy in my life? I need a freakin' break from guys, not someone else!"

Mario follows her past her easel to the foot of her bed. Closing in, frustration and anger overrun his mind. He can't stop it. He wants to shove her back on the bed—push her down with his entire weight—tear off just enough clothes that he can enter her—reclaim her.

"I know what you're like, Whit—sooner or later you're going to want another guy—"

"So he can do what, Mario—so he can *fuck* me to death?"

Mario grabs her and she begins to struggle.

"What are you doing?" she asks—but clearly knows. "Why are you—" she starts to ask, but stops.

Falling to her bed, she lies beneath the crushing weight of Mario's urgency. And she feels his desire fully formed at its center—already pushing, already probing through her clothes.

"Get off!" she chokes—her voice muffled by his pressured kisses.

She can taste him now—tastes herself. She can smell the heat off Mario—can smell herself. And she hates that heat, the pressure, and all the wet parts to the point she starts to claim them—even though she won't let him know. Instead, she reaches up beneath his shirt and claws his back—reaches up and grabs his hair—bites his cheek until he wrenches it away. With all his strength, Mario forces his body into hers. But she knows better—knows that she's brought him to this, even as the awareness is fleeting. Hate, love, lust. All at once, all together. All of that and they don't care *how* or *why* anymore—and no one's thinking about it anyway. All the merging—the savage meshing of rightness and wrong. They travel like this for a long time, until they finally get off together.

*

So that's what it takes for Mario to discharge his anger, his fear. That's what it takes for Whitney to complete her unspoken game with him. That's what it takes for Mario to stop raving about *the truth*. That's what it takes for Whitney to end it all. After their huge but separate sleeps, they climb out of bed. They arise to a bright gray light flowing through the *morning window*—the kind of light that best sheds reality on a canvas, a painting. They take turns at the toilet—take turns washing their faces. Whitney opens her fridge and pours a glass of orange juice for herself and one for Mario. She wonders how best to say it to him. Some further justification or apology for breaking up.

But before she can open her mouth, his cell goes off again. In order to answer, he excuses himself—steps outside to the small wooden landing. He closes the door, but even so—the truth of the conversation seeps through the cracks between the door and frame. Propped against the counter, Whitney muses over matters of *honesty*. She listens to Mario's conversation with his mother—has never heard the nature of their exchanges before.

She picks up on a certain cadence, a certain familiar rapid-fire flow of syllables—listens to the trill of "r's" that sounds like small explosions. From high school lessons, she identifies a pleasing musicality, even though it rides the swells of internal distress. Something about Mario's brother—something about getting in trouble. Something about *la migra* and the fear of deportation. *No toda la familia....* And Whitney hears the way Mario's voice gradually settles—eases into a quiet, reassuring tone. *Todo saldrá bien, Mamá....* Mario's voice—measured, comforting. A tone she recognizes from some time ago. And Whitney thinks to herself—*so much for the truth.*

When Mario reenters her studio, he apologizes for his mother's intrusion. It's something about his younger brother, Fredo, again. More trouble, and their mother needs his help in dealing with the school administration. Another meeting, another appointment with the school counselor.

Whitney gathers up all his words—notes the different

rhythm now, the different sounds—the "r's" that fail to roll, but simply flow.

"Mario," she says to her soon to be former boyfriend, "you talk so much about the truth, but you're not even the person you say you are. Hearing you on the phone, I found you out—I've got the truth on *you* now." Setting aside her empty glass—"It's no big deal if you're not Italian—you're not white, whatever. That whole ethnic thing—it's so totally bogus, such a joke. But it hurts that you kept on lying to me. I guess you never planned to tell me you're really a Mexican—an undocumented one at that—"

* * *

Alex—

I remember it was January—1982. Lisa and I had just spent the night at my parents' house. It had felt really strange—thought I'd get at least a funny look from my mother. But I guess they must have considered me an adult by then. I enjoyed the New Year's festivities, the ceremonial stuff—much more than usual. That's because Lisa was there to take it all in. Always such a good sport—

After a special breakfast, we drove back to campus—I'd gotten both my car and my own place that year. I relished the privacy of my little room—liked arranging it exactly the way I wanted. Or, I should say—pretty much the way I wanted.

Lisa had given me a poster as a gift—Rodin's *Prodigal Son*. I got the feeling I should put it above the bed. I went around the room holding it up in different places for her to see. It was like that game—the one where you're told if you're getting *hot* or *cold* based on your proximity to something. So in the end, the anguished figure of the *Prodigal Son* came to rest above the headboard. Honestly, I preferred the Modigliani nude I had up there before. That gorgeous odalisque was far sexier, with more seduction value. So yeah, I have to admit—there were a couple of other women who came by to see me that year.

But getting back to that day in '82—it was Lisa's senior year and my first in grad school. When we got to my place, it had already started to rain. We'd enjoyed the ride and both of us were in really good spirits. I wish I was more clear about how it went that afternoon—that is, after we got into bed. All I know is that afterward—Lisa was absolutely radiant. And she was so sweet, so tender—and that was the first time she used the word *love* with me.

I suppose a guy should say something like *And I love you too*, or at least *thank you*. Of course, I knew that. But the irony was, I cared so much for her, I just couldn't manage to say the word. I could have said it because I *did* love her. But it wouldn't have been exactly the way she'd meant it. And I'd known for quite some time, there was this—disparity. If I'd returned her *love*, I knew I'd be misleading her.

So what did I end up saying? I feel like an idiot now—but I said, *love is a big word*. And I still cringe when I remember her face—how she could look both surprised and hurt at the same time. I said that maybe we should go for a walk—maybe we should talk about it some more.

So we got dressed. I was feeling awful, and so was she. I almost couldn't get the car started—that damn Camaro. But eventually I drove us back to her dorm. We got out—I went back and rummaged through the trunk and found an old umbrella, one with a balky mechanism. The wind was strong, and the rain was falling harder. Holding the umbrella over both of us, I walked with her up to the Knoll—the old, ivy-covered music building. From there we took the short path down to Lake Lagunita.

That afternoon, all the surrounding oaks looked like battered umbrellas, too—protective canopies in the midst of utter failure. The rain made the sky so dark, we could hardly see the opposite shore and the rolling hills. We were silent for a long time—unusual for us. Then, I tried to explain that we both—what? Nothing I could say was of any good for what Lisa was feeling. And so, yes—I finally said that I loved her too. But with all the equivocation, she knew it wasn't the same feeling for me. And about a half mile around the bank, we were both shivering—our pants damp from the knees down. And in that small space between the umbrella and our shoulders, I could see her quietly crying. And it broke my heart—that is, whatever my heart was made of at the time.

She said something to the effect—"When we get close like that—it's only natural for a person to fall in love." And then, for the first time I heard a tone of bitterness. And she kind of scolded me—even as her voice remained small. Said something like, "You shouldn't do that Alex. You shouldn't do that to a girl— Shouldn't make her feel that way when you're making love—not if your heart isn't up to it."

And then later, she apologized to me for saying that. But I didn't want an apology—didn't deserve one.

A couple days passed, and it started raining again in earnest. For three days, it rained so hard in the San Francisco Bay Area, there were something like eighteen thousand landslides in the region. And the worst damage happened right in Santa Cruz County. A catastrophic storm—the worst loss of life from a natural disaster in recorded history here. At the time, I didn't know the names of some of the affected places. But the river flooded—the San Lorenzo River. Twenty-two people died in the storm, mostly because of landslides. At Love Creek, twelve miles north of Santa Cruz—a quarter-mile section of hillside gave way—burying houses and killing ten. The bodies of two small children were never recovered.

When I moved here later, people warned me not to live in the Santa Cruz Mountains. Anyway—it was too far from the university for an easy commute. But I listened to what people had to say—respected all that. And I can hardly believe that next year—it will be thirty long years since that storm.

15

The house on Escalona Drive

Through billows of vapor, Alex exits the shower—heads for the glass triptych overlooking the counter. Wiping off the main mirror, he confronts his face. Here he is again—that central person in his life—the one in the spotlight of his own making.

Checking the time, he ponders what clothes to wear. Given the stealth required tonight, only dark attire will do. Although he would like to work on his art, he knows that's only part of the picture. So why is he returning—going back to the scene of a potential disaster?

It's not that he wants more of what the young woman, Whitney, has already provided. The specter of her nude body actually overwhelms him. Beyond that, she was a student of his, a female further removed by an entire generation of possibilities. It's something else—something greater that makes her so compelling. Something about her soulful essence, her fierce coupling with art, that suggests that she could possibly understand him. *Like looking for a twin*, he smiles to himself. Something about the pain behind her work pulls him toward some essential *source*. In any case, he leaves his house a half hour early.

At the Art League, Alex reclaims his table, the one in the most obscure corner of the room. A woman takes a seat to his left, a man to his right. Peeking about, he spots the large body and even larger presence of Tom, the guy he recognized at Stripe.

When Whitney arrives, she shares a jovial moment with the fellow. She looks *cute* in her abbreviated clothes, even as Alex admonishes himself for noticing. Cecil addresses the class on some odds and ends—updates the schedule. Right at 7 p.m., Whitney emerges from behind the screen, wearing a white terry cloth robe.

With a slight sashay, she seems to welcome the soft murmur—a physical buzz in the room. Looking about at the collective gaze—she slowly slips off her robe. Atop the stage, she stands tall—loosens her shoulders, shakes out her arms. She rises up on the balls of her feet, then settles—rotates slowly back and forth.

Alex looks away, looks down, then looks directly across at her. At Cecil's request, she takes an open stance, hands on hips, arching her back—head tilted up. Alex notes a certain pride in her face, one that the rest of her pose embodies. Pencil engaged, he struggles at first with a balky arm. In time, the discordant parts settle into a more cohesive flow. His line takes on a pleasing rhythm. From a wild orbit about the figure, the pencil homes in on the truth of the pose. No need to erase, the lines become increasingly honest.

Keeping her gaze above the students, Whitney's attention appears to drift to the upper reaches of the gray ductwork. But with the sound of Cecil's voice, her focus returns to the class. As directed, she faces the opposite wall—steps boldly forward with her right foot, then stops midstride.

With her one arm reaching forward, the other trailing, Alex enjoys a view of her left profile. From beneath a breast, he traces the elegant line from rib cage to pelvis, thigh to knee, shin to foot. The orb of her buttock rises above a soft crease. He discerns something vaguely different about her body, her presentation. He's not sure what, but it has something to do with that gently elevated part of her.

But now, Cecil asks her to change poses again. Introducing a chair, he places a drape over its back. Taking time to stretch her limbs, she turns about in half-circles to scan the people in the room. Caught off guard, Alex dips his head. His attenuated gaze reveals once more that something seems different about her body. At the same time, Whitney's face appears to freeze—as if struck by the weird notion—there's something different about the people in the room.

Alex strains for a better view of the part of her that puzzles him. Examining her bottom, it starts to come clear. As Whitney spots an oddity in the corner—Alex notes a change in the tattoos gracing her butt. When Alex looks up—Whitney looks down. Their eyes lock. Surprise meets shock—shock meets horror, horror leads to a small cry that escapes her mouth.

"Why—why are you here?" she stammers. "What's going on?"

Seeing her distressed—Alex wants desperately to explain himself.

Whitney pivots—snatches the drape off the chair with such vehemence, Cecil looks shocked.

"Something the matter?" he asks.

A couple of students have witnessed the encounter. Clutching the drape to her body, Whitney paces back and forth as if caught in a cage. Tears erupt.

"What's the problem, hon?" asks Tom, standing.

Without answering, she gathers herself and steps off the stage—marches stiffly to where Alex sits.

"How could you?" she asks, standing before his desk.

Alex opens his mouth but makes no answer. Backlit and draped, she's cast in shadows—her tears reflecting the only fragments of light. Reaching down—she seizes Alex's sketchbook. Turning, she charges off to the dressing area, even as her backside remains exposed. Amidst gasps from the women, Cecil follows to assist her—still unclear of what's just happened. Tom struts to where a frantic Alex gathers the rest of his materials.

"What the fuck, man! Hey," he says, "haven't I seen you before? Like, wasn't it back at Whitney's show?" Eyes big—"Man, I thought you were some kind of relative. What are you trying to pull, you perv?" Tom leans over the desk—fakes a headbutt—then storms off to comfort Whitney. When he reaches the dressing area, Carlos is already there.

Alex bolts to his feet—hurries to the door. Terrible looks

follow him, terrible judgments. All in attendance make him feel stupid, horribly ashamed.

Face red and sweaty—*God, you idiot—you goddamn idiot!* Alex jumps into his car, takes off, heads for the hills—the *city on the hill*, the university—drives up through the east entrance to one of the remote parking lots, sits there for a long time.

* * *

Mario's place, Soquel

Not sleeping—who would think Whitney's nightmares were contagious? In nocturnal flight, he finds himself hiding in dirty canals or drowning in rivers. Sometimes he's caught by *la migra*—sent back across the border to a place he barely remembers. And if he were taken, what would happen to his mother and sibs? Who would look after them all? Or maybe because of him and the delinquent Fredo, the whole family gets rounded up and deported.

But this is Santa Cruz, California—a *sanctuary city* at that. Same for Watsonville. The local sheriff and police departments refuse to enforce federal immigration law. Even so, raids by Immigration and Customs Enforcement continue throughout the state and country. Just ask Mario's mother— still traumatized by the ICE round-ups in the Beach Flats area some years ago.

So, he ponders—*what exactly does an illegal alien look like?* Through years of trepidation, how could he have put on a charade like this? His height, his stature, the light-colored features—not at all unusual for Jalisco, Mexico. As he gets into his car, he thinks of Mr. Joseph Verlatti, his third grade teacher. An educator and a compassionate adult, he noted Mario's promise when others seemed not to care, or were too burdened by the load of so many other English learners. Mr. V. nurtured his mastery of the language—focused on his burgeoning writing skills. For starters, he had Mario remove the warped little stick of a tilde over the "n" in his last name. Just like that, it seemed—how easy to become an Italian American success.

Mario takes the freeway to Morrissey Avenue. On the way, he notes uneven patches of paint on the retaining walls signifying graffiti clean-up. In addition to everything else, he feels frustrated. Repeated sweeps of graffiti hot spots have yielded no other sightings of the writer known as DRAZ. It's been a random exercise—totally futile. But today, he pursues a lead from a young writer he met at the Davenport ditch. It turns out that the skate shop, Bill's Wheels, has long supported graffiti art by sanctioning a legal graffiti wall. Maybe someone there can direct him to the writer he's searching for—the guy he so desperately wants to size up.

Mario enters the parking lot off Soquel Avenue. He finds impressive graffiti pieces to both left and right. His heart leaps when he spots the name *DRAZ* blazing into the side of the shop like a comet. Directly opposite looms the cholo-style script of an intricate tribute wall. Through a Golden Gate Bridge motif, he spies the name *DRAZ* in the brilliant sunset. Feeling crazed, Mario's caught in an echo chamber of images— the reverberating, visual display of his rival's name. The man named DRAZ taunts him while staking his claim to Whitney. Mario scours both designs, desperate to locate an example of her tattoo. He knows it must be there, but can't find it. He hates the man behind the pieces—would *beat the shit* out of him if he could.

Once in the building, Mario marches straight to the front desk. At the register, a thin young man assists one of the teenage customers. Mario can't help but confront him. The flustered cashier, not at all rude, simply can't process both tasks at once. A few minutes later, his patron leaves with a custom new skateboard under his arm.

"Like I said," spouts Mario—"do you know anything about the graffiti wall outside?"

"You mean, like—do I know who owns it?"

"I mean—do you know the writer who put up the pieces outside?"

"Oh, that? Oh yeah—that's Joey. He did all that."

"You mean the DRAZ guy—the guy who writes DRAZ?"

"Yeah, that's right."

"Tell me again—Joey's the guy who writes DRAZ?"

"Yeah."

Mario places both hands on the counter. "So, where can I find this guy?"

"Oh, he's here today. He's out on break."

"You mean he works here?"

"Sure does."

"So, when does he get back?"

"Should be here any second."

Rattled by the exchange, the cashier peers over Mario's shoulder to the front door. "In fact, there he is. There's Joey."

Turning, Mario's eyes spot a tall, lanky man with tussled hair, a hooked nose—unshaven face. *Wow,* he thinks—*the guy must be forty years old. No, mid-forties.* Joey's appearance takes him aback, but also reassures him. At the very least, the image disarms him. *Looks like he's had a pretty tough life.*

"Hey Joey," says the young fellow, "this dude's been asking for you."

"Oh, is that a fact?" Engaging Mario with a quick grin— "So, what's it gonna be today, my man?"

"Well, I'm a reporter from the paper—the *Courier.* "I'm doing an article on street art in the community. Includes graffiti art."

"Go ahead, shoot—if you wanna know somethin'. I've been a writer for a shit-load o' years."

Mario muses—*This guy can't be after Whitney, can he? For sure, he's not someone she could really get into, could she?*

"The kid here says you're the one who did the pieces outside. Is that right?"

"Oh yeah, I did. I'm makin' a comeback, man. It's been quite awhile, but I just had to get myself up again. Truth is—I ain't gettin' any younger—know what I'm sayin'?"

"So, you're the guy behind DRAZ."

"Oh no—I ain't behind nobody, bro. I *am* DRAZ."

Mario pulls out his phone, asks permission to record.

"Feel free if you like."

"Okay, Joey—if it's all right to call you that—where else do you like to write?"

"Oh, all over town. If this here was San Francisco or New York, they'd be callin' me *all city.* Fact is, they'd be callin' me a *king*. Here in Santa Cruz, you'd have to call me *all county*. Smiling—"Whatever, though—I'm still a king."

"Well, you'll probably like to know," says Mario, "I've already seen your work in other places. Looks like you also got yourself a crew. Other names attached to your pieces."

"You could say that," Joey laughs. "Yeah, you could say I got me a crew."

"So, how many people in your crew?"

"Oh, really now, just one other cat."

"So, how do you two work together?"

"Well, tell you the truth—I'm the guy who does it mostly. But I appreciate the interest, the company. You know—my main man helps me in other ways."

"Is that his name on the bottom of your pieces—the thing that looks like a tag?"

"Oh yeah—he's gettin' better though. It's been a big stretch for him."

"How's that?"

Pausing a moment. "All this talk now—it ain't gettin' no one in trouble, is it? Fact is—writing is seen as a crime by most, if you catch my drift."

"I promise you, I'm just trying to get the story."

"Okay— But you gonna keep the real names off them pages, am I right?"

"Of course. I won't do anything to mess up my sources."

"Well then, my guy—he's a real interesting story in hisself. A real live professor up at the UC. Teaches art history—a real smart cat you could say."

"And so, how did you guys manage to meet?"

"Turns out—we got a basketball connection. He plays ball—I ref through the city parks and rec. It's the *over the hill* seniors league, but a lot of the guys still got skills."

"So I guess you also connected around art."

"Oh yeah—he totally gets it. Fact is—he's got more potential writing now than he's got as a baller."

"What do you mean?"

"Well, he's been practicin' a lot. His hand style's startin' to look pretty good. And a while back, man, he turned me on to this sign—this image I use. We call ourselves the *MPB crew*. Stands for *Make Piece, Bro*. He turned me on to a cool-ass design—like a double-duty palm tree, seein' how it also looks like the palm of a hand.

Mario can't believe his good fortune. "So, what's the guy's name, the guy in your crew?"

"I call him *Professor*. *Professor A-wry*. Mostly though—people call him Alex. An older guy, like—older than me."

Mario processes the new lead. "You think I could meet him someday?"

"Oh sure you could. You might want to drop by at the next game. Saturday night hoops at that funky little gym at Pacific Collegiate. Eight o'clock I think. Season's almost done, which is fine with me. I plan to take a break—go up to San Francisco for the time bein'."

"Any particular reason?"

"I'm goin' back to my old neighborhood. I'm done practicin' here in Santa Cruz. I'm returnin' to the big time—wanna get myself up again, just like things was in the '80s. I want everyone to know, DRAZ is comin' back to the City—back to where it all started for me."

"That's cool, Joey—hope it goes great for you. Can you give me your number, if I need to talk to you again?"

Mario turns off his cell, but the audio in his head keeps playing. *Professor, Professor A-wry, Alex.* Something familiar about the name. *How could a guy that old be scheming on Whitney? It's the art thing, of course—the art connection. The professor must know her through the university.* But whatever the reason—the professor is a guy, and however old, guys never give up on women. Of course, Mario won't give up either—will do whatever it takes to track the professor down. As he exits the skate shop, a certain irony overtakes him, but not in a way he would consider funny. Just as Mario now struggles with his own identity, he vows to unearth the truth of another man, a man whose cryptic signature also shows he's hiding.

＊＊＊

Lisa—

I recall what a mixed bag of emotions it was. I knew Alex cared a lot for me, but just didn't have the same feelings I did.

And I felt kind of foolish in a way. Being *in love* with someone, *falling in love* with a guy who wasn't going to be there in the end.

After graduating that summer, I went home to Altoona. I was just miserable—kind of moped around. My father was stuck in bed—sicker than ever before. My anxious mom was even more anxious. She tried her best to feed me back to health. I actually lost a lot of weight, which, on my frame—just made the bony angles stick out more.

After about a month, though, I started to come around, started picking up steam. Of course, I needed to work if I was going to have enough money for grad school. In the meantime, I was accepted to New York University—the School of Business. A great program—closer, but not too close, to my family. I knew Alex was going to stay in California—and I knew the distance would help me get over him.

Toward the end of summer, I was feeling much better. I looked forward to the adventure of living in Manhattan. At the same time, I was also scared about making the move. Maybe I'd bitten off more than I could chew. The big city—the mix of all those people, the crime, the danger—

On the spur of the moment, I wrote Alex a letter—asked if he might want to fly out for a visit. He could help me set up my new place, while getting a chance to do some research. I wanted to reassure him I wasn't trying to win him back—that this wasn't some kind of trick I was playing. I said it would be like our last date together. A nice, long, memorable one. To my surprise, I got a quick response three days later.

I probably should have just gotten a room in one of the university residence halls. But the thought of being in a dorm again just wasn't appealing. I started to get excited—maybe a little expansive, even. I'd saved up my money and decided to splurge. So I found a place in Greenwich Village—right on MacDougal St. It was on the top floor, six steep flights of stairs from the bottom. The apartment was just a narrow slice of an old building—all the rooms in a tight row. All the way back, the last room was just big enough for a double bed.

Alex flew in a week later—took a bus in from JFK. He really liked my place—loved the area. His enthusiasm gave me a real shot in the arm. We spent a few days exploring the neighborhood, visiting thrift shops and buying what I needed for my new household. One night we went through two-thirds of a loaf of bread—along with some peanut butter and jelly, some Provolone, and dry salami from a nearby deli.

Alex took me to some great places in Manhattan—several of the big museums. He liked traveling by subway—something about how smart it was, and how colorful. To me, though— all the crowds, especially in the stations and in the trains, were scary at first. I didn't like getting jostled about—being in contact with strangers and not knowing their state of mind. It was humid and smelled of fumes, just felt dirty and gritty to me. And everywhere I looked there was graffiti. It looked like some hoodlums had taken over. It was right in your face—you couldn't get away from it. Just this aggressive energy. It was always a relief for me to walk up the stairs of the station and resurface.

The day before he left, Alex spent the afternoon playing basketball at some outdoor courts on 4th Street—a place called *The Cage*. I couldn't believe it—him bringing his basketball shoes and shorts to New York. But it had always been a dream of his to play something he called *streetball* or *schoolyard ball*. I went to watch, and it looked really different from anything I'd seen before. It was pretty much all black guys, and I remember the spectators kept yelling something like, *Get back! Get back!* after someone did something special to score. Alex wasn't good enough to play on the main court, but off to the side he did pretty well. In fact, I'd say he played like a man possessed. When he was finished, he was so excited he looked like he'd just done the best thing possible. And I had to smile, because he seemed even happier than when he was in a museum— rhapsodizing over the art.

That last night was really tough for me—for both of us. We'd spent the week being so upbeat and happy. And being in a new city, a new apartment, a new bed—all just added to a certain craziness. The next morning we caught a cab to the Eastside bus terminal. From there, it really felt like such a short ride to the airport. When I saw him off at the stop, we both cried. We hugged each other really hard, and a lot of beautiful words were exchanged between us that day. I don't know how it happened, but I'm pretty sure—I ended up comforting Alex more than he seemed to comfort me.

✳ ✳ ✳

Center Street, downtown Santa Cruz

It has to do with dark water. It has to do with storm clouds— full, floaty, voluminous containers of water. A summer squall strikes—short lived. A flash of lightning—a flash of gold, an unraveled thread that causes the sky's soft panels to disassemble.

Why now? she wonders—why is it happening now? Why do her dreams spill out of the night, into morning, drenching an entire day? Before, she could keep them safe in the stormy compartment of her sleep. That's what vessels are for, aren't they? A nocturnal cloud opens, and a dormant Whitney gets soaked. When it cinches back shut, everything goes dry again. Oh sure, she remembers her dreams come morning. But this isn't about memory—at least not *that* kind. It's more about the freakish new dreams that happen when she's fully awake. How confusing, asleep or awake—these last few days, there've been times when she can't tell the difference.

On her way home from the farmers market, she waits to cross the street. Her canvas bag swells with lettuce, carrots, honey, and oatmeal cookies. When she steps off the curb, she suddenly feels it—the bottom of her bag drops out. Or maybe it didn't drop, but only took a dip when she left the curb. But when that sensation strikes—she immediately feels her *own* bottom falling. Terror-stricken, she's a child again—can't talk, her pink bottom fully exposed as if there were something wrong with it—like it needed changing. And someone else's hands are there, snatching the soiled piece of cloth, the dirty bedding. Someone removes the messy turd—that bad pressure that only went away with some grunts and cries.

In the *day*-dream, it's not so much that she sees this, but that her body remembers it all. Her body's stored away sensations, the scary kind. And she's sick to her stomach—feels like throwing up. She wants to purge her body from the inside out. She doesn't know how she's kept it in so long, why it hasn't poured out before. But the internal walls can no longer save her from a raging, overdue torrent.

* * *

Hello Whitney,

I am extremely sorry for what happened at the drawing class. I should not have been there, and I feel very bad about what I put you through. Before you could possibly forgive me, I think you deserve an explanation. As it turns out, the motivation for my visit is something I struggle with myself. I know you are upset with me, and that further face-to-face communication might sound repugnant. However, I hope you will please afford me the opportunity to address this poor behavior on my part.

Sincerely,
Professor A

Alex castigates himself. What he's done to Whitney is a gross violation—something that should have been obvious from the start. What the hell was he doing, cloaking his prurient interests in the guise of improving his art? Yes, that's the word he would use, *prurient*. Alex is a sick, *dirty old man* taking advantage of a young woman who was simply trying to support herself with a job. And, of course, she's not just any woman, but a former student, for heaven's sake. What a *goddamn idiot* he is.

And just beyond this professional travesty, something else—something cultural, possibly genetic—makes this transgression that much worse. Alex evokes the stereotype of the polite Japanese. And part of that script is to never intrude on another's boundaries. So reticent are the Japanese, so indirect in communication lest someone be made uncomfortable. Poking fun at his *own people*, he imagines an initial meeting between two Japanese families, the entire day spent deferring to one another. But families aside, in modern Japan, people are used to crowded conditions. Even when packed into subway cars, they maintain separation. Even as flesh impacts flesh, they're able to remove themselves, separate from the rest—go silent. And the lack of intrusion feels like politeness, but also serves as self-protection—a means to not get involved.

As a third generation American, he's clearly acculturated, even as his internal discomfort goes deeper than it might for a lot of his fellow citizens. Alex, the *perverse idiot*—never seems to grow tired of calling himself names. He feels so terribly bad, but *so what?* Whitney must surely be suffering, now what can he do?

16

Whitney's place, downtown Santa Cruz

*I*t's happening again. Passing the tilted easel, her body feels tilted too. She goes to the sink, turns on the water. As it gushes out, she feels something gushing out of her. When the cold water splashes her face, she feels like she's plunging into a deep pool.

So, which will it be today—the older Whitney, firmly in charge—or the young child lost to the recent flood of physical memories? To stay whole, she tries to anchor herself in this small world of her own making. But her body transports her back in time—back to sensations she'd completely forgotten. Is she truly safe in Santa Cruz, or is she in danger once more of being swept away?

Whitney trudges to the foot of her bed—stares at her most recent canvas. The familiar face of a man stares back at her. Just last week, those eyes appeared kind and good, but now they look strange and threatening. And now—they exude a sort of penetrating *evil*.

Ever since that night at the drawing class, she's been operating in a kind of fog. And just like the marine layer, the grayness comes and goes. When her body isn't trying to tell her something, it feels *numb*—as if she's been out in the damp too long. She would like to cry but can't quite access the tears. Then, all of a sudden her feelings pour out, and she cries hard.

Why was the professor there? she asks. *What did the man want?* Didn't he know it was wrong to be in that place where she felt good about herself and her body? Didn't he know it was wrong to see her that way—to look at her like that? She lets out a wail, long and hard—lets loose a painful keening.

To think, she actually liked the professor—thought he cared about her painting. But she knew all along she shouldn't trust a man—especially in terms of fairness. Men have their own agenda—one that always starts and ends with a *fuck*.

Now she needs to look for something—the thing that's been lying on the floor since class. And it's lying exactly where she threw it, even though she can't recall where. The professor's sketchbook—his collection of drawings of her from the nude. Somewhere in the room lies the record of the professor's *twisted* interest in her.

Jumping to her feet, she scours her place. Beneath some rumpled clothes in a corner, she finds what she's looking for. Grabbing the tablet, she marches it back to her bed. Slamming it down, she tears it open—systematically rips out the pages.

At first, she destroys a series of still lifes, followed by landscapes and caricatures. Her rage feeds on the torn pieces of the professor's attempted artistry. Then, somewhere near the end—just as she reaches the final pages—she comes to a complete stop. There, she unearths a drawing of a young woman, a woman whose pose exudes a kind of *pride*. Whitney's surprised by the flowing lines, the pleasing proportions, the subtle shading of the musculature. The artist captured not only the body, but something of the emotions inside. Having seen other studies—especially from the men—she's noticed the occasional focus on breasts and ass. The drawing in her hands reveals a strong attention to the model's face—especially the expression of her eyes.

Now, Whitney evokes the professor's eyes, retrieves the kindness she thought was reflected in her latest study. She doesn't know which eyes to believe anymore—which pair to follow. Even so, she welcomes a growing sense of equilibrium. She stops her destruction—puts the sketchbook off to the side. Collecting herself, she walks to the fridge—pours herself some orange juice. She watches as the tumbling liquid settles in its glass. For the moment, she feels whole again—her body all in one piece, fully present and accounted for.

* * *

Mario's place, Soquel

On the high school baseball field, Mario never played dirty—just played hard. He never let anyone get in his way, be it a pitcher throwing inside heat, or a second baseman trying to keep him away from a steal. Involved in a number of on-field fights, he always got the best of it. But he paid a heavy price for his aggressive play, losing his final season to injury.

Still working hard, he splits his time developing two quite different stories. For his article on street art, he has all the resources and information needed. As for his second piece—the one about Whitney—he feels at a complete loss. It's a perplexing tale, one he keeps reworking in his head. So far, he's managed to track down a Mr. Joey Militich. A prolific graf writer, Joey clearly identified the man who exposed Whitney's tattoo for public consumption.

Upon learning the professor's name, Mario went online. On the university website, he found a photo of the distinguished historian. *Oh yeah, I've seen him before—at Whitney's show. Not bad looking—but he's got to be old.* Then again—*If he's her professor, what about the tattoo? She likes to wear crop tops—maybe he saw her in one of those. Or, he could have gone to the drawing class, but no,* he laughs—*that would have been ridiculous.* Disturbingly, it doesn't take much to imagine the two of them in her bed. *Some kind of weird daddy thing.* And as for professors—*They sleep with students all the time. Just one of the perks.*

Mario continued his search by Googling the professor's name. The screen lit up with reams of professional material. Educational background—quite impressive. Three well-received books and a large number of other publications. Associations, awards—positive commentary from students.

Following Joey's tip, Mario attends a game in the city league's senior basketball division. He's surprised at the competitive level of play. Unfortunately, neither of the teams is the one to which Professor Arai belongs. It could have been so revealing to see the guy play. So much about a man comes out on the battlefield of sports.

Back home, he emails the professor, asking for an interview. He says he's writing an article on "modern memorials." In case his name might sound familiar, he changes it to "David—" the same as his late father's, but with a different accent.

He knows it's a long shot. Fall quarter doesn't start for a month, and how many vacationing professors answer requests like this? But a deadline looms, one that doesn't have an actual date. It's a deadline to finish the story of Whitney's tattoo as soon as possible—to define what's going on between her and the professor. And somehow it feels like a competition—an aspect of a game involved. He can't shake that desperate fear attached to the specter of losing. In order to *win*, he'll play with aggression. He feels like he's back on a baseball field again, playing as hard as he can—mindless to the risk of injury.

* * *

Porter College, UCSC

In the bright courtyard, Alex sits on a concrete wall that borders the koi pond. Across—a leafy haze obliterates the tops of three Japanese cherry trees. Wearing professional clothes, he looks poised to deliver a lecture. But he has no confidence in what he plans to say. No control over the material—no control over the next half hour or so. Peering down and to his left—

From the perspective of underwater— About a dozen glimmering koi inhabit the large triangular pool. Elegant fish—supple bodies slip through the water. A bright orange specimen passes by—followed by a black, a white, a multi-hued calico, and one the color of old gold....

Looking up, he spots Whitney approaching the courtyard. From his angle, he spies his father's memorial looming behind her. With contorted figures reaching skyward, he should warn her of the danger—a wave of bronze about to break over her head. But her bobbing form remains untouched, her hair in a casual mess. She grows in small bursts as her feet kick out over the cement walkway. Wordless, she takes a seat on the wall beside him. Bowing her head, she stares into the pond—dips her fingers through the surface.

Several koi ease through the water—approach the disturbance that sends out ripples. From the perspective of fish—do the ripples look the same from below? Air ripples? The fish respond to simple things—a shadowy figure, a quick movement in their direction, something falling, and then the primal promise of food….

Alex starts. "I'm so glad you came today."
Retrieving her fingers—"I wasn't sure if I should."
"These last couple weeks must have been hard for you."
"Oh yeah," she says, as if by rote—"but I'm okay, really. I'm fine."
"Whitney, I apologize to you for what I did. I feel terrible for having caused you pain. And obviously—it's completely my fault."
To fully face the professor takes incremental steps. Brief glances, quick looks—then more prolonged exposure. Finally—"You're right," she says. "I've been really upset. You being there— It was like a guy in my family seeing me *naked, nude*—*whatever.* It was so totally wrong—like an *uncle,* a *brother,* a *father!*"
Mortified—Alex fights the urge to reach out. "Again—I'm extremely sorry. What you just said—it was completely inappropriate what I did to you."
"Well you messed me up. You took away a place that was special to me. And now, it's not safe anymore!"
"I—didn't mean to."
"Of course you didn't. I hate what you did to me. In fact, I probably hate you too!
"I don't blame you."
"So, why didn't you just leave when you saw me in class?"

Alex hesitates. "I was kind of in shock. The longer it went, the more I thought I'd be discovered—thought that would make things worse. So—I hid. "

"You hid, but you kept on *looking,* didn't you?"

"I told myself I was working—working on my art."

"What a crappy excuse—"

Alex wants to apologize for *both* his visits—including the one she doesn't know about. All part of the same violation, he figures. "At the time, it seemed almost right—to be in the presence of someone so passionate about art. Strangely—and I know this is wrong—it almost felt like we were working together."

"That's totally *weird*. It's not like you even asked my permission—"

"You're right—I didn't. I was just deceiving myself—trying to rationalize what I did. That connection was part of some—*perverse* attraction. I was acting so stupidly. Such an *idiot*—"

For the moment, Whitney goes silent. Maybe it's because of what she's managed to say. A sense of relief, perhaps—knowing she's spoken her truth. But then, she spends the next few breaths berating him—extracting further halting replies.

"I thought you'd blame me," she says. "Tell me it was all my fault. Maybe something about me flirting with you."

"Oh no, no—it's all on me. I'm ashamed of myself for how I treated you."

Another pause follows. "I guess I didn't expect this kind of reaction. Didn't think you'd be so pissed-off with yourself."

Alex detects a shift in her eyes—some kind of softening. Just as quickly, he dismisses the thought as another *dumb idea*.

But Whitney's voice settles a bit. "I guess it's been hard for you too. That is—because you screwed up, is what I mean. But part of me really wants to get it—I want to understand where you were coming from. If I could, maybe it would help me, too."

Alex can't quite believe what he's hearing.

"When I saw you in class," she says, "everything got totally crazy. I knew you were wrong to be there, but then later—I started to doubt myself. Was it really *me*—was I the one doing something wrong? Like—maybe I was doing something wrong with my body, with myself—as far as men were concerned.

And then, my body started doing weird things—like bringing back stuff from the past. And I should blame you for all that's happened, and I do. But something tells me, maybe I need to go through all this. That if I do, maybe I'll be better off somehow."

Alex feels grateful for her words. This is so much better to be clothed and talking. So much better than he could have hoped for.

"It's like what you said," she continues, "it's good to know the history of something. I've always blocked out my past—kept it as far away as possible."

"Maybe working through it could be a good experience."

"Oh no—it wouldn't be easy. I'm totally afraid to look."

"Well, I admit—my own life has been pretty easy. It's only a few parts that have been painful for me. Sometimes I feel a lot younger than I am—like I'm just stuck reliving that old story. I guess it's no surprise I'm a history professor. I really need to get beyond all that—need to commit more to the present, like you."

Whitney dips her fingers back into the pool, stirs about—watches the koi rise to the surface. "I wonder if you can help me too. I don't mean figuring it all out, or whatever. I'm just saying—you kind of got this process started. Maybe you can just be there for me, in case I need you—whatever that means. Actually, I don't even know what I'm asking for."

* * *

Phone call from Mario—

"Yeah—Joey, I'm glad you answered. I've been trying to get a hold of you all week."

"Well, half the time I ain't carryin' this thing. The other half, it's out of juice—you know what I'm sayin'?"

"Right—but it's great I got you. Are you still up in the City?"

"Oh yeah—been up here for a while now. Stayin' with a nice lady friend of mine. She's got this place—and it ain't much. In the Tenderloin, but a good location. That's cuz it's just around the corner from a graffiti art gallery."

"Really, there's such a thing?"

"Definitely man. It's called One AM. You might think that

stands for the late hours us writers keep. But it really stands for the First Amendment—our rights to self-express. They got all the goods—all the caps, all kinds of Montana paint behind the counter. Anything I want—I can get, that is—if I can afford it."

"Sounds great, Joey. Say look—the reason I'm calling is—you know that professor you mentioned, the one in your crew?"

"You mean Alex?"

"Right— I've been trying to track him down for this article I told you about. Problem is—I can't find the guy. I got his email address up at school, but no answer. I even drove up to campus a couple days ago. The office person said I just missed him. He was meeting with one of his students, I think. Anyway, I left a message for her to pass on. But I'm not feeling too optimistic."

"Okay man, just tell me what I can do."

"I was wondering if you might have his number—cell, landline. Or maybe you've been to his place—maybe you know where he lives."

"Yeah, well—I got his number, got it somewhere. Ain't never used it though. As far as where the cat lives, your guess is as good as mine."

"Well then—can I just get his number from you?"

"You sure can—as soon as I find it."

"So, where do you think it is?"

"Probably back in Santa Cruz, I don't know. Probably with all my papers, official documents, if you catch my drift."

"So, when are you coming back?"

"Not for a few more days, man. It's been great up here—really has. I've been gettin' up all over the City. Some of the old sites—some crazy new ones. Met me some cool dudes—young guys rockin' some great new shit. Man—I'm in heaven."

"Well, when you get back, do you mind giving me a call?"

"Not at all. Fact is—I can show you pictures of my new pieces."

"Hey, terrific—I'd love to see your latest work. By the way, have you ever put your stuff on the Internet?"

"Oh, no man—I ain't predisposed to doin' that stuff, the computer stuff is what I'm sayin'. But hey—if you'd be willin' I'd be more than grateful. That's the ultimate these days. Some toy goes over your pieces, man—but the photos—they're already out on your website and all. That's what's makin' things international. Cats all over the world could be gettin' off on my style."

"Sure, Joey—I'd like to help. Let's get together when you're back in town. I can get you seen by a lot of people. In the meantime, if you happen to find this guy's number, could you please give me a call?"

"No problem man, we'll stay in touch."

* * *

San Francisco Bay Area
In their words—

"It's vandalism. I like vandalism—I'm a vandal. Most writers are just punks. That's how I started. I just got sophisticated—changed and adapted, 'cause it's something I like to do. It's good therapy for me. It's my release in life."
—REYES

"I had everyone tell me, 'you're a fuckin' idiot.' I just kept doin' it and doin' it. It's like some superhero shit, you know, like—you just fuckin' fly out and do your shit and come back like you're just a mild-mannered reporter, you know?"
—NORM

"Late nights, early mornings—trips to go steal, trips to go paint. Someone told me something when I was a kid, and they said being a graffiti writer is probably the most quintessential thing you can do growing up—you know, to have an identity. Thought it was kind of silly when he said that, but now when I look back in history, it definitely combines a lot of different elements of life. And balance is important, you know? I will never stop doing it 'cause it's just me, you know? I'm a lifer. I'm gonna do it forever."
—REYES

＊＊＊

Washington Street near Elm, downtown Santa Cruz

Mario sits in his beat-up Corolla. He's pushed the seat back to stretch out his legs. He keeps the windows wide open because of the summer heat. He's got a sandwich—chicken salad from Zoccoli's on the Mall. These past couple weeks have been so demanding, so stressful—his full-time job, his deadline with the *Courier*, his mother's calls about his brother Fredo. And now, today—a rare afternoon off. He's just finished his story on street art—has sent it back to the paper. He hasn't heard from his mother in what—a couple days?

It comforts him to be parked beneath the shadow of a robust tree. Just a half block up—Elm Street intersects Washington on the right. If he were to take that little turn, he would find the yellow house where Whitney lives. But Mario doesn't need to go there today—doesn't need to risk a confrontation. In fact, he doesn't even know if she's there. Just to be close to her apartment is enough for him. To be *somewhere in the neighborhood*—knowing that the woman he loves lives just around the corner.

The fact is, there's nothing pressing for him to do. Simply being here feels like doing enough. And what exactly *is* he doing? Just resting—certainly not doing anything wrong. He's definitely not following his former girlfriend—not spying on her like some psycho on the prowl. He has no intention of causing a stir. He's simply minding his own business.

So when Whitney emerges from Elm on her bike—he's genuinely surprised. He's also shocked, delighted, and a little afraid. As she peddles off in the opposite direction, he wonders where she's going. To follow along would simply be a matter of curiosity—again, nothing to do with stalking. It's all just a matter of chance—of serendipity.

Sitting tall atop her bike, she travels at a casual clip. She makes a looping left down Lincoln Street, followed by a sharp right onto Chestnut. Lagging behind, Mario frequently pulls to the curb. He worries for her safety, as parked cars pilfer one-half of the bike lane. It's a straight shot for several blocks before the steep uphill to Mission Street. As she engages the incline, several cars go rushing past.

Waiting at the bottom, Mario obsesses about her destination. To get to campus, she would normally take the bus. Where could she be going between downtown and the school? The intersection atop the hill involves the main Westside thoroughfare. As she disappears over the crest, he reenters traffic.

Reaching the top, he finds her safely across the tangled lanes and turning right onto Highland. When the signal changes, he crosses as well. Just in time, he sees her coasting into the parking lot of the Abbey Coffee Lounge.

Pulling over, Mario catches a clearer view of what she's wearing. Simple jeans—no torn look, no gaps and slices. A white jersey top—nothing suggestive or revealing. As she steps inside, he enters the lot—backs into a space where he can easily monitor the front door.

Mario thrusts an elbow out the window. The rest of his sandwich lies on a crumpled wrapper. No more appetite, for sure—he waits and ponders. He conjures up multiple stories about who Whitney's seeing.

Forty minutes pass, as he snaps to attention each time someone appears. Finally it happens. Whitney emerges—somebody clearly pushing open the door. Turning, she watches as Alex Arai crosses the threshold, smiling. She returns the smile as a kind of reflection. And now the two of them cross the lot, walking closely enough together to be a couple.

The pair approach a beige-gold sedan. *What about her bike?* Mario wonders. When the professor opens the door, Whitney climbs in without hesitation. Soon after, the professor eases himself into the driver's seat. Stunned, Mario observes the car taking off. Upon crossing traffic, it enters a quiet residential street. Mario follows—maintains a safe distance. Spotting a street sign, he makes out the name *Escalona*. For the next half-mile, he travels the gentle turns, the ups and downs of the pleasant street. He notes the impressive houses along the way.

Finally, he sees the other car slow. With a smart pivot, it heads up a steep driveway. Mario passes the entrance before making a quick U-turn. He parks under a substantial shade tree, hands still tightly gripping the wheel. In front and to his left, some forty feet up a landscaped hill, stands a redwood-sided house—three stories tall—part of which rises over an imposing oak.

The garage door closes to the gold sedan, concealing both passenger and driver. Mario might as well be gazing up at a citadel—a fortified structure that looms high above. So once again, he finds himself sitting in his beat-up old car. Sometimes he folds himself over the steering wheel—sometimes he falls back in his seat. Sometimes he looks up at the big house— mostly he looks straight ahead. Sealing his windows in spite of the heat, he occasionally notes the smell of his spoiled lunch.

Fighting a peculiar lethargy, he admits to being stuck at the lower end of a vastly tilted playing field. *How unfair*, he thinks, that the well-born, the privileged, can take whatever they want. Fantasies of what Whitney and the professor are doing now drive him wild. Even so, he finds himself strangely immobile. Periodically, he checks the time on his cell phone. For the next two-and-a-half hours, Mario sits and fumes.

17

"*H*ello Alex—are you there? I'd appreciate you picking up. I tried calling a couple days ago. Tried again yesterday. Not sure why you haven't called back. Like I said, I really need to get together. It's about my retrospective. I also got some sketches for my new Sendai memorial. Before I go on, I want to check them out with you. You can help me with your thinking on memory and narratives, like what Carter was saying. Anyway—give me a call as soon as you can. And, thanks, Alex."

✳ ✳ ✳

Lisa—

I recall what an empty feeling it was at first. A huge roller-coaster drop from when Alex left. I just got myself busy—threw myself into my new studies. But, it was a lot to get used to—I mean, here I was in New York City, and I felt so alone. The Village itself was quite amazing. Over time, I established some local favorites—the Bleeker Street Bakery, great for cannoli—a falafel place called Mamoun's, the deli on Bleeker and Barrow. Mostly I shopped at the Pioneer Market for groceries.

In my kitchen, I kept two chairs beside the table. I'd make some tea, sit down in one. I could pretend Alex was sitting there

165

in the other. Pathetic, actually. But I got to wonder—how long does it take to get over someone—someone you care that much about? No answer, of course—and I eventually got tired asking that stupid chair.

After an initial period of *paranoia*, I started to open up to the new people around me. I made friends with a couple women, fellow students—one from western Pennsylvania, the other, local. They were both more outgoing than me—more fun-loving, I guess you could say. Rachel was from Brooklyn and liked to stir things up. Sarah liked to tag along, and pretty soon, I was tagging along too.

Rachel took us on walking tours of different Manhattan neighborhoods—was especially fond of the East Village. There was quite a nightlife going on there—lots of young people out on the streets. Lots of artist types—filmmakers, theater folk, and musicians. Just the energy—I have to admit I was afraid at first. There were hip hop guys break dancing on the corners—boom boxes going full blast. Graffiti everywhere. I went to some bars and nightclubs for the first time in my life. Managed to check out the Roxy, Negril—the Peppermint Lounge. Because of my dad, I never really drank before. But Rachel called me a *sissy* and Sarah was giving me static, too. So, in keeping with this new chapter in my life, I started having a few drinks. Turns out I really liked vodka tonics, but limited myself to only two in a night.

And yeah, there was some serious dancing going on. Lots of guys—really hot guys. But unlike my two friends, I never went home with any of them. I never accepted any of those slick or sloppy invitations, that is—except this one time. I think that night—I managed to get an extra drink in there somehow. The guy was really tall—had an open-collared shirt, tight jeans. And I was just all worked up—was really missing physical contact with a man. So, we danced for a while—all crazy, then we got close and danced slow, even though the music kept going fast. We kissed each other on the dance floor. We actually started making out. It felt all floaty and good. But when we headed for the door, Rachel and Sarah both came over to stop us. Rachel yanked me away—must have told the guy to get lost. She'd seen him around before—knew something about him. It was that time, you know—the first half of the '80s—when crack cocaine had hit town. She said the guy was into drugs, was bad news. We talked about it later over mugs of coffee. We also talked about the strange new AIDS epidemic. Sarah laughed about it—which wasn't very nice, of course. She said she was just grateful to be young, single, and a heterosexual female.

It might sound like I was pretty wild, but I wasn't. I knew I was putting a career together. I was on my way to becoming an expert at something. Maybe not exactly a professor, but an expert just the same. I was feeling better about myself. Sometimes at night, I realized I wasn't really missing Alex. And the pain of it all, as it receded, was replaced by a sense of freedom and an excitement over possibilities. I began appreciating some of the young men in my program. I enjoyed talking to guys who were into the material as much as I was. And a number of them started showing an interest in me—especially in my *long legs* and *pretty hazel eyes.*

Over the three years I was in New York, I had two special relationships with men. They weren't the only ones I slept with, but they were the two I really cared most about. I think I needed some time to experiment around with sex. I wanted to know what it was like to be with other men. It's not like I slept around a lot. I was actually quite discriminating. I found out how different men could be as lovers. Some were sensitive and liked to please, like Alex. A couple of them were so perfunctory—had so little awareness of what the experience was like for me. It's not that they were bad guys—they just didn't seem to get it. And then there were those guys who seemed completely wild about women, guys who were great in bed, but after the act— didn't really seem to *like* women that much.

And apart from the sex, I wanted to know what it felt like for a man to fall in love with me. That happened twice, and they were the relationships I held onto longest. In both cases, I couldn't honestly say I loved them back, and I developed some empathy for Alex. I mean—I cared a lot about each one, but didn't love them in the same way. It felt overwhelming at times. And worst of all, those two relationships overlapped. They knew about each other. And the pain I caused them was almost unbearable to me. I even thought of writing Alex—getting his input on the situation. But, the most I revealed about other men was this one time I was feeling a bit expansive. I think I wrote something about having "taken a lover." That seemed to trigger a flurry of letters from him.

By the time I was into my last year of grad school, I'd say I'd pretty much gotten over Alex. That is, if you had asked me then. So, getting back to that question—how long does it take to get over someone—someone you care about so much, someone you actually love? I guess the answer for me would have been something like *two years*. As it turned out, I also learned that the issue of time has everything to do with *timing*. Because right after I started my last term, Alex called me on the phone one evening. It was funny in a way—I was just getting ready to spend the night at my boyfriend's. But it was quite a shock—hearing the voice of a man I had finally gotten myself free of. In fact, I was surprised—taken aback by how happy I was to hear from him. It was the first time Alex had ever called me in New York City, and he really needed to talk.

✳ ✳ ✳

The house on Escalona Drive

Sunlight filters through birch and alder, dapples the redwood deck in back of the house. An open rectangle, it forms a generous platform nestled in a garden of slumbering azaleas and rhododendron.

Whitney delights in the Japanese cherry tree on the left. To the right, white oleander marks the drop-off to a year-round creek in a small ravine. The rushing water forms an unseen cloud above the yard, drizzling a soft aural rain. Before her stands the cinderblock wall that keeps the hill from sliding down. The *Wall of Mistakes*, as Alex calls it, forms a riotous band of color across the middle of the composition. The first time Whitney saw it, she was taken by surprise. Today—she appears delighted.

Alex offers her a seat—takes the one opposite her at the redwood burl table. If there were an audience inside the house, the two would be seen as occupying center stage. From where they sit, the retaining wall looks like the painted backdrop to a play.

Alex smiles. "I feel like saying I *racked* some paint for the occasion."

"Well, go ahead. I guess we don't have to act so formal anymore."

"Actually, I didn't really *rack* the paint—that would have meant I stole it. But I found all this at a local art supply shop—a bit of a surprise." Opening the paper bag at his feet, he produces several cans of Montana 94. "This is the stuff I told you about—what real writers use."

"I appreciate what you explained last time. It was like you were still being my professor— It was really cool, though. I even got off on the history—the stuff you're going to use in your new class."

"I've been practicing a lot on this wall. Can't wait for you to try it."

"Oh—I don't know. I'm not so sure anymore. Your girl-friend, Lisa—your partner. She might not like it. This is her wall too."

"Lisa's been great about my interest in graffiti—sees it as a hobby of sorts. She just wants me to keep it in the backyard."

Reaching for a can of red paint, Whitney reads the label. "Nice to have someone understanding like that."

"Lisa's fine about giving me support. The thing is, she's not an artist—she's not someone I can talk to about the process."

"Well, okay—so she doesn't make art. But I bet she shares a lot of other stuff with you. Like, what about kids—do you guys have any?"

"Oh, we thought about it some. Lisa felt she'd already done the parent thing, having been the oldest child in a big family. And even though it's different than raising kids—I always had a special relationship with my students." Grabbing a can of purple paint and a new cap—"Why don't we go over to the wall and try out your hand?"

"Okay, I guess. Well, actually—I'd love to." Rising from her chair—"I did bring my ratty clothes today."

Alex squares himself to the wall that once represented mistakes and limitations. Of course, the mistakes continue, but now they occur in the context of pursuing his art.

"Okay—this is how you shake the can."

"Oh come on—I'm not a dummy."

Removing the top, she vigorously starts her shaking. Alex hands her a virgin skinny cap, just like the one he's using.

"All right—let's check it out," he says.

In little bursts of red and purple, the sound of aerosol paint permeates the air. Before he can offer instructions, Whitney begins to spray the wall.

Scrambling verbally to catch up—"You've got to hold the can upright. Yes, try holding it closer to the wall. Yes, about an inch or so from the wall."

Remarkably, that's all he needs to say. It's not long before she produces smooth straight lines and curves. He completely marvels at how her hand, her arm flows—how her body moves so gracefully as a unit.

"This is so much fun," she says. "Now watch this!"

After practicing some circular motions, she produces a beautifully arcing *W*. With a couple of drips, the letter is far from perfect. But before Alex can help correct the problem, she renders two more versions without the flaws.

"Good God—congratulations. You're a natural!"

And now, a strange ambivalence overcomes him. It definitely involves a certain pain—the pain of being in the presence of a talent greater than his own. But countering that—he exalts at finding a potential artistic partner. He's already discarded his authoritative style with her. In her youthful presence, he finds another internal change—one that welcomes the expression of his own small self. Alex is excited to engage her in a new kind of play.

"You know—I'm still getting used to calling you *Alex*. This is such a cool experience."

"I have to agree—it's a lot of fun." Feeling both excited and silly, he directs her attention to a series of symbols just a few feet to her side. "Here's something I've been working on. It's a tribute to you as you can see. Hope it's all right. Actually, I hope you like it."

Whitney stares at a part of the wall that's been shaded all afternoon. "Oh-My-God!" she exclaims—her body jolting at the sight of a masterful rendition of her first tattoo. "Have you been out in public doing that stuff?" Turning to him—"Were you the one spraying my tattoo all over town?"

"Oh no—I did it only once. But if there's a problem, I could go buff it—get rid of it if you want."

"My old boyfriend, Mario. He said he saw it in more than one place."

"Well, I wouldn't have been involved in that."

Bolt upright—"But you *did* use my tattoo, even before I saw you at the Art League. Like—how many times did you come to my class?"

"Okay, well—it was only twice total."

"That makes it so much worse!"

Whitney's overcome by a daunting spacyness. Something to do with a loss of balance, a loss of power. Something about being *used*. The wall before her grows massive. Her own body becomes a wall, too—fixed, rigid, difficult to move. She feels like someone's smearing her up and down with something wet—or is she simply sweating?

"Are you okay?" asks Alex.

Dropping her can, she slowly backs her way to the table. Now the ambient sounds pour into her ears—the white noise of the creek grows louder, the sound of water fills her head. And taking her seat, her breathing gets harder—she struggles as if she *can't* breathe. Alex grows frantic as if she were drowning. He shouldn't touch her, but takes her hands and cradles them anyway.

"Whitney, I'm terribly sorry—I wasn't completely straight with you. I didn't bring up the other time—thought it was part of the same bad behavior. Again, it's *my* fault. I need to help you—I need to try."

Letting out a huge exhalation, she begins to cry. And with her crying, her breathing recovers its primary purpose—the regular in-and-out of air. As harsh as it looks, the wracking of her body seems so much better than the specter of suffocation.

Alex keeps his place until she finally slows, finally loosens up and her tears cease. And when she's able to pull away her hands—she takes her *self* back. Silently, he punishes himself. He would like to scoop her into his arms, but decides not to. Now, the air cools as it always does when evening approaches. Feeling the chill, she might like to be held but doesn't speak. Locked together without touching, no one moves. No one disturbs the stark tableau, as the soft folds of the marine layer come drifting in—close on the deck and the long, looming wall.

* * *

Alex—

I remember, it was like a sinkhole or something. In a way, it felt like it came out of nowhere. I guess the conditions were there—had been there for a while. But it felt so sudden, like a street or avenue had just fallen through, caved in.

I thought I was doing well—in fact, I was. I was enjoying my cozy academic environment—the place that felt more like home than anywhere else. Studies were a pleasure. Writing was hard work, but rewarding.

As for my social life—it was a great time to be a young, unattached man in the Bay Area. Lots of art-related activities, and I met a number of intriguing women. That quest of mine—that desire to connect with some artistic, spiritual *twin* kept me busy. I got involved with a couple of artists—got to share my art obsession with real practitioners.

It was a woman named Erica who captured both my heart and imagination. Strange thing, since we got into so many struggles. She was born and raised in Minnesota. Coming to California was akin to a punk rocker having escaped the Heartland the first chance she got. She had a place in San Francisco, and was quite the specimen. Definitely impressive in a striking, Valkyrian way. And she was very analytic, conscious about history—serious about her art and where she fit in the broad scope of things.

She started off as a Photo Realist painter—did large-scale works in oil. But at the same time, Postmodern developments were forcing painting into a kind of hibernation. Everyone seemed interested in the new technology—like camcorders and the use of monitors. Some artists were creating installations and performances outside the gallery. Some were making earthworks and other environmental art.

Immersing herself in the latest trends, Erica searched for a new direction. This led to a lot of discussion between us—heated arguments at times. I thought she should continue her painting because she was so talented—had worked so hard to become a first-rate painter. Why not extend the medium in a creative way—help steer it through those crazy Postmodern times?

Instead, Erica developed a method of her own by taking each of her paintings and surrounding it with a second *frame* of found objects. Their composition provided the context for the image inside—usually topical or political in nature. For example, a painting of an impoverished urban child might be encased in a halo of street detritus.

I thought this was a fine extension of the medium, fit for contemporary purposes. But with each successive piece, the effect became more like that of collage. And, over time, that original image shrunk to the point of non-existence. By then, our theoretical concerns had spread to the rest of our relationship. I couldn't help but think that the disappearing painted figure was a stand-in for me. About the time that mantel of objects had claimed the entire canvas, our relationship was over.

I was upset, disappointed—devastated in my own way. I'd been absolutely wild about her—keenly in love. In Erica, I'd found someone who actually engaged me—challenged me— even fought me with an equally passionate commitment to art. I saw her as heroic—driven by the same ambition I associated with Modern artists. When we finally broke up, apart from the heartache, I felt a strong sense of defeat.

And then, of course—while all this was happening—another big stress was brewing. A major item—the biggest challenge I would ever face in my professional life. Throughout school, I studied and wrote whatever I wanted. But as I looked to the future—my desire to become a professor—I started bumping into significant resistance. I was surprised at the pressure applied to minorities to pursue an academic course reflecting their ethnicity. The pressure was of institutional proportions and pervaded the entire art world.

The thought that I could be controlled, channeled—forced into a direction not of my own choosing was outrageous. How dare anyone define me and my interests, activities, my life's work? But by the second year of grad school, I realized no major university would hire an Asian American whose primary focus was Modern Western Art. Getting a tenure track position would be impossible.

I was dumfounded—felt foolish, felt I'd been naïve. All my life, I never believed that race or ethnicity determined my value—certainly not in the world of academics. Here I was—patting myself on the back for being a totally acculturated American. But alas, in the world of fine art—the Canon belonged to white people, entrusted to the care of white critics and historians. As I think about it now, it was kind of like getting interned all over again. I was being removed from where I grew up—from the shining citadel of Modern Art, and sent to a camp made up of the artwork of my own people. What the hell was I supposed to do? Evidently—find myself some ethnic artists I could study. I'm ashamed to say this—but at the time, it felt less like being sent to a concentration camp than being sent to an artistic ghetto.

Bottom line is, between Erica and the prospect of being an unemployed scholar, I began suffering bouts of anxiety. I got to feeling very strange inside—really shaky. It was that sinkhole feeling of *having the earth fall out* from under me. And of course, I obsessed about things all the time. I also had trouble sleeping—had bad dreams. And so, it was feeling like this that made me give in—not in the sense of losing function, of course. I mean, I finally broke down and gave Lisa a call.

Graffiti Free Santa Cruz...

...is a volunteer-based program that will help you in your efforts to remove and report graffiti.

The program offers:
graffiti hotline
free graffiti removal supply kits
instructions on removal methods
group paint-outs

Graffiti and the Law:
Graffiti is a crime. It is a felony if the damage is over $400 and is punishable by up to a year in jail and a $10,000 fine. It is a misdemeanor if the damage is less than $400 and is punishable by up to a year in jail and a $1,000 fine.

Report the Crime:
Call the Graffiti Hotline at 420-5303
Call 911

If you see someone "tagging" or suspect vandalism is going to take place, do not hesitate to call 911. Police will always prioritize life-threatening calls. Your quick reporting helps us to catch criminals and keep Santa Cruz Graffiti Free.

* * *

DONDI— Donald Joseph White
[4/7/61–10/2/98]
Birthplace— Brooklyn

From Style Writing to Art
by Magda Danysz in collaboration with Mary-Noelle Dana

During the summer of 1980, and encouraged by his friend KEL 139, DONDI is a part of collector Sam Esses' Studio project. Heartbroken by MTA's stubbornness to erase all graffiti from its network of trains, Esses has financed a project to allow a number of writers to work in a studio, to transition to canvas and to gain artist status. For DONDI, the experiment is a success, inspiring a new artistic orientation to his career. Between 1980 and 1981, he paints some of his most beautiful work on trains, in addition to producing a great number of canvas pieces. Thanks to his collaboration with The Soul Artists, he takes his first steps in the art scene, with a few collective exhibits in the East Village and at the Fun Gallery, which will present his solo show in 1982. That same year, he's in the movie, "Wild Style," and is hired as a consultant for the television film, "Dreams Don't Die" before participating in the European "New York City Rap Tour."

While New York's MTA is busy treating graffiti writers like criminals, California and the rest of the world can't get enough of them. In 1982, the University of California at Santa Cruz invites DONDI along with FUTURA and ZEPHYR to present 25 pieces all born at the Esses Studio. Santa Cruz's transit authority actually gives the artists a bus to paint.

All Gone Awry

* * *

Santa Cruz/Capitola

tart with the garden out front. Snapdragons, petunias, and little bursts of marigolds. Follow the driveway on the right, the narrow corridor hedged by rose bushes. Just to the left—a flight of stairs and a casual pile of rooms like a child's building blocks. The man ascends the steps on the tips of his shoes. He probably shouldn't be here—but here he is. Aboard the small landing, he knocks on the door—waits. He doesn't knock again.

When the door opens, Whitney's face glimmers in the late light of the dipping sun. Squeezing past the door, she slips out onto the landing. The man, Alex, follows her down the stairs. It's been a warm afternoon, and now cooling breezes flit through the heat like so many swallows. Observing from behind, he's relieved to see the cohesion of her body, her resolute strides. Spotting the car beside the curb, she opens the passenger door—simply enters.

*

Finished at the bookstore, Mario heads for traffic. Once on the freeway, he comes to a complete halt—slams his steering wheel with a fist. Some kind of accident up ahead, he guesses. *What else could go wrong today?* He hates being late. Then again, is Joey Militich the type who's ever on time? Mario's got a meeting at Bill's Wheels to select photos for a website he's making. Joey wants to go really big—go international.

*

Alex cuts through a maze of neighborhood streets, heading for the Eastside. Cautiously—"How have you been this past week?"

"Oh, I've been okay."

"Again, I apologize. I should have known it was wrong to

177

use your tattoo. And that business of returning to your class—Once more, I'm sorry for my behavior—*all* of it."

"You apologize too much," she says. "You should think about things beforehand. Seriously—you really ought to think more."

Noting the irony—"Yes, I really ought to do that—"

"I just don't get it. It's because of you my body acts so strange sometimes. But then, you're the only one who can make me feel better—better in the moment. You're the only one who gives me some kind of—hope."

*

Caught in a crawl, Mario approaches the obstruction. It's not an accident, but an emergency nonetheless. A young man on the overpass stands sprawling against the chain-link fence. Thick dreads float about his head like a blond halo. Several patrol cars wait below—their roofs providing metal stretchers should the man actually jump. Two policemen attempt to talk him down. Mario feels bad for the man, wonders if it's drug related, then wonders about his own brother Fredo. He also can't help but think the unfolding scene would make for a great story.

*

Alex pulls into Bill's Wheels—parks in a space just past Joey's car.

"I think what we're doing today is going to help. When you meet this guy, you'll know he's okay—that he's got no weird agenda when it comes to you."

"Well, I hope not. Some of these guys—they're pretty creepy. You know, on the other side of the law."

A likely candidate rounds the corner. After a hearty laugh, he steps to the car where Whitney's face appears to be floating behind glass. Smiling widely, Joey stoops to peer inside.

"You gonna come out, or what? I ain't no freak, if that's what you're thinkin.'"

Whitney immediately opens the door, forcing Joey back. Standing defiantly, she tosses her head—shakes the hair away from her face.

"My name is Whitney B. I'm an artist."

"Glad to meet you Whitney B. I hear you're a painter—like a really good one."

"Yes, thank you. I like to paint."

"No matter if it's from a tube or spray can, it's all paint and it's all good—you know what I'm sayin'?"

"Yes," she says firmly—"paint is what it's all about."

*

Arriving opposite Bill's Wheels, Mario fidgets as he waits to enter. Peering through traffic, he notices two cars in the parking lot. The closer one looks small and battered like his own. The one just beyond is bigger, more angular—has a golden sheen to the finish. At first, he can't believe what he sees—sits rigidly at the wheel. Then again—*Being Joey, it makes total sense.* It looks like he plans to introduce Mario to Alex this evening—however much Joey plans such things. By complete chance, the time has arrived for Mario to meet his adversary.

*

Alex and Whitney admire the graffiti pieces on a wall behind the main building. "These are great," says Alex," but you can't see them from the street or even the lot."

"Yeah, but a wall's a wall. Just another opportunity." Turning to Whitney—"I heard it was causin' you problems—me usin' that sign, that tattoo of yours. You got to believe me—I had no idea it was such a private thing. My man here—he didn't fill me in on no details. I'm truly sorry."

"I appreciate you saying that. Alex and I—we're trying to work through a—misunderstanding."

"Well, you got my word—I won't be usin' it no more."

"Thank you."

*

Scowling hard, Mario reenters traffic. *How can I confront the professor with Joey there? What if things turn ugly—physical?* For that, he needs some strictly private time, one-on-one. No witnesses. As he maneuvers the next few blocks, second thoughts overcome him. Suddenly, his mind makes a U-turn, followed closely by an actual one on the street. *So why not check out the guy? I'll get his number—get permission to call. Better yet—I'll make an appointment. Besides—I've been waiting too long for a chance like this.*

*

"Hey man," says Joey smiling—"I got somethin' for you too, Professor. Happens to be this cat I met. He's a writer for the paper. He wants to meet you—wants an interview. It's all on account he's doin' an article on graffiti. Nice enough guy—kinda intense, though."

Whitney immediately knows who he's talking about. "What do you mean—are you going to arrange some kind of meeting?"

"Nah—I ain't gonna be arrangin' no meetin'. Fact is—I already did. This guy—his name's Mario. He should be gettin' here anytime now."

"Well, we've got to go then," she insists. Turning to Alex—"We've got to go right now!"

Scooting to the edge of the wall, she peeks around the corner to the street.

"So, what's wrong?" asks Alex. "It's just some guy looking for a story."

"No, you don't get it. That guy—remember my show at Stripe? That's where you met him before. Your girlfriend Lisa was there too."

"Well, he's still your boyfriend, isn't he? What's the matter?"

"He's my ex—and it didn't end well. And now he's out to find the guy who used my tattoo—used it for graffiti. He really wants to confront you. I don't know, but maybe he wants to beat you up."

*

Mario's mind continues to rev, even as his car idles. He struggles with what he plans to say. Nothing inflammatory unless the professor says something stupid. Then again, the investigatory questions keep churning—*What the hell's going on with you and my girl? She went to your place—have you been to hers? How many times have you done it? Do you like her in bed—does she like it too?*

*

Led by Whitney, the trio scurries towards Alex's car. As two of them tumble in—"Say," asks Joey, "are you guys still plannin' to do what you said you was?"

Rolling down his window—"Yeah, we are."

"Then the girl's got on the wrong kinda outfit."

Glancing over, Alex ponders a light pink sweater top.

"Here, just a sec," says Joey, scrambling to his car. "Here—she can use one of these." Hustling back—"Take it," he says—handing over a big, black hoodie. "You oughta put it on now, but don't you worry. I got me an extra."

*

As Mario approaches the skate shop, he sees what looks like the Volvo pulling out the entrance. Several cars ahead—his vision gets partially obstructed. *How weird*—he thinks. *Why's he leaving?* Ignoring the skate shop and his date with Joey, he watches the car nudge its way through traffic. *Back to the freeway,* he assumes. As he fights for a peek, something else about the vehicle surprises him. *Why in the world is Joey inside?* He's definitely seen that black hoodie of his. *What a total flake— must have blown off our meeting.* And then it dawns on him— *Maybe they're going out tagging tonight—"getting up," as they would say.* Here's a chance to catch them at work—a chance to see the crew in action. He accelerates down the street before giving chase onto Highway 1.

*

With a description of Mario's car, Alex scans the visual swatch of his rearview mirror. He asks Whitney more about her former lover before taking the exit to Aptos Village. At the first stop, he finds himself stuck behind a large silver Suburban. A virtual billboard, it features stickers and decals from all over the country. Although ecologically lapsed, the owners are politically liberal, have an outstanding junior high student, a baby, and a love of Dobermans. Relief comes when the sport-ute lumbers off the road in search of more gasoline. Passing the shopping center, Alex crosses the bridge into the village—claims the only space left in the parking lot of the Britannia Arms.

*

Mario follows the two off the freeway. A couple turns later, he watches them take the bridge and disappear at the entrance to the restaurant. Wanting a good vantage point, he stops short of the span—parks in a lot across the ravine from the restaurant's service area. From here, he gazes over some fifty yards of open space.

In the center of his vision, a cement wall stands beneath the railroad trestle. Just below, steel piers support the structure over a brush-covered plunge. Graffiti litters nearly every structure. In fact, Mario can barely make out DRAZ's piece on the wall—the piece with Whitney's tattoo. At the moment, everything's quiet on the other side. *Having dinner, those guys. Drinks for sure. Must be discussing the details of tonight's project.* Mario can afford to wait—he's not hungry.

*

The Britannia Arms proves lively tonight with its friendly waitresses and free flowing pints of beer. But instead of soccer matches, baseball flickers from all the corner monitors. Halfway through a turkey pot pie, Whitney asks—"So tell me more about you and Lisa."

"What do you mean?"

"Well, you said you met in school—went separate ways. And then you got back together."

"That's about right."

"So, what does she do? What kind of job does she have?"

"She's big into marketing—a key person over at Xerox. She's been there a long time. Feels like she's been doing it forever."

"Lisa sounds cool. Does she know we're having dinner tonight?"

"Not really. She's actually in L.A. this week—has some important business down there."

"Does she like her job?"

"Yeah, she likes it a lot. She deals with the latest technology—meets a lot of interesting people. People from all over the country—all over the world."

"Kind of a people person."

"I suppose. She wasn't always, but I guess she is now."

"Sounds great—the way she changed and all. Now, let me go ahead and pay for dinner."

"No you're not."

"Yes I am. I'm a working girl too, you know."

*

Once again, Mario checks the time. He leaves his car to stretch his legs—paces the narrow ledge just beyond the parking lot. Coming to a stop, he glares across the gorge to where the two men must be wrapping things up. Inhaling the cool air—*I mean, what else can they be talking about?*

*

Alex and Whitney exit the restaurant, pass through a mingled veil of dusk and early moonlight. Stepping briskly, they follow a concrete retaining wall that leads to the trestle. Turning the corner, they're met with a narrow dirt pad, thickets of blackberry and manzanita—a cavernous ravine and stream below, a thrust of steel and railroad ties overhead.

Whitney stops. "Oh shit, this creeps me out!"

"But check out all these tags and pieces," he says. "Just be careful, it's a long ways down. So many writers—it's like a huge art gallery to me."

Together, they admire the permutated letters, even as darkness drains much of their color. Alex points to the wall behind them, as if to a projection screen in his lecture hall.

"Now let me show you Joey's piece. Here's his graffiti name—*DRAZ*—right over here, the finest creation in the whole place."

"How cool is that? I can't believe he did it without a brush."

"Just like you—a lot of talent and tons of work."

From deep in the bushes, a gruff snort erupts—Whitney freezes. Gathering himself, Alex peers through the overgrowth and spies the same dirty love seat he had found earlier in the year with Joey. And he finds the same filthy man wrapped in his overcoat lying on the sofa. Clearly drunk, he looks recently passed out.

"Just some poor fellow down on his luck—"

Whitney finds what she's been looking for. Flanking a separate tag are two versions of her own creation—the one that looks like a palm tree.

"Oh, come on," she says, "what a total mess!"

"Sorry."

"The lines are shaky—and those sloppy drips!"

"I was in a rush. Was scared out of my mind to be honest."

"Wished I could have seen it—losing your cool like that."

"Got to admit," he says—"poor optics all around."

*

Mario spots the two cloaked figures fronting the concrete wall. He thinks the taller of the two carries a backpack. As Mario waits for the crew to start, he allows for some interesting thoughts to surface. *What would happen if I called the sheriff—report the two? Would the deputies respond? Would the officers make an arrest? If so, what would be the fallout? Probably no big deal for Joey—but what about the professor? Maybe an arrest would cause serious problems. Maybe it could cost him his job—maybe his career. Maybe Whitney would be upset with him. Maybe....*

Mario watches as the two men approach the piece by DRAZ. Reaching for his pocket, he pulls out his cell phone—calls 911. Doubts surface. *Nobody cares about the train trestle—the place is covered with graffiti.* Cradling the phone, he keeps a steady eye across the ravine.

"Yes, I want to report a case of graffiti vandalism. Yes, it's taking place right now. It's under the Aptos trestle by the Britannia Arms. I think they just tagged the restaurant, too. My name? My name's David—David Verlatti. Well anyway— please hurry."

*

Unzipping his backpack, Alex extracts a can of silver paint. After a thorough shake, he leans across and starts to obliterate Whitney's signature design.

Looking more than a little disappointed, she watches it disappear. Squatting, she removes a can of red paint, shakes the contents—tests the flow the way she's been taught.

Hesitating—"Why can't we have a do-over? Let's paint it together this time—make it into something new."

But Alex is lost to concentration. Shrugging, she huddles to the left of DRAZ's piece and prepares to write the opening *W* of her name. And just then—just as the paint softly kisses the surface—she hears a man's commanding voice explode from Alex's direction—

"This is the sheriff's deputy!"

Swallowing a scream, Whitney drops her can.

"Fuck—oh fuck," she whispers to herself. "My parents are going to kill me!"

Scrambling, she takes off in the opposite direction.

Alex hears the same voice—shares the same panic. Following her around the corner, he passes the disheveled drunk. A second officer now appears. Turning on his flashlight, he orders the two to stop.

Terrified, Whitney slips off the edge of the dirt pad—skids, then falls down the steep slope. Alex knows he should hold his ground—deal with the law, act like an adult. But it's the youth in him that's brought him to this place, this act, this vandalism disguised as play. And he fears for the girl, fears for Whitney—and so he scuttles over the lip to find her. Losing his footing, he plunges down the same sheer drop—brambles and bushes tearing at his clothes, his skin. At the same time, the broken beam of a flashlight gives pursuit—chases him down the precipice.

"Over here—" yells one deputy to the other. "There's a guy over here on the sofa."

The old man has just come to—says he feels *all fucked up*—feels *sick*. He staggers off the love seat, while the officer grabs him before he can fall. Even with support, the man stumbles forward several feet. Bending over, he heaves something dark all over the ground.

In the meantime, the other deputy calls down the gorge. "Hey—are you guys all right? Has anybody been injured?"

There's only silence.

"Did you get a good look?" asks his partner.

"Not really," replies the first. He grabs his radio—calls in the paramedics. Sizing up the drunk man—"We got us a sick one here."

Both of the officers are standing now. "Those taggers—just a couple of punks. Say, look at that—" one of them says, shining his light on the wall. "They only just got started."

The other deputy helps the man back to the couch. "A case of prevention tonight."

The officer with the radio walks back over to the ledge. Trying once more—"Say—is anybody hurt down there? We've got an ambulance coming. If you tell us you're okay, we'll leave you alone this time—let you go. Next time, you won't be so lucky."

*

Mario slides into his car. Excited—definitely. A certain exaltation—a soaring emotion he associates with sports. For him, it's like the thrill of hitting a home run—a walk-off homer no less. But another part of him feels disturbed by the scene—something about frightened trespassers being rounded up by authorities. Clearly now, somebody's been hurt. But, *why should I care?* Let the men in charge do the dirty deed. Injuries are a part of the game, he thinks—a necessary part. Buckling his seat belt, he drives off as unobtrusively as possible. Still struggling with a nagging agitation, he reassures himself—*Why the hell should I care? If the professor's hurt, he totally deserves it.*

*

Some twenty feet below the pad, Alex lies in a peculiarly vertical position—caught in the savage undergrowth. A lot of pain—a lot of body parts hurt, but mostly his right leg. He wants desperately to find Whitney, but still tries to hear what the deputy is saying.

One of the officers starts picking his way down the side of the ravine. As he does, the sound of the emergency vehicle blares from across the bridge. The officer above gets another call—a vehicular accident on Highway 1—a possible injury scene.

Calling off the search—"You know these kids," he says to his partner, "got every inch of this place wired—know it like the back of their hand."

"Hey we tried," says the other—"you can write that down."

As soon as the paramedics take charge, the deputies take off.

Alex shifts his weight—calls out in a whisper—"Whitney—are you all right? Where are you?"

Off to his left—"I'm over here."

Whitney's chest hurts, and her right thigh feels like it's been torn open. Checking for blood—there's something slick down there. She's trapped in some brambles—saved by some blackberry bushes from a fatal fall. She wonders why she isn't crying, but the truth is....

"Don't move, I'll come and get you."

Alex slowly untangles himself from his own nest of blackberry brambles and thorny manzanita—rugged plants that have saved him as well. Grabbing a hold of rock and branches, he makes his way in her direction.

Whitney watches as Alex struggles. She knows she could free herself, but decides not to. The racing of her heart is due to fear, but the truth is…. The pain she feels throughout her body is definitely strong, but the truth is…. And when Alex, out of breath, reaches her—when he brings her close, when his face hovers before her, a look of relief…Whitney parts her lips—takes his mouth into hers.

*

So the minutes creep by, but the time passes quickly. Under the trestle. Extrication—the prolonged climb to the top of the ridge. The mutual trudge back to the car. And then the long drive back into town. Not much communication, until—

"Park over here," she says—pointing to the driveway. "Go all the way back."

In the light of the landing—"You're hurt. Why don't you come upstairs for a while?"

The key clicks, the door opens—the door opens to a dark room.

Walking to her bed, she reaches for a small incandescent lamp. As she flicks it on, the front of her body lights up. Removing Joey's black hoodie, the entire room glows pink. Whitney's hair looks as wild as the ravine—her face abraded, smudged with dirt. A black gash runs down her right thigh, the denim below wet with something.

Alex takes a step into the room. "You're hurt, too," he notes softly.

Returning his gaze, she has the strange sensation of looking into a mirror. Beside the torn sweatshirt and ripped jeans—something about Alex's face. An expression she clearly recognizes. The look of disbelief, displacement—the mask of shock after one's whole world has gone upside down. At a loss—no explanations.

Stepping to the sink, she takes a clean dish towel and soaks it. Approaching him, she locates several scratches on his face. Tenderly, she dabs at the streaks of blood and dirt. Her desire to touch him like this removes anything tentative about her. She leans forward—kisses him a second time.

Alex responds with a wry smile—"I guess you couldn't kiss me again without cleaning me up."

"Oh no," she replies. "I don't need you clean."

"Fine with me," he says.

Although she takes him by the hand, he doesn't feel like he's being led. For the first time in a long time, he doesn't think. He doesn't clutter the moment with high-minded thoughts. He tells the voice in his head to shut up. And because he does, he finds himself looking forward to being with Whitney. No, not being with her, but making love to her. Whatever fantasies he's entertained, nothing is as real as this tiny room, this small light, a meager addition of the moon through the window.

Now the hands let go, and the two turn to face each other again. And it's a kind of synchronicity of movement, a kind of silent choreography. Whitney lifts the hem of her top, just as Alex takes hold of his sweatshirt. For a moment, Whitney pauses in her bra, as Alex unbuttons the top of his shirt. When his fingers reach the middle of his chest, she unhooks her bra from behind. Now Alex's shirt drops to the floor—just as her breasts fall open to the light. A moment later, two pairs of shoes and socks go flying. Then Whitney undoes her jeans, just as Alex unzips his own. She utters a small gasp as her pant leg scrapes the wound in her thigh. Echoing the sound, he eases out of his own torn denim. Now a tiny triangle of panties, slithered off. A pair of briefs disappears. Standing silently, the two of them fully absorb the sight of each other. For Whitney, some terrible imbalance rights itself. Before her, this man— this authority, the professor—the one who unfairly saw her nude before. And it pleases her to see him naked now—without the professional clothes, the desk, the lectern. And it pleases her because he looks beautiful in the light—trim, athletic, his cock already starting to rise. And for Alex—Whitney appears like a revelation—so unlike the naked girl, the nude model, the one he'd studied in class. More than just a physical woman— but one animated by some deep, soulful essence.

And so she pulls the covers from her bed. Climbing atop, she sprawls out on her back. Such a fine and clear invitation.

Despite the pain, he goes to join her. Settling in the space between her legs, he starts to kiss her mouth. Slick and wet, her lips begin a dialogue with his. He likes her taste—a bit of sweat adding to the mix. She likes his scent—an aura that now envelops her body. He works his way down her neck, using his tongue like the tip of a brush. He generously paints the ridge of a collarbone, the small indentations of her sternum. He renders the fullness of each breast and traces the concentric rings that define each nipple. He follows the shadow of her abdomen, the rise of her pubic bone—then drops still farther to where she glistens.

Whitney receives. Whitney feels everything. Whitney shudders. And when Alex hears the harsh exhalations, it reminds him of when he's heard her sobbing. Only this time the source is something other than pain, he thinks. Little does he know how much her chest, her ribs hurt—how the torment goads her into the relentless pursuit of relief. Now she reassures him—says she takes something for contraception. And so he enters her, and when he does, she wraps her damaged thigh around him. And the inflammation grows so intense, she finds herself coming before she wants to. But Whitney continues to hold on to him, keeps her hold on him, and so she returns to the same level of pain and pleasure until her next release coincides with his own. Alex finishes with a sudden, internal roar—flares externally—goes deep into every recess of her body. And the satisfaction he feels is beyond any immediate comprehension. He feels grateful—feels so fortunate. He wants to thank her, but instead, uses his mouth to gently kiss her. Enfolding her, he embraces how very dear she is to him. She nestles in his arms and lies there in her own sublime disbelief. Together, they fall asleep like this, will spend the entire night together—will find out in the morning to their great surprise, the shared resonance of their dreams.

19

Seattle—home of Alex's aunt

Kaz's older sister studies the weathered photo album—family pictures from around 1940. In one portrait, her mother wears a black silk dress with lace collar—her dapper father, a three-piece suit. Haruko, or Haru, was fourteen at the time—wears a scalloped-hemmed dress and pearls. Standing proudly in his sailor's outfit, Kaz is almost five.

Stiff, formal—their pose suggests a family of means. Haru says her folks ran a hotel in downtown Seattle—the Marion Hotel on 6th Avenue. They leased the building, because they couldn't legally own it. Most of the tenants were *hakujin*—Caucasian. The rest were first generation Japanese, some with children born in this country. Thanks to an immigrant's work ethic, Mom and Pop did well for themselves—were good providers. Theirs was the first Japanese family to own a refrigerator, the first to buy a car.

After the Great Depression and before the war, life was tough for many of their friends. Beyond community service, Pop often drove neighbors around—those with errands to do in other parts of the city. He also made loans to a number of people—never expected to be repaid. Always said—if you give a person money you should treat it like a gift. On a loan of $15, he once received a white cat in return.

Pop liked to take the family on outings. Haru recalls picnics at Lincoln Park and Lake Washington. In the summer, he would take the kids to the waterfront with nets and gunny sacks for shrimp. They would drive over to "Hoover Town" to catch fish in ponds—stickle fish. One winter they bought skates at a Japanese sporting goods store on 4th Avenue—skated on a frozen lake near Sears, Roebuck. Pop also knew that the Fairmont Dairy had the best milkshakes in town—and that the best hot dogs came from street vendors in Pioneer Square. On weekends, he might take the kids out for a treat. Sometimes— he would just surprise them.

Mom was ever resourceful, good with her hands. Like many women back then, she was a competent seamstress. Haru says that she always had nice clothes to wear—pretty dresses her mother would create for her. Mom was artistic in a practical way. It was probably her sense of design—her *eye* that Kaz inherited.

Mom also held to old Japanese practices. Once, when Haru became very ill, Mom called in a Japanese doctor for an emergency visit. In addition to Western treatments, he allowed for traditional interventions. When close friends suggested that Haru eat raw snails and earthworms, Mom arranged for that to happen. When asked how she responded, Haru would say—*Of course, I ate them. They told me to.…* She was further advised by friends to drink the fresh blood of a rabbit. Fortunately, the Arai children had a pet bunny named Wellington. When Haru finally recovered, her grateful mother picked up the rabbit in her arms. Gently stroking the beneficent ear—*Thank you, Wellington*, she said in English.

Haru finds a photo of the family taken in early 1941. They're picnicking at the foot of Mt. Rainier, sharing a *bento* lunch with other families. She says that before the war, she doesn't remember any negative racial encounters. With the attack on Pearl Harbor came a huge anti-Japanese backlash, but she can't recall any incidents of prejudice against herself. There was, however, some hushed talk about a neighbor's letter to the *Seattle Times* editor—one with the byline, *Jap family next door.*

When the FBI came to the hotel, everyone was in the living room. Fortunately, Pop had just gotten rid of his picture of the Emperor. According to Haru, the agents ransacked her belongings. In so doing, they found an old report card she'd been hiding from her folks. But Pop was known as a community leader and was a member of the local hotel association. About two weeks later, the agents returned—this time taking him away. Later, the family paid him a visit at the immigration building on Dearborn Street.

From there, Pop was sent to detention in Bismarck, North Dakota. The family wasn't reunited until five months later at the Camp Harmony assembly center in Puyallup. When Pop finally showed up in the middle of summer, he was wearing the sweater Haru had knitted for his birthday. It never occurred to her, she says, to ask why her father had been arrested.

Earlier that year, when Executive Order 9066 was issued, life was terribly altered. With her husband gone, Mom decided to sell the lease rather than having someone else run the hotel. When the day came to leave home, each person was allowed to take only what he or she could carry. The family had *hakujin* friends who owned the Panama Hotel—used their basement for storage. Haru packed away all her dolls in boxes—her two Shirley Temples, her Patsyette—her favorite Deanna Durbin. To this day, she deeply regrets that she never got any of them back.

As for her little brother, Kaz—Haru says he was a good boy, kind of spoiled, but then again, so was she. Six years old at the time, it was probably a kind of adventure for him. Kaz had no responsibilities and was usually in his own head anyway. Leaving Seattle, he brought all his crayons and colored pencils—made his mother carry the extra sketchbooks that wouldn't fit into his suitcase. From the assembly center, the internees boarded a train to Idaho. The day of departure was very quiet, recalls Haru—quiet and orderly. *We did what we were told.* On the train, she says the window shades were kept closed. Among the things she remembers is her brother silently drawing pictures of the inside of the car.

Kaz, himself, recalls Minidoka the way many other children would. For example, the huge sandstorm that greeted anxious evacuees was a cause of wonderment for him. He hardly remembers certain other aspects of the ordeal—like the commotion around the weekly showers back at the assembly center. To stand outside in a long line—naked—must not have engendered the same humiliation as it did for adolescents and adults. At Minidoka, sitting on one of the eight holes used for toilets—no partitions—must not have been a problem for him either. He does, however, recall a curious bit of conversation between two older boys. *Hi, Jimmy, what are you doing?* The sarcastic response—*What the hell do you think I'm doing?*

Normally, Haru doesn't like to talk about the relocation of her family to Idaho. When her own kids were growing up, she rarely mentioned anything about that part of her story. The occasional comments referred to the experience simply as *camp.* No modifiers like *internment, relocation, concentration.* More like—*Back in camp*—or, *When we were in camp*— She might as well have been referring to summer camp, as far as her children knew.

It's been a number of years since younger generations started asking questions about the internment. Although hard at first, Haru obtains a certain relief having permission to address this part of her life. Now in her eighties, once she gets going—it just feels good to talk. She no longer minds sharing her memories—adds her voice to so many others. She says it's kind of like returning to some old hotel—like going back down into a dark basement somewhere, to retrieve things—to clean things out.

* * *

San Jose—phone message from Sumi to Alexander Arai

"Hello Alex—this is me calling. Hope you're okay—hope the weather's good over there. I meant to tell you, Mrs. Kihara—she passed away the other day. It would be nice if you could send a card to the family. You remember—*koden*—something like fifty dollars should be okay. Services at the church this Sunday, but I don't expect you to attend. I mean, you knew her kids from high school, but anyway—

"So, yes—the reason I'm calling you is, well—it's about your father. He's been trying to reach you for a while now. It's about that retrospective coming up. A really big deal for him.

Anyway, he thinks it's getting kind of late. You know how he is—how uptight he gets.

"And believe me, I understand. Sometimes your father is hard to deal with. Sometimes, it's like he's the only one he thinks about. But you know—the Japanese American community looks up to him. He's given them something to be proud of. So, anyway—I know you don't want to let him down, or disappoint all those other people.

"And, gee, Alex—I'm sorry this is taking up so much space, but—well, if you could just do it for the family's sake. It would be nice if you just gave your father a call. All right? Of course you understand. Anyway—hope you stay in touch. Bye."

∗ ∗ ∗

The house on Escalona Drive

Extreme stress along internal fault lines—the forces build. Alex feels a painful tension between major chunks of himself. Plate tectonics—significant pieces threatening a violent shift. It feels so much more than being pissed off. All the expectations, the control that others exert on him—telling him who he is, what to do. Long hours researching—cobbling a course on Contemporary Art. It's been quite some time since he's crammed like this—working on a term project worthy of a lowly grad student. And then, of course, there's the matter of his acclaimed father. Kazuo Arai, that mad dog—barking away from across a mountainous fence—still nipping at his heels with frequent electronic messages. *Okay*, thinks Alex— *so everyone wants something 'Contemporary,' something a little 'Postmodern?' No worries—you'll get what you want. All of you—*

But now there's something new in his life. Something that gives him pause, like a fresh green landscape in the midst of physical and cognitive abstractions. Alex cherishes the time he's spent with Whitney. He wonders how his own recollections compare to the physical memories that sometimes derail her. He thinks of the artist she is—so gifted and skilled as a painter. He thinks of that wild moment when she unleashes her furious truth. Something soothing about her unsettled self. While evoking her, he feels fortified—solid. In fact, he actually feels grand at times, believing anything is possible now. Just as he hates the constraints that bind him, he knows that creativity and courage are his way forward. So Alex continues his rumblings into a night of disrupted sleep. In quick succession, he dreams of—

Two sumo wrestlers— Alex is one. No, he's actually *both*. After arduous training, a painful apprenticeship, he crouches in anticipation. Alex confronts Alex in the moment of truth. Alex charges—meets himself in the middle of the ring—a resounding, massive collision.

A baseball player— Alex is a Japanese baseball player in the American big leagues. After so many seasons rising through the system, he stands in the batter's box—faces an imposing pitcher. The pitcher winds up—delivers a fastball down the middle. The moment of truth. Does Alex swing?

A samurai in the castle of his disgraced lord— After a life obeying the code of *bushido*, a life of loyal service—Alex unsheathes his knife, the finest in all the world. He must plunge the blade into his abdomen—slice all the way through to the right, then up. Ritual disembowelment. He has prepared his mind and soul for this. The moment of truth—the knife, poised and ready.

An Imperial Japanese fighter pilot— After perilous training, multiple missions over the Pacific, Alex rides the *divine wind*— *Kamikaze*. He looks below at the enemy destroyer. In the name of the Emperor, he is ready to kill American boys. The moment of truth. He thinks it first, then cries aloud—*Banzai!* May you live *ten thousand years!*

An American soldier in Italy— Alex is a dirty, buck private getting set to storm the impenetrable Gothic Line. After months of bloody battles for freedom and democracy—months away from his home in a concentration camp. The moment of truth. Alex and his brothers *go for broke*. And as he charges uphill toward the frightened Germans, he too will scream *Banzai!*

Trip east Day 1—Lower Manhattan, New York City

*A*lex takes a straight shot at "Ground Zero," walking south along Church Street. A week before school starts, a week after the National September 11 Memorial opened to the public. He has long been awaiting this opportunity—wants the version in his head to collide with reality. His target awaits, hidden by a multitude of skyscrapers.

What strikes him most is the great commotion of people. All kinds of people. New Yorkers at work in the financial district, New Yorkers at work building the replacement parts to the World Trade Center. And tourists everywhere, so much like himself. People of every shape and color, age, gender—what have you. People from every part of the country, the world. As America observes the tenth anniversary of the terrorist attacks, everyone either remembers that day, or obtains those memories from someone close. And now, an official memorial stands ready to further that process—a new, national icon to evoke the traumatic narrative. Alex hopes the site will provide tools for addressing the wounds. He wants an opportunity to heal. His mission is all about healing in the end.

Peering from outside the memorial's perimeter fence, he sees nothing. *Funny*, he thinks to himself. Wasn't there another time when he'd experienced something like this? Years ago, stepping out of the Cortlandt Street Station—hadn't he looked up toward the towers and seen nothing? So tall and silver-white—they obliterated the entire skyward view. And in spite of their looming presence, they seemed to dematerialize into the heavens.

Today, he joins a long line of visitors snaking about in Disneyland fashion toward the entrance. Arriving at the spacious new plaza, he looks left, right—straight ahead. Once more, there's a great commotion of people. On the periphery, he fails to locate a focal point. Nothing monumentally *vertical*. Just a matrix of young trees beneath which he spots clusters of kinetic visitors. Alex assumes they're gazing into one of the two signature fountains that define the footprints of the towers.

Pressing forward, he approaches the former site of the South Tower. There, he finds a wall of people blocking the low lying parapets. Given the inverted design, there's no such thing as a graduated perspective of the fountain. Like the event itself, there's no way to experience a modulated approach to a tragedy. A brief opening—he bellies up to the waist-high bronze border. He's immediately engulfed by the gravitational pull of the pool. Water, unrelenting water—he hears a constant, static-laden roar. Nothing soothing about the sharp white noise that surrounds him. He traces the flow from beneath the railing before it plunges over a sharp edge into the square pool thirty feet below. Denied any peaceful refuge, the water inexorably runs to a small hole in the center, through which all of it disappears. The bottom of the shaft can't be seen, and the water vanishes in a tumult of spray. As Alex scans this vast cavity—his eyes go corner to corner, tracing the endless curtains of water. Distressingly, they remind him of the way the towers collapsed in showers of concrete and melted steel.

Ten years ago, he stared into his television screen and watched as everything fell. Now, he mouths the title of the memorial—*The Reflection of Absence*.... The pools were meant to evoke *the presence of absence*. Looking skyward—he experiences a sense of tangible nothingness where the towers once stood. His mind creates a three dimensional Rothko—a voluminous void rising high above the plaza. No upward thrust—the vertical elements tumble downward, plummet beneath street level to God-knows-where. He registers the pool as a sinkhole, and at worst—some kind of ongoing, flushing toilet. As if the city were bleeding out, he bears witness to the uncontrollable loss of life's energy flowing into oblivion. And it won't stop.

Acutely depressed, he turns his attention to the perimeter of names that frame the pool. Each name has been punched out of bronze. Again, each life noted by an absence. Standing on a side that lists first responders, the Irish and Italian names jump out at him. As he tours the railing, he recovers names from all manner of ethnicities. Mostly as individuals, some side-by-side with a partner. Names of several women note, *with unborn child*. Alex feels the weight of all those empty letters. He decides that the power, the human spirit of the memorial, resides in the names. He concludes his visit by paying tribute to the names on the North Tower pool. Today, he has managed to hit his mark—the new, national memorial to September 11. Through its minimalist components, he re-experiences the trauma of that day's events. He's not certain about any healing, though.

*   *   *

Day 2—Lower Midtown

Just around the corner from the United Nations, Alex sits on a smooth wooden bench. The seating is part of two long rows lining the broad Dag Hammarskjöld Plaza. On a pleasant day beneath swaying alders, he's about to visit the Japan Society building. The five-story creation of Junzo Yoshimura was the first major building in New York City designed by a Japanese architect. Although started earlier, The World Trade Center by Seattle-born Minoru Yamasaki was completed six years later. Alex admires the grid-like façade of metal and glass, so in keeping with the Modernist aesthetic. Its system of panels and window screens evokes bamboo shades and paper *shoji*.

Leaving his bench, he ambles across 47th Street. As he enters the building, Japanese elements infuse the interior with a formal simplicity in complete accord with Modernism. Adding to his delight are pieces of furniture designed and built by George Nakashima. Also from Seattle, the well-known craftsman was interned in Minidoka, Idaho—the same camp as Alex's parents.

A Modern exterior. The question becomes—*How deep does a surface have to go to reach a Japanese interior?* Stepping outside, he locates a modest sculpture in a small nook to the right of the building. About ten feet high including the black granite pedestal, it depicts a *Nikkei* man heading off to work. Commissioned by the Japanese government in 1996, the memorial honors Japanese Americans who endured World War II while preserving traditional Japanese values.

The inspiration for the figure is Sontoku Ninomiya, the so-called *peasant sage of Japan.* A farmer, philosopher, and government administrator, his social movement helped to improve rural conditions in pre-war Japan. Sculptures of him were placed in elementary schools to inspire children to both study and to work hard. The present depiction is a bronze figure astride a stainless steel bridge, symbolically spanning the Pacific Ocean. In one hand, he clasps an open book. The satchel on his back overflows with mechanical items like the grill of a car, the nose and wing of a jet, the prow of an ocean liner. Instead of traditional country garb, the figure wears a Western office shirt and tie—sleeves rolled up, with sharply-creased slacks over business shoes.

Beneath the dedication on the pedestal, the Japanese words for *diligence, cooperation, deference to authority* and *thrift* are carved—along with the English translations. While skirting the sculpture, Alex notes how the figurative water laps at the bridge with shimmering, serrated peaks. Contrasted with the dark bronze, the glass waves look ethereal.

* * *

Day 3—Lower Midtown

The time has arrived, and as it would happen—the time is 2 a.m., or thereabouts. After so much preparation, so much practice, he has no control over the few people still out. Random vehicles pass in the dark. Alex spots what looks like the same yellow taxi circling the block—circling him. Walking onto Dag Hammarskjöld Plaza, he enters a vast expanse stretching up, down, left and right—like air space. His eyes strain as he maintains his course down the long promenade. Above, treetops hover like black clouds—sodium light sifting through, the color of the moon.

All of his senses are switched on—the flashing gauges of a cockpit, ablaze in the night with jumping dials and bursts of dire warning. Piloting his body, he feels like he's in an airplane—or he is the plane itself. His fuselage fully pressurized—a bay of guts wanting to dump—the taste of acid in his mouth, precursor to vomiting. His head pounds—all the volatile blood within him wants to explode. Everything in-side and out-side—bizarrely fused, jumbled. Sometimes he finds himself peering through a kind of canopy, one in which his mind feels trapped. He can't really tell who's guiding the plane—the adult in him, or is it the boy?

But now comes the time to cloak himself—time to go stealth. He unfurls the rumpled cloak he's clutching, that dark piece of clothing—the black hoodie that belongs to Joey but carries Whitney's scent. Drawing it over his body, he hides his head.

Finding the Japan Society building, he focuses on the target just to its right. Brandishing a loaded spray can, he makes an initial pass at the monument—the sculpture designed and cast by his father, Kazuo Arai. After skimming the length of the street, he banks sharply around. Now, as he makes his final approach, he wants to be *huge* with anger—wants to feel *consumed* by the rage that propels him. But somehow the fear is too great—the interfering *terror*. Alex feels *terrified* of being caught—*terrified* of the authorities, *terrified* of his father, actually—*terrified* over what he's about to do. The fear is so strong it completely perverts his anger.

Finally reaching his father's memorial, his body falters, his knees buckle—he can't think. In the quiet of the plaza, there's only chaos in his brain. So he thrusts out his arm as he's trained himself to do. He attacks with a *pssst, pssst* sound, and the smell of spray paint jolts his mind. In this moment of truth, he renders an elegant silver line—gives birth to the interconnected letters of *AWRY*. And the flow is so beautiful, he sees it, receives it—a *revelation*. And from the midst of great terror soars an even greater joy. Alex writes his name—writes it again. Thrilled by his hand, he writes all over his father's creation. And as he steps away, he notes for the first time the heaving fullness of his breath. Taking his leave, he dips through a shadow and then under a light. And as he coasts down the street, he turns once more to the receding figure. Alex marvels at his name as if just discovering it—a fresh constellation in a night sky of darkened bronze.

* * *

Day 5—The National Mall, Washington D.C.

"Injustice anywhere is a threat to justice everywhere. We are caught in an inescapable network of mutuality, tied in a single garment of destiny. Whatever affects one directly, affects all indirectly."
—Alabama, 1963

Carved in stone—*The National Martin Luther King, Jr. Memorial*

Alex approaches from the main entrance behind the new sculpture. Delayed by Hurricane Irene, the official dedication takes place in a month. Walking down a paved corridor, he looks up at the two towering stones that flank him. Facing away, the figure of Martin Luther King, Jr. stands just beyond— appears extracted from the very gap. As he enters the plaza, the Washington Memorial rises to the distant left. The tranquil dome of the Jefferson Memorial floats above the expansive Tidal Basin ahead. At the venue's center stands the thirty-foot monolith from which Reverend King is rendered.

Already, streams of people fill the plaza, small eddies washing up against the base. Young voices, old voices—people speaking in a variety of languages. Although visitors hale from all over the world, African Americans predominate. As he passes the right flank of Dr. King, Alex reads the inscribed words: *Out of the Mountain of Despair, A Stone of Hope.*

Rounding the corner, Alex views the sculpture from the front. He's immediately taken by its monumentality. The blocky composition consists of squared shoulders, a thick chest, a set of angular folded arms, and a rigidly upright stance. With its bulging veins, the sinewy right hand looks disproportionately large from below. The partially obscured left hand squeezes a roll of documents. The overall impression is one of strength and power. *For godsake*, Alex puzzles, *why is a style associated with totalitarian regimes used for a civil rights leader? Why is a man of the people defined by an authoritarian vernacular?*

Having absorbed the mass of the torso, he gazes up at the face. He finds that the two eyes convey very different emotions. The one to his left exudes a subtle warmth. Beneath a more arched brow, the one to his right projects a definite sternness. The specter reminds him of the Great Seal of the United States—the eagle's talons bearing a sheaf of arrows on one side, an olive branch on the other. Indeed, like the eagle—King directs his gaze toward the peaceful side of the written word rather than favoring the heavy hand.

As for the color of the central figure, Alex would describe it as a gritty oatmeal rather than the gleaming white of polished marble. The fact that the black civil rights leader *reads* white doesn't disturb him. He's studied more than his share of subjects—human, animal, mechanical—rendered in various monochromatic stone. For the sake of balance, the whiteness serves to bind the sculpture to both the Washington and Jefferson Memorials.

Walking back through the plaza, Alex approaches the wall of quotes behind King's statue, contemplates each one. The words are what bring out the man's greatness, as much, if not more than the sculpture towering nearby. The words evoke so much history, tap the memory of so many events in the narrative of American civil rights. Despite the specter of continued despair at the entrance, Alex takes ample time to appreciate the man, his words—the deeds that led to greater justice for all.

* * *

Day 6—Constitution Avenue and 1st Street

Alex frets. From the top of the Supreme Court steps, he gazes below to a small plot of land across the street to the right. Southern magnolias spread themselves over the paved courtyard as if trying to hide a secret. Alex asks himself—*At what level is justice achieved?* Korematsu, Hirabayashi, and Yasui all stood their ground—disobeyed one or both the military curfew and Executive Order 9066. They argued that both curfew and exclusion orders were unconstitutional and discriminatory to American citizens.

The three men were charged and convicted of violating military orders. Subsequent appeals went all the way to the Supreme Court, which upheld the original decisions. Forty more years would pass before the convictions were finally vacated. During that time, another generation of Japanese Americans reached maturity. Young Sansei attorneys worked to fight the injustices that befell their parents and grandparents. In 1987, the United States Court of Appeals ruled that the government's actions toward Japanese Americans were wrongful, and Congress issued a formal apology in 1988. Financial reparations followed at the amount of $20,000 per surviving internee or heir. Fred Korematsu, Gordon Hirabayashi, and Minoru Yasui—all inspirational lights for the community. In 1998, President Bill Clinton awarded Korematsu the Presidential Medal of Freedom, the highest civilian honor in the United States.

At the corner of Constitution Avenue and 1st Street, a triangular courtyard rests beneath its green canopy. Black marble benches border two sides. In the center stands a twelve-foot-high memorial honoring the redress movement and the three Americans who refused to go quietly when their civil rights were violated. Dedicated in 1999, the sculpture proper stands atop a welded stainless steel base shaped like a stack of legal books. On the pedestal rests the bronze depiction of a large shattered porcelain plate. Some of the shards jut skyward, as if they were flames. From this jagged ruin, the nude torso of a young man rises up like the proverbial Phoenix. With arms triumphantly raised, he holds aloft a shimmering glass plate bearing the names of the three civil rights heroes. The bronze of the sculpture bears a golden patina—one which the creator, Kazuo Arai, found particularly appropriate.

Alex descends the white marble steps of justice. In planning his next attack, he locates a pair of park rangers in front of the Library of Congress. One says the city's absence of graffiti is due to the respect most people have for the nation's capital. She directs him to certain adjacent neighborhoods where examples of graffiti are readily found. The other ranger notes that grounds keepers remove graffiti as soon as it's discovered, thus minimizing the payoff for vandals.

Tentatively, Alex concludes that few in Washington would expect a memorial to be defaced. Still, he knows he must be careful. Surveillance cameras are plentiful according to the rangers. If not a mark for graffiti bombing, the capital remains a terrorist target since the Pentagon was attacked during 9/11. The rangers do their best to reassure him the capital is indeed secure.

*

Dark now, but not too late. Alex doesn't want to stand out—doesn't want to be the only one walking about Capitol Hill. He thinks to himself—*At what level is justice achieved?* This mission is not an attack on Korematsu, Hirabayashi, and Yasui. This mission is not an attack on the attorneys who worked so diligently to right a wrong—who honored their forebears with a deep and relentless gratitude. *No*, he asserts—*this is about personal justice, an issue between my father and me.* Wearing Joey's hoodie, he lifts the hem to his face—draws in a prolonged breath. Fortified, he crosses Constitution Avenue, takes a grassy walkway to the courtyard on 1st. The memorial up ahead looks strangely dim and subdued. Partly because of minimal lighting—partly due to the magnolia trees and their generous shading. For tonight, he welcomes the added protection. He considers the enormity of what he's about to do. To act within a stone's throw of the Federal Judicial Branch feels daunting enough.

As he gains momentum, terror grips him just as it did in New York City. His eyes flit about as he struggles to keep his objective in view. He feels like a helicopter pilot about to dive through a tight breach in the mountains—a tilting canyon. Limiting himself to a single shot, he has one opportunity to get it right. Clearly, he must minimize exposure to the cameras wherever they are. Through a perimeter of shadows, Alex bursts into the courtyard. Immediately ahead—his father's memorial. With spray can drawn, he identifies the least-lit part of the sculpture. Hovering, Alex strikes—aiming for the figure's lower back. Using the on-off flow of a bus hopper, it takes a mere four seconds to get his name up. Retracting his arm, he whirls away—briskly exits the scene. Back in the shadows, the attack seems unreal. It happened so quickly—did it happen at all? Resisting the urge to check, he disappears into a nearby clump of trees—tries to settle himself. For the time being, he huddles in the dark—makes himself small. Trembling, he silently exalts. Even as he appears to be cowering, he exalts. Lying low, hiding—he crouches beneath the heavy branches and the towering Supreme Court building just down the street. Whatever guilt inside him seems like a mere abstraction. For the moment, Alex feels above the law—even as he finds himself beneath the level of the three names on his father's glass plate.

✳ ✳ ✳

Trip south—Little Tokyo, Los Angeles

From Tokuji Ono, veteran of the 100th Infantry Battalion and docent for the *Go For Broke Memorial*—

"An ordinary company had two hundred—around two hundred men. But in saving the *Lost Battalion,* my gosh, I-Company and K-Company—they took a beating. 'Cause the mountain ridge was so small it would only take two companies. But I-Company went in there with a normal—say, one hundred eighty, two hundred guys—and they came back with just five riflemen. The rest were all killed or wounded. K-Company was about the same. The Germans—they knew about the *Nisei* soldiers— really feared us. The 100th/442nd had built a reputation of being good fighters.

"A-Company was the lead company of the 100th in the battle to break the Gothic Line. And Sadao Munemori was in my company, and he—he was the only one that got a Medal of Honor until the year 2000. The only one out of the whole regiment. Then the rest were upgraded—twenty-three more Medals in all. While we were away from Italy, we fought in France for the Lost Battalion, and battles in Biffontaine and Bruyeres. At the same time, the Allies were completely stalled—hadn't moved for six months against the Gothic Line. The Germans were dug in—up in the Apennine Mountains—trying not to get pushed out of Italy. That's why Mark Clark wanted the 100th/442nd back in Italy to break the Gothic Line. It was supposed to be a secret to the Germans. And the 100th Battalion—we were assigned to the 92nd Division, and they hadn't moved, and we replaced one of their infantry regiments.

"And so, together along with the 442nd, we pushed forward and we broke the Line. They said it took only a half an hour, but I—I really don't know how they judged the time. But once we got 'em moving, well—you know? 'Cause over here on our right was Mt. Folgorita, and the 442nd—they had to climb that mountain from the night before to be on top for the 5 o'clock—you know—when the battle started. So then, they actually caught the Germans sleeping up there. And so the 442nd was comin' from the back, and we were comin' from the front, and then the Germans had no choice but to retreat. And little by little during the month of April, into May—that's when the war ended."

In Little Tokyo, Alexander Arai decides to abort his mission. Actually—he alters his mission before returning home to Santa Cruz.

✱ ✱ ✱

Trip north
Interstate Highway 84—east out of Boise

Cruising the freeway, Alex contemplates the so-called *loyalty questionnaire* given to persons of Japanese descent during their World War II internment. Obsessed, he ponders the choice of available answers to the two key questions—

#27. Are you willing to serve in the armed forces of the United States on combat duty, wherever ordered?

#28. Will you swear unqualified allegiance to the United States of America and faithfully defend the United States from any or all attacks by foreign or domestic forces, and foreswear any form of allegiance or obedience to the Japanese emperor, or any other foreign government, power, or organization?

Lots for Alex to think about. A flight from San Jose to Boise, Idaho—and now the 140-mile drive to Minidoka. Almost seventy years ago, a seismic wave struck the Japanese living in the western United States. Out in the Pacific—Imperial Japan had just bombed Pearl Harbor—killing over 2,400 American boys. With that naval explosion, bad news spread like a giant tsunami striking the mainland and *heart*-land of America. In no time, *all persons of Japanese ancestry* disappeared from the coast. Many found themselves high and dry—in the parched deserts of the interior. From Los Angeles, they were sent to Manzanar, California and Heart Mountain, Wyoming. From cities like Seattle, Portland, and Anchorage—Idaho awaited them with some thirty thousand acres of barren land.

Alex looks out through the tinted glass of his rental car. The highway unfurls without turbulence, and at seventy-five miles an hour—today's trip is swift and smooth.

...Back in Little Tokyo, Alex identified his next target—the next victim of his next *sneak attack*. Just across the street from the Japanese American National Museum— *How odd,* one might think. Why would a memorial by Kazuo Arai *not* be displayed in the sweeping space in front of the building? After all, most of the museum's content spoke to the Japanese American narrative of World War II. Inside—one could find a reconstruction of a barrack room, made of actual pieces recovered from Topaz, Arizona. Inside—one could view photos of the Medal of Honor recipients from the 100th Battalion and the 442nd Regimental Combat

Team. What was a memorial by Kazuo Arai doing across the street—separated from the museum by four lanes of busy traffic?

From behind the wheel, Alex surveys the distant vistas—a 360-degree panorama. As a cradle of volcanism, Idaho consists of tall mountains and high desert built up through eons of lava flow. And over all that time, the sculpting winds blew incessantly. And the body of the Snake River flowed continually—cut the land to its own writhing specifications. So many years after the internment, metal windmills harvest invisible energy from out of the air. Farms and dairies extend in every direction, in ever increasing numbers.

...Back in Little Tokyo, Alex understood the score. It all came down to the questionnaire given in early 1943 to all internees seventeen years and older. The survey was meant to determine which among them were fit for military service. Questions #27 and #28 were the most confusing and controversial. How a person answered them would determine the rest of his or her life. To answer, *Yes, yes*, was to be seen as a loyal American, many of whom went on to serve in the U.S. Army. To answer, *No, no*, was to be judged disloyal and a potential threat to the United States.

The civil rights group, the Congress of Japanese Americans, had taken a central leadership role. After advising the community to cooperate with the relocation, they pushed for the questionnaire to be answered in the double affirmative.

Of the so-called *No-no boys*, the distinction was never made as to the reasons behind their responses. The older *Issei* were already barred from becoming U.S. citizens. Some feared that answering in the positive would nullify their Japanese citizenship as well—thus leaving them without a country. They also reasoned that to answer in the negative might lead to their immediate deportation. Some internees may have indeed maintained their loyalty to the Japanese emperor. Some young men may not have wanted to serve in the military—sometimes the result of maternal persuasion. But many of them bitterly protested the relocation and incarceration as unconstitutional and racially biased. Some would later resist the draft and end up with prison terms.

Whatever the case, the No-no boys were removed from their respective camps and sent to either McNeil Penitentiary or the Tule Lake Segregation Center in California. Those born in the United States were pressured to renounce their U.S. citizenship. And so, with the two questions creating a harsh new fault line, a painful rift ensued within the Japanese American community.

Nearing Twin Falls, Alex takes exit 173 off the freeway. After heading north on Highway 93—he turns right on Highway 25. Even at a rapid clip, the drive has taken nearly two hours—has covered a lot of territory. *How far*—he wonders to himself. *How far did the Japanese have to go to make the country safe? How far did the U.S. Government have to go to make the country safe?* Alex imagines the interminable train ride from the Pacific Coast, window shades drawn—the worn buses hauling prisoners the last few miles to camp. As he takes a left onto Hunt Road, he marvels at the number of green fields surrounding the area today. The North Side Canal of the Snake River surges beside the pavement—just as it once hemmed a part of the barbed wire fence surrounding the evacuees.

...Back in Little Tokyo, Alex visited his father's memorial—a controversial one for the Japanese American community. The memorial was titled, *No-No,* and was commissioned by a group of individuals, all grown children and grandchildren of the No-no boys. During early proposals, the National Japanese American Museum refused to accept it. Subsequently, the group purchased a small plot of land carved out of a parking lot just across the street. For the site, Kazuo Arai created a ten-foot bronze sculpture on a modest stainless steel base. The memorial depicts a strapping young man in the midst of struggle. Arms outstretched—he grapples with the tall, vertical members of a guard tower made of dark bronze and textured glass struts. From his fists, small fissures explode into the main supports. When examined closely, the word *NO* can be seen in block letters made from broken segments of the structure. At the foot of the figure lies more frame-like pieces—more fractured sections of the guard post. Once again, the fragments spell out the word *NO*. As a young child at the time, Kazuo Arai never had to face the loyalty questionnaire. But he gladly agreed to memorialize the courage of the No-no boys—those who protested racial prejudice and the violation of their constitutional rights.

Alex approaches the entrance to the Minidoka National Historic Site. What exactly was he expecting to find? He'd seen old photos taken upon the evacuees' arrival—photos seeming to glare back at him in the oppressive August heat. In them, he found a desolate landscape stretching in every direction— covered with sage brush, roughened by volcanic outcroppings. He saw row upon row of tarpaper barracks whipped by winds and dust—then subsequent pictures where everything had turned to mud and slop with the first rains.

Today, Alex takes in the scope and scale of the environment. The initial feeling is one of *vastness*. The landscape appears essentially flat—nothing tall until the desert meets the distant mountains. Low-lying brush clings to the ground, the occasional tree looking somewhat stunted. Scrubby grasses dominate the terrain—a gold-brown color, a remnant of summer. And above this layer of land, a vast blue sky—as if the ocean had also been transported here and left to hang. Alex wonders if the sky in its blue form made the occupants yearn for the peaceful waters of home. Or maybe it was the gray sky of fall and winter that called them back. And what of the giant white clouds now moored above? No barbed wire fence could keep the imagination from boarding them—setting sail on them. Alex thinks of his father.

...Back in Little Tokyo, Alex prepared to vandalize another of Kazuo Arai's memorials. The problem was—to do so could be misconstrued as an overt political act. Namely— to deface a sculpture dedicated to the No-no boys could be viewed as an attack by those aligned with the "loyal" *Nikkei* honored just across the street. The Japanese American narrative had little use for those who refused to serve their unjust government. Simply put—the official story featured racial discrimination and victimization followed by triumphal redemption through valor and blood.

Alex decided to cross the street. Skirting the museum, he continued down a long walkway, past the Geffen site of the Museum of Contemporary Art. Toward the end, he reached a well-kept plaza featuring a checkerboard motif. There in front of him stood the *Go For Broke Memorial,* honoring the veterans of the 100th Battalion and the 442nd Regimental Combat Team. Behind a large mock-up of the unit's combat patch rose a forty-foot staff bearing an American flag. Backing that—a wide, canted cone of black marble. The feature reminded Alex of the volcanic origins of the Hawaiian islands—birthplace of the 100th Battalion and home to so many *Nisei* soldiers. Just for a moment, he considered tagging both the No-no memorial and the one directly before him. Perhaps that way, his name wouldn't be associated with taking sides.

As he mulled things over, a spry bespectacled man in a docent's shirt approached him. Former private first class, Tokuji Ono, introduced himself with a smile and an extended hand. No more than five feet tall, and in his nineties—the Nisei veteran welcomed Alex to the patriotic site. Over the next half hour, Mr. Ono gave a personal account of some pivotal battles in Europe. He also led his guest to the back of the memorial where all the soldiers' names were engraved. Alex's maternal uncle, Yoshi, was killed while fighting in France. With paper and pencil, he made a rubbing of his uncle's name.

By the time the encounter was over, Alex felt like a complete *ass* for having ever considered defacing the structure. He expressed his deep gratitude to Mr. Ono, his own uncle, and all the others. He thanked his guide— walked off the property. However substantial were stone and metal, nothing could be a more powerful memorial than a person who actually lived the events.

At the entrance to Minidoka, the remains of a guard station and receiving room stand to Alex's right. The red basalt walls overlook the swift current of the North Side Canal below. Across the road, the same volcanic stone forms remnants of a rock garden built by internees.

At the trailhead proper, a memorial by Kazuo Arai dominates the site—obscures a second structure some fifteen feet beyond. Trying to ignore his father's work, Alex spots the white panels of the more distant *Honor Roll* mural. Topped by a proud eagle, it bears the names of camp soldiers who served during World War II. Examining the tableau, when taken together— two symbols of Minidoka form one of the most iconic images of the Japanese American narrative. The theme of *victimization* dominates the front as symbolized by Kaz's sculpture. Ultimate *triumph* stands in back—written large in the names of the veterans. Alex has long been critical of this cobbled *assemblage*. The memorial in front overwhelms the one in back. A matter of scale, the sad story of the relocation still dwarfs the sacrifices of the soldiers. If challenged, Kazuo Arai would dismiss any hint of imbalance. He would likely declare—*I was here,* as if to say—*I know this place. This is my Minidoka.* It was not the suffering involved—certainly not the little triumphs of everyday life that made this memorial so large. It was all about Kaz's ego—that distortion of self that led to other self-aggrandizing distortions in his art. At worst, his vision of himself resulted in the public skewing of the ethnic narrative.

Kaz decreed that three tall figures rise up from the Idaho desert. Claiming inspiration from Rodin—he placed each one on a shallow plinth of Corten steel. Although set at ground level, the plane of the common citizen, he created three grandly oversized figures—the tallest of which loomed thirty feet high. Cast in burnished bronze, the tragic figures represent a husband, wife, and their young son. Dressed in period clothes, each carries a single suitcase. The clothes themselves appear as weighty as the cloaks and the binding rope of *The Burghers of Calais.* The pathos of the hands and faces proves every bit as dramatic. Backing the figures stands a tall, *shoji*-like screen of glass. Across the panels—etchings of mountains and ocean evoke the Pacific Northwest.

When Alex first saw the initial mock-up, he was horrified by its theatricality. He even refused to participate in the dedication some five years ago. In person, his father's memorial, *Displaced*, only enhances the overall sense of injustice for him, because of its perverted style. The memorial looks garish, or *hade*, to borrow a Japanese term—counter to *shibui*, the preferred aesthetic defined by an *understated elegance*. Alex feels offended—incensed. Kazuo Arai has uprooted his people from the clean and subtle design sensibility to which they were linked. He has succeeded in *relocating* his people to a stylistic wasteland as alien and unrecognizable as this desert place.

...Back in Little Tokyo, Alex retraced his steps down the long walkway. Across the street, he passed through a corridor of shops and restaurants to the Miyako Hotel. At two in the morning, he reemerged, feeling disturbed— black hoodie beneath an arm. He approached his father's memorial, but kept moving. He crossed the street and passed the dark red sandstone walls of the museum. Then came the Geffen annex on his right—and finally, the *Go For Broke Memorial*. Performing an about face, he donned his protective garb—inhaled the scent of a sleeve. He returned to the very middle of the walkway—the perfect midway point between the *Nisei* soldiers and the No-no boys.

Alex stood in front of the Geffen—site of the past summer's biggest exhibition on street art. His heart kept time with the severe pain throbbing in both temples. *Certainly, they wouldn't mind, would they?* Even if cameras caught him. For Alex, everything was becoming an issue of style. *How could MOCA object to a Contemporary aesthetic? How could they condemn an example of street art?* The decisive moment arrived once more. Dropping to his haunches, he shook his can of purple paint and in long sweeping letters—wrote his name on a scale as large as a throw-up. *A*, *W*, *R*, *Y*, spreading like a tangle of dark veins—a birthmark—all across the flat concrete face. In a fit of inspiration, he added a sprawling *M-P-B* to the side. As Alex stood up, he stood tall. Then he walked off—no, actually, he trotted off—his aching skull now filled with a pulsing laughter—filled with himself.

Alex takes a stroll all about the historic site. It's the middle of the afternoon, and not a single other person is here. He has all of Minidoka to himself. *Where have all the people gone?* Nine thousand—almost ten thousand people. A ghost town empty of their bodies, their movements, their thoughts and feelings, their conversations. Empty of their work, their play, their births and deaths—their rights of passage. And for a moment, he can almost see his father as a child, running free within the barbed wire fence. And he can almost see his mother, an even younger child, with no knowledge of the boy, the man, she would one day meet and marry. And for the moment, Alex can't help but feel sad.

But today, he can't afford any tears. He can't let his emotions disarm him. And so he walks back down the dusty trail, past open fields, past more sage brush and grass. He walks back to his rental car—opens the trunk. Reaching inside he pulls out a spray can—the one filled with silver paint. Leaving behind his black hoodie, he dispenses with the need for concealment and stealth today. Without another soul around, it occurs to him— there are probably few who would even care.

Marching off to confront his father's memorial, he's still provoked by the sight of it. Taking his time, he studies each of the suitcases held by the evacuees. He doesn't mean to desecrate Minidoka—doesn't mean to dishonor anyone who was incarcerated here. But it feels like a compulsion—something he has to do. What he has planned for today constitutes an attack of style on style. It's *Postmodern,* if you will—the painted obscenity on the body of property, an assault on authority, the introduction of chaos into the constructs of Modernity. One significant difference, though—graffiti writers maintain their esthetic concerns. *In the eyes of the beholder,* he muses—*how beautiful does my tag need to be?* That is—how beautiful does it need to be in order to make up for the crime—to be welcomed somehow by its victims? Alex removes the universal cap on his can—replaces it with a fresh skinny cap from his pocket. Then, in the most graceful script he knows—writes his name on each of the three suitcases.

21

[re: art]
"Commitment to your work takes guts. If you got them, stay with it. Only don't forget, a painter's got to kick the world in the ass, and if he's real he won't even know he's doing it. He's got what it takes, that's all."

[re: creativity]
"An artist knows what he's doing, or should. It's not something you talk about, only feel—deep, deep inside. What I do, I unite parts of a union into a bigger whole. With enough, that created whole turns into being. But I don't talk about it— If I do, I'll lose contact, and with more than just that canvas on the floor. You know, when you lose contact with yourself, living gets to be just jerking off. The creative act has its own life, better had. The unconscious turns it into art, because the unconscious is the source of all art. Only you got to let your unconscious be, same time staying with it. I don't know how to say it right, just that it works. For the rest, let those wise bastards—critics and professors—make a living out of it."

—Jackson Pollock

* * *

Whitney's place, downtown Santa Cruz

Whitney keeps her hands busy—has a lot to do. She's getting ready for the school year, her final year—looking forward to Senior Studio. Today, she organizes her paints and brushes, pencils and sketchbooks—everything she needs to take to campus.

She also thinks a lot about Alex—thinks about him more than she would like. Feeling stronger—perkier. So much closer to who she thought she was—more intact, her body parts all of a single mind. Mostly, she's able to stay in the present—not the past. Sure, she would like to see him again, but he happens to be too busy. Preparing a new course on Contemporary Art—flying cross-country for research. Her chest continues to hurt, but not as much. The wound in her thigh—scabbed over, healing from inside out, or outside in—it doesn't matter.

Grabbing rubber bands, she binds all her brushes together—tries to recall the history behind each one. Some were gifts, but most she bought herself. She also wonders about the strange bond between Alex and her past—why he's been a conduit to so many horrible sensations. And why those flashbacks have mostly stopped—ever since they had sex on the bed over there. Pretty easy, wasn't it? So maybe now, she doesn't need to *fuck* him anymore. But she truly likes him—feels attached in a troubling sort of way. Finds herself worried about the plane rides he's taking all over the map.

* * *

Coffeetopia

A grandmother turns to her daughter—"It seems like it's getting worse. Those kids have no respect anymore."

"Kind of disgusting," comes the reply. "Not like when I was up there."

A blondish guy turns to his friend—"Seriously? You've got to be kidding. What the—? I can't wait to see!"

"Check it out," the young woman replies, handing him her phone. "They found it over the weekend."

Whitney feels a definite buzz in the room. Stopping on her way to campus, she's waiting for her friend Julie. Finding the paper on the communal table, she scans the front page. The lead story concerns a shooting in Live Oak. Just below—

"Graffiti Attack: Vandal Strikes Japanese American Memorial on UCSC Campus"

Whitney reads—

At Porter College, a spray-painting vandal attacked a bronze and glass memorial by the renowned sculptor, Kazuo Arai. The vandal used purple and silver paint to repeatedly 'tag' the work titled "Forever Manzanar." A tribute to Japanese Americans interned in the Manzanar concentration camp during WW II, the sculpture has been a campus landmark for the past eighteen years. "It's very sad," remarked Provost Ann Leland Chandler. "Whoever did this not only defaced a work of art but struck at the very core of our community. The travesty of the Japanese American incarceration must not be forgotten." The provost said that the offensive graffiti would be removed as quickly as possible pending police investigation.

It is believed that the vandalism took place in the early hours of Sunday night and Monday morning, the first official day of classes. It was discovered by a maintenance worker who immediately reported it to authorities. Police at the scene are considering the possibility of a hate crime. According to one officer, the actual 'tag' has not been released in order to minimize its impact. "The letters form a kind of name," he said, "and there are clues for sure, in figuring out this person's identity."

An accompanying photo shows the memorial as it was before the event.

As Whitney looks up, a lively brunette enters the café. It's Julie—

"Hey," asks Whitney, "have you seen the news?"

"No, I haven't. But it must be crazy, cuz you're all worked up." Skimming the article on the front page—"So—so what? I mean it's really too bad—but that kind of stuff happens, like—all the time."

"Yeah, I know. But let's get to campus as soon as possible."

"Hang on a sec."

After Julie gets her coffee, it's a quick drive up to school. By the time they arrive at Porter College, a large crowd has gathered around the defaced memorial. Lots of energized students—a few teachers and administrators, police officers examining the site.

"Wow, that's awesome!" says a guy with a scraggly goatee. "Is that the only thing that got hit last night?"

"Oh yeah," says another young man, "that graf looks totally sick!"

"Such a travesty!" remarks a female student. "Some guy goes off like that. You *know* it's a guy!"

A school official overlooks the scene. "What a way to get the year started. Oh my—here come the media, cameras and all."

Whitney approaches the chaotic scene—a strange cross between a techno concert and a student demonstration. "Oh-my-God," she mumbles to herself. "Oh-My-God!" she exclaims to Julie.

Standing before them, the three tragic figures of Kazuo Arai—the anguished grandfather, his grown daughter shielding her baby—both adults reaching skyward with their arms. From top to bottom, she finds a riot of four-letter tags in a multitude of styles—some she recognizes. Harsh and angular to loopy and lyrical. Purple or silver—purple *and* silver. It's like colorful patchwork on the dark bronze and the trailing veil of blown glass. The effect shocks her—takes her aback. But then comes a surprising turn. In a bizarre way, the sculpture looks beautiful—looks revived. The figures appear refreshed—newly animated.

"Oh, Alex…."

"What kind of a douche bag?" says Julie. "I mean the guy's good—but, he could've done this on a wall somewhere. Either way, it's a crime."

"Oh come on," says Whitney, mesmerized. "It's really artistic. The writer went totally psycho on that thing."

"It's vandalism—that's what it is. You can be really talented—do things like that. But you cross the line when you do it on someone's property without permission."

"Yeah," agrees Whitney, still admiring the effect. "That thing about art and vandalism, it's not just one or the other. Something like this—it's definitely both."

The camera crew sets up, just on the periphery of the milling throng. With a mic in one hand, the Latina reporter settles her hair with the other. She moves to a nearby spot for better light.

From a balcony of the adjacent faculty building, Professor Alexander Arai observes *everything*. Standing tall, he presides over the work of Contemporary Art evolving before him. He even casts Whitney and her friend as part of the necessary audience. But when he catches her peering in his direction, he steps behind a convenient corner. A few seconds later, he reemerges. Commanding a beautiful autumn day, Alex enjoys being awash in brilliant sunlight—soaks in the amusing spectacle unfolding below.

* * *

The house on Escalona Drive

It's hard for Alex not to feel smug about recent events. Mission accomplished. He's managed to tag nearly all of his father's memorials. And now, he enjoys the fruits of his final endeavor. The *bombing* of Kaz's first major commission—the one coinciding with Alex's obtaining tenure. Of course, *Forever Manzanar* will far outlast him—will continue to stand long after he's retired and gone.

Still, he marvels at his ability to carry out the attacks. And how convenient it was—the inadvertent collusion of others. No doubt, city and park workers across the country have long since removed all evidence of his string of crimes. He can't help the smile erupting across his face. He's gotten away with it— the perfect transgression. He's made a statement against his father's tyranny—made an artistic assault on his father's style. Musing over the *spree* in the term "crime spree," he savors the frightfully illicit *fun* that resulted. Now he can afford to stand back, watching as events continue to play out. Alex can hardly wait to hear his father's reaction.

* * *

All Gone Awry

At the home of Kazuo Arai, the camera crew sets up again. One hand on an earpiece, the reporter awaits her cue.

Reporter— "As you know, yesterday—an act of vandalism occurred on the UCSC campus. Many were outraged when a memorial to Japanese Americans unjustly incarcerated during World War II—was tagged with graffiti. Here with me now is Kazuo Arai, the celebrated creator of that memorial. Mr. Arai, tell me—how did it make you feel when your memorial was attacked?"

K.A.— "Well...uh—I guess I wasn't too happy when I got the news. That was my first big commission, you know—"

Reporter— "Your memorial was the only one on campus involved. Some people suspect the tagging represents a hate crime. Your thoughts?"

K.A.— "Oh, I don't give it much thought, really. But I suppose—the way it was done and all. The police said the so-called tag was like a *perversion* of my name, I think they said. It's hard not to take that kind of thing personally."

Reporter— "An ongoing investigation is taking place. Do you have any ideas or clues about who's responsible for this act?"

K.A.— "No, not really."

Reporter— "And what about the Japanese American community? How do you think they'll respond?"

K. A.— "Well, of course, as you put it—probably a lot of people are going to get real upset. That memorial of mine represents a lot of suffering to those whose civil rights were violated. That's the end result—that's our legacy, you know? Goes back generations."

Reporter— "Lastly, Mr. Arai—what would you say if you could, to the vandal—the perpetrator out there?"

K. A.— "Oh, I'd, say—show your face—turn yourself in. At the very least—stop doing things like that. I mean you're defacing a work of art, for crying out loud."

Reporter— "Okay—thank you Mr. Arai. Well, there you have it. A sad situation indeed. A possible racially-motivated hate crime in the beautiful redwood hills of Santa Cruz. Reporting live from San Jose, this is Courtney Zamora—Channel 8 News."

* * *

Mario's place, Soquel

Since he got home from work last night, he hasn't been able to put the newspaper down. Oh, he set it on a sink, a table, a chair—placed it on his bed. Moving from one spot to the next, he kept the flimsy pages close beside him. Sometimes, he just had to read the front page story again. Agitation, suspicion—Later, while trying to sleep, he heard the coyotes yelping through the misty air outside—a solitary owl.

Early this morning, Mario drives to the UCSC campus. At Porter College, he enters the crowd. Amidst the chatter, the occasional laughter—his suspicions are confirmed. Frozen in place, he gawks at the sheer brilliance of *AWRY*, spread out like an angry rash all over Kazuo Arai's memorial.

Mario jogs to McHenry Library. Opening his laptop, he Googles the sculptor's name, and on a hunch—makes a list of all his significant public works. The reach of the projects impresses him. The sites include New York City, Washington, D.C., Los Angeles, and a former internment camp in Idaho. Mario wonders if any of the other memorials could have been hit. Checking the major newspapers online, he finds no mention of graffiti vandalism anywhere. Clicking on an Idaho map, he locates the Minidoka National Historic Site—nearest city, Twin Falls. Scanning the website of the *Twin Falls Eagle-News*—he discovers—"Minidoka Memorial Defaced." A front page story from yesterday's edition—right side, bottom—

> It was a disturbing sight that greeted Mr. and Mrs. James Sato and family yesterday at the Minidoka National Historic Site. Seattle natives, the couple and their three children were on a pilgrimage to honor relatives incarcerated at the former WWII concentration camp. Upon approaching the impressive

memorial by sculptor, Kazuo Arai, they found its pristine surface marred by graffiti. "It was quite a shock," noted Mr. Sato, a civil engineer. "You'd think America had gotten past all that. It goes to show that minority people have to keep their guard up. No matter what we do as citizens, I guess some people will never see us as part of this country. What do we tell our children?"

Park rangers are taking the incident seriously. Cooperating with the local sheriff and other law enforcement, they hope to track down the perpetrator. Still, the task appears daunting. No clues were left at the scene besides the vandal's so-called 'tag.' The silver, spray-painted letters appear to spell out the word, 'Awry,' a possible cruel corruption of the sculptor's name. If anyone has seen any suspicious individuals or activities this past week, they are encouraged to contact the park ranger's office at...

Immediately, Mario places a call to the number provided—identifies himself to the staff person as a journalist from Santa Cruz, California. Affecting a professional tone, he asks for the contact information for Mr. James Sato. It doesn't take long before he makes a live connection.

"Very upsetting," says Mr. Sato—"very upsetting to us all. At first, I felt too ashamed to tell anyone else, but...."

Mario gathers information about the family—their community status and social ties. Mr. Sato plans to contact the Congress of Japanese Americans—the largest and oldest Asian American civil rights organization in the country.

Mr. Sato sounds clearly upset—"I heard how bad it was for our people when the war broke out—the way they were treated. After all this time, in some people's eyes—I guess we're still just a bunch of *dirty Japs.*"

Taking note, Mario truly feels for the man—identifies with the disillusionment and bitterness expressed. Of course, he also asks Mr. Sato if he's taken any photos of the vandalized memorial.

"Sure—sure. I'll email them over to you right now. Tell me your name again—"

"Yes, my name is Mario—Mario Patino. Here's my email address. Thank you so much for your time. I'll keep in touch."

Mario can hardly contain his excitement. In a matter of minutes, he sits—*stands*—as a flurry of attachments arrives. Before his eyes—three silver tags written on their respective suitcases. *A little different,* he thinks to himself. Not like the bold tags up on campus. *Kind of a finer line,* he notes. *Almost elegant.* Still—as applied to the suitcases of the displaced and weary, what a travesty—almost *comical,* really. Like some colorful travel patches documenting a cross-country lark. But Mario has come upon valuable evidence—has managed to enhance his case against Professor Arai. He places a call to the *Courier* office, but not the police. He wants to speak to the chief editor—wants to schedule a meeting ASAP. He knows he has the makings of a big scoop, even as he admits more research is still required. But the blockbuster story is his, he believes—and there's no way he plans to let go.

The house on Escalona Drive

"You what? Don't tell me Alex, you did what? Here—let me see that." The paper flies from him to her. "What were you thinking, Alex? What were you thinking!"

Lisa's a quick reader, a quicker study—but somehow she's managed to miss all this. "Will they be able to find out? Will they be able to know it's you?"

Handing her another issue of the paper—"Here, get a load of this—"

"Well, it says there's a demonstration planned. Representatives of the C.J.A. and the J.A. Veterans Group. For godsakes—and then students from Campus 10—representatives from the various ethnic student alliances."

"Okay now—look Leese, it's all going to blow over. Don't worry— They'll have their big media event, whatever. Then it'll all disappear."

"What're you saying? Are you completely nuts?" Like a pinball, Lisa bounces from sofa to love seat to chair. "What if they figure it out? You know you're going to get crucified—lose your position at school!"

Standing his ground—"But they'll never find out—I completely covered my tracks. They'll never trace me back to all the stuff I've been doing."

"And what exactly do you mean by that? Don't tell me you've done more than just tag your father's memorial."

"Just make that plural. The operative word is *memorials* with an *s.*"

"But that means the East Coast—it means L.A. It means up in Idaho, doesn't it?"

"All of the above," says Alex. At the moment, he teeters between a pleasurable rush and the torment distorting Lisa's face.

"So that's why you've been traveling so much."

"Well, sure—"

"Why didn't you tell me about your plans beforehand?"

"I thought about it, but I didn't think you'd understand. To tell you the truth—I thought you'd be really against it."

"That's just an excuse!" Returning to the love seat—"You know you've got a position, an important one at the university. You're a tenured professor for heaven's sake. This would be a huge embarrassment to the school—to everyone associated with it. Faculty, administration—students, even."

"But only if they find out it's me."

"And how about your family—did you think about them? You'll cause them enormous shame. And you'll be the laughing stock of your whole community. Isn't that the worst thing that can happen to a Japanese—a Japanese American?"

"So it is. I know you're worried for me, but you're getting way too upset."

"Well it's a matter of judgment—a *lack* of judgment, actually. You realize you're putting me in a bad place too—putting me at risk as well."

"Look—I appreciate being partners in the big things we do. We love each other, but we live in different worlds. I'm all about art—you're about high tech and marketing. We've got a solid thing here, but our lives run on parallel tracks."

"But people will find out—they always do. All my colleagues. Especially in this age—everyone's connected to everyone else. I'm sure this is all over social media."

"Well, it is."

"And people will judge. *How did you let that happen, Lisa?* It's like being a terrible, neglectful parent. A bad mother."

"Oh, come on—"

"No, I'm serious. I had no idea this was going on—right under my nose."

"Again, Leese—it's not like you're around all the time."

"I know," she says, wrapping herself with her arms. "I guess I just can't leave you alone. Can't trust you. Can't leave you alone without supervision."

"Oh stop being so funny—"

"But I'm not kidding—that's how I feel. How can you keep such a huge secret from me?"

"Well, I guess I should have told you, then. Of course you're right—I'm sure you are. I'm sorry for not including you."

"I bet you are."

"I mean, I see your point. But I've been pretty good at pulling things off—stuff that takes some creativity."

"So far so good," she smirks. "But sometimes you just get lucky." Looking sad for the moment, wistful, maybe. "I just don't know. People can't get away with things like that—hiding the truth forever."

Absorbing the absurdity of it all, she can't quite pull off a smile. With several prolonged breaths, she tries to clear herself. "I've said it before, you always had a way of surprising me—with your projects, that is. It's just that—there's got to be some limits on what you can do." Scooting over as Alex joins her on the love seat—"I suppose your father's going to get a lot of airtime over this."

"Yes, he is." Carefully now—Alex settles atop the small gap between the two leather cushions. He places himself so the side of his body just touches Lisa. Upper arm to upper arm—hip gently against hip. Turning to his partner—"My dad's been invited to speak at this weekend's demonstration. And guess what? So have I—"

✳ ✳ ✳

Senior Studio, UCSC

So, what's going to happen now? Especially in the middle of it all—in the middle of *everything*. Not to mention all the stuff that's already happened. So messy with the overflow of feelings.

And it hasn't been easy getting ahold of Alex. Cell phone calls, texts—emails. Finally connected, there's not a whole lot he can safely say with his electronic voice and touch. Something uncertain looms overhead, and today—storm clouds drench the hills as he approaches the studio.

Whitney adjusts her easel. A fresh canvas clears a chair—lands in the center of her vision. Pondering its hidden images, she stands awhile—her head and hips tilted. A box of light—she inhabits a big box of light. And now, with the clank of a door, more light enters near a corner of the room.

Whitney speaks first. "I'm SO glad to see you Alex."

"And I'm happy to see you, too."

"I got all worried when you hinted at your big *adventure*. Are you okay?"

"Oh, I'm fine. In fact, I'm *more* than fine."

"It's been so long—I know you've been dealing with stuff."

"An understatement," he smiles.

"I thought you'd be all stressed—but you look happy."

"It's because I'm here today. You know—I've missed you."

Carefully, now—"I missed you, too."

Grabbing a stool, he takes a seat beside her new canvas.

"So tell me about it," she insists. "Tell me everything—"

Happily complying, he enthralls her with stories of his cross-country trips—his swift campaign against a terrible foe, an enemy both far-flung and close to home.

"So, how did you feel?" she asks. "How did you feel when you did all that?"

"I felt terrific—way beyond anything I'd felt before. It's like I had a monitor in my head. And I wanted it to tell me what was going on inside. And it spelled out everything from *fearful* and *cocky* to *rage* and *joy*. And then the words got all jumbled up—blew up in my face. I can't quite describe it."

"But I know what you mean. It's like when you asked me about my art—how I take an image and go *crazy* on it—"

"And, one of the best parts of it all was feeling close to you—"

Words, revelations—laughter between them. With such an easy back and forth, no one needs to touch just yet. And all the while, the studio takes on grander dimensions of its own. It's volume seems to grow beyond the roof and into the sky.

Somewhere above the storm, the sky turns blue. And it may be the same blue that a child uses when she hems the top of the page with color. She signifies how something as big as the sky looks unreachable.

For Whitney and Alex, there's nothing but air and light right now—nothing but space. Nothing but soaring ideas. Nothing but talk about the next canvas, the next project—the ones that can now take shape together.

* * *

Mario's place, Soquel
Three phone calls

1. From the features editor of the *Santa Cruz Courier:*
"Look, Mario—this has turned into a hot story. People up and down the coast are tracking it. People from as far north as Seattle—south to L.A. Wherever there's a lot of Asian Americans around. This is a story for a staff writer, not an intern."

"But you've liked what I've written before—"

"Yes, you're outstanding. But making assignments—you know how it goes. We've got a structure here—protocol. If you'd like, you can help with research—work closely with the news desk. Sounds like you might have some good leads."

"Okay, I'll do whatever. But I promise—I'm going to get to the bottom of this."

Hanging up, Mario thumps the wall with the side of his fist—thumps it again. He'll have to keep on working his sources—collect his own facts. And while he's at it, he might as well write his own treatment of the story.

2. From Mr. Joey Militich:
"Say Joey—thanks for returning my call. I guess you heard about the big graffiti case up on the hill."

"Oh yeah, right— Sounds like somebody's got a big beef with that statue up there. What's the problem, man—somebody don't like the style? Heard it got bombed big time the other day."

"So tell me Joey—did you hear anything about the specific tag?"

"Nah, but I think the police—they're actin' all crazed up there. Withholdin' the cat's name. He ain't gonna get no fame—the police bein' petty like that."

"Well, I guess that's the point. But you *know* they're trying to track down the guy who did it."

"I suppose."

"So, what if I told you I know who it is?"

"Is that a fact?"

"That's right. And, what if I told you—*you* know who the guy is too—"

"Ah, you're shittin' me man."

"No, really, Joey."

"Well, then...."

"The guy getting up wrote the name AWRY all over the memorial."

"Oh, fuck—you gotta be kiddin'. No way would a guy like Alex do somethin' like that. Didn't I hear that statue was made by his old man?"

"That's right. And I was wondering if you might know why the professor would do a thing like that to his father."

"I got no idea. Professor A-wry—he's got too much to lose to be taggin' his own school, you know what I'm sayin'?"

"Did he ever say anything to you—tell you he was going to do something like this?"

"No, man—never."

"Well, there's got to be a reason somewhere."

"I got no clue about that. 'Speculatin' is what I call it. So what do you plan to do with all your suspicions and what not? You ain't gonna turn him in, are you?"

"I haven't decided."

"Well—he's a good man. I wished you and him could have got together—talked it over somehow."

"I know there's a story behind all this, and I'm going to get it. Give me a call, Joey—if you think of something."

"Sure thing. I'll be back and forth between here and the City. Might have to borrow me a phone, though—I'm runnin' out of minutes. But I'm gonna check out that statue first—gotta see if it's for real, if you know what I mean."

3. To Professor Alexander Arai:

"Thank you for taking the time, Professor. I've been covering the story about the desecration of your father's memorial. I've got a few questions I'd like to ask. First off—please tell me who you think could have committed such a crime."

"Well—by definition, it's some kind of vandal, a criminal—someone outside the law."

"Maybe you can share some additional insights—"

"The guy who did this—and he's most certainly a young male—strikes out from a position of disempowerment. He's definitely an outsider—someone who can't make his statement through the usual channels."

"And what kind of statement is he making?"

"It's clearly an anarchist statement. In the broadest terms, he's taking on the so-called *Establishment*, or the *System*. The crime he commits is an attack on property. Vandalizing property goes to the heart of the System—whereby the ownership of property equates to power."

"So, how does that broader view apply to what just happened at the university?"

"Let me answer that question in a stepwise manner. The Art World—here in the West—forms an integral part of the Establishment. It's the repository of value for a certain type of art—*fine art* that embodies tremendous financial worth. On one level, the Art World functions as a market-driven business—based on the commoditization of art works. Graffiti originates from outside this structure. It can't be bought or sold. It can't enhance the investment portfolios of the power elite."

"But Professor Arai, the art work in question doesn't look like it was chosen at random. Specifically, it was your father's memorial—one that honors the sacrifices of Japanese Americans interned during World War II."

"Of course, that's true. And so, now—getting to specifics. This graffiti writer is making a highly personal statement in his attack. The irony, of course, is that the name he uses is a pseudonym—so he's still in hiding. He apparently has some old vendetta—deep resentments over the Japanese American people. He's attacking their narrative, their identity—how they want to be seen and remembered. Maybe he's lost a family member in the Pacific war. Maybe someone killed during the attack on Pearl Harbor."

"Professor Arai—that was a long time ago. You already said the vandal was probably somebody young."

"That's certainly true—but the legacy of war can impact even distant generations."

"Well, then—could the tagging have been a more personal assault in terms of the target? That is—could it have been specifically aimed at your father?"

"I rather doubt that. He doesn't have any enemies I'm aware of."

"Maybe issues with other artists, gallery owners, dealers—critics, even?"

"That would be rather funny, actually. Critics don't need to vandalize art works—they use their electronic *pens*. And as for the others—they have the power to make or break an artist if that's what they want. Beyond that, can you imagine one of them wielding a spray can?"

"Well, the reason I ask about a motive involving your father is because of recent findings. So far, we know that the same writer also vandalized your father's memorial in Minidoka, Idaho. Efforts are being made to check the status of other works around the country."

"Oh—is that so? Well, I don't know who would want to do that to my father. Knowing about other targets—it's still consistent with an ethnically-based attack."

"I realize this is a strange question, but I've got to ask. Excuse me, but—how do you and your father get along? I hope I'm not being out of line—"

"Not at all. What I mean, is—if you're aware of my papers and presentations, you'll know I've been his chief proponent. Fact is, my father depends on my critiques to solidify his position in the arts."

"I see."

"Well, then—it's very clear how I fit in that Establishment I just described. I'm an integral part of the Western Art World. I suppose you could say that the vandal who desecrated my father's memorial—also attacked me."

"I guess so—that's an interesting point. And how are you personally feeling about all this?"

All Gone Awry

"Oh, I'm upset—truly upset for the Japanese American community. And as for my father, I'm more than a little worried for him, you know—his health and all. He's getting older, and I'm sure this has all been very stressful for him."

"Of course, I'm very sorry. Still, there's something about all this I don't understand. I'm just not sure. Maybe something else will turn up as the investigation proceeds."

"Well, yes—we'll just have to see about that."

"All right, Professor, whatever happens—thank you for your time today. If it's okay with you, I'd like to stay in touch."

"No problem, Mr. Verlatti. It was a pleasure."

* * *

The house on Escalona Drive

In the third floor nook, Alex sets his laptop off to the side. He's decided to go low tech today with an old-fashioned binder made of recycled fibers. Easily stashed, he can keep his thoughts safe from prying eyes. Today, he officially acknowledges the organic nature of his graffiti tags. The phenomenon excites him—the fact that his artwork grows larger than he had anticipated.

But as part of art, he wonders, is it acceptable to promote a fiction/deception/lie? To promote untruths feels terribly inauthentic—but then again, can authenticity be achieved through a lie? What kind of artist is Alex if his message is based on misinformation? Like the use of a pseudonym, his answers to the journalist, his complete disavowal regarding his own art, his own motivation. *So, big deal,* he thinks. *I perpetuate a ruse, a trick, a joke on all the powers that be.* Following a long pause, Alex records the definitive aspects of what he now refers to as—

Action Live:

I.   Definition: Art. By virtue of Marcel Duchamp, anything I declare as art is such.
II. Time frame: Brief, ongoing, *ad infinitum.*
III. Intent: To promote a hoax. To let a personal attack on my father be interpreted as an ethnic hate crime. To allow it to

inject anarchy within the Japanese American community and in its relationship with the dominant culture. Why? Both these entities serve to define who I am in ethnic terms, leading to a constriction of who I am and what I can be. Ethnicity, when used as a primary source of identity and possibility, is limiting.

IV. Process:
   A. To apply graffiti tags to all of Kazuo Arai's memorials. [done]
   B. To await and monitor outcome. Some tags will "die" quickly at the hands of private and city service workers. Others will survive through a combination of <u>fitness</u> and <u>chance</u>.
   C. As an organism, each surviving tag replicates through photos and media references, grows through its influence on viewers and any others who are interested.
   D. To note the <u>meaning</u> found by individuals in each tag, particularly in regard to ethnicity.

V. Principles at work:
   A. <u>The art instinct</u> as discussed by Professor Denis Dutton.
   B. <u>The meaningfulness instinct</u> as discussed by me.
   C. <u>Darwinian principles</u> in which the two instincts above confer both selective and sexual advantage.

VI. Notes on the artist:
   A. Modernist beliefs: [Modernism seen here as a general cultural trend, within which Modern Art is created]
      1. Belief in <u>Meaning</u> based on the autonomous individual.
      2. Belief in reason and science as exemplified by "V" above.
      3. Belief in pragmatic living based on a practical "know-ability," unlike living with the paralysis of Postmodern thought.
      4. Belief in the value of <u>novelty</u>.
   B. Postmodern beliefs: [Postmodernism as a general cultural trend, within which Postmodern Art is created]
      1. Belief in the <u>elusiveness</u> of Meaning, but not in an absolute Postmodern sense.

2. Appreciation of <u>ambiguity</u>, <u>ambivalence</u>, <u>irony</u>, <u>playfulness</u>, <u>sarcasm</u>, <u>humor</u>, <u>nihilistic tendencies.</u>
3. <u>Skepticism</u> toward the grand narrative of Western culture with its associated Euro-centric, male, elitist orientation.
4. The primacy of <u>concept</u> in art.

Setting down his pen, Alex didn't intend it to be this way. Tagging his father's memorials was supposed to be just that—a personal statement against his father. But the surprising aftermath forces him to consider the broader implications and consequences. Up to this point, he was only vaguely aware of a certain resentment toward his ethnic community. Those well-intentioned, brave people who—in righting a wrong and vigilantly protecting their good name—still served to promote a restrictive identity. It galled him to think that the defining moment for his "people," and thus for himself—took place some seventy years ago. That the internee and the Nisei Vet— the narrative of victim and hero—ironically served to confine him. In the meantime, Japanese Americans had transcended World War II to become teachers, engineers, doctors, lawyers, judges, politicians, generals, even. He knew his own life was bigger as well—his professional accomplishments went far beyond the events of the war.

Of course, he feels like a complete ingrate thinking like this. Without that segment of "the greatest generation," he would never have been able to accomplish what he had. But Alex took steps beyond the war—built a name for himself right in the midst of the majority culture and its precious Art World. Now, another forged name—a *forged* name—the tag *AWRY* takes on a life of its own. *Action Live* will be whatever it is—will persist, then die—whatever happens. Really—in the world's great scheme of things, no big deal. Closing his notebook, he inserts a copy of his personal statement deep in the gap between two massive tomes on art history.

23

Porter College

*H*igh on a hill above the city, UCSC opened its doors in 1965. Originally comprised of six colleges, it was purposely scattered about the redwoods. Without a central plaza, there was no large site for student gatherings—so concerned were regents that they not spawn another Berkeley, that problem child an hour-and-a-half north of here.

Today, about a couple dozen students surround Kazuo Arai's memorial. Not at all grim, angry or anxious. No *down with The Man* vibe today. The noon demonstration feels tame compared to what Alex recalls of the '60s and early '70s. At any given moment, several participants are lost to electronic devices. Consulting his watch, he turns to the crowd.

"It's time to march," he announces. Placards rise into the September skies. Hand-painted signs proclaim *Stop The Racist Graf! Don't Forget the Japanese Americans! Say Yes to Ethnic Studies!*

Alex's job is to lead a march of solidarity from Porter College to College 10—site of the official rally. Volunteering for the task, he hopes to engage more fully in his creation, *Action Live*. He directs his spirited band to the fine arts section of campus—then up a long rise past the sciences. Meandering more than marching, group members make friendly call-outs to cyclists and the occasional motorist. About twenty minutes later, they arrive at the College 10 Multi-Purpose Room—a boxy red building evocative of a large barn.

Cheers and applause greet the students as they flood the room. Joining some fifty of their cohorts, they disperse among rows of dining hall chairs. At the front, administrators and faculty mingle with the honored guests. A few media folk mill about—a camera set up in one of the central aisles. Alex locates his assigned seat, two chairs down from his father. He savors the effects of the spirited trek—heart pumping to complement a light sheen of sweat. Relaxing—he feels like some kind of puppet master awaiting the next *act* in his own surreptitious show.

The emcee, an angular Asian student, approaches Alex. She informs him of a change of program. Instead of having him address the history of graffiti, she simply wants him to introduce his father—citing his importance to the community. Although disappointed, Alex reminds himself that *chance* and the *unexpected* are both parts of his artistic process. *Let the work organically unfold,* he tells himself.

With its theme of "social justice and community," College 10 proves the perfect host for the program. Sponsored by the Asian American/Pacific Islander resource center, the rally is titled, "Buff Out Racism!" The emcee begins by introducing the Vice Chancellor of the university. She, in turn, welcomes guests and provides a heartfelt apology for the defacement of the Japanese American memorial.

The Vice Chancellor says—"I feel a terrible sense of shock and sadness over what appears to be racist graffiti desecrating our campus. Such hateful vandalism will not be tolerated, and we shall go beyond simple letters of condemnation from administration and faculty. I am open to all suggestions for addressing this problem. For starters, I am calling for a university-wide town hall meeting to cover the topic of racism on the UCSC campus."

Next up—an Asian American politico from San Jose says—"We must never forget the injustices done to minorities in the past. We must learn from the travesty of the Japanese American internment. Especially in post 9/11 times, we must learn from the example of American concentration camps in order to prevent such constitutional violations from ever happening again."

A representative from the Congress of Japanese Americans says—"Through our own investigation—we know of other attacks on Japanese American memorials by Kazuo Arai. One in Minidoka, Idaho. Another in New York City, where a camera found what looked like a white man in a black hoodie engaging in suspicious behavior. The C.J.A. has notified the federal government—the Department of Justice. Upon receiving further evidence, this case may be referred to its own hate crime unit. The C.J.A. Anti-Hate Program empowers victims of defamation and related offences, while promoting greater understanding about the value of tolerance and diversity."

A representative of the Student Union Assembly says— "Forget about catching the vandal, whoever he is. What we need to do is to educate people. A one-time event or rally won't get the job done. We need to formulate a strong ethnic studies program here on campus. I believe I speak for all of the students here at the rally."

Professor Alexander Arai says—"It's my pleasure to introduce the sculptor, Kazuo Arai, creator of the memorial, *Forever Manzanar*. Mr. Arai is a prominent voice within the Japanese American community because of his iconic works. With his unique style, Mr. Arai confronts the World War II incarceration of over 110,000 persons of Japanese descent, most of whom were United States citizens. His work has been crucial in perpetuating his people's narrative."

Kazuo Arai says—"It's a big honor for me to be here today. As you might know, *Forever Manzanar* was my first big break— my first major commission for a memorial. Some of you might ask why I was chosen—why should I be the one commemorating those terrible times? Well, you see—I was there—there from the start. As a young child from Seattle, I was one of those poor unfortunates—uprooted with my family and sent to the concentration camp in Minidoka, Idaho. My father was being detained by the FBI. My mother and sister carried whatever clothes they could in the one suitcase they were allowed each. I guess you could say I was an artist even back then. Instead of clothes, I brought my meager art supplies with me to camp.

And that's how we referred to it over the years—*Camp.*"

Alex feels embarrassed—*mortified*, actually, as his father rambles on about his experiences at Minidoka. Hands tensing, he would like to give his father the gaff. But he also perceives how quiet the room has become—recognizes that special silence that comes with the rapt attention of a crowd. And no, not just any crowd—but a veritable classroom of students.

Kazuo Arai says—"Well, you see, a couple young boys—they must have been five or six. They drowned while trying to swim in the Snake River canal. That's when authorities had a small lagoon built—a swimming hole for us kids." And—"The food was horrible. To this day, I can't stand the sight of French toast. They'd have this big wash tub full of it—would just sling it at you. All cold with that Caro syrup and the white Oleo margarine. Tasted so bad, I've never been able to eat French toast since." And—"The wind was something terrible, you know? I got an extra blanket, but it was mostly my mother who kept me warm." And—"What about the vandal who's doing all this—attacking all of my memorials? For cryin' out loud—you know he's a coward! Why doesn't he come forward—show his face?" And—

Alex can barely contain himself. He watches his father holding court—regaling the audience with stories—working himself into a lather with scathing tirades against the perpetrator.

Students pipe up to ask questions. Clearly, Kazuo Arai enjoys the limelight, savors the attention—the various solicitous and inflating comments cast in his direction. From his front row seat, Alex feels totally helpless—his artistic creation veering out of control. He tries to reassure himself—tries to appreciate the effect of the *unexpected*—of *chaos* rearing its head in his father's verbose, though surprisingly colorful accounts and exhortations. How strange, he thinks. He's never known his father to be such a raconteur, such a firebrand.

Once more, Kazuo Arai upstages him—just as he had when *Forever Manzanar* was dedicated eighteen years ago. Once again, here on campus—Alex's territory, his turf. And somewhere in the midst of an agonizing, internal soliloquy—he thinks he hears his name being called. It's his father's voice— Something about, "my son, the professor over there— he should know—" And Alex really hasn't heard the question directed at him—doesn't know who did the asking. And as he feels everyone's eyes trained on his back, he finds himself at a complete loss. Alex doesn't know what to say.

* * *

Phone call from Joey to Alex—

"Yeah, yeah—this is Joey. I know man, my phone went out— ran out of minutes. This here's my girlfriend's phone. Yeah, I know—it's pretty shitty. What did you say?"

"Hey, man—like the reason I'm callin' you is, that guy I told you about—he's thinkin' you tagged your father's statue."

"So, this guy—oh fuck it. Yeah, this guy—funny thing, I was gonna introduce him to you— remember?"

"What's that? You sayin' you need some help? Well sure— I'll be back in town pretty soon. Got me some big plans, bro. Still gotta get up some more—got one last place in mind. Yeah, I know—before I can get some rest."

"So, what was you askin'? Yeah, I know—there's some crazy-ass things you can do, if you don't wanna get buffed and all. Yeah—like usin' a sharp tool, like a jeweler's tool or somethin'. Yeah you can etch glass and plastic—no way it comes off. But that's like heavy duty damage, bro. 'Specially that—a cat could be put away for a long time."

"Hey look, the signal keeps breakin' up. I mean—so what're you sayin' to me? You wanna know how to do it on metal? So what're you exactly talkin' about? Did you really tag your old man's statue—up on the hill? So tell me—why did you do that, man?"

"Okay, shit—I'm breakin' up again. Like I'm talkin' straight into a wall or somethin'. Like my head's buzzin'—know what I'm sayin'? Yeah, let me give you the number, but first—oh fuck it."

"Look—the guy's name is Mario and he knows you were the cat who did it, all right. Do you hear what I'm sayin? Alex— Professor—Professor A-wry...."

240

All Gone Awry

***

Whitney's place

A lovely evening, cool and clear
  and Alex walks down the stairs.

            But just before that
        he turned and closed the door
            gently, quietly.

            And just before that
        he donned his clothes, piece by piece
            followed closely by his shoes.

        And just before that, he eased out of bed
      fully naked, yet sheathed in her damp residue
    and his own. Bearing the sheerest of bedclothes
      the kind two people share if close enough
        caught in that minimal space between lovers.

    And just before that, he rested on his side—facing
            her sleeping self.
      He took his hand and caressed her back—
          the various provocative curves.
  And he started with the nape of her neck—her ruddy hair
            tussled about, lying
      in some formation that spoke to recent abandon.
          And he let his fingers run the length
  of her back—the tips of his fingers feathering her spine
    past the flare of ribs to the small of her back—just
above her dark tattoos. Then up and over the rise of her rump
right to the place where the sheet now brought him to a stop.

Andrew Kumasaka

And before all that, there were cries and entanglements. And
some cries were sharper than others.
And that was because of this docking arrangement—this
locked position and the urgent manner with which they
forced themselves together, a rhythmic contact—
fleeting separations, so despite
the wildness of contact, they would not come
undone. And they somehow found the perfect pitch
and angle, and at the perfect time
they told each other exactly that.

And just before that—rising above the sheet, he started
to enter her.
He, on top—wondering if it was still
all right with her. Was it *all right*, he wanted to know.
And she answered him firmly with open arms, skewed legs.
And her hands flared—and her fingers
splayed to bring him closer.

And before all that, she sprawled back—
pushed the sheet from below her neck
to below her shoulders, to below her chest.
She pushed the sheet past the dip of her belly,
past her hips, until it came to rest on her thighs.

And just before that, they turned to each other—
still hidden by the sheet.
And for a while, they searched each other's faces—propped
on pillows. And as pillows merged
they approached each other's mouths, the source
of all their previous words. And they stopped watching
as they kissed—pressed each other's lips to prove
the depth of the moment.

All Gone Awry

And just before that, they each waited for the other to move—
still parallel, side by side. Each
covered to the chin beneath the sheet. And their minds drifted—
hovered above her passionate paintings
as they continued waiting.
And they imagined things. And they wanted things.
But neither of them talked
about the wanting.

Because just before that—she told him of her chance encounter
with an old boyfriend. At a function—
a public function up on campus.
And she enjoyed herself, had learned so much—
had sat in the back so as not to be discovered
by those presenting. And the ex-boyfriend felt menacing in a way
like he was still angry at one of the men speaking.
And the ex-boyfriend looked so handsome—so terribly
attractive—reminded her of some fiercely
passionate times together. And so, she said—
she found herself responding, even though she didn't want to.
She said she found her body responding—
but somehow managed to turn away.

And before all that, he shared ideas from his most recent creation.
Told her in detail of the ruse involved. A project so clever
so devious, it made her smile. And she wanted to know if she could
somehow be a part of it. And so he assured her she already was.
And when she asked him if he could stay the night, he told her—
told her that his girlfriend, his partner, had plans for dinner.
The partner had prepared to make dinner tonight.
He said he was sorry but he would have to go home.
And she said she was sorry too—but couldn't hide the fact
she was hurt
and angry.
And so he tried to reassure her
saying he felt sad as well.

Andrew Kumasaka

And just before that, they rose from the counter
fingered their clothes as they approached
the bed. They enjoyed watching each other strip
to essentials—each in the process of exposing a truth.
But when they took their places in bed—they found themselves
staring into the evening void above their faces.
And they clutched at the crumpled sheet to cover themselves
parsed themselves atop the narrow space.
And then they began to share their concerns—
she worrying for his safety—
he having questions about the contents
of her heart.

And just before that—they talked about a myriad of things,
some mundane and some
amusing. They laughed at times. In fact, they laughed a lot.
They drank orange juice together—talked of places
they might someday visit
together.
And then one of them glanced at the bed—
And then the other one followed with a glance at the bed.
And then everything went completely silent.
And they sat at the counter for what seemed like a long time—
because it had been such a long time since she'd asked him here.

24

Pacific Collegiate School gym—
   city league basketball game, over-40 division

What a tiny gym, thinks Mario to himself. Definitely not up to standards. But maybe the shortened court helps the old guys—cuts down on the running, easier on knees. In any case, he needs to be sneaky—can't afford to blow his cover tonight. Certainly, nothing new for a guy in his situation.

Mario crosses the linoleum floor—maneuvers the rows of clattering bleachers. Apart from the players, the gym looks mostly empty. Spectators include a girlfriend here, a couple spouses over there—a few kids running around. Ready for competition, he enjoys watching what guys like to do—establish dominance. Who wins and who loses? Who's alpha, beta, gamma, or whatever else lies below? Who gets to exalt in the end, having won the prize, or maybe—having finally won the girl?

Checking his phone, it's clear that the game's behind schedule. The team in front wears white jerseys—looks significantly younger than the team to his right. The team in black looks a bit subdued—spends much of its time on the floor stretching. Mario listens to what the players are saying. A guy in white jogs toward a woman sitting directly below. Approaching the stands, he grows taller in an exponential way. The man has to be about six feet eight by Mario's reckoning. From a distance, he would have never guessed, because the bronzed Adonis appears perfectly proportioned.

"Yeah, babe—watch us kill those old bastards."

Returning his kiss—"Do it babe— Go Posse!" Retaking the court, the big guy knocks the ball away from a teammate. Corralling it, a stocky, hirsute guy fires it back. "Cut it out you guys," he says. "Time to get serious."

"Remember the last time we played them?" asks Adonis.

"Yeah," says the guy who reminds Mario of a Neanderthal. "How about that point guard they got? Man—the guy went totally nuts on Joey."

"That was hilarious, dude."

Crossing half court, *Neanderthal* looks like he's stalking pray. "Hey Silver Backs!" he bellows. "It's getting late. Joey's not here. Let's go ahead without him."

After a quick huddle, the Silver Backs send out the black guy in the gold shorts. Returning Neanderthal's challenge— "Fine—let's do it. We've all got other things to attend to."

Mario watches the two teams gather at center court. It's painfully obvious who's going to win. Sure enough—the much younger Posse pulls out to a commanding lead. Mario's particularly interested in how Alex Arai and Neanderthal play each other. The latter deploys a very physical style—puts a body on his foe every chance he gets. If Alex feels bothered, Mario can't see it—at least not in his face. But as an athlete, Mario appreciates the controlled aggression being returned. *The game still means something to him—* Alex's jump shot looks decent, even though there's virtually no *jump* left in his *shot*. Besides distributing the ball, the best thing he does is to occasionally drive to the basket. Defense is another matter though. As much as he hustles, he's no match for younger legs, hearts—younger *everything*. Guile gets him only so far. Every time Neanderthal posts Alex low, the hairy guy leads with a shoulder—backs his opponent deep into the paint for an easy shot.

The game proves no contest, but there aren't any emotional explosions today. No outbursts of frustration, anger—no railing against injustice and misguided authority. Afterward, the two teams exchange various versions of *fives* and *fists*. Even Alex and Neanderthal share a respectful nod, as they towel down.

While the two teams mill about, Mario gets up—shuffles carefully down the bleachers. Avoiding discovery, he quickly crosses the court. Shoving open the metal doors—he leaves the gym.

* * *

The house on Escalona Drive

Morning shadows graze the hill—swept back like drapes from the face of the retaining wall. Alex sits at the redwood table, a box of spray cans resting on the deck. He watches the sun brighten the deviant wall—the *Wall of Mistakes*. Until today, he never considered it a potential memorial—every tag representing a moment in his life. A non-linear narrative, but rather—the *layering* of moments. And the writing shines both clear and cryptic—that art of crafting a name out of an oversized sense of marginality. How ironic, the desire to be seen, but not *really*— To *get up* is to create a name for oneself—but a name that expresses a beautiful lie. It's a shame, but for the sake of protection, Alex must buff his wall completely clean. And when the final curtain of gray paint falls—the tag dies, his identity disappears. And memory recedes as it tends to—lost without formal prompts.

It takes several hours, but he doesn't mind the mess. Nearing the midpoint, he stops at the juncture of his last purple tag and a beautiful, arcing *W* in red. He examines the points of contact—the intriguing overlap. And he hates destroying the casual, spontaneous glyph—a symbol of something else he wants to preserve. And so he stands there and stands there—a roller in one hand, bleeding gray. And as he continues to stand, he hears a discrete *click*. And the sound of the click might as well have been an explosion. It might as well have been the crack of a gun. He pivots sharply—

An athletic young man commands the deck. An angry man—Whitney's ex—but this time his face looks calm. Mario raises his phone again—takes a second shot of his subject standing beside his name.

Depositing his roller, Alex straightens his back—forces himself to look his foe directly in the eye. "What brings you here?" he demands. "You've got no business coming to my house, taking pictures."

Returning the glare—"I'm a reporter, Professor Arai—I'm here to do a story."

"Well then—you should have called first. At the very least, you've got bad manners." One step forward—"Do you care to have a seat?"

Noting a familiar sense of cool, Mario accepts.

Claiming the chair directly opposite—"So, what kind of story are you writing?"

"Oh, I think you know. I think you know exactly what my story's about."

"Well, let me see." Pointing off to the right—"It appears you're interested in the artwork over there."

"That's correct."

"So, what exactly do you want to know?"

Being seated reduces the height disparity, so Mario extends his chest. "That incident up on campus—the defacing of the Japanese American memorial—I've researched the whole thing—put together a lot of facts surrounding the crime."

Alex affects a relaxed pose. "I'm sure you did. So, why don't you just knock off the pretenses. Go ahead and tell me what you've got."

"Fine then. What I've got is—I know you're the one who attacked your father's memorial at Porter College. I also know you vandalized his sculpture at Minidoka, Idaho. Back in New York City, at the Japan Society building—they reported your father's memorial getting tagged. Too bad they cleaned it up so fast—no one got any pictures. Funny thing, though—they're right around the corner from the Trump World Tower—share a long driveway in between. Cameras from the Tower caught suspicious activity the night before the graffiti was discovered. A guy dressed in a black hoodie. Speculation was that the guy was white—but all that means is, he wasn't very dark.

"And then following that—there's Washington D.C. Someone hit up your father's memorial a day after the New York incident. Video showed the same thing. The park service took a set of photos—the tag's definitely yours."

Mario pauses to gauge the effect.

Alex folds his hands to keep them still. "Go ahead then. I'm sure you're not finished."

Resisting a smile, one corner of Mario's mouth lifts in a sneer. "Oh yeah, I've got more. I checked with the Japanese American Museum in Los Angeles. They had nothing for me at first. For some reason, you didn't tag your father's memorial across the street. I emailed photos of your *work* to them, but they didn't know anything about it. Then a few days later, someone from the museum was walking over to the *Go For Broke* memorial nearby. On the way, he happened to find a huge tag of AWRY written in front of the Geffen campus of MOCA. The only difference besides the scale was that you wrote the name of your crew, MPB, right beside it. I've got the pictures stored away with the rest."

All Alex can do now is to get to his feet. It's no longer an issue of trying to appear cool. On the other hand, Mario feels like he's on a huge roll—continues his relentless attack.

"Professor—you must admit. I've got a tight case against you. And it's going to make for some great reading, this exposé of mine. All I need to know now is your motivation for doing it." In total command, he leans forward. "But the tagging's not my only issue with you. The other one might be even bigger. I'm sure you're familiar with a certain Whitney Willis—Whitney B. In case you forgot, she and I were involved in a serious relationship. Then you showed up—used your position, your power, to get her in bed with you!"

Slamming a forearm onto the table—"You know, Professor—you know what I feel like doing?" Rising to his feet, he shoves the table. "You were wrong to *violate* a student—and soon enough, you'll be arrested. So, what are you going to do—call the police?"

Mario makes a move in Alex's direction. At this point, Alex should run. But there's something about all the sports he's played—something about the way a guy should handle himself in the face of a physical confrontation. Something about winning and losing that won't let him quit.

Mario makes a fist—

Alex holds firm—"Before you continue, I've got something to show you as well."

Walking to his box, he extracts a can of silver Montana 94.

Returning to the wall—"I'm sure you're acquainted with this...."

With several deft strokes, he reproduces Whitney's palm design from her tattoo.

"What the hell?" spouts Mario. "That belongs to Whitney, and yeah—I know you've used it before."

Alex continues. He sprays a version of her second tattoo—a fierce, stylized tiger.

Mario's other fist goes hard. "Now you're just trying to mess with me."

But Alex continues. He sprays a version of her third tattoo—a cyclone turning into a waterfall. "You know, tattoos are harder to remove than graffiti—"

"Okay, that's it—you're paying for it now!"

Mario stomps in Alex's direction. One yard away—

"Hold it Mario—I heard you out. Now give me the courtesy to finish, goddammit."

Alex returns to his box—replaces the silver can with the one filled with gold. Facing the wall, he uses short, linear strokes to produce what looks like a pyramid—a step pyramid. And just below he writes the three letters, *W—O—P.*

"What the hell's *that* about?"

"You know what the term *Wop* means?"

"Yeah, of course—got called it a few times when I was a kid."

"And this step pyramid—where can a person find one of these?"

"I don't get it. What are you asking?"

"I'm not trying to be pedantic, but this one's Mayan or Toltec—definitely from Mexico."

"And so?"

"And so, Mario—if this symbol refers to you, the fact is, I believe you're a guy *without official papers.* You're an *illegal alien*—the harsh way to put it. And furthermore—you're not even an Italian *Wop*, are you?"

Mario stays silent.

"No, you're actually *Mexicano.* You're undocumented—not supposed to be here. And you could be deported back across the border—if someone were to turn you in."

Now, Mario's the one who struggles to move—stands bolt upright. Both of his fists begin to unfold—his hands going completely limp.

"She talked to you—told you about me."

"Yes, she did. She told me a lot about you—and about your family—"

"So, that last design—you just make that up?"

Alex expels one final *pssst* before returning the can to the box.

"Why no, Mario," he casually answers. "That design on the wall—*I* didn't do it. That happens to be Whitney's latest tattoo—"

* * *

National Oceanic and Atmospheric Administration (NOAA)—

"Tracking Marine Debris from the Japanese Tsunami" Debris from the tsunami that devastated Japan in March could reach the United States as early as this winter, according to predictions by NOAA scientists. However, they warn there is still a large amount of uncertainty over exactly what is still floating, where it's located, where it will go, and when it will arrive.

As the tsunami surge receded, it washed much of what was in the coastal inundation zone into the ocean. Boats, pieces of smashed buildings, appliances and plastic, metal and rubber objects of all shapes and sizes washed into the water. The Japanese government estimated that the tsunami generated 25 million tons of rubble, but there is no clear understanding of exactly how much debris was swept into the water nor what remained afloat.

The worst-case scenario is boats and unmanageable concentrations of other heavy objects could wash ashore in sensitive areas, damage coral reefs, or interfere with navigation in Hawaii and along the U.S. West Coast. Best case? The debris will break up, disperse and eventually degrade, sparing coastal areas.

✳ ✳ ✳

Porter College

Scattershot. Shot and scattered. That's how it looks to Alex—that's how it feels. In isolation, sitting behind his academic desk. From this tight spot, he admits his efforts have blown apart—have gotten way out of hand, strewn in every direction far beyond the confines of his original concept. It was, at best, a creative explosion—the birthing of surrogate, pseudo-progeny, organisms meant to populate the world or to die trying. Alex reviews *Action Live*. The tags that once spanned the country—three states and the District of Columbia—cease to exist, have all expired. But in going *terminal*, their ghostly images continue to haunt via the electronic network. Dejected, he feels like the proverbial pebble dropped into a pond. Although he might have *jumped* in, he lies inert at the bottom now, while the ripples spread to infinity. And following the initial splash, his father rides the disturbance, welcomes a seemingly endless wave of media attention. If Alex had planned to make his father more famous—he couldn't have done a better job.

Through electronic media, the tag AWRY now serves as an entry point, a portal to his father's own work. Images of his sculptures, both major and minor, waft through the Web—hover about like electrons in a probability cloud. Now, school children fortify lessons on the Japanese internment with the very memorials Alex finds so stylistically offensive. At the moment, Kazuo Arai is the best-known, most celebrated Japanese American artist in the country—if not the world. As Alex sits, his father travels the country making appearances sponsored by a consortium of civil rights groups and the art establishment. The next big event on his *national tour* takes place in Minidoka.

On occasion, Alex admits to having gone too far—but how much further out can he get? It all comes back to that scattershot sensation. At times, he feels as deconstructed as his far-flung, artistic offspring. He knows he should simply count his blessings—accept the outcome of his brave assault on his

252

father. Then again—he craves one final deed, one last decisive moment, to claim some ultimate triumph. Coupled with that—a more permanent outcome is what he needs to restore a sense of wholeness inside. Within the confines of his tiny office, he collects himself around his computer.

* * *

Mario's place, Soquel

If Alex feels scattered, then Mario passes the time feeling *small*. How can a guy so strong and virile—feel so deflated? The phone goes off—it's Mario's mother. Once again Fredo's in trouble. Once again, the panicked mother casts a distress signal—loops the entire family back together. Mario's not used to jumping when the ring tone sounds, but a new vulnerability clearly resonates with his mother's alarm.

Fredo's backpack was searched today. Absent of all schoolwork—what had the counselor found? Just a couple of silver Krink markers and a spiral notebook. And on those pages, devoid of lessons—dozens and dozens of tags. And not just any tags, but slick versions of *Goofy* and *Shy Boy*, *Payaso*, and *Chino*. And which of the many names is Fredo? By the sheer volume, it must be *Caballo*. And what about the section in back of the binder—the one where he mimics a fine and official looking *cholo* script?

Mario can't seem to get away from it—the graffiti. In the process of chasing a tag line, the tags have been chasing him. Now he's become a connoisseur, a collector of sorts. For the past two weeks, he's met with the C.J.A. and the city police to glean what evidence they might have. Just before his showdown with the professor, he dropped a few hints about a person of interest *closer to home*. A bit of a teaser on his part—one he now regrets. At the time, no one knew how close he was to finishing his exposé. All he needed was a decent motive and a couple more photos to complete his case against Alexander Arai. But now he finds himself in an equally precarious place.

Mario fears that law enforcement has sniffed out the very same trail. And so, in a bizarre way, should the authorities conclude that Alex Arai is Alex AWRY—his own illegal status could come under scrutiny as well. No doubt, the professor will return the favor—trade in one deception for another, one bogus identity for another. Once again, the phone rings—jumps in Mario's hand. Yes, he promises his mother—he will help Fredo. He will find a way to steer his brother onto a safer, more law-abiding path.

25

San Francisco

Joey awakens to a beautiful day. Autumn in the City—*his* city. The bright sun cleaves an alleyway deep into a block of gritty buildings. Somewhere in the gap, a tiny apartment cracks open. Through a fractured window, light scatters on a makeshift table. Beer bottles, spent weed—sandwich wrappers, chips.

"Gotta go, girl—"

"Nah, babe. What time you comin' back?"

"Got me some work to do. I'll be late—*real* late. Don't wait up."

Grabbing his backpack, Joey kisses his girlfriend good-bye. A virtual tornado out the door—he whirls down three funneling flights of stairs.

Outside, a chilly wind greets him. Whipping through blue skies, it scours the nearby canyons of downtown and the financial district. Here in the Tenderloin, the wind scatters any random refuse, but spares the long-term stains and grime. Joey passes a seedy tableaux—an old man leaning against a wall— pisses the sidewalk. A homeless woman sitting by a grate— spews out epithets like a string of broken teeth.

Joey dashes across Market Street, just as the light turns yellow. Saturday traffic has already backed up. Passing a grocery and liquor store, he ambles down 6th Street to Mission. At the

Triple X Arcade, he cuts right—sprints through staggered cars to the busy bus stop. Soon, he boards a silver #14 headed for the Mission District and Daly City beyond. Changing seats, he's never been a passive rider in his life. Of course, years ago he'd be whipping out a marker—searching for a spot on the ceiling to wedge in his name. So much fun for the young outlaw trying to get known. With zero chance of gaining fortune, a little *fame* would have been nice.

A few minutes later, the bus curves south to enter the Mission, a neighborhood with the highest concentration of public murals in the country. Several hundred works brighten the thirty or so blocks of the district. Just past 17th, he catches a glimpse down Clarion Alley. *Been twenty years,* he thinks—this small stretch of pavement—host to *a ton* of street artists and their different techniques. Traditional muralists—graffiti writers—the alley has been a crucible for diverse, sometimes conflicting, artistic visions.

Up ahead, the chaotic flow of shops and other mixed-use buildings continues. Painted façades reflect the nearby murals, some of them truly spectacular. Beyond the beauty, he respects the social and political statements being made. He recalls having helped a friend paint a *tight-ass* mural on the Longshoreman's Union Building downtown. Aside from that, Joey, DRAZ—has no use for brushes—defines himself strictly as an aerosol writer. Today, he exits the bus at 24th—crosses traffic in the direction of Lilac Street.

*

Twin Falls, Idaho

Kaz awakens to a beautiful day. Sunshine floods the third-floor room the moment he splits the motel drapes. One door down, his sister, Haru, reminds Sumi of the correct time. How nice of Kaz to include his older sib on the final stop of *the tour*. Of course, Haru has already been up awhile—has already showered and dressed. It's not often she leaves Seattle, and when she does—she tries to keep a step ahead. Twenty years have passed since she last visited Minidoka. And that was before her husband passed away.

With his camp cohorts, Kaz enjoys a complimentary breakfast of bacon and eggs, toast, and coffee. Over-imbibing the fresh brew, he tries to counter the fatigue of travelling the East Coast. New York City and D.C. were thrilling stops, and the reception he got was impressive. Not only did he speak before the Japan Society, but he attended a personal reception at the Guggenheim.

"Sumi," he says—oblivious to the conversation she's having with Haru. "When was the last time you talked to Alex?"

"Sometime before we went back east. Actually, it was even before we went down to L.A."

"I tell you—I'm so disappointed. He never returned my calls. No more feedback on the retrospective."

"He's busy, too," notes Haru. "Besides, you depend on him too much."

"I suppose." Pushing away his coffee, Kaz ogles a platter of pastries. "For gosh sakes, it's just about words—that's all. Just words. And I'm talking a lot on this tour of mine. It's like I've found my own voice, or—I've gotten a new one. And people like what I'm saying." Nibbling on a cherry Danish—"Isn't that funny? You're probably right—I shouldn't depend so much on Alex. Maybe I just don't need him anymore."

"Well...." ventures Sumi.

"He's your son," says Haru. "Sometimes you make him sound like part of your staff. That is, if you were important enough to have one!"

Breakfast done, the trio meets with the event planner, a young man from the C.J.A. After a respectful greeting, he leads them to the rental car—drives them off to the site.

On the way, the young man stops at the Perrine Bridge so the party can enjoy a spectacular view of the Snake River. The bridge itself looks downright flimsy. Its single arch appears to have been pencil-sketched across the vast chasm. Below—hundreds of feet and eons of time give way before the eyes reach the sinewy body of the river.

Kaz doesn't like heights at all. As the group descends a flight of stairs, the cold wind rushes up to strike him. *That wind*—he thinks to himself. Then—"Sumi, Haru—remember this wind?"

"Oh boy," says Haru—"do I ever."

The two women clamber about a narrow ledge beneath the roadway. The wind and the void force Kaz to stoop to the ground. He reaches for the dirt, so he won't confuse the buffeting of the wind with vertigo. Sumi remains at his side, while Haru leans over the waist-high wall for a better look. It's clear to her there's more than one *snake* that's worn through the layers upon layers of lava. There's the visible one of relentless water. Then an invisible one made of wind—one that uncoils—jumps its banks in unpredictable ways.

Badly shaken, Kaz stumbles as he climbs the stairs to the roadway—slumps into the car. Settling in, the two women return to a topic they were enjoying back at the motel. On the short drive to Minidoka, all are surprised by a pristine golf course to their right. For unspoken reasons, they're not so sure what to make of an oversized American flag towering on the left.

*

Santa Cruz

Alex awakens to a beautiful day. Actually, he *stumbles* into a beautiful day from out of a troubling dream. Something about the quake in Japan, the following tsunami. Details fade—bleached by the sun deflecting off the bedroom mirror. After a shave and a quick shower, he drives down the hill toward Coffeetopia.

At the communal table, he finds a jumbled copy of the paper—text and photos in disarray. The rough handling of the news disturbs him, like aftershocks from his bad dream. Finishing his coffee, he heads for campus. Dropping his window, he lets in a rush of air. The self-induced wind chafes his face. Taking the East entrance, he maneuvers his own bit of turbulence up the road.

Alex parks in a shady lot overlooking the gym. Its adjacent pool unfurls towards a broad field for soccer, softball, and ultimate Frisbee. Leaving his car, he heads for the track that rims the field. With a slow jog, he reaches the southern end of the loop—takes in the spectacular view.

In the distance below, all of Santa Cruz stretches before him. Finding the cluster of downtown buildings, he traces the Pacific Garden Mall to the Municipal Wharf. And just beyond— his eyes settle on a shimmering expanse of gray-blue water.

Time, distance, and volume, he ponders. First sculpted some two hundred miles to the south, how long did it take Monterey Bay to ride the San Andreas Fault to its present location? And beneath those recreational waters lies a vast underwater trough deeper than the Grand Canyon. Alex stares to the point of going blank. He can't imagine the void disguised in the distance—can't imagine the volume of that huge and mysterious emptiness.

*

Joey passes Mickey D's—the planters brightly painted as part of a work that covers the entire building. Just beyond, Lilac Street emerges from the right. Entering, he gazes up at a vibrant mural covering two full stories of cinderblock wall. The vivid colors are *way cool*—resonate with Joey's work in Santa Cruz. A fiery woman in yellow and orange soars above the massive, silver-blue form of a semi-recumbent man. The woman could be viewed as the sun—but with her feathery wings, she could also be seen as an avenging angel. Or maybe she's a female Icarus, her naked figure burning as she reenters the atmosphere. Below her, the man's upper body rises like a wave—a fish sprouting from his neck. Maybe the man represents Neptune—maybe he's the feral ocean ready to receive the female sun.

Joey inspects Lilac Street—actually, a narrow alley. If he pulled out the camera from his backpack, he might pass as a scruffy tourist. But Joey plans to get up tonight—somewhere here in this vital section of town. The group, Mission Art 415, coordinates the space—arranges for all the work that's done here. Maybe he should talk to those nice folks, *Lisa and Randolph*—get a legitimate spot on someone's garage door. But Joey has no patience for that. He wants to be spontaneous, completely free. Recalling the past—*Man, this place was messed up before. The bums, addicts— Drug deals comin' down everywhere.* Part of inner city blight, the alley was lined with dead-end people. With its dirty needles and human waste, Lilac was a place where desperate beings could skulk and hide in the dark. But graffiti art changed all that, or so it seems.

Stepping along the piece-lined corridor, Joey feels like an outsider. *Like I'm takin' a walk down a fuckin' museum.* He never got as famous as these other guys—never was part of any historic crews. *My stuff from Psycho City—that was some crazy shit. Me and these other cats. I was rockin' Franklin Auto, too.* But that was nearly thirty years ago, and he regrets not having taken more pictures back then. *Oh man,* he says to himself— *check out that piece with the biker chick—her ass just starin' up at you on the seat.* Joey moves in for a closer look. *Oh yeah— that's a BODE piece, man. Gotta like them lacey red panties.* Continuing along—*Nice thing about legal walls—less chance of gettin' buffed. Kinda off limits for most.*

Joey enters the loading area behind a small Chinese restaurant. Staring at a piece inspired by Mexican motifs— *Yeah, it's like doin' a mural.* In fact, the piece in front of him depicts an Aztec warrior as masked superhero. With spear and shield, he straddles a jaguar. Taking up an entire wall, the work is a tribute by graffiti writers to Mission-style muralists. Four *traditional* graffiti pieces surround the central figure done by BODE. Four brilliantly-colored names—*CUBA*, *TWICK*, *TERMS*, and *STAN 153*.

Farther down the alley, Joey encounters a wall done by MPC—*Masterpiece Creators. That's NATE, for sure,* he notes— admiring the pulsing name done in lime-green and pink. Along with *CRAYONE*, the names are awash in a watery turbulence of cresting waves. In a violent sunset above, the red inscription reads—*FUCK THE BLUE ANGELS & FUCK COLUMBUS!*

Continuing his walk, Joey recognizes pieces by *ESTRIA*, *BAM*, *KING 157*, and tattooist, *D. VINCI*. At the end of the block, a tall wooden building posts a haunting tribute wall, titled *ROCK IT DON'T STOP*. Purple figures point to the names of beloved writers who have died. So many writers, as transient as their art—*DONDI, KASE 2, IZ THE WIZ, SK8, DASH, RESEK, REGRET, VITEL*—and of course, *DREAM 1*, the *Michael Jordan* of Bay Area graffiti.

Ah shit, that's sad, thinks Joey as he turns around—heads back in the direction of 24th Street. *Ah man—all them writers, what a shame, gone forever— Rest in peace bros.*

*

The rental car crosses the North Channel of the Snake River—makes a quick vault over the rushing water. Peering through the windshield, Kaz prepares himself to receive the most magnificent sculpture he has ever created.

"There it is," he announces. "There it is—" like a ghost rising up from the high desert—bright light dematerializing the shiny bronze skin.

And he catches flashes of sunbeams off certain angles, certain surfaces. Pride wells up—grows in proportion to the three heroic figures thrusting skyward from the barren land.

"Sumi—Haru," he calls out, awestruck.

It's as if Kaz were just another visitor—coming to Minidoka for the first time. It's as if he's never seen the memorial before. Filled with genuine wonder, he registers the full impact. He's overcome by admiration for the creator of such a powerful work. No doubt, he *is* the creator—but for the moment, he almost forgets.

Cold, windy—a day that portends the hardships of winter. And the weather serves as a memorial too—one of nature's enduring features. Haru shakes beneath her overcoat—an emotional trembling extracted by the harshness of the surroundings. It's the rocky remnants of the guard house she studies—not so much her brother's sculpture. Crossing the road, she ignores the shimmering figures—points a finger off to the left.

"Over there," she says. "The military police had its headquarters there, and the hospital was just beyond."

Then Haru reminds herself—Kaz and Sumi were little kids at the time and probably don't remember. For the next ten minutes, the two women watch as Kaz repeatedly circles his design. Reverently, he reviews the powerful modeling of the surfaces—the expression of the faces. He approves of the way the *father's* visage exudes both pride and determination. The *mother* looks painfully distressed—appropriately so. The innocence of the *child's* face strikes him as particularly poignant.

While waiting for her brother, Haru approaches the Honor Roll wall, a number of feet behind the memorial. Fourteen-years-old at the time of internment, she recognizes a few of the names of those who served in the armed forces. She certainly remembers the commotion over the so-called *loyalty questionnaire*. Some 97 percent of Minidoka residents answered the key questions with, *Yes, yes.* Haru finds the name of one of the older boys from her block—block 26B. He went off to fight in Europe, and she still wonders what became of him. She turns from his name, as Kaz and Sumi approach her.

"They'll be putting up a sound system next to my sculpture," her brother says. "Should be driving up any second. Got till twelve to get things working."

The three decide to take a walk around the site. More than for the others, it's a kind of *memory lane* experience for Haru. Kaz voices interest in what his sister recalls.

"Gosh, I appreciate it—really do. The stuff you remember— I've been using it when I give my talks."

"I don't mind," says Haru, passing the large volcanic pieces that once helped to define a Japanese rock garden. Ignoring the perversion of the traditional form—"Yes, the rocks were hauled in and they made this big *V for Victory* shape." Farther down the walkway—"The post office used to be right here. I wrote letters to a couple kids back in Seattle. Funny how the ones I got back had black marks all over them. One of the letters had cut-outs even."

Winding past an abandoned fire station, the trio examines an old root cellar. Haru points to some lower lying areas farther below. "Well—that's where a block of barracks used to be. In fact, the next set of barracks—that's where we lived."

"So, what else do you recall?" asks Kaz, gazing off into the distance.

"Oh, I was young. I had my friends."

"What about the hardships? What about those dust storms, for cryin' out loud? Pretty bad, weren't they?"

"Well, that's true. There were tough times. You know—Pop said he could understand being put away, he and Mom being born in Japan. But for us kids—we were citizens. He thought that was wrong. All that turmoil—the uncertainty." Turning to Sumi—"*Shikata ga nai, neh?*"

Sumi nods in understanding.

"Now if I had been older," says Kaz—"I'm sure I would have stirred up some trouble. You know, like the riot they had at Manzanar. Or the *No-no* boys—stuff that happened at Tule Lake. I do remember the folks using that phrase, though."

"Well," says Haru, "that's how we are in situations like that—that's what we say—*Shikata ga nai. There's nothing we can do about it. So make the best of it.* No use complaining. Keep going—do the best you can."

"Yes, that's the attitude," he says. "I bet the same thing—it's going on in Japan right now."

"Makes sense," says Haru. "That's what we did. We went to school, church, had Girl Scouts—sports teams. We had our music. Amy next door—she was a little older—had a real swell collection of records—best on the block. All the young guys would drop by—wanted to hear that swing music."

"Any dancing?"

"Oh sure, we had sock hops—sometimes big ones."

"And wasn't there this nice boy you liked—Tommy—Tommy Shibata?"

"Sure was—really good-looking and a great dancer. He worked as a swamper, unloading trucks. Worked outside of camp too—on the farms nearby. Told me one time—he got a rabbit dinner for a full day's work. The farmers around here really appreciated the help from camp. The guys made something like 50 cents an hour."

"So, tell me something else you remember," Kaz urges. "Something else I can use for my talk."

"Oh, I don't know. Tommy and his friends—they used to cut the barbwire fence from time to time. And yes—the authorities got real upset, even electrified the fence for a while. But a couple times, a bunch of us kids—we snuck out at night. You know that place called Eden—a small town not far from here? We would walk all the way to this little restaurant—get hamburgers and fries. Maybe even a chicken dinner."

"Wasn't that a dangerous thing to do?"

"No, not really. Nothing bad ever happened to us."

"You could have been hassled—maybe shot. You know there was a war going on."

"No, the people were okay."

"Well—with what's happening to my memorials, sometimes I think we're still in a kind of war." Kaz sticks his hands under his arms. "Maybe we should head back to the entrance now. I've got to prepare some more—want to take a look at where I'll be standing. After that, I'm going to the car—get some rest."

*

Alex takes a seat by the campus swimming pool. With a sweep of a hand, he motions Whitney toward the water. He doesn't want to interrupt her routine. Surfaces— A young woman sheathed in a one-piece swimsuit. Her untamed hair soaks in the sun—gives off a burnished glow. Tussled sunbeams fall onto tan shoulders, chest—spill over the waterline of her blue outfit. Will she jump in, or will she ease herself through that skin of unblemished water?

Whitney lingers, dips a toe, a foot—looks for Alex's response. Delighted, she lowers both feet, both calves as she settles her bottom on the concrete edge of the pool. Alex is intrigued by this gradual emersion. Flipping around, she lets her knees vanish while supporting herself with both forearms. And now her thighs go under, and then her rump—water rising to just above her waist. Pushing off, she stretches back in a long arc—arms extended. And as she cleaves the liquid plane, long folds of water envelop her chest, her whole body.

Surfaces— A veil of water atop Lycra. Lycra caressing tattoos. Tattoos gracing the skin—skin applied back to water. Alex notes the efficient windmill action of her arms. He follows the compact splashes at her feet. And everything in between appears so calm. Even her face looks relaxed as she breathes rhythmically in tune, in *time* with the rest of herself. If there was ever anyone made to swim, to occupy water—it must be her.

When the final lap ends, Whitney rises—pulls herself out of the pool. And as she exits, she looks all shiny and slippery, and the water falls away, even though some of it still clings to certain parts. And the water returns to what it was before. All the turbulence gone—all the ripples and wakes—all the slapping against floats and the sides of the pool. Surfaces return, reconstitute, regain that faultless look—as if no one had ever entered.

*

Joey slips inside the McDonald's. Moving to the counter he finds a mix of people milling about—no obvious pattern.

"Say, bro—you waitin' in line?"

Noting a nod, he steps behind the stocky Asian guy—Giants cap snug over a splay of dark hair. Those to the side must be waiting for their orders—most of them staring straight ahead. Shifting her weight—a black woman flaunts a letterman's jacket, as a white guy twitches in a flannel shirt. Things seem to move pretty quickly.

"Next—" calls one of the all Latina front staff.

Stepping forward—"I'll be takin' a Number 1. Make that super-sized."

"Drink?"

"Gotta have me a Coke—"

Joey pays, then leaves the counter—waits beside a Latino couple, children in tow. In time, he collects his food—locates an empty seat facing the service area. Chewing his burger, his eyes elevate in that placid look of someone enjoying his meal. Maybe some type of prehistoric behavior—an animal gazing up from its kill to scan the horizon for other predators. But focus returns when he notices the wall by the exit. *That design, man—it really rocks.* Smiling to himself, he finds three crimson hearts taking flight, each with a pair of wings and feathered tails. Finishing his meal, he approaches for a better look. In the corner, it reads © 1998 Precita Eyes Muralists.

Feeling satisfied, Joey jaywalks 24th Street—heads for the opposite corner with Mission. It's not just the food, but the added *high* of finding beauty—of exploring a neighborhood where street art grows wild. Crossing the plaza above the underground BART station, he takes a seat on a bench by the sheltered bus stop. Undoing his pack, he extracts his black sketchbook and colored pencils. He plans to create a piece for Lilac Street—one he can render late tonight. From his vantage point, he views the endless string of buses as they head downtown.

From behind, Joey hears a small commotion—turns to find three young men huddled about—drifting sideways. Things go quiet, then turn loud again. One thick fellow sports baggy jeans—dreadlocks whisking the broad expanse of his black ski jacket. He's in a heated discussion with a smaller guy wearing a baseball cap, gray hoodie, and equally baggy jeans. A skinny fellow simply watches—a raggedy beard further pinching his face. He's the only one whose jeans look oversized due to his emaciated condition. *If it's a drug deal,* thinks Joey—*they be makin' too much damn noise.* Returning to the task at hand, he's got plenty of ideas in his head—plenty of preliminary sketches. Now it's time to pull it all together.

*

The young event planner approaches Kaz as he paces in front of the car.

"We're sorry Mr. Arai, the bus—it got delayed. Over at the Minidoka visitors center—the one in Hagerman."

"So what's the problem?"

"Something mechanical. I'm not sure. Actually, *they're* not so sure, either."

"For gosh sakes—what're you going to do? Call off my presentation?"

"Well, no. However long it takes, we'll wait. That is, if it's okay with you. I know it's a terrible inconvenience."

"So—you've got no idea how long it'll be."

"No, I don't. But the people—they're from all over. A big contingent from Washington State and Oregon. And they really want to hear what you have to say."

"Is that so?"

"Oh yes, Mr. Arai—your reputation as a speaker precedes you."

"But I'm sure they're getting lots of information, right where they are."

"Well, it's not the same, and they know it."

"So, tell me—why is the visitors center for Minidoka forty miles away in Hagerman?"

"Probably had some extra space in the building. Really, I don't know."

"Isn't that place mostly for old fossils?"

"Yes, that's right. The Hagerman Fossil Beds National Monument."

"Still seems kind of strange."

"Well, as you probably know, Mr. Arai—there's a fundraising effort to build a visitors center right here on this site. Right here in Minidoka."

"That's all just fine. But I'm afraid it won't be doing me any good."

"Again, I apologize. We've sent for some hot food from the motel. If the wait gets much longer, we'll just head back and stay in our rooms. I mean—I realize it's been kind of cold out here."

"It's just that I'm getting tired, you know? And I'm starting to get a headache. Things like this didn't happen in New York, Washington D.C., L.A.—"

"Those are big cities."

"Well, I've got to admit, the C.J.A. has done a pretty good job—up to this point."

"We're really trying, Mr. Arai. This is so—unfortunate."

*

Alex departs the pool area—drives the loopy ups-and-downs of the campus road to Porter College. Once there, he trudges the final incline toward the office buildings above. At the top stands the bronze edifice of *Forever Manzanar*. The farther he walks, the bigger and shinier it gets. The burnished surface disburses light as if the work were a fountain spraying water. The piece now stands as much a monument to his father as it does to commemorate the trials of a people. Absent his graffiti, Alex marvels at how clean the sculpture looks. That, plus its sheer size confer upon it a kind of *rightness*, a kind of *moral authority*, even. Avoiding its shadow, he pivots left into the courtyard containing the koi pond. He glances up at the cherry trees—two seasons removed from their transient blossoms.

Once inside his office, he takes out a tablet of notebook paper. Pencil in hand, he sketches the latest versions of his tag—symbols of his alter ego, his *nom de plume*. He rips off one page—begins another. Over time, the papers scatter—a slow motion explosion of his tablet, while he and his pencil hold the center.

In the midst of his frenzy, Alex stops. What's this exercise about, anyway? A kind of madness, really. And he swears to himself—tonight's act will be the final time he engages in such nonsense. And like every other *child*, like almost every other adolescent writer that's gone before him—he sees the endpoint where his wild graphic ravings must come to a stop. It's a matter of growing up, of getting or keeping a job—of resigning oneself, accepting the name that was given him at birth. Only those few with enough talent, enough luck, can take their art still further.

*

So, how many people have come to the bus stop on 24th and Mission? How many people have boarded the #14 headed downtown? Joey doesn't know—doesn't count. He's busy putting the finishing touches on his new design. It's turning into a good-sized piece—all about a big mandala. *Yeah, a wheel of sorts—a wheel showin' the progress of my life.* The day passes quickly—the whole afternoon. Looking up, he spies yet another set of bus wheels—another group of people being whisked away. Colder now—darker. In fact, the sky over the Mission takes on a deep orange glow. *Kinda pumpkin colored.*

Repacking his bag, Joey saunters back to McDonald's. He orders another supersized meal with a Coke. Burger in one hand, he splays his piece book with the other. The *Wheel* he's created begins at the top—starts with a star portraying him at birth. A radiant silver, it embodies all of his untapped potential. A little to the right, a female figure representing his mother falls from the arc and into a black void. At three o'clock, two contrasting forms depict Joey's father. The first lies shrunken and folded inside a syringe. The second looks tall and athletic—lifts up a tarnished version of the star.

As the mandala continues, the star brightens again—develops a face and limbs. One hand carries a spray can. At six o'clock, an image of Psycho City anchors the piece. A little to the left, a jagged rift breaks the circle—represents the quake of '89. The silver star writes *DRAZ* in one of the *pits*—the underground spaces left after razing downtown buildings. Around eight o'clock, Joey's father tumbles from his spot, and the graffiti halts. The rest of the loop lies empty until just before reaching the top. The star reappears on a segment comprised of a beach scene and forested hills. Turning to the vacant center of the wheel, Joey outlines the name *DRAZ*, as it hurtles into whatever space lies beyond.

*

Alex takes a break. He's settled on the design he plans to use—a simple tag with an angular elegance. Walking to the door, he breaks the seal—notes how much the ocean air has cooled. From his backpack, he removes his black hoodie—drapes it over his shoulders. He heads for the stairs, then makes a soft descent to the courtyard below. In order to avoid his father's memorial, he banks left—follows the path up a grassy slope overlooking the bay.

On the gentle crest, Alex finds the squiggly red sculpture known to students as the *IUD*. Sitting on its base, he gazes at the meadow below. Family student housing nestles at the bottom, the College Eight campus tumbles to the left. From his privileged perch, he beholds an enormous sunset. *Everyone knows—the most beautiful sunsets happen here in October.*

A big black night seems to hover above the California coast—a big black bird with vast, outstretched wings. And the wings form a wide, feathery arch over the blazing orange sun. And parts of the wings light up with fire. And the wings slowly descend, engulfing the sun, joining with water—ready to extinguish the day.

*

"I'm sorry Mr. Arai for this terrible inconvenience. It's best we head back to the motel."

"You know—I slept all afternoon in this damn car—got a crick in my neck."

"Don't worry, it'll be much more comfortable back in our rooms. I'll drive you there as quickly as I can."

"So, what's the schedule?"

"The bus should arrive at Twin Falls in the next hour or so. We're arranging to get everyone dinner. After that, you can give your talk."

The trio returns to the motel without incident. Re-crossing the Perrine Bridge, Kaz can manage only a brief flash of fear. He's almost too tired to care—and more and more, he looks forward to the end of the trip. It takes him a couple of tries before clearing the car's sill. Sumi and Haru follow him back to the lobby—the young rep primed to trigger the doors.

Once on the third floor, Haru approaches a bank of windows to inspect the view. Looking back in the direction of Minidoka, she remembers a Japanese word she once heard her mother use. Haru contemplates the vast orange sky—murmurs the word *kangeki* to herself. Once more—*kangeki,* the word that means *the deep emotion you feel, when watching the sun set....*

*

Nighttime in Joey's city—nighttime in the Mission. The spraying of artificial light on dark walls—buildings with neon signage look covered in tags and throw-ups. Joey searches for a good site. Starting at the far end of Lilac, he inspects a corner laundromat. Although the wall facing the alley is smooth and wide, it's too close to the main thoroughfare. Halfway down, a streetlamp illuminates a rare unmarked dwelling—the façade guarded by a cyclone fence. *Man that cat's gotta be a hater—* Continuing on, beautiful pieces line the corridor even as their colors have gone ghostly pale. Out of respect, he won't consider covering the work of writers he's known.

Approaching 24th again, he examines two additional sites. A warehouse to his left bears a few crude tags and irregular gray patches from recent buffing. To his right—three flawless garage doors front a refurbished triplex. The wood siding looks brand new, the mocha paint, pristine. He would love to plant his piece on one of those doors, but a camera and downlights preclude it. He also knows that graffiti on newly-gentrified property is the first to go. So he settles on the marred, industrial wall to his left. Thanks to the opposing residential fixture, the illumination proves just right.

On the cusp of light and shadow, Joey opens his backpack—pulls out his camera. After taking a flash-lit *before shot*, he exits the alley for a much needed leak at Mickey D's. *Got me a tight-ass design,* he tells himself. *Fits right in—just as good as all the others. No way they gonna buff it— Gonna be around for a long time.*

*

Back at his office, Alex sits and waits. He waits as a deep darkness engulfs the campus, merging with his internal state. And with the growing dark, the tremors at his core finally reach the surface. His hands fumble with an outsized bin in his desk. Inside, he seeks out the coldness of metal—the unambiguous feel of solid metal. Unlike the gentle contours of spray cans—the cylinders of mystical paint, capable of flow, of rise and dip—of nuance and subtlety. He removes three pieces of forged steel, blunt in their intention, but sharp in potential application. Atop his desk, he arranges his implements—two flat head screwdrivers and a stylus for etching art prints. He prepares himself for a surgical strike—one intended to slash the surface, the skin of a bronze abomination. No scalpel as such, but humble, honest instruments. Tonight, he will leave a tell-tale scar on the body of his father's work. He will alter all the false, personal narratives. He will leave his mark in the deepest, most permanent way his art allows.

*

Kaz should be asleep by now. Instead, a commotion fills the so-called banquet room of the motel. A makeshift staff deconstructs and hauls away tables. Several guests busy themselves by setting up rows of chairs. It's late—*ridiculously late,* he thinks. *Makes me mad—* And it also makes him think about possible conspiracies—wondering who could be behind this delay, this mess. It's hard not to take things personally—as if the chaos, like the graffiti vandalism, were being done to him in a malicious way. He tries to assess the mood of his audience—these sixty or so people have been on the road most of the day. Just an hour ago, they were hauled in by bus—deposited in the parking lot with their travel bags.

Just like when they first brought us to Minidoka—except it's dark outside. And the darkness of the high desert is something he really does recall from childhood. It was amazing to the young artist how that big black sky could carry so many floating stars. On the spur of the moment, he decides to speak to the voluminous nights from camp. *But they better hurry up if they expect me to talk.*

Sumi brings her husband a mug of tea. "The only green tea they have is decaf. I brought you some of this black tea instead."

Kaz reshuffles his notes—

*

Joey can't resist another Coke. He takes a final look at his master drawing—slides the piece book into his pack. Fortified, he heads for the exit—flings the glass door open. Actually, a cold blast of air opens it for him—spirits him away. Turning onto Lilac Street, he faces the imposing corridor—a pink-orange fog drifting over static black pools of shadow. Behind him, the two figures of the guardian mural loom above like apparitions. For the first time, he seems to recognize the female form, falling and burning. He might even identify the male figure lying below her—lost to turbulent waters. Shaking off the associations, he reenters the alley—strides defiantly toward the wall of his choice. He feels so young, even more so now—feels like a kid. He's all excited and a little bit scared. But tonight is special. Tonight, DRAZ will be *rockin'* Lilac Street—will unleash a *crazy-ass* piece fit for a king. Tonight, Joey will claim his rightful place among the most famous writers in town.

*

Alex dons his black hoodie—places the stylus and screwdrivers in the front pouch. He won't have to worry about the rattle of spray cans, or the sound of aerosol paint. Just the random clinking of steel tonight. It's been quiet on campus for a while. The hubbub of *Action Live* has died down. Returning to baseline, the student body is probably planning for Halloween. Whatever the case, campus police have retreated to their normal routines. No more nightly presence here at Porter.

Still, his shakiness persists, coupled now with a strange rhythm to his heart. He sometimes feels the boom of an extra big beat—followed by a long pause. The sensation scares him to the point he's not really sure what troubles him most tonight. Could his heart seize, stop, blow up? So much violent movement inside his body. Leaving the office again, his breath labors as he makes his way through the chill.

*

Finally, Kaz gets up from his table to speak. Usually, he would enjoy the lavish words by the C.J.A. host. This time, the intro seems a bit long-winded, even to him. How annoying—the lack of a formal lectern. Addressing the audience, he realizes he's dealing with a captive crowd of sorts. *Japanese people are very polite.* He imagines that even the younger ones are, even the *hapas*—the ones with mixed blood. Not too sure about the *hakujins*—the whites—though. He gazes out at the weary faces—people gallantly showing interest. *Yes, Japanese people are good at sitting up straight.* In truth, he feels resentful for having to go on with the show. It's been a long trip, and he can hardly tolerate standing in place, his mind exhausted, his aching body with nothing to lean on—nothing to hold onto. Irritation—just *irritated.*

Kaz ignores his standard speech—lets himself ramble, lets himself vent— "So yes—I guess you know how it feels to get detained—herded around and all. Well, we didn't like it—*I* didn't like it. In fact, some of us actually cut down parts of that barbed wire fence. The army—they even tried electrocuting us. And it wasn't enough just to work in the camp—the concentration camp. I was a swamper—heavy work unloading

273

trucks. But I also worked in the fields outside for white farmers. Fifty cents an hour, as I recall. Was nothing, really. All day long, for gosh sakes— Once they paid me with a rabbit dinner...."

*

Alex descends the stairway—his feet feeling distanced from his head. The irregular, heart-felt pounding inside must surely register in his skin, his clothes. He would certainly look unstable, if only he could see himself. Is he ready for what he's about to do? He hopes so. The time for debate is over. Leaving the courtyard, he turns in the direction of his father's memorial. As he steps forward—he notices something strange up ahead. Someone's *there*, crouching at the base of his father's sculpture—someone's there doing *something*. Alex's mind freezes—thoughts out of sync. Surely students have left mementos, but not *now*—not anymore. Pausing in the dark— he can barely contain the pressure in his chest. One step forward—Alex hears something, he actually *hears* it— The rattling sound of a spray can....

*

"I'm sure you're tired—really tired. And I'm tired— In fact, I'm exhausted. And it burns me up that you couldn't see my memorial in the light of day. So let me tell you some things about my work—tell you what I was thinking." And as Kaz describes the "powerful but elegant figures," the modeling of surfaces that "go way back to the French sculptor, Auguste Rodin," an amazing surge takes hold, informs him—a wonderful kind of intoxication. Filled with himself, his head grows bigger and bigger. He appears to rise as tall and grand as his three heroic figures. In fact, as their sole creator—Kaz is even grander. And it's as if he looms over the Idaho desert, certainly, he towers over his audience—all of whom are fully awake now, eyes *round* in a mixture of awe and a touch of alarm. And from his ongoing detonation of words, Kaz ascends still higher, hovering—a kind of nuclear cloud—one that no one can avoid—a presence from which no one can look away.

*

Alex sprints to his father's sculpture.

"What the hell are you doing?" he shouts.

Startled, a tallish man uncoils—dark clothes, scraggly hair—big bent nose. Grabbing the guy, Alex yanks him to his feet. Staggering, the intruder waves his spray can—points the cap directly at Alex's face.

"Give me that, you idiot!" Alex demands.

The guy strikes back—a frantic blow with his free hand. His darting eyes—impossible to track. Focused on the spray can, Alex ignites. Enraged—and now he says it—"How dare you vandalize this memorial!"

*

"It's ironic you know? The criminal who attacked my work—he's made me into kind of a star." In the rarefied air of his own making—"All over the world, people know me. I got a global following now." Temples pulsing—"A curator at the Guggenheim—she wants to put on a show, a big show in the future. And gosh—that gives me a great idea. Let's all get together in New York City when it opens. I'll keep you up to date with the progress—"

*

Alex explodes—attacks the guy with a fury he can't explain.

"Are you crazy, old man?" Grappling—"Get the fuck off me!"

Alex tries to snatch the spray can—gets a gust of paint on his arms and hands. Incensed—he manages a glancing blow to the side of the intruder's face. The tallish guy gives up the can— seizes Alex by the throat. Choking, Alex reaches for his pouch— grabs the first item he finds. With all his strength, he thrusts the screwdriver into the man's gut—catches a flap of jacket on the way. With a sharp cry, the guy lets go—slams Alex against the bronze sculpture.

"You're fuckin' nuts!" spits the wounded man—takes off running.

*

For twenty minutes, Kaz has held court. "And with the help of the C.J.A. and law enforcement, we're going to find the vandal—find the guy who assaulted my memorials—assaulted my memorials to Japanese Americans. He's not going to get away with this, for cryin' out loud. He's not going to get away with this—this attack on my people! He's not going to get away with this attack on me!"

Kaz has done a fine job—has utilized all the memories appropriated from his sister. He knows he's a big artist, a big man. In fact, his head has gotten so big, so full— In the midst of closing remarks, a horrific pain explodes in the back of Kaz's brain. Staggering—he reaches down with both hands—seeks out the table—anything for support. And with this ungainly bow to his rapt audience, everything in Kaz's mind goes blank—

*

When Alex comes to, he finds himself sprawled—his right arm wrapped about his father's sculpture. His left hand lingers on the cold bronze surface beside his cheek. His heart now quiet, he lies dumbstruck from the fall—the blow to his head. Feeling strangely empty, he tries to push himself up. He tries. He pushes himself up—sees what appears to be a freshly-painted tag on the surface—and a long line, a *gash*, actually, across the side of the closest figure. And Alex feels something odd in his right hand—feels something hard. And so he grips whatever it is—grips it tightly as he tries to remember what it is. And Alex hears the strident voice of a man, a different man—ordering him to get up off the ground....

*

Joey has worked at a rapid clip—has finished the main design of his wheel. All this time, he's been moving to the rhythm of Bone Thugs and Harmony. No need for a boom box or one of those iPods he'd like to buy. He's got it all playing in his head. And the music, the beat—keeps him on track, keeps the adrenalin from feeling like fear. But he still can't stop from jumping at times, as random people filter through the alley. The occasional drunk, the homeless girl—a *sweetheart,* really, asking him for the meaning of his piece.

But now he takes a much needed break, steps away—contemplates both ends of Lilac Street. And when he returns to his circular life—Joey feels just a little sad. And he doesn't know exactly why, and he's not the kind of guy who tries to put a finger on it. So he gazes at the elaborately painted wheel, examines the central void of non-descript color. It's an open space reserved for his name—ready to accommodate *DRAZ* in all its glory. And as he stoops to check his spray cans, he hears another set of footsteps fast approaching. Probably some other *bum* passing through. One of them *drunk-ass, high, fuck-ups* searching for a place to hide, to sleep. Sure enough—it's this skinny cat, running down the pavement, stumbling through shadows.

Standing, Joey tosses him a greeting—"What's up, my man?"

So out of breath, the fellow can't even answer. He doubles over—hands on knees, panting away. When he looks up, Joey studies the hollow face—the tangled beard.

"Say—ain't I seen you before? You know—at the bus stop, by the BART station—"

"Shit," comes the answer, "don't know, man." When the skinny guy opens his mouth—it looks like a busted-up grate. "Hey man," he says—"you got some change?" Looking to his right from where he came—"Anything's good man—anything's good."

"Well, ordinarily I don't—but tonight…." As Joey opens his pack, the guy gets edgy— "Make it quick, man. Gotta get outta here—know what I'm sayin?" Checking to his right once more— "Oh God—oh fuck!"

Someone's spotted him. The skinny man starts to run again—stops short as he finds a second figure trotting from the opposite direction. "Oh shit! Fuck it—fuck!"

"What's goin' down?" asks Joey—even though he already knows. Joey's from Holly Park Court Projects up on that hill—ran around a lot in the Mission. "Just like old times," he says out loud—says to the man now cowering at his feet.

Joey watches as the two men converge—right here in front of his piece, right where the skinny guy lies crying.

"Say you two—I know you got business. But my man here—he needs some help—" Joey holds up a couple of tens.

"Shut up mother fucker!" says the husky one—dark ski jacket covering his top-heavy frame.

"Yeah—shut the fuck up," says the smaller one—a weasely face protruding from beneath a baseball cap. Walking up to the prone man, he swings one oversized pant leg—kicks the guy in the ass.

"Hey man," yells Joey—"that ain't cool! I said I could help—"

The big guy takes a step forward—"Didn't I tell you to shut up, mother fucker? We takin' care of this here mother fuck—Fucked up big time!" The big guy goes over to the man on the ground. "Hear that *bitch*? Let me see them hands of yours! What you got?"

The man complies—stretches out his empty fingers.

"Just what I thought, mother fucker!" The big man delivers a powerful kick to the man's exposed gut.

Now something goes off in Joey—and what goes off goes all the way *back* to when he was growing up in the projects, caught up in drug wars. *Back in the day,* when he was protecting *civilians,* as he used to call them. Joey grabs the big guy by the shoulder—turns him around.

"Say what? What's wrong mother fucker—you tryin' to throw hands?"

"I'm warnin' you two—take this money and get the hell out."

"You talkin' big for an old mother fuck—but you ain't shit!"

Just for the moment, the guy in the jacket bends at the knees, hand extended—as if to help the man balled up on the ground. Suddenly, the big guy explodes straight up—puts his whole body into a punch to Joey's head. But Joey knows all the moves—thinks this guy's a *punk*. Stepping away—the would-be blow only demolishes air. Joey feels like a young man again—

strong enough, *bad* enough to take both these characters down. Take them *out*—just the way his father showed him— Now the big guy lunges at him. But like a phantom, Joey's no longer there. He lets out a laugh, but just a little. The next time the guy winds up, Joey decks him with an efficient right cross.

Standing back from the fray, the smaller guy watches. At first, he's quiet. Joey knows to be careful with small guys, quiet guys.

"Okay, man," the small guy says, "I think we gonna be leavin' now—" Helping his buddy up from the pavement, he turns to Joey. "Just gimme the bills, man—we'll leave this sorry-ass bitch alone—"

"Oh no," says Joey, "you lost your chance. Now, get the hell out, or I'll beat the shit outta both of you."

"I said give me the money."

"No way, man."

"I said give me the money."

"No way—"

The small man's eyes begin to widen—open to the point where the whites completely surround his pupils. Reaching into his waistband, he pulls out a gun. Hands together—he blasts Joey once in the chest.

The big man picks up the bills. Both thugs run out of the alley.

The skinny guy lies on the ground whimpering—Joey lies silent. He lies in front of his piece—his partially completed, beautiful piece. The wheel is a clock, and the clock has stopped before Joey can finish it the way he intended. Claiming the wall where his name, *DRAZ*, should be—a splattered mess of dark red blood.

26

"UCSC Graffiti Vandal Nabbed"
    In a bizarre twist, a long-time professor at UCSC was arrested early Sunday morning and charged with the graffiti vandalism of one of his own father's memorials. Dr. Alexander Arai of the Department of History of Art and Visual Culture was apprehended at the Porter College site of "Forever Manzanar." The memorial by well-known sculptor, Kazuo Arai, pays tribute to Japanese Americans interned in U.S. concentration camps during World War II. At the time of the arrest, it bore a freshly-painted 'tag' as well as the beginnings of what is believed to be an etched version. Several graffiti tools were found in Dr. Arai's possession.
    Campus police have been keeping an eye on the memorial ever since it was heavily 'bombed' three weeks ago with similarly painted tags. An investigation by police and the D.A.'s office has focused on the possibility of the initial incident being a hate crime. Yesterday's arrest seems to throw that contention out the window. In a statement released by the D.A., similar attacks on memorials by Kazuo Arai have turned up in various other parts of the country. "If related, the motive for these attacks remains unclear," notes one

official close to the investigation. "By all accounts, Dr. Arai has been a champion of his father's work over the years."

Other puzzling aspects involving Sunday's incident pertain to the physical and mental condition of the suspect. Dr. Arai appeared to be injured and somewhat dazed at the time of his arrest. He was initially taken to Dominican Hospital to be evalutated for a possible concussion. He was then transferred to the city jail and booked on suspicion of felony malicious mischief.

* * *

The house on Escalona Drive

*G*od—*you idiot,* he thinks to himself. *What a goddamn idiot,* he perseverates. Flat on his bed, or more accurately—lying in a disordered heap. Whatever the case, he feels terribly ill. Unable to curl himself up—no fetal position in this womb of his. Distant sounds—vague pulses from the falling stream outside. Something maternal about that sound. And so, he wonders—*who'll be taking care of me now?*

Spending time yearning for Whitney, he wishes he could see her, be with her—that special *twin* of his. But as vital as she's become, she can't function as *family* for him. Instead, he listens to the voice of the loving woman just outside the bedroom door. Someone else who's not technically family, but *should* be—

"Alex, honey—you've got to come out. I'm making some soup and toast—you'll feel better."

The words would console him, if he wasn't so ensnared in anxiety. Lisa, herself, has settled a bit since her initial barrage—

"You're WHERE, Alex?"

"You're WHAT?"

"Just hold on—I'll be driving back over the hill."

"Don't worry Hon—we'll post bail. You'll be out before the sun's up."

Then later—"What were you THINKING, Alex? You should have quit while you were ahead! You're going to lose everything now! You're going to lose EVERYTHING!"

But that was yesterday morning. Today, Lisa plans on staying home. She's canceled her whole work week, just as Alex seems hell-bent on cancelling his entire future.

"Come out, Hon—you need to eat sooner or later. And you need to return these calls, these emails from Carter and Nita. They're awfully worried about you."

Alex wants no contact with his friends just yet. It's a matter of supreme embarrassment. *What a fucking idiot I am!*

"All right—I'm going to look up some attorneys for you. The arraignment's set for four weeks."

Alex can't formulate a *thank you*— He's too busy anticipating the horrible backlash—that terrible consensus about to wash over him. So much for *Action Live.* Here he is, Professor Arai—the artistic creator of his own disaster. What is his father going to think? What about his mother? What about the university, *for godsake?* Funny how these questions strike him as novel. Funny how they managed to elude him for so long. But of course, he was beyond all that—*above* all that. He was so swept up in the size of his ideas, his plans—their implementation. He was so swept up with a kind of grandiosity he usually associates with his father. What a *disgusting thought* to contemplate—

"Hon—you might want to come out and check this out. It's a text to me from your brother. Says he's been trying to reach you since yesterday. Says to check your phone—check your emails. Something about your father—sounds important—"

"Last thing I need is to hear about my father." *And Henry— the last guy I'd want to talk to. Always the smart one—always the guy with the right answers.* Suddenly nauseous—*Oh God, of course— I bet he's found out about me—*

A weak autumn sun hangs over the house, dappling his retreat, his final bastion. Unable to respond to the pressing needs, he feels momentarily safe, somehow protected. After all, it was his *actions* that got him into trouble, not his thoughts per se. And now, inactivity feels so right—an indecisiveness that once kept him out of danger. He welcomes a sense of containment as he luxuriates in utter inertness. Once more, in the periphery—he hears Lisa's footsteps. This time they seem to fade. Now he detects the sound of a door opening—maybe the front door? A minute later, it's Lisa again—

"Alex honey—it's the police." With a voice turned grim—

"You better get up. They've got a search warrant. They're coming into our house."

✱ ✱ ✱

UCSC, Senior Studio

"Did you hear what happened to Professor Arai?" asks the female student with the shaved head.

"Oh yeah, I did," says her stubble-faced friend. "That was totally crazy—like what's he doing getting arrested for graf?"

"I took his class—the guy's good. But seriously—a professor tagging campus property—how awesome is that?"

Abandoning her easel, Whitney finds the *Courier's* website on her phone. *Shit, oh shit!* She would like to stay calm, but her skin betrays her—a tingling sensation of *embarrassment*. Even though the shame belongs strictly to Alex, for some reason—it feels like *hers* as well.

Exiting the building, she places a call to his cell. No response. Trying again, she struggles not to leave a message. It's just like the last time he left town—when he flew across country on his big mission. It feels like that, only so much worse. How long will she have to worry about him? How long will he be unreachable this time? She hates the loneliness of fretting over someone she can't contact, can't see. Someone who was close enough she could have sex with—make love to.

Back in the studio, no one's working. The students are all busy critiquing the behavior of Professor Arai. And the opinions are split roughly fifty-fifty—one half saying that the man is a *nutcase,* the other half saying—*how dope—how totally cool!*

Finding her station, she props herself atop the stool. Returning to her canvas, she stares into the green eyes of her latest subject—contemplates the unruly red hair. For the first time, she's chosen to paint a self-portrait. Not as an assignment—but because she wants to. She's decided to treat herself as an interesting, if not meaningful, subject of art. But this canvas is only one in a set of two portraits on which she's working. Whitney studies the one before her, knowing that the second exists on an easel back home. The separation of the two troubles her now—makes her feel split inside—like part of her is missing. To complement the face in front of her—the portrait of Alex Arai.

* * *

Mario's place, Soquel

Mario slams the paper to the floor—starts pacing to the extent the small room allows. Just a converted storage shack, devoid of any farm tools now. But Mario has a computer—the contemporary tool of choice. With its keyboard and screen, and especially all the *letters*. Strange how those trusty characters have led to so much trouble lately. That use of letters to create names—the misuse of letters to create *false* names. What's in a tag—what's in that painted alias? And, for that matter—what about his personal exclusion of tildes? Somehow, he's got to compose a way to save himself with those very same symbols. The police arrested Professor Arai. Soon enough a jury will convict him of a crime. And believing that Mario was key to the outcome, the professor will respond in kind—*rat* him out. So now that AWRY reverts to "Arai," Mario Patino becomes Mario Patiño once more.

Slumping at his desk, you'd think it would be easy to just tell the truth. Something about that old saying, that old *lie*—that the truth shall set a person free. Addressing his screen, Mario returns to what he was reading just before the paper arrived. *So—who is Jose Antonio Vargas?* The answer—*The man's a journalist, a Pulitzer Prize-winning journalist.* Not Latino—but Filipino. And until June of this year, he was leading the closeted life of an illegal alien. Mario studies the man's out-coming article in the *New York Times*.

Sympathizing—he's sick and tired of all the rhetoric surrounding immigration reform. He knows the rocky history of the federal DREAM Act. *No way will they ever pass it,* he mutters to himself. *Dreamers dream on—it'll never happen.* Last time the bill was considered, it was buried under the weight of filibusters—avalanches of more words, more letters.

Rising from his chair—Mario struggles to find a plan. Lies

and truth, truth and lies. All in the service of identity. The one you were born with, the one you create for yourself. The one you want to be known by—the one by which you'll be remembered. And lies and truth, equivalent tools—in the service of self-preservation.

*　*　*

Dear Al,

From all the media coverage, we hope you're doing okay. Please be assured you will always have our support. Call us whenever you'd like. We can do lunch, dinner, whatever. We'd also be happy to stop by.

Our love to you and Lisa always,
Carter & Nita

"Alex. Call me immediately. It's about Dad. Henry"

"Alex where are you? Call me. Henry"

"Alex—how in the *hell* did you get arrested? *Huge* embarrassment for the family. Tried talking to Mom, but she refused to believe it. Call me. Henry"

"Look Alex—Dad had a cerebral hemorrhage. Appears to be getting worse. PICK UP YOUR PHONE. Henry"

"PICK UP THE PHONE GODDAMMIT."

*　*　*

The house on Escalona Drive

It irks Alex. It irks him severely. Once more—Kazuo Arai manages to upstage him. Arrested by police? On the verge of losing career, livelihood—his reason for being? That's not good enough, it seems. As he teeters on the verge of professional and personal ruin, his heroic father lies dying in a Boise, Idaho hospital. And despite all the public humiliation, Alex finds an extra modicum of shame for thoughts like these. *My father, Kazuo Arai—the late, great sculptor. Oh God,* he slams himself— *how can you think like that? What's wrong—what kind of a man are you, anyway?* Through his newfound art, he successfully made an overdue statement—registered a complaint, corrected a wrong. His tags expressed his *true* feelings about his father's work. Sure he was furious—a lifetime of resentment kindled. But Alex didn't mean to *kill* Kaz. He didn't mean to *kill* his father.

There has to be something more to it—some other aspect to his feelings. Of course—that reaction he had when he caught the copycat tagger in the act. *It enraged me when that guy attacked my father. This fight—this struggle with my dad— It was "our thing"—not for anyone else.* In fighting for his father, for the both of them—he welcomes a feeling of connectedness with Kaz. A closeness that stirs a place incredibly deep. And suddenly, he admits to an impulse to shake his father's hand, embrace him, even. And it feels so foreign, so very strange—but welcome.

Scooting from his bed, Alex grabs the sandwich Lisa made, before she took leave for the day. Climbing to the loft, he enters a kind of jewel box steeped in soft gray light. He gazes through the picture window—searches out the bay. Then he dips a glance at the topmost leaves of the old oak tree. Alex remembers the expensive remodel that built this airy perch of a room. And he thinks about the towering giant he refused to cut down—so many years ago.

* * *

Seattle, Washington
December 7, 1941
10 p.m.

My diary begins today. I intend to continue writing until the day peace returns. I will keep writing until the
day when Japan and the United States shake hands

again. I keenly hope that day will come as soon as possible. As I envision the constant torment we will have to face, I see that we will need to be both extraordinarily courageous and patient. It will be a blessing if our family can somehow survive the grave difficulties that lie ahead. I put down my pen to reflect upon the situation. My heart is full to bursting. In a moment, we have lost all the value of our existence in this society. Not only have we lost our value, we're unwanted. It would be better if we didn't exist.

The cold wind of December did not blow directly on me until yesterday. It's now blowing right through me. Even the wind doesn't approve of our existence. I feel cold. So cold.

> Stricken on a journey,
> My dreams go wandering round
> Withered fields.

This poem comes to my mind. *Stricken on a journey...on a journey...on a journey. ...*After more than two decades, we believed this place had become a second home to us. Were we merely travelers on a journey all this time? I suppose we were. Or were we really?

—Kamekichi Tokita, Issei artist

＊＊＊

Horizon Airlines terminal, Boise Airport

Having registered his brother's calls, Alex can't seem to get to Boise fast enough. He's convinced he was the main factor in his father's demise—a trigger to a previously unnamed medical condition. Kazuo Arai—the man who harbored an arrogance both pneumatically and hydraulically treacherous. That—plus an aneurism at the base of his brain, a blood vessel ready to pop—one the doctors suspect might be familial. Under extreme pressure—the artery burst, releasing a deadly spray of red. Now the father lies comatose in the hospital. Brain scans detect smatters of activity—tiny deflections when approached by people he knows. And although Alex hates to think of himself at a time like this, he wonders—*could this happen to me?* And he wonders if maybe some terrible version already has—that due to his own grandiosity, his world has blown into pieces.

The UC Committee on Privilege and Tenure has placed him on indefinite leave. Pending the outcome of the legal case, he has too much time for his thoughts. He feels like he's going to court today—facing arraignment before a judge, before his father. He's about to hear the charges, only this time—the magistrate can't speak. Today seems more like a matter of sentencing.

Outside, the snow-laced Sawtooth Mountains crest like a wave behind the city. From the sweep of the highway, downtown Boise looks quaintly small for its spacious setting. His rental car strikes him both bland and unobtrusive—save for the faint smell of cigarettes. And the scent now reminds him of Whitney—even though she doesn't smoke. It's more the suggestion of something combustible, burning—something that leaves traces of itself no matter how hard one tries to extinguish it. Not that he wants to.

Arriving at St. Alphonsus, he jogs to the entrance, a stream of second-hand breath trailing behind. In the lobby, an emotional heaviness overtakes him, a heaviness that grows until he finally identifies it as *dread*. He stands in front of the elevators for what becomes a long time.

Third floor, ICU—Alex approaches the station. "It's my father—he's here on the unit. He's suffered a cerebral hemorrhage."

This is old news for the lanky young nurse. With her long dark hair and angular frame, she reminds him of Lisa. Per her instructions, he finds a row of glass panels fronting the patient's rooms. Collecting himself, he heads for the one marked *3212*.

Clearing his breath, Alex enters. Two steps in, the imagery explodes in his face. Head of a man that looks like his father. Odd colors—the skin sallow under harsh fluorescence. Neatly combed hair, but parted bizarrely down the middle. Eyes closed—how unusual. Prominent brows—something familiar to grasp onto. And, swarming about the head—all manner of devices for keeping a dead person alive. Cords, lines, hanging fluids—a tube thrust down the man's throat—forcing air. And a persistent hiss emits from the bedside machine, along with the constant beeping above. A telemetry screen perched on high, monitors proof of residual life—justifies the commotion about the bed.

With a murmur of excitement, Alex's mother stands. In a quick aside, he nods in return—his eyes still trained on his father. *Where to begin?* he asks himself. Hadn't he prepared an official statement? Alex—so meticulous in planning, so particular in dispensing verbiage. And now, his speech escapes him. He has no words to give—offers only a lengthening silence. Nothing in his jumbled mind can spark his inert mouth—the normally facile connection failing him.

Finally—"Dad.... Dad, it's me. It's me—Alex, Alexander." The only truthful thing he can say in the moment. After a stretch of painful dumbness, he takes a seat beside his mother.

Alex spends the rest of the day in the cramped room with his parents. The hours pass in silence—a familiar, *familial* silence. Several times, he rises—walks to his father's side. He wants to engage, but ends up just staring. He can only observe the disturbing specter of his father's face. All the same features, but lacking cohesion. The coma causes the pieces to drift apart, then collide—resulting in a fractured display. And the man's hands—disconnected, un-tethered—two small fragments floating on the bed, the same color as his face. And Alex feels responsible for this horrible installation—feels guilty for transporting his father here. Feels guilty for having reinterned his father just down the road from Minidoka. In a moment of escape, his mind scrambles in the pursuit of additional meaning. He feels like an involuntary prop in a Kienholtz assemblage. Like the one memorializing an abortion scene—or the one involving fornication in the back seat of a Dodge— *Oh, cut the references,* as Whitney might say.

Once more, Alex sits. Once more, he climbs back out of his chair. Standing at the foot of the bed—the right words seem no more accessible. He remains at full attention as his legs begin to ache. Forcing himself to stand straight, he looks his father directly into his lid-covered eyes. What he wants to say is—*Dad, I'm sorry you're in this bad way— I'm sorry I put you through all this suffering— I'm sorry I'm the one who tagged all your memorials. Sorry I hated you for the way you treated me—all my life, as if I had no value of my own. I'm sorry we couldn't spend more time knowing that—we're like each other, in certain ways.*

And through a mist of hospital vapors, a mist of disbelief—maybe Alex hears himself saying exactly those words aloud. And he sees his father as a child now—the displaced child. He sees the small boy who roamed the dusty camp in Minidoka. And Alex feels profoundly *bad* for what he's done.

"Guess I can't ask you to forgive me. It's way too late now. And what about me forgiving you? Probably not even the right question. How can I talk about forgiving you, after I punished you like this? I did the same thing, you know—used *our people* for my own purposes, used them in order to get to you—"

And Alex imagines the young boy with crayons in hand—drawing vivid pictures in the desert. He imagines the boy following his own, evolving line—asserting his name all over the otherwise worthless scraps of paper. He would like to say, *I love you Dad*, but this—he doesn't hear coming from his mouth. Maybe it's because it's difficult to feel that way right now. Or maybe it's because Japanese people never say things like that, or maybe—it's just *him.*

He reaches out to touch his father's hands—wonders if this is the first time he's ever done so. Neither warm nor cold, the hands reflect one final, fragile transition. Pulling back, Alex returns to sit beside his mother. His mother appears so stiff and astonished—like someone rendered in exclamation marks. She's heard all the words spoken by her son—all the words meant for her husband. She looks both shocked and angry at Alex, but doesn't address him directly. Standing, she walks to her husband's side.

"*Ganbatte ne!*" she says to him in a firm voice. "Do your best—don't give up."

Downtown Santa Cruz

*A*lex sits before the polished mahogany slab. As a new client, he's grateful for the airy space—so much larger than his own office. The framed prints on his attorney's walls are all reproductions—mostly abstractions. Judging from the angular Mondrian, she must be a linear thinker. Then again, the bright yellow grid of the painting lends a frenetic energy to the work. Behind her analytic prowess must be a lively spirit drawn to dance. The title of the work is *Broadway Boogie Woogie*. No doubt, the attorney loves jazz and swing—loves New York City. Hopefully she knows something about art—maybe a lot. Anything for a genuine connection—

While lost in his little projective test, the door opens. In walks a stately woman in her late forties, wearing a smart gabardine pant suit. Horn-rimmed glasses project a certain bookishness—the slash of bangs subverts the softness of her honey-colored hair.

Trying too hard to break the ice—"I like your artwork— looks like you're drawn to Neo-Plasticism. As you probably know—that was Mondrian's bird's-eye take on New York City taxis in traffic."

With a hint of a smile, the attorney responds—"You *must* be kidding. You can ask my partner on the choice of artwork.

I confess—I'm more the literary type." Extending a hand, she introduces herself as Helen Strickland.

Alex—"I truly appreciate you taking my case."

Settling at her desk, she opens a manila folder—scans a set of documents. "So, how have you been holding up these past few weeks?"

"Oh, it's all new to me. I've never been in trouble with the law before, ever— The possible consequences scare me to death."

"Well, you certainly are a respected professor on campus—for quite a while, it seems. How have you liked living in Santa Cruz?"

"I love it here, and for the record—I'd really like to stay."

Returning her attention to the papers, Ms. Strickland reads aloud the charge of malicious mischief—reviews the police report with him. "So," she asks, "what have you got to say about this?"

"Well—technically it's all correct. I mean, the officer found me in front of my father's memorial. I had those items on me, or they were on the ground. I was dazed, but still managed to cooperate. After that, they took me to the hospital. Of course, I denied having anything to do with vandalizing the sculpture. I was actually trying to protect it from this guy—this tagger. I just happened to surprise him that night—"

"Can you describe for me how he looked?"

"He was on the tallish side—long arms and legs. Some facial hair, I think. It was dark and we were scuffling—so I didn't get a great look at his face. Something about his nose being big. And his hair was pretty scraggly, I'd say."

Alex assumes Ms. Strickland will challenge his story—try to poke holes in it. The attorney does nothing of the sort—doesn't ask any other pointed questions, doesn't even comment on Alex's account. Instead, she simply nods while he speaks, as if she agrees with everything he's saying.

After he finishes, she explains the scope of her professional services—details the financial arrangement for payment. She asks him to sign the necessary papers for her representation. The attorney says she will need more time to investigate the case—will see what the prosecution has. She says her office will call to schedule the next appointment.

Briefly, Ms. Strickland smiles at her new client. Taking this as a cue, Alex tries to wedge himself in a bit more. He wants to know his attorney better as a person, a human being—wants her to know him. Wants more the feeling of a mutual partnership.

"Well," he says—"for what it's worth, a nice piece by Paul Klee would look great in that corner over there." Pointing—

Smiling again, the attorney shakes her head—collects the papers and slides them back into their folder. Standing, she reaches out her hand once more. She tells Alex how pleased she is to have met him, and how she will do her best to represent his interests.

Alex rises—measures himself against this woman, this woman who's roughly his height. Taking her hand, he notes the strength of her grip. He tries to imagine her dancing, maybe ballroom dancing—something that involves a coordinated pair. He tries to imagine dancing with her—understands full well, who must lead.

✳ ✳ ✳

Alex—

I remember, Lisa got a great position at Xerox, while I was still struggling. We lived in a little apartment in Mountain View—kind of like being in the dorms again. One big difference—Lisa was supporting the both of us. I felt bad—completely dependent on her, and I didn't like it. She was very understanding, though. So much enthusiasm in that girl—happy with her new job, happy to be back in the Bay Area—happy to be back with me.

Then, at the beginning of '89, I received some really great news. I was offered a position at UCSC, and there I was—my first step to becoming a professor. Oh sure, we celebrated—took a jaunt over Highway 17 to Santa Cruz. Back in college, Lisa and I had driven there several times in Rhoda Rambler.

So, the question came up about where to live. Not much of a discussion really. Lisa said she wouldn't mind moving to Santa Cruz because it was such a pretty town. She also said she could handle the commute. I felt like the two of us were stretching out as a couple. Like we were claiming new ground—new territory. She had Silicon Valley, and I had the coast, and between us—we had both.

At first, we lived downtown—one of those little granny units that've multiplied out of control. Fun neighborhood—close to the Pacific Garden Mall. Anyway, we spent our weekends exploring the town—got a feel for the Westside and the Eastside of things. We also went on long hikes in the beautiful redwood forests nearby.

One day, we drove up the coast past Davenport. We were heading up Highway 1 to Pescadero and San Gregorio Beach. But I saw this sports car slow down in front of us—took a left into a parking lot hidden by a curtain of trees. I thought, *why not—let's check it out.* As I hit the brakes, Lisa's hands flew up to the dash. We started laughing as I made a sharp turn. *Full of surprises today*, she might have said.

The place was called Greyhound Rock, and the parking lot was nearly empty. What we discovered was a little gem—one easily missed by fast-moving traffic. On a high bluff were picnic tables that looked out on a spectacular view of the coast. To the left, a large cove welcomed a festive procession of waves to the shore. In the center of the view rose the long smooth hump of Greyhound Rock—sleek as its name.

Lisa was all excited at the discovery and so was I. We grabbed our stuff and headed down a steep trail to the beach below. Reaching the sand, I dropped the picnic basket and started running. Lisa gave chase, and each time she tried to grab me—I managed to break away. Finally, I turned and hit the ground—wrapped my arms around her legs and tackled her. We rolled around for quite a while—wrestled in the soft, warm sand—sand in our hair and down our shirts, up our shorts—everywhere. Sitting up, she laughed hard—said we looked like a couple of gingerbread people, covered in sugar. *Sweets for the sweet*, I think I said. Lisa called me her *sweetie pie*. We got up and brushed the sand off each other's lips—shared a sweet kiss.

Then, she took my hand and led me to where the water met with some rocky grooves that fell from the back of Greyhound Rock. The tide pools were teeming with creatures. Barnacles, mussels, limpets—a purple star fish, a red one. We stepped lightly over the pools, careful not to slip on the kelp and seaweed. Then Lisa pointed high to her left and said, *Let's climb the rock!* Normally this would terrify me—that rock—some sixty feet high and a couple hundred feet long. Made of shale—judging by the crumbly shards that so easily split off from the next layer below—

But in that moment, I realized something—something about my feelings for Lisa, feelings that had grown so slowly over time. And it was such a surprise to discover them—the fact they were so *big*. And so I trusted her to lead me up this hulking mass of unstable rock, until I finally peeled my eyes off that small patch of footing I kept before me. Looking around, it was like I was standing atop a mountain in the middle of the sea. Or, I was standing on a continent—the narrow spine of some great continental divide. The wind swirled all about. I held Lisa close as if I were protecting her—keeping her upright, when I really needed her to do that for me. And to one side was the cove, the beach and the cliffs of the California coastline. And to the other side was a sudden drop into the surging ocean. And the fear suddenly dissipated—gone like the marine layer that tends to obscure everything from sight.

After a long while, a long bracing while, Lisa and I climbed back down from the rock. We re-crossed the fertile tide pools. Famished, we devoured our lunch. I lay back—must have fallen asleep. When I came to, I saw her sitting in front of a large pile of dampened sand. She was concentrating hard. She was building a big sand castle— Right then and there, I just nodded to myself. Right then and there, I knew it was time to make another commitment. The next couple weeks, Lisa and I continued our trek through Santa Cruz. But this time, we were looking with a realtor.

* * *

The house on Escalona Drive

"Come to bed, Hon—"

"Oh really? First you tried to get me out of bed—and now you want me back in?"

"It's the daytime, nighttime thing, Alex. You know—sunrise, sunset."

"Doesn't seem to make any difference. Can't get away from my thoughts."

"Well—everyone's got to get some rest, sometime."

"But the mess I've made—for both of us. It's not funny, but in a few more months, maybe a year—we'll be back in the same place we were twenty-some years ago."

"What do you mean?"

"I mean—I'll be sans job again. I'll be broke. I'll be living with you, depending on you to support me."

"I guess we'll just have to make do."

"I wonder if it means I won't be a professor anymore. Of course, I'll still have my diplomas and all. But functionally—I'll no longer enjoy that special position up on the hill.

"You'll still have your books, your articles—"

"Oh yes—books and articles, those arcane little memorials. My father used bronze and glass—I used paper. And now the paper has turned into electronic texts—something even less tangible."

"You'll still be leaving quite a legacy—both of you will."

"And a part of mine has to do with him. Now that I've pretty much done away with the old man."

"You didn't mean to—"

"Well, it doesn't matter. Mom and Henry—they must hate me now."

"Look Alex—anyone who knows your father would understand your feelings about him. On some level, your mom and brother have to empathize. Things are just too raw right now. Anyways, it's late—time to sleep—"

"But I'm afraid. I keep getting bad dreams."

"How about we just cuddle some?"

"That would be nice, even though I feel like a burden to you."

"Well, now's not the time to worry about that—you need your rest. Come on, Hon—just come to bed."

28

Downtown Santa Cruz

*C*ontrary to her previous denial, Ms. Strickland is something of an artist today. She stands beside a pad of paper set on a metal easel. She directs her client to its clean white surface—a kind of blank canvas the two will share. The attorney brandishes a black marker—confidently slashes Alex's name at the top of the page.

Nice hand style, he smiles to himself—*good pen control. Would probably be great with a spray can.* Yes, Ms. Strickland is a practiced artist—has done this many times before. She works with concepts—is a *conceptual* artist. She starts with all the circumstantial evidence against her client. *Pieces of evidence—like found objects in art.* Of no intrinsic value, they lie about—until someone declares them of interest. And now the attorney flips the page—regroups the evidence on a fresh sheet. She arranges it so that the two can create meaning together. And meaning will not be a simple matter of black and white, but will require interpretation and legalistic flare.

The attorney wants to tell a story with the so-called facts—the same story Alex wants the jury to hear and believe. For this to happen, the two must shape the evidence—steer the narrative in the direction of innocence. As he views the darkening pad, Alex feels skeptical at best. The attorney says this is just a start. By devising enough plausible counters to the evidence, they can remove each piece in turn—having literally explained it away. And over time, each subsequent page will grow less encumbered. And in the end, they will achieve the effect they want—a perfectly clean sheet or *slate*, as it were.

Alex keeps his own notes. In working with the attorney, he finds one part of their interaction quite strange. With all that's been garnered from the police, he keeps waiting—waiting for her to ask him certain questions. Alex wonders—*When does she hit me with that point-blank query—"Did you do all this?"* Listing the various cross-country crimes—*when will she demand to hear "the whole truth and nothing but"?* Doesn't an attorney need to know the actual truth? Doesn't she need to know what honestly happened?

The black marks continue to grow. Beneath his name—

Local evidence

1. Arrested on site

2. Black hoodie

3. Spray can of Montana 94

4. Screwdrivers x 2

5. Artist's stylus

6. Fresh tag of *AWRY*

7. Gouge on memorial surface

8. Fingerprints on all items above

9. Second set of prints on spray can

10. Previous photos of *AWRY* on campus

Elsewhere

1. N.Y.C. report of tagging—vague video of 'white man in black hoodie'

2. D.C. photos of *AWRY* tag, video of a man in black hoodie

3. L.A. photos of *AWRY/MPG*

4. Minidoka photos of *AWRY*

Ms. Strickland says Alex's case pertains solely to his arrest in Santa Cruz. The D.A. can only pursue the local charge of felony malicious mischief. The other crimes involve different jurisdictions—each with the power to consider legal action separately. Somewhat relieved, he asks the attorney why the other cities still appear on the list of evidence. She says the prosecution will look for *similars*—similar crimes in order to establish a modus operandi, or M.O. By defining a signature pattern of criminal activity, the D.A. will make the case for a single perpetrator. Should Alex's case fit that pattern, it will be easier to persuade the jury of his guilt in the local matter.

The attorney continues her list—

Results of subsequent search warrants

1. Nothing on personal computer except drafts of essays on the 911 memorial in N.Y. and M.L.K. memorial in D.C.

2. No incriminating calls on personal cell phone, land line, UCSC phone records.

3. Credit card account shows purchase of round-trip plane tickets to N.Y., L.A. and Boise, all within the past three months. Records also reveal round-trip train ticket from N.Y. to D.C. and hotel bills from all four cities.

Keeping pace with the attorney, Alex feels overwhelmed with the work taking shape in front of him. The theme of the evolving story clearly looks like *guilt* to him. He suspects Ms. Strickland must surely believe he's the perp behind all the vandalism. And yet—she never inquires into his possible involvement. When he asks the attorney to assess his case, she says it will be a *challenge*.

✷ ✷ ✷

Mario's place, phone call to San Francisco

"Oh, I'm sorry—maybe I dialed wrong—"

"Like, what do you want?" asks a scratchy, female voice.

"Well, I'm trying to reach this guy I know."

"Oh—you tryin' to reach my Joey?"

"Joey Militich?"

"That would be him—"

"Well thanks—I'm a friend of his. My name's Mario. Is Joey there, please?"

"If you're askin' me that—I guess you ain't heard."

"Heard what?"

"Joey, my baby—he was found dead."

"What? What are you saying?"

"It's true, it's true. I been cryin' like this for a week now—"

"What happened?"

"The cops—they found him, over in the Mission."

"So—what did they say?"

"Said Joey was in this alley—was gettin' up this piece. Was gonna be special, Joey told me— Some punk musta came up and shot him. Murdered him!"

"Oh no—I'm SO sorry—"

"A fuckin' bullet. One fuckin' bullet— Oh God, oh God!"

"Excuse me—but, did anyone see it happen?"

"Nah, there's nobody seen it go down—"

"Does anyone know what the reason was?"

"The cops—they think it was a hold-up. Somethin' to do with drugs, probably. Thing is—Joey never had much cash. Even so, they still gone and killed him—killed him for what? My poor baby, my baby—Joey...."

"I feel so bad stirring things up—"

"Nah, nah—don't you worry. I been needin' to say somethin'—needin' to talk. Joey, you know—he ain't got no family left."

"Yeah, he told me some interesting stuff about his life."

"Like growin' up. Him and his mom—him and his dad. His grandpa bein' messed up cuz of the war—"

"I know he fought a lot just to survive."

"Well, my baby—he was a sweet guy too—no angel, mind you. Me and him—we both had our share of tough times."

"It took a lot of courage. And he found something he liked to do."

"Sure loved his writin'—Joey did. He was an artist, no doubt about it."

"Oh yeah—a really terrific artist."

"Can't get over this—can't get over the pain. And it's like—it even makes my leg worse, too. I got this sciatica thing—goes down my whole leg, you know what I'm sayin'? Got disability for it—but it's just about killin' me now."

"I'm truly sorry—it sounds terrible."

"Gotta get me some help, that's all I know. Gotta get me some relief—"

"Look, I better go now. Again, I'm sorry to hear about you losing Joey."

"Like I said, it's fine you called. Glad he had friends. By the way—what was you gonna say to him—what was you gonna say to my Joey?"

"Oh, it wasn't much really— I just wanted to talk to him. I was going to ask Joey about a favor, that's all—"

***

Downtown Santa Cruz

Alone, composing her legal argument, Ms. Strickland enjoys creating a story—something even whimsical in the telling.
...*Let's try this for a title*—

"Alexander Arai and his Doppelganger"
Main characters—
1. Professor Alexander Arai
2. Kazuo Arai
3. The District Attorney
4. Helen Strickland, attorney at law
5. The Doppelganger

...*How about this*—?
[Once upon a time] there lived a highly esteemed professor of Modern Western Art. His name was Alexander Arai, and he worked in an [ivory tower] on the campus of the University of California, Santa Cruz. Dr. Arai had impeccable character and was a well-respected academic. Of special significance, he composed numerous critiques in homage to his father, the

sculptor Kazuo Arai. As a true and loyal [vassal] to his father, Dr. Arai served with distinction over the years.

A few weeks ago, at Porter College, an [evil] graffiti vandal attacked Kazuo Arai's beloved memorial, *Forever Manzanar.* Dr. Arai was working late that night. As he left his [chambers], he surprised the vandal in the very act of desecration. While the professor tried to protect the sculpture, the vandal—described as a *tallish, scraggly-haired man*—brutally assaulted him. This violent attack led to a blow to Dr. Arai's head and a momentary [trance] or [spell]. When the professor awoke, campus [minions] mistook him for the actual vandal and falsely arrested him.

...The nature of the case against Professor Arai— Time to get serious now.

The District Attorney cites several items found on Dr. Arai's person or in the general vicinity of the crime. The D.A. also cites evidence from crime scenes in other parts of the country. The D.A. will contend that similar features link all these incidents together. By establishing a modus operandi, the D.A. can point to a single perpetrator. Should similar features be found in Dr. Arai's case, the D.A. will argue that he *is* that perpetrator, guilty of the crime in Santa Cruz.

...All right, so—

Dr. Arai was arrested at the scene wearing what is described as a black hoodie. Just because a similar garment was spotted on surveillance video at other sites does not mean that Dr. Arai is a graffiti vandal in Santa Cruz. One might ask, *What exactly is a black hoodie?* Certainly the term bears negative connotations of street urchins and gang bangers. Beyond that, such a garment is quite generic and ubiquitous. At the time of his arrest, it was cold outside. Dr. Arai was wearing an appropriate piece of clothing, namely a black-hooded cotton wrap. Furthermore, it should be noted that the vandal seen on one video was described as *a white man.* Clearly now, Dr. Arai is not white.

A can of purple spray paint was also recovered at the local site. True, Dr. Arai's fingerprints were found on the can, but were minimal compared to the overwhelming preponderance of a second set of prints. Dr. Arai states that during his struggle with the true vandal, he attempted to wrest the can away, thus, appropriating it. A fresh graffiti tag was found on the memorial, a tag bearing the letters, *A, W, R, Y.* Various versions of the same tag have been photographed at other sites. According to the D.A., the gouge on the surface of the memorial is an attempt to permanently deface the work. Judging from photos, the mark proves much too crude to be of any artistic or expressive value.

Dr. Arai was using a metal implement in order to defend himself. Although he cannot clearly remember, he believes the sculpture was harmed when he was thrown against it. As for the possession of the two screwdrivers, Dr. Arai was simply returning home after some minor repairs at his office. Beyond that, the artist's stylus only highlights the fact that Dr. Arai is an artist himself. It should be noted that nowhere else is a metal tool implicated in the defacement of the other memorials.

As for expense records seized during the investigation, several charges for plane tickets and hotel stays were noted. The destinations appear to coincide with the sites of other acts of vandalism referenced by the prosecution. Dr. Arai maintains he traveled across the country in order to conduct research on various memorials. Entries found on his computer represent actual drafts of scholarly work on two of the most important memorial sites.

...Of course—the issue of motive.

The D.A. has so far been unable to establish a motive for Dr. Arai committing the crime with which he has been charged. What reason could compel Dr. Arai to deface his father's memorial on the professor's very own UCSC campus? What reason could compel him, as inferred by the D.A., to attack his father's memorials in other parts of the country? Throughout his career, Dr. Arai has been a staunch champion of his father's work. One could go so far as to say that Kazuo Arai's success is due in no small part to his son's scholarship. Unfortunately, Mr. Arai has fallen seriously ill and will not be able to testify on his son's behalf.

...So, in conclusion—

Why would a tenured professor in art history engage in such a ridiculous crime, directed at a father he so clearly loves and admires? As the D.A. contends, it may be possible to establish an M.O. regarding the serial vandalizing of Kazuo Arai's memorials. However, the M.O. fails to fit Dr. Arai in any way, but for his choice of clothing on a cold Santa Cruz night. Any M.O. the D.A. establishes points to a different person as the perpetrator. Clearly, it points to the tall, scraggly-haired assailant described by Dr. Arai. It points to a man with nothing to lose, a person with a vendetta against the Japanese or Japanese American people, someone who possibly harbors a vendetta against Kazuo Arai and even perhaps, the professor himself. It is clear that Dr. Arai is not the perpetrator of a crime, but an actual hero having protected his father's work at the cost of a brutal physical attack. He is also the foil in an unfortunate case of mistaken identity by the police. Far from being a criminal, Dr. Alexander Arai is the actual victim here.

...And finally, jury willing—

After I, Helen Strickland, vanquish the D.A. [the all-powerful smiter of graffiti], Dr. Arai will return to the university, [and live happily ever after].

The End.

* * *

Center Street, downtown Santa Cruz

Like bobbing in water, bruised by currents. Whitney feels completely adrift—a hundred miles from shore. And it's odd, because she's completely immersed in crowds of people today. Wednesday afternoon at the farmers market—a definite time and place, a definite *here*. But all of the people, all their clothes— all the bags they're carrying, all their hair— Everything runs together. Everything ebbs and flows in her vision—everything gets blurry. And what about her own clothes—her own dirty jeans, her crumpled tee? Maybe it's her green down jacket that allows her to stay afloat. But the dream-like thing is happening again. Her body remembers—retrieves sensations from the distant past. She'd like to know the meaning of it all, but she's too busy righting her capsized self.

The long rows of tables—the posts and awnings. Wherever she looks, they're the only structures stable enough to call to her. As solid as sections of coastline, like friendly beaches. But she can't get help as people tumble—a brush here, a nudge there. She can't get to those steady shores covered with the produce, berries, fruits, and breads she needs to save herself. Her hands reach out—arms outstretched as if trying to swim to shelter. With no true course, she flounders in the midst of an ocean, lost at sea.

And as the sun starts to set through threatening clouds, it dawns on her—how alone she is. In the middle of chaos, how completely alone. And she wants to grab at the sun—wants to raise herself, raise her arms so the sun can somehow pick her up. And there's something familiar in all this—a repeat of long ago times. She knows it now—can feel it. Somehow, she's been a *bad girl* again—a *very* bad girl. Maybe it was the fuss she made— Maybe she cried too loud out of hunger—or maybe she refused to eat. Maybe her stomach hurt—maybe she just needed changing. But nothing she imagines can account for what consumes her. She feels so sad, so terribly *guilty*—it feels like she must have *killed* someone. That's *crazy* thinking she tells herself, but she can't let go of the thought. It's like a long rope cast in her direction, but no one's holding the other end. So now it's her turn to be punished—her turn to be left behind, to drown in a horrible riptide of fear.

And the sun goes away, she knows. It always goes away. The sun goes away—leaves her behind. The red-haired sun finally abandons her. And then it gets cold and black.

* * *

Mario's place, Soquel

Mario sits at his table.

Mario writes.

Outside, the December sky shines a bright, bright blue.

The sun is a flash. The bay looks spotless—a metallic sheen in the distance. The power plant fifteen miles away lifts its smokestacks into the air. The big wind— Sometimes the sound proves steady. Sometimes the sound is a surge. Sometimes the surge up the canyon is like the surf. The surf is an extension of the ocean—a shove of sound, the break and crash of acoustic waves. The wind forces the beachhead back—thrusts the beachhead up to a place hundreds of feet above the bay. This is new territory for the frothing air, the blustery ocean. The slim eucalyptus bends then springs back straight. The cluttered oak trees shimmy. Frayed manzanita sway, then wrench— A tinkling sound, a crackling. The snap of a limb, like the shot of a gun—a scattering effect. Nectarine trees from an abandoned orchard hold firm to the slant of a canyon. The trees ripple, a wave of supple greenery rises to the crest of hills, then the wave repeats. For a brief moment, everything goes still, goes silent. Then the invisible charge of weather starts once more. Reaches far inland—clutching and receding. Reaching, advancing— Grasping again at all loose ends, tearing apart anything not rooted to the ground.

Mario sits at his table.

Mario writes and writes. Mario writes in concert with the wind—writes at the speed of the wind—writes to the rhythm of the wind—

"What is crime and what is not?
What is justice? I think I forgot!"

—lyric from "Squeeze the Trigger"
Ice-T

"What is crime? What is not?
What is art? I think I forgot!!!"

—text from "Crime" piece
PHAZE 3

* * *

Santa Cruz County Courthouse

For the third straight day, it threatens rain. Alex passes through security as if it were routine. What's different this time is he's come alone—Lisa unable to skip another crucial meeting at work. As he skirts the crowd outside the courtroom, two young women break free to accost him.

Cell phones extended—"Professor Arai, did you really tag your father's sculpture? What was your reason for doing it? Were you the tagger who also—"

Pushing past, he barges through the courtroom door. What seems like an escape now feels like a trap. He fixes on the judge's stand—still backed by the state and national flags. The bookshelves on the left seem to loom even higher. The jury box on the right looks even more ominous. His eyes settle on the two large tables in the space between. Descending the aisle, he passes rows of curious onlookers. Opening the vestigial knee-high gate, he heads for the right-side table, the one where his attorney parses papers.

As directed, Alex takes a seat. *Everyone's laughing at me,* he thinks—such a culturally determined, kneejerk reaction. He repeatedly tugs at his blue tie—adjusts the lapels of the sincerest suit he owns. Once again, Alex looks sharp, but hopefully not *too* sharp. He desires the jury's respect, not their suspicion. He craves their sympathy, not some deep-seated distrust of the intellectual and cultural elite.

A tall young man represents the District Attorney's office. It surprises Alex when the man leaves his post and heads in his direction. Crossing what should be an inviolate line, the man now stands before the defense table. He actually speaks to Ms. Strickland, as she rises from her chair. *What about boundaries?* Alex wonders. What about *us* versus *them?* To his horror, the two attorneys stray in the direction of the judge's empty stand. They whisper to each other—share a laugh. Such strange intimacies between adversaries. What's Ms. Strickland doing—cavorting with the enemy? As they stand in tandem, the two appear almost identically dressed. Sharply tailored, matching suits—clothes which look, for all purposes, cut from the same cloth. The visual affinity between the attorneys makes them look like members of the same club. *They can't be in cahoots, can they?*

The overhead fluorescence drenches the room with an intense light. Quickly now, the bailiff crosses the floor—opens the door to the right of the judge's stand. In walk the twelve jurors—the most important people in the entire courtroom. Alex studies this group of everyday people—this jury of his peers. And who exactly are his peers? Six men and six women—a full spread of adult ages, ten white and two Latino. No blacks, no Asians. Funny how he thinks about race in this context.

During jury selection, Ms. Strickland had asked an older Japanese woman if she had any reservations taking part in this case. The woman had responded *no.* Ms. Strickland asked—*The fact that this case involves a Japanese American man charged with vandalizing a Japanese American memorial—does that make it more difficult for you to be unbiased?* Again, she answered *no.* Ms. Strickland asked the woman if she had any family members who were incarcerated in U.S. concentration camps during World War II. The woman responded with a litany of names. Pressed further, she said that one of her uncles had served as a member of the Military Intelligence Service—had acted as a translator for U.S. forces in the Pacific. Upon further questioning, she said that her husband was a member of the Congress of Japanese Americans, and that they received the monthly J.A. Veterans Group newsletter. Finished, Ms. Strickland thanked the woman for her cooperation, then used one of her peremptory challenges to excuse her.

Now the bailiff asks for everyone to rise. From the door to the left, the judge enters—a wiry man in a black robe—chin tilted up. Taking his seat, he addresses the court in the matter of "The State versus Dr. Alexander Arai." The judge's voice sounds firm and paternal. It's a voice that projects authority without ever resorting to volume. Alex can't help but have mixed feelings about a man who could be his father's contemporary.

The judge instructs the jury on matters of procedure and rules of law. He then asks the attorneys if they're prepared to deliver opening statements. Over the course of several minutes, Alex listens to the prosecutor as he presents the gist of the state's case against him.

Approaching the jury's box, the attorney deliberately paces back and forth before turning to engage the jurors. With one outstretched hand he begins—"Folks—the defendant shouldn't have done it. He shouldn't have vandalized his father's beloved memorial up on the UCSC campus. He shouldn't have taken a spray can and defiled this tribute to Japanese Americans wrongly imprisoned in U.S. concentration camps during World War II. But the defendant did exactly that. He took a can of purple spray paint and wrote a cryptic version of his name on that beautiful bronze and glass sculpture. He did what so many criminals have done not only in Santa Cruz, but in towns and cities across this country. He did what so many other vandals do—he tagged a piece of property that wasn't his.

"And what exactly is a *tag* you might ask? A tag is the ugliest, most disgusting version of the graffiti writer's so-called craft. It's a signature—it's his name. It's what we find sprayed all over abandoned or derelict properties. It's what we find on highway structures, on legitimate businesses—on homes even. Tags invite crime, the criminal element. They often represent gangs. There's nothing good for a community or neighborhood when tags start showing up.

"And not only did the defendant use spray paint on that night six weeks ago, he went so far as to leave a gash in the side of his father's memorial. A gash produced by one of two screwdrivers found on his person at the time of arrest.

"But that's not all, folks. No—not by a great stretch. You see, the prosecution has compiled evidence from four other sites across the country—evidence that four other memorials by the defendant's father have been defaced with the very same tag. Yes, folks—this is big. Bigger than just Santa Cruz. By pointing out similarities in these crimes, we will demonstrate a modus operandi—a pattern of criminal behavior, that points to a single perpetrator. And that perpetrator is Alexander Arai. *Why?* you might ask. *Why would a university professor engage in such criminal acts against his own father? What could possibly be the motive?* Even if the reasons remain unclear—experience tells us that some of the most heinous crimes occur between people who are closest to each other.

"We can only prosecute the defendant on the local matter. But in bringing him to justice in Santa Cruz, we can help provide closure to those other offences as well. And that is exactly what I will attempt to do as we complete this trial. Once again, I will stand before you and ask that you find the defendant, Alexander Arai, guilty of the crime of felony malicious mischief. Thank you."

Alex doesn't like what he's just heard. Adding to the humiliation, he doesn't like being so forcefully confronted—defined. Knowing the entire truth, he can't help but be swayed by the attorney's words. And he knows full well his father is more a victim than anyone here could ever imagine. How can anyone protect Alex, when even he feels like throwing himself at the mercy of the court?

Now, Ms. Strickland steps before the jury. She strolls the length of the box while making eye contact with each of the twelve jurors. In response, some sit straighter while others lean forward.

"Members of the jury—the D.A. has got it all wrong. As you will see, Dr. Alexander Arai, a man of impeccable character, a highly respected academic—did not commit the crime with which he has been charged. The defense will show that another individual was at the crime scene, and was—in fact—the actual vandal—"

Glancing up, Alex winces at the overhead lights—the fluorescent downpour growing. His mind bounces all about for a way to escape. Off in the periphery, he registers a muffled voice—

"The presence of the *tall, scraggly-haired* assailant will introduce much more than reasonable doubt—"

Staring at the judge—Alex can't read his expression. Darting to the flags, his vision climbs to a set of windows up high.

"By the end of this trial, you will rightfully conclude— Professor Arai is not the perpetrator of a hateful crime, but an actual hero...."

Alex wants to bolt out the small wooden gate behind him— rush up the aisle splitting the audience in two. He wants to flee the courtroom—charge down the halls. He wants to run out of the courthouse into the streets. It seems only Alex can free himself in this matter. He needs to escape this holding tank— even as a deluge of water awaits him.

✱ ✱ ✱

"The art world bores me to tears. I cannot truly feel connected to it until all my hooligan friends are running the system or actively destroying it. Soon."

"I believe [destruction]—it's the only thing left that shakes the public from its daily ritual of working and consuming. It is a fabulous joy to work on something so hard only to see it destroyed in a blink of an eye."

—Barry McGee, TWIST

* * *

The house on Escalona Drive

Lisa minces her way down the steep wet driveway—picks up the Sunday edition of the paper. Back in the kitchen, she settles at the table—stacks the sections by her toast and tea.

No longer the lead story, Alex's trial resumes in the lower right corner of the front page. The police department's graffiti expert swears that the tag in question is identical to one from Minidoka. In fact, he says, all the tags from various sites appear to be the work of a single man. The detective sounds like a handwriting expert—points to the recycling of certain *fonts,* the similarity between various loops and embellishments. He maintains that the vandal is clearly right-handed with a tendency for tilting his work slightly up and to the right.

The prosecution's progress in establishing *similars* feels discouraging to her. As she unfolds the section titled *Opinion*—a long white envelope tumbles out, one with Alex's name on top. Carefully extracting three typed pages, she examines the contents. When finished, she scrambles to the loft to join him.

"Take a look at this," she says. "You won't believe it—"

"Say, Leese—I said I don't want to read the paper. No more rehash of the trial—"

"I know," she replies—"but look what I found stuck inside. Here's something that will knock your socks off—"

Taking the pages, he sets them on his lap. For starters, he finds a full-color picture of a graffiti piece—one he immediately recognizes. Looking at the heading—

"Could Joey DRAZ have gone AWRY?"

"The death of a local graffiti writer—more than a remembrance"
By Mario Patino

"Wait—wait a sec— What's this?" Alex lifts the papers from his lap. "What the hell's going on?" Continuing—

Joey Militich was left for dead. In the Mission District of San Francisco, in a gritty alley known as Lilac Street.

"Oh no—you've got to be...." Bringing the papers closer to his face—"This can't be *our* Joey—can it?" Alex reads on—reads fast—as fast as he remembers Joey talking.

Once an example of inner city blight, Lilac Street now hosts an all-star gallery of prominent graffiti writers. Six weeks ago, Joey was found shot to death beneath his unfinished graffiti piece. Police are unsure of the motive, but speculate robbery, possibly in relation to drug activity in the area.

I first met Joey while on assignment for the *Santa Cruz Courier*. At the time, I was researching a story on the local street art scene. I found him to be a generous source of information, a colorful character who had an animated, *hip hop* way about him. As I got to know him, he also shared some amazing stories about his life growing up in a tough San Francisco neighborhood during the '70s and '80s.

As a young teen, Joey considered himself to be a *soldier*. That's the word he used to describe himself, living in a kind of war zone caused by successive waves of drugs. Early on, he was known to be a good fighter. He was recruited by *civilians* whenever a battle broke out, whenever some gang lay siege to the housing complex. He called it a *true miracle* that he somehow managed to survive. First, it was basketball that took him away from the fighting. But it was hip hop culture that ultimately saved him. In 1984, he discovered the allure of New York-style graffiti. Writing graffiti became his passion. For the first time in his life, he felt truly good about himself.

Although Joey escaped the projects, he couldn't leave all his experiences behind. For years, he suffered symptoms consistence with Post-Traumatic Stress Disorder. Beyond flashbacks of terrifying intruders, he had nightmares of being back in his old neighborhood fighting for his life. From what Joey reported, his father also suffered from PTSD. A heroin addict, he used drugs partly to suppress memories of physical abuse from his own father, Joey's grandfather. To complete the picture, the latter was a veteran of World War II and endured severe symptoms of PTSD, as well. In fact, he was stationed in the Philippines when the Japanese invaded. Although Joey never heard the details, he remembered the name *Bataan*. He also recalled phrases like *slanty-eyed yellow bastards* and *dirty Japs*. That's what his father relayed, while trying to explain the older man's afflictions. Joey's father described terrifying screams in the middle of the night. He remembered the grandfather pulling the drapes whenever the weather was hot. There was the matter of the loaded rifle and the canteen of water hidden under the bed. There was the ranting and raving— the physical battering that erupted seemingly out of nowhere.

I'm writing today about Joey Militich, or DRAZ, as he would like to be known, because I liked him, respected him, and I will miss him. I also write because of some strange events that have happened recently in Santa Cruz involving graffiti. Specifically, I am referring to the vandalizing of Kazuo Arai's Japanese American memorial at UCSC and the subsequent arrest of his son, Dr. Alexander Arai.

As I thought about Joey's life alongside the incident in question, I began to wonder if the two might be connected. I admit, it seemed rather far-fetched at first, but still worth considering. The defense argues that a person other than Dr. Arai committed the crime on campus. What if someone like Joey Militich was found to fit the evidence at least as well? At the time of his arrest, the professor appeared dazed and confused. Could his vague description of a *tall, scraggly-haired man* actually refer to Joey?

If so, what would be the motive behind this act? Could Joey/DRAZ have been so ravaged by three generations of PTSD as to explode? It might seem disloyal to associate him with such an event. Why would I risk damaging the reputation of a man who can no longer defend himself? But as Joey taught me:

the *name* of the *game* in graffiti is *fame*. What better way to honor Joey than to enhance his visibility? Why not help DRAZ *get his name up* through traditional media and the Internet? Why not help him go viral?

My own research into this case has brought up some interesting facts. Consider the photograph on the first page. It was taken at Cabrillo College and provided to me by Joey himself. In it, you will see the name, *DRAZ*, along with the words, *Make Piece Bro*, referring to his MPB crew. You will also see the tag, *AWRY*, along with *J-Boy* and *#3*. Despite his crew, Joey often worked alone. He regularly included both *DRAZ* and *AWRY* in his pieces. Is it possible that he created a clever second name in preparation for an eventual graffiti assault? At the very least, this picture demonstrates a clear connection between DRAZ and AWRY. Another photo taken under the Aptos trestle again shows the names together.

In Los Angeles, a sweeping version of both *AWRY* and *MPB* was painted on the sidewalk near the Japanese American National Museum. A surveillance video from New York City shows a *white man* acting suspiciously at the site of vandalism there. How likely is it that Joey drove so far as Idaho or the east coast to tag Kazuo Arai's memorials? It is known that he took an extended leave from work around this time. Unfortunately, he kept no expense records, but his car was found to have exceedingly high mileage.

Finally, there is a little known but crucial fact that I have just provided authorities, along with a set of photos and the above information. It is true that Joey Militich had a cursory relationship with Dr. Arai. The connection in this case happens to be basketball. Joey was a referee in a recreational league in which Dr. Arai regularly took part. Within the last year, an ugly incident occurred between the two. As a result, Joey ejected Dr. Arai from the game. Could this incident have been the tipping point, the precipitant to the graffiti crime spree? Did Joey know of the closeness shared by the professor and his father? Was an attack on the father actually an attack on the son? But why wouldn't have Dr. Arai recognized his assailant? No doubt, darkness and the blow to the professor's head may have made identification impossible. Even so, the description provided is eerily similar to Joey's appearance.

Although I implicate my friend, Joey Militich, in a possible crime, I also choose to honor him. I've decided to do this for the very reason that the incident is so highly publicized. And now that I have shared my points, I trust that the legal system will arrive at the proper decision. Because even if Joey DRAZ is not in fact Joey AWRY, he will still be able to reach more people, be known by more people than he ever could when he was alive.

Alex sets down the three pages. "What the—? What the hell was that? Poor Joey—I had no idea. Guess I haven't played ball in—what? Same as for watching the news. Joey was so good to me—taught me so much."

Flabbergasted, Alex shakes his head. "What a *weird, strange, bizarre* story." Looking up—"You won't believe it, Leese, but I know the person who wrote this—"

30

Santa Cruz County Courthouse

*I*t's all in the jury's hands now—twelve jurors busy shaping the truth, formulating opinion. The jury deliberates— seeks consensus. After hearing all the evidence, all the expert testimony—do they like the D.A.'s version of the story? Or will they prefer the clever rendition provided by his attorney?

Ms. Strickland ushers her worried client out of the courtroom. She informs Alex that the trial has gone well. The new evidence provided by the *cub reporter* clearly confuses matters, and confusion is good. For Alex to beat the charge, all that's required is the presence of "reasonable doubt" in the jury's mind. Thanks to the young journalist, there emerges another potential suspect. And not just an apparition, but one who actually has a name. And unlike Alex, the new suspect has a plausible motive.

Ms. Strickland is pleased at how she massaged the timeline to include Mr. Joey Militich. Regarding his murder, the coroner acknowledged a couple hours leeway in the actual time of death. That was all the opening she needed. She argued that the graffiti writer had more than enough time to tag the memorial, then drive to San Francisco to paint in Lilac Alley. Her injured client's confused state had provided a vague description of his assailant, one consistent with Joey's physical appearance. The *brutality* of the encounter now made sense, given his history of PTSD and the acrimony between the two men. So, whether it be Joey Militich or some unknown copycat tagger, someone other than Alex could have committed the crime.

Now the jury must weigh two possible interpretations of the evidence. Either Alex vandalized the memorial, or someone else did. As per the judge's instructions, if more than one plausible explanation exists for the commission of a crime, the jury must choose the one consistent with the defendant's innocence. All that's left to do now is to await the jury's decision.

Alex thanks his attorney—heads to the parking lot for a much needed break. She'll call him back to court when the jury finishes its deliberations. On his way to the car, he feels euphoric. All the stress, the obsessive worry—all the worst case scenarios clear like the unpredictable coastal weather. Once inside, he locks the door. He starts to laugh—laughs like he's in on an insider's joke. Secretly, he laughs in a way that hardly makes a sound, just the release of his breath in short, explosive bursts. He can't believe he's about to get away with it—the *it* being his entire crime spree. With the verdict of "not guilty," *Action Live* will lead to a fabulous conclusion. And although no one but Whitney will appreciate it, the triumph will feel complete. He would like to celebrate the occasion with her, but he also wants to call Lisa before she arrives from Chicago tonight.

Alex needs to get out of the parking lot—leave the courthouse behind. Traveling along Soquel Avenue, he passes Charlie Hong Kong's. Maybe the direction he's driving isn't so random after all. He clearly remembers the last time he was there, the time Joey was doing a piece honoring the names of Bay Area crews. Alex decides to visit Bill's Wheels just up the street. He wants to pay homage to Joey's work—show appreciation for DRAZ and all his generous instruction. And most of all, he wants to thank Joey for saving him today from total disaster—jury willing.

Alex turns into the skate shop's parking lot. Even before he looks for a space, he's aware of something terribly wrong. Slowing, he gazes out his side window. On the wall facing the skate shop, he should find Joey's tribute piece. Instead, a swatch of gray paint has obliterated the entire work. Someone has completely buffed the piece. And on the darkened wall, a writer using the name, *JEST*, has gotten up an impressive piece of his own. The figure of a court jester wearing a crown dominates the center of the work. Written below with an emphatic script— the phrase, *THE KING IS DEAD—LONG LIVE THE KING!!!*

Alex now peers through the passenger window at the external wall of Bill's. He can't find Joey's piece that features the cosmic basketball. Once more, a sheathe of cheap gray paint has covered all evidence that DRAZ has ever been here. Replacing his fiery design, a series of four names appears, done in a trite knock-off of 80s *wild style* graffiti. The work of the *FDT* crew, the names are the product of *toys* as Joey would call them. Alex feels a surge of rage, a surge of insult and rage— profound sadness, and rage. *How dare they do this? How dare they do this to Joey!*

As he slumps in his seat, his head overflows with images of DRAZ and his pieces. And now those images merge with those of Kaz and his sculpted memorials. All the various creations converge right here at the skate shop. And Alex thinks of his father, lying comatose in the hospital—more famous than he could have ever dreamed. And Alex thinks of Joey, of DRAZ— lying dead in the ground—with more fame than he could have ever imagined. And Alex thinks about himself and what his art has finally become. Sitting in his silent car, he waits. He sits and waits, waits for his attorney—waits for a phone call that never gets placed today.

* * *

The house on Escalona Drive

Under the covers of night—what was once easy months ago has turned into a terrible ordeal. Alex knows he needs to sleep— craves sleep. But every night presents a battle. And he dreads having to fight his way through the hours, struggling toward another impossibly distant morning. Now his dreams have captured him—have taken control. They've issued him marching orders, an enforced march through the dark night. It's as if he's gone back in time—back to the Philippines, back to the *Bataan death march*. His captives allow him to fall asleep, only for the torture to begin. With any halt in consciousness, the dreams attack—force him back awake. Tonight, he dreams of—

A battle in the South Pacific. Alex, himself, is a Japanese soldier dressed in fresh fatigues like he's ready for a movie. In fact, the director of the movie says to *take five*. It's time to drink a Sapporo, time for a box lunch. A picnic by the blue tropical waters— When shooting resumes, Alex awaits direction. There's no script, so he's going to have to wing it. As cameras roll, he spots a man coming into view above a sand dune. It's an American soldier and he's ready to fight. He carries a flame thrower that looks like an acetylene torch. To Alex's surprise, the soldier is actually his father Kaz. Alex knows what he has to do. Tossing his rifle, he pulls out the family samurai sword. As he charges up the dune, he wants to yell out something appropriate, but can't remember the word, *banzai*. Instead, he moves silently—slashes at his father's wrists. Now the torch falls away, hands still attached. And the sand is soaked in red—

* * *

Santa Cruz County Courthouse

Hopping up the steps, Alex hears his cell phone ring. Ignoring the sound, he turns it off. A half-hour ago, Ms. Strickland called to tell him the jury had finished its deliberations.

Straight to voice mail—"Alex pick up. It's Henry. I know the trial's going on, but Dad's condition got worse last night. Whatever's happening—I hope it goes well for you today."

Once more, Alex passes security. Pocketing his keys, he almost wishes he had a lucky charm. But he really has no faith in luck—isn't superstitious—believes in preparation. He trusts his attorney, and that's about all. Avoiding reporters, he takes a seat on a bench around the corner.

Straight to voice mail—"Alex— Dad had a really high fever this morning. The doctor examined him—ordered an X-ray. Turns out he's got pneumonia. I'll call you back later this afternoon."

Looking up, Alex welcomes Helen Strickland. Her face looks promisingly flush beneath her bangs. After shaking hands, she leads him back to the courtroom.

At the appointed time, the bailiff starts the proceedings. Alex studies the jurors as they file in. Do they look sad, happy, angry—relieved? Maybe they look a little weary—deliberations having taken longer than expected. And now the bailiff heads for the other door. As people rise, the judge enters—marches straight to the bench. After addressing the courtroom, he turns to the jurors' box.

"Have you, the jury, reached a verdict in case #F-26355—the people of the State of California versus Alexander Arai?"

The foreperson—a female social worker, juror #9—stands. "Yes, your honor. We have reached a verdict."

"Will you please hand the verdict to the bailiff—"

Upon receiving the form, the bailiff hands it to the judge—who, in turn, passes it to the clerk. The judge intones—"Will you please announce the verdict to the court—"

The clerk's voice commands the courtroom— "As to the charge of felony malicious mischief—we the jury find the defendant, Alexander Arai—not guilty."

Alex's heart nearly drowns out the foreman's statement. Pivoting, he hugs Ms. Strickland—offers up various ecstatic versions of *thank you*. The attorney shares his jubilance—tells him she's more than happy to have done a good job for him. Alex feels he could soar to the ceiling—feels he could fly out the windows atop the front wall.

Reviving his phone, he calls Lisa at her board meeting—leaves the message she's been hoping to hear all day. Noting Henry's calls, he extinguishes his cell once more. Bounding down the hallway, he exits the building—jogs to his car.

Straight to voice mail—"Alex, look— Dad's breathing has gotten worse. His oxygen level keeps dropping. They're culturing him up for whatever's in his lungs. It's a bad sign. I asked one of the doctors— Said you should come up pretty soon. Call me when you get this."

* * *

Andrew Kumasaka

Boise, Idaho

Alex should have checked his brother's messages earlier. Now it's too late—just a few short hours too late. His father lies in the same hospital bed where Alex had left him. No more coma, he lies in state—the site of their last meeting, their one and only heart to heart. Of course, there wasn't much of his father's *brain* back then.

But now he's gone, no longer fettered by probes and tubes. The nursing staff has freshened him up. He doesn't look peaceful so much as relieved. Now someone has combed his hair the way it should be—the way he liked it when he still had an opinion. And beyond the parts left behind—where has his father's *spirit* gone? Alex has no idea—has never taken to instruction on matters like that. For now, it's simply time to dispose of what's left.

Alex approaches his mother sitting on a chair beside a raised table. On the surface rests a box of tissues at a perfect right angle to a magazine. Soiled tissues are nowhere to be found. Bending at the waist, Alex reaches to console her. As her left hand opens, her right one drops a damp but neatly folded tissue into her purse. With both hands now, she receives her son. She nods as if to say, *thank you—thank you so much for coming.* She nods as if to say, *I understand how you feel about your father. I understand why you did what you did.* She squeezes his hands as if to say, *all is forgiven.* As if to say, *you will always be my son.*

Henry and Haru join Alex and his mother. Stepping away, Alex avoids the judgment in his brother's face. It's not until Lisa arrives that Henry's expression finally softens. Having flown in from Portland, she gives each person a gentle hug. After one last encircling of Kaz's bed, the family repairs to a hotel in downtown Boise.

Sumi welcomes everyone into the room she and Haru share. She prepares green tea with the hot water maker on the counter. From Seattle's International District, Haru has brought several bags of *osenbei*, the little rice crackers shaped like cherry blossoms. She's also brought a box of handmade *manju*— the specialty rice cakes filled with a sweet bean paste.

Henry starts the reminiscences. In time, everyone has something to say. Even Alex's mother shares the story of how she and Kaz officially met after the war. It was in Japantown, San Jose—shopping for New Year's ingredients at Dobashi's. Lisa expresses her admiration for Kaz's *moxie* and drive. She says he serves as a role model for steadfastly pursuing one's vision.

Alex has to agree, even though his sense of guilt prevents him from saying too much. What he does say—"I apologize to all of you in this room—for how my actions might have affected Dad's health. So much for being single-minded, like him— But also like him, it's hard to apologize for pursuing my own reasons—doing what I needed to do."

Everyone nods in silence, including Henry. Patting Alex on the shoulder—"Glad you got that legal stuff resolved."

The following morning, everyone meets again in Sumi and Haru's room. It's a full two weeks before New Years—too early for them to officially observe. On the other hand, when will they all be together again like this? Haru brought a red lacquered *sake* service from Seattle. She packed a small bottle of Kurosawa *sake* in her suitcase. They decide to go ahead this morning—celebrate the new, dispense with the old. Henry and Alex dislodge the desk—position it between the twin beds.

"What's the proper way to sit?" asks Lisa.

"Oh, just sit anywhere," says Haru. "We don't have to do it the *honto* way—that is, the real, traditional way. We gotta adjust."

"As I remember," says Lisa, "we're all supposed to walk into the room one at a time—starting with the men, then finishing with the women. Also—it was done in the order of age. At least that's how Kaz liked it."

"Of course he liked it that way," replies Haru. "That's because he got to drink his *sake* first."

"First in everything," notes Henry.

"Okay," says Alex. "If it's not going to be traditional—how should we serve?"

"Let's shake things up a bit," offers Lisa.

"Yes," agrees Haru. "Just serve the person on your right."

With three on the edge of one bed, two on the other—an impromptu pouring of *sake*—

Turning to Henry, his mother says—"Why don't you do the honors? You're the oldest son. You're supposed to drink to your father."

Already flush with the moment, Henry raises his cup. "Let's just make it a round, why don't we? Go ahead, Auntie Haru— why don't you start? You're the only one Dad ever listened to, anyway."

For the next few minutes, it's gentle chaos. Chaos and the sound of laughter.

31

Whitney's place, downtown Santa Cruz

The gap keeps getting longer. The void grows wider, deeper. She feels it on all sides of herself—the *space*. And it makes her feel small, insignificant—inconsequential. All her life, Whitney has never thought she was reason enough for people to stay. Even so, they always managed to leave their mark—leave ample evidence of their wanting, needing—*their* needs always bigger than hers.

She's lost weight—hasn't eaten much. But she doesn't do the vomiting thing—never has. And it's not that she thinks she's fat—just that she doesn't deserve the usual portions. Her clothes sag—her tops having grown a size too large. Her jeans droop, the waist slung at a lower orbit about her hips.

In spite of her minimized self, she continues to paint—her art the one thing that gives her release. Certainly more than what men can do for her now. More than a *particular* man can do, the man whose face appears on the canvas in her room. Of course, he's been too busy with important matters as of late.

From memory, she'd created a new portrait of Alex—a way for him to stay close to her, even while in absentia. She liked to pretend he saw her pour her morning orange juice. That he saw her wash the dishes—wipe the counters. Liked it when he watched her exit the shower—climb into her clothes. And she felt reassured by his steady vigil each night when she went to sleep.

But now, she's really *pissed* at him. She's *mad, crazy*—whatever. Now the focal point of her room simultaneously annoys her, depresses her—angers her, makes her *sad*.

It's cold in her room as she listens to a hard rain. Barefoot, she tugs her jeans to pull the hems up from under her heels. She exchanges a worn tee for the warmth of a green flannel shirt. Restless, she approaches the crash cart where she keeps her paints—extracts the desired colors. She squeezes two large dollops onto her palette—looks for her long, hog bristle brush.

True to the moment, she stands tall—stares at the portrait of Alex. Without naming the incendiary forces, she simply turns them loose. In a fury, she scoops up a glob of black paint—savages Alex's hair. She makes his hair grow long and longer—down both sides of his face—down past his chin. She compels the blackness to fly in every direction—wild black hair flailing against the restraints of the angular canvas. Her hands dart about as quickly and unpredictably as a hornet, as frenzied as an angry bee—*Whitney B.* And as her hand attacks the periphery, her eyes go straight to the face in the middle. It's a kind face, a receptive face—the mouth offering a hint of a smile.

But now comes time for the red paint. Whitney reaches for a second brush—an old brush that's mostly splayed. Soaking up the redness, she prepares for the next assault. As she steps forward, her body registers a subtle rush—a quick *shiver* from someplace deep down *low*— Surprised, she welcomes that pulse of arousal that sometimes triggers when she paints. Extending her hand, she slashes a narrow streak down one side of Alex's face. A second stroke follows along the other side. Bright red parentheses, like taut labia—bracket the eyes, the nose, the mouth. Harshly, she scours those red parts—fills in all the space around his most sensitive features. She fully engulfs him, making the merger complete. Tossing the brush onto her palette, she backs off—backs away.

Whitney settles atop her bed—arms stuck at her side, legs together. To loosen up, she expands her chest with deep breaths. Now her arms relax as well as her legs—her limbs beginning to part, just so. Silently, she welcomes the urgency of her *own* wanting, her own needs. It's a matter of directing herself—of having her own power. It's about her body providing the kind of wholeness she craves and deserves.

Unbuttoning her shirt, she slips a hand between the soft panels. She slides her fingers up her breast bone—finds a budding tenderness off to the side. As she touches the spot, the pain turns electric. Tracing circles, she draws out every spark. Now her other hand follows the dip of her stomach—enters the space between denim and skin, a space that flutters with her breath. Undoing a snap, she follows the sound of a zipper as it works its way down the rest of her crotch. Using both hands, she tugs her jeans from beneath her bottom—slides them down then flails them off. Bending at the knees, she raises both legs—doffs a pair of panties, skimpy as a scent. As one hand lingers, the other drops low to address the blush—the small plush parts demanding her attention. It's both a revelation and a reminder. The fact that she can make herself feel *this* good. And so it goes like this. It goes like this for a while. It goes like this until matters verge on the obvious. And in the throes of a self-fulfilling conclusion, she finds herself complete.

✳ ✳ ✳

The house on Escalona Drive

It's an innocent thing really. To drive off for coffee—to get back into a routine. Relax with a copy of the *Guardian* and take in the bustle of the morning. But for some reason, Alex feels uneasy as he backs out of his garage—inches his way down the long driveway. That shadow there—darting across the pavement—tumbling over the trunk of his car. Was it there all along? He puzzles at the source of the sudden darkness. Could it be from the big oak tree? Riding his brakes, he wonders if the sidewalk's truly clear—wonders if a jogger might suddenly appear, or a cyclist, or a skater—

Driving west on Escalona, he hunches over the steering wheel. Who knows if a child will come dashing forth? A child on his way to school, his mother in tow, screaming out a warning. How dangerous the road appears today. Even parked vehicles look like hazards. Maybe that van up ahead will lurch into his lane. Maybe that oncoming truck will suddenly veer—cause a head-on collision—

As he turns left onto Laurel Street, his eyes scuttle back and forth. It's all about *fear*—the fear of something bad, unexpected. It could be a sinkhole in the pavement. It could be a dog or cat leaping out in front of his tires. *What's happening?* he asks himself. *What's happening to me?* He feels feverish, his damp shirt starting to cling.

At Mission Street, he's all but paralyzed. So much traffic—more than he can recall. But in truth, there's nothing unusual about the fitful gridlock of a Monday morning. Alex makes a tentative right. *What's going on?* he wonders. *Why does the street look so different today?* The car seems heavy—balky. The steering wheel groans in the stranglehold of his hands. A half-block down, he slams on his brakes. He thought he saw someone entering the crosswalk. Immediately he hears the unnecessarily *long* blare of a horn. Rattled, he stomps his brakes again—nearly misses the entrance to the parking lot. Now a line of cars opposes him, as he waits to make his turn. The driver behind must surely be *pissed*—another irritating glitch in his morning commute. A second honk of his horn will no doubt follow. Alex cringes—braces for the blast of disapproval. Suddenly, he spots a break in traffic—hits his accelerator, cranks the steering wheel hard to the left. He clears the breach—only to find a white-haired Asian man in his path. The man staggers, steps sideways. Alex mouths an apology as he squeezes past—half expects a shaken fist in return.

Creeping down a row of head-first parking, he finds a space, but it looks too narrow. It probably isn't, but he doesn't want to take any chances. Just as he's about to give up and leave, a large SUV backs out, barely missing his bumper. *Get a hold of yourself,* he fumes, as he pulls into the vacant slot, pulls back—pulls forward, then stops. Relieved, he exits his car—checks both sides for adequate spacing. It's not that he fears his vehicle being hit. He just doesn't want to cause an inconvenience. He doesn't need another person getting angry at him this morning. After a short trek up the sidewalk, he opens the door to Coffeetopia—careful not to get in anyone's way.

All Gone Awry

West Cliff Drive

After two weeks of fretful driving, Alex parks his car at Natural Bridges—takes a winding stroll along the cliff. *So far, so good*— He's not hit a skater, slammed a walker, inconvenienced a biker, struck a jogger—

Finding a dirt path, he crosses a patch of ice plant to a tiny bluff overlooking the tides. In the middle stands a sculpture made of Corten steel and translucent acrylic. About one-and-a-half times the height of a man, it's shaped like the gnomon of a sundial. For the time being, a triangular shadow signals a late afternoon. Off to the right, the Pacific Ocean flows into Monterey Bay. This is where the tsunami entered a year ago, having vaulted the earth's vast curvature. And somewhere on the other side of the earth, Japan still works to recover.

Alex feels a need for a time out. Feels like a child being *put* in time out. A bad child. Ever since the trial—ever since he was found not guilty, and properly so. In order to win his case, so much of the truth was distorted. *So what?* he counters. So what—except for the informal punishment that's followed. A kind of sentencing that has nothing to do with the court. As it turns out, to be a *bad* child is to be a *sick* child. How else can he explain the anxieties, the nightmares, the sense of accidental tragedy about to happen? On perpetual alert, he could commit a terrible act at any moment, it seems. And who imposes these consequences? He has only himself to blame. It's enough to make a person want to tell the truth—to come clean, to cure himself. ...It's *almost* enough. For now, he believes he deserves these symptoms for having—*what?* For having egregiously *lied.*

Alex studies the shifting waters. Some twenty feet below, the surf crashes into the cliffs, undermining this small outpost of land. He rethinks the destructive handiwork of *Action Live*— perseverates over the outcome. *What a dirty trick,* he thinks to himself. A trick on his father, a trick on his ethnic community. And what about the deception, the *dirty trick,* played on Joey? All examples of true treachery, something a *sneaky Jap* would do. It's enough to make a person want to tell the truth—to apologize publicly, to clear the names of people he's harmed. ...It's *almost* enough.

Alex examines the sculpture standing to his left—a surface of artful corrosion. At the tip, a small bit of translucent material protrudes from some kind of essential core. Each day, the sun does a dance around this piece, this work of art that can't help but address the passage of time. And he knows he can't change the dreadful perceptions he's created—the way people define him now. Everything's been transformed, thanks to the media—their outpouring of memorabilia, a memorial of print and sound bites. Now he'll be remembered as the graffiti vandal with the fancy doctorate—the guy who most likely attacked his father, but got away on a technicality. Alex, the *coward*—the one who couldn't face his father man to man. It's enough to make a person want to tell the truth—to own up to the sleights of hand—to stake claim to his own motives—to stand up and declare himself for who he truly is. ...It's *almost* enough.

Alex detects a commotion below. A flock of seagulls suddenly appears, rising above the edge of the cliff. A beautiful sight—like white caps freed of the ocean—soaring to infinity. That's how he'd wished to be seen his entire life—by a set of adoring parents—by *everyone*. From his first drawings to his last— That reflection was what he sought when "breaking into" his father's studio so many years ago. And to be seen now forever attached to an alias, a *tag*—feels to him like a monumental letdown. Why couldn't his art have been good enough to sign with his *real* name? And as for the biggest irony of all? As a criminal, he's forced to disavow his own creations. It's enough to make a person want to tell the truth—to explain the brilliance behind his concepts—to prove that his tags were the expression of a greater art. ...It's *almost* enough.

Alex recognizes the start of a long sunset. Even as the sun still rides so high in the distance. He looks back in time—is blessed with a good memory. As if in a gallery—he strolls through a display of all his works. Memory as memorial—a hedge against growing old, growing *dead*. He counts the good and bad—scans a list, a ledger. In the moment, memory *becomes* Alex. For all he's done, he feels disappointed. For all he's done, he doesn't like himself right now. And of course, once he's gone, none of this will matter to him anyway. But until then, he must be able to abide, respect—live with himself. Needs to be able to look in the mirror and not turn away. Alex struggles with the cracks in the internal construct of how he sees *himself*. It's enough to make a person want to tell the truth—

* * *

The house on Escalona Drive

From out of the kitchen into the fire—"You're what Alex? You're thinking of what?" Lisa deposits two plates on the dining room table. BLTs—freshly made for lunch. "Run that by me again—I couldn't quite hear—"

In a measured voice, Alex responds. "I'm going to tell everyone the truth."

Lisa can't believe what she's hearing. Doesn't believe. "Look Hon—that's not even funny. You shouldn't be making jokes like that."

"But I'm not kidding—I really mean it. Here, have a seat—"

Lisa would comply, but a part of her wants to back away—retreat to a neutral corner of the room. Wants a safe distance, so she can simply glare at the man. "You can't be serious—"

"But I am. I'm completely serious."

"You won your trial—don't you get it? You're home free—"

"That's what you'd think."

"Of course—that's exactly what I think. Are you *crazy?*" Lisa's question borders on the literal.

"Yeah, you could say that. But this decision is about who I've become. I can't stand who I am anymore."

"So, is telling the truth going to fix that?"

"I don't know—but it's something I believe. I've got to be honest—got to be *real*. That's the only way I can live with myself."

"Look Alex, talk to Nita—she can help you out. Help straighten you out is what I mean."

"I already know what Nita would say. She'd say I've completely messed up my life's story, my narrative. That I suffer for being a—complete fraud. She'd say I need to correct the story. She'd encourage me to...."

"Hey, wait a sec," Lisa murmurs. "Wait—" She knows she's forgotten something. "Oh yeah—the soup, I left it on!" Rushing to the kitchen, she charges the stove. "Oh damn—I burned it!"

In the meantime, Alex studies his beautiful sandwich—itself a work of art. And a testament to Lisa's love, her support of him through all the dark times.

A clatter from the kitchen. "Say, Hon—do you mind? Do you mind if I just open a bag of chips instead?"

"Not a problem." Alex appreciates what he's doing to her life—to *her*. "Say, Leese, not to worry. Come on back and have a seat."

Still mumbling to herself, she reappears. She smothers his plate with chips, neglects hers—takes a seat opposite him.

"Look," says Alex, "I know any decision I make has big consequences on you as well. I'm sorry this is really upsetting to you."

"Well, of course it is. You're not even considering the practical things—the huge practical implications." Glaring into her partner's eyes—"Didn't you tell me how worried you were? Didn't you tell me you were terrified about losing your job?"

"I did."

"So what about that? Weren't you feeling bad about yourself—feeling terrible about being dependent, about becoming a burden to me?"

"I was."

"Well, what about now?"

"Leese—I *am* worried. But if I manage to put myself back together, I'm sure I'll find work—somewhere. I'll do whatever it takes. I'll do whatever I have to. But at least I'll have my integrity. At least I'll be living my truth."

"Living your truth?" she scoffs. Sadly, she adds—"The truth's overrated."

"I'm going to make it up to you, Leese. And you won't have to wait long. I'm going to make it up to you big time. You'll see—"

Lisa can only shake her head. *What will he come up with next?* Placing her hands on the table, she reaches for the most tangible thing she can find. Some smooth, reassuring surface that connects them. Something shared and solid between them—something with a common history. Lisa splays her fingers—searches for substance. One table top—two untouched meals.

* * *

Mario's place, Soquel

Mario pursues Jose Antonio Vargas. Fiddling with the radio, he seeks out one of the most outstanding of his fellow undocumented immigrants. Somehow, Mr. Vargas seems lost in the airwaves today—a dismembered voice concealed in all that static. The man has a message for Mario—an invitation really. A chance to join his group, *What's American*, and help elevate the discussion on immigration.

So, why can't Mario find the right frequency? Maybe the problem is in the numbers—mere analogue approximations. *How about this?* Something promising emits from where—*FM 88.5?* The host of the show—a woman—sounds like she could be coming from the campus radio station he's seeking.

"Hi folks, this is Molly Mendez.... Say—why don't you check out Jenny and Johnny at the Rio this Friday? You know...Jenny Lewis, the cute redhead from Rilo Kiley...slim-Jim boyfriend Jonathan Rice...."

The signal continues to wax and wane—

"Okay—you're listening to.... Today, it's my great pleasure.... Once again, welcome to the show. I see you're still a sharp dresser.... And I'm trendin' a cool calico rain slicker over black tights.... All right, I hear you've got an agenda today. Why don't you go ahead and start...."

Finally, the radio stands perfectly tuned. What catches Mario off guard—the voice of the guest sounds surprisingly familiar. Too familiar to be Jose Antonio Vargas. In fact, the voice is *shockingly* familiar.

"As your listeners probably know, I've been involved in a legal case with the State of California and UCSC."

"Sorry to interrupt you professor, but that seems like an understatement."

"Again, as you might already know—I was found not guilty of the charge of felony malicious mischief in a case of graffiti vandalism. The target was *Forever Manzanar*, a Japanese American memorial created by my father, the late Kazuo Arai."

"A truly heavy event, professor. Sorry for your dad's passing, but seriously—I'm so glad you were cleared. Most of my colleagues feel the same way."

"Well—thank you very much, Molly. But today, I'm really here to set the record straight—"

Mario grabs a seat—can't believe what he's hearing. *What the hell's he doing? Why's he stirring things up again? I mean— the jury got it right this time.* Mario wants to snatch the radio— wants to shake it—wants to knock it around until he gets the professor to shut up. Hadn't he provided the man with an out? Hadn't he personally delivered him from the hands of the prosecution? *What the fuck?*

"Beginning in the month of June—I, Alexander Arai, embarked on a campaign of graffiti vandalism that involved four other sites around the country...."

Mario bashes the table—once, hard. As a journalist, he had compromised himself for this man. In a profession dedicated to the truth—he had suggested a terrible lie. *What a total nutjob*—as if the professor had made him do it. *And now he's screwing everything up!*

"...In New York City. At the site of the Japan Society Building...."

Mario drops his head. He had betrayed his craft in order to protect himself and his family. To avoid deportation, he reasoned, that's what most people would do. And besides, he was just one of several million other liars. What he did was simply an extension of how he normally lived.

"...In Washington D.C. Near the Supreme Court Building...."

Mario cringes. He had promised himself this would be the only time he would write the untruth. This would also be the last time he signed off with the name, the alias, "Patino." Never again would he present to the world without an honest tilde.

From that point on, he swore to tell and write the whole truth and nothing but—

"...In Los Angeles. In Little Tokyo...."

Mario scowls at the radio. He imagines silencing the professor with a punch to the mouth. But as the program continues, the tension in his face begins to lessen. He had always wanted to know the motive behind the serial taggings. Here's his opportunity for finally discovering the *why*.

As the internal criticism stops, he listens like the reporter, the journalist, he is. He learns all about the relationship between the professor and his father. And he hears about a kind of pain, a type of estrangement that strikes a resonant chord. *Yeah, there must be lots of ways—lots of ways to lose a father.* And he grudgingly admits to how hard it was—to grow up so young after his own father died. Mario listens to the point where his internal roiling subsides. He listens to where his deeply personal anger diminishes. For some reason now, when Whitney enters his mind, he doesn't feel *quite* as upset over the professor's involvement. Of course, he still *hates* the man for what he did. But it's not as hurtful, coming from a guy who seems disadvantaged in a familiar sort of way. A guy in the process of cutting himself down to size. Doing so, publicly.

And as Alex finishes, there's a stretch of dead silence, normally a *deadly* silence when a radio show is live on the air. But Molly is silent. And when she finally speaks, she offers her guest a quiet and heartfelt thanks.

Mario flicks off the radio. Pulling out the morning paper, he checks the *Local-lifestyle* section. He discovers he's a complete day off on the radio program he's seeking. But he's really okay about the mix-up—has gotten something valuable in return. He's come to understand the professor better, having found a certain kinship between their two devious lives. Satisfied, he's done enough for today. Tomorrow promises another opportunity to turn the page in his pursuit of Jose Antonio Vargas.

32

"C.J.A. strongly condemns Dr. Alexander Arai"
Sacramento, California.

The National C.J.A. has been an active partner with law enforcement in the criminal investigation of Dr. Alexander Arai. He was previously charged with felony malicious mischief in a well-publicized crime on the grounds of UC Santa Cruz. Earlier press releases have documented our efforts in providing evidence for this case.

We are now disappointed to hear that a jury in Santa Cruz has cleared him of the charge. We have also learned that following his trial, Dr. Arai came forward to admit his involvement in a series of graffiti crimes around the country. We strongly urge other jurisdictions to initiate charges and to seek justice in this matter. Dr. Arai's confession does not absolve him of the vandalism that has made a mockery of the unjust wartime incarceration of American citizens of Japanese descent.

All Gone Awry

*

From the J-A Times—

Column—"The regrettable case of Alexander Arai"
With his recent surprise admission, the bizarre behavior of Dr. Alexander Arai continues to raise eyebrows
nationwide, and causes further consternation within
the Japanese American community. Needless to say,
this is the same community into which he was born,
a community that has nurtured and encouraged him
throughout his life.

We trust that Dr. Arai has never suffered the in-
dignity of having his loyalty to this country questioned.
He has enjoyed the privilege of attending good schools
and excelling in the discipline of his choice. He has not
had to take a back seat to anyone due to his ethnicity, as he pursued his career. If not for the sacrifices of
previous generations, his story would be very different
today.

We do not pretend to understand Dr. Arai's motives. In explaining himself, he cited the need to rectify
certain 'issues' with his late father. With all the benefits he received from his family, how could he behave in
such an ungrateful manner? His graffiti antics not only
embarrassed the community, but brought great shame
to his family.

Is it possible that Dr. Arai suffers from some deep
psychological problem? Maybe he struggles with the
phenomenon known as 'internalized racism.' Maybe he
hates himself for being Japanese, or Japanese American. Maybe he feels compelled to attack cultural values
in order to disavow or destroy that part of himself.

We at the paper condemn Dr. Arai as a true outlier,
one who rejects his cultural identity and the history of
his own people. We would urge him to pursue the obvious and to cease all participation within the greater
Japanese American community. In our humble opinion, the sooner the better.

Andrew Kumasaka

*

From the Japanese American Voice—

Letters to the editor—"Comments on a JA traitor"
I've been avidly following your coverage of the vandalism case involving Alexander Arai. Like so many other JAs, I was initially enraged at the desecration of these sacred sites. What hateful man would do such a thing? Of course, I assumed it was some kind of racist. When I found out it was 'one of us' I became even more enraged. Finding out was kind of like a Bernie Madoff moment. It was about being a traitor to your own people. My grandfather had a name for a guy like that. It was 'baka' or 'bakatare'—a fool.

I'm a third generation Sansei from Los Angeles. My parents were incarcerated at the Manzanar concentration camp. Only with much encouragement did they tell me about such things as the 'loyalty questionnaire' and the way it split up the community. Both my parents answered, 'Yes, yes.' My father volunteered for the service but had a medical condition. With hesitation, my parents told me about the 'No, no boys,' guys who were mostly seen as troublemakers. They didn't go on to prove their loyalty to the country by shedding their blood and giving their lives. They didn't go out and fight for those in camp, to prove we were loyal Americans.

With his acts of vandalism, I believe Dr. Arai is a traitor too. He took his selfish needs, his personal vendetta against his father, and dragged the whole JA community through his childish acts. He embarrassed us all and deserves all the shame that comes his way. If I were still a young man growing up in the sixties, I would say let's picket his classes. Let's hold up placards saying 'Dr. Arai—the JA Bernie Madoff.' 'Dr. Arai—the new No, no boy.'
Chad Matsui, Cincinnati C.J.A.

*

From the Nikkei Progressive—

Column—"Alexander Arai Follows Proud Footsteps"
Let's get some perspective here. It's true that Dr. Arai
defied the law. But isn't that exactly what Korematsu,
Hirabayashi, and Yasui did nearly seventy years ago?
And what about those other young men who later
resisted the draft? Of course, the professor wasn't
challenging an unjust government and defending his
rights as an American citizen. He wasn't acting in the
service of a common good. He wasn't breaking the
law in order to assert an even higher law, that of the
Constitution of the United States. And yet, the three
civil rights heroes and their fellow dissenters were
all making statements of personal identity as well.
Through courageous acts, each man defined himself
while facing wartime hysteria, racial prejudice, and
even backlash from his own community. What Dr. Arai
did, as strange as it seems, is not that fundamentally
different. With his own defiance of authority, both
paternal and legal, he has brought the JA community
into current times. Korematsu, Hirabayashi, and
Yasui—and indeed, the draft resisters—all fought to
be considered true Americans. Freely acting on his
personal issues, Dr. Arai apparently never doubted
that he was.

*

The University of California, Santa Cruz—

"The Faculty Code of Conduct as Approved by the Assembly of
the Academic Senate"

Part II of this Code elaborates standards of professional conduct, derived from general professional consensus about the existence of certain precepts as basic to acceptable faculty behavior. Conduct which departs from these precepts is viewed by faculty as unacceptable because it is inconsistent with the mission of the University.

Pertaining to—
A. Teaching and Students
    Ethical Principles—
    Types of unacceptable conduct—
B. Scholarship
    Ethical Principles—
    Types of unacceptable conduct—
C. The University
    Ethical Principles—
    Types of unacceptable conduct:
        3. Unauthorized use of University resources or facilities on a significant scale for personal, commercial, political, or religious purposes.
D. Colleagues
    Ethical Principles—
    Types of unacceptable conduct—
E. The Community
    Ethical Principles—
    Types of unacceptable conduct:
        2. Commission of a criminal act which has led to conviction in a court of law and which clearly demonstrates unfitness to continue as a member of the faculty.

*

"University Policy on Faculty Conduct and the Administration of Discipline"

Section II— Types of Disciplinary Sanctions
The types of discipline that may be imposed on a member of the faculty are as follows, in order of increasing severity: written censure, reduction in salary, demotion, suspension, denial or

curtailment of emeritus status, and dismissal from the employ of the University.

* * *

University Terrace, Meder Street

Swish—game over. Alex and Carter head for one of the buff-colored concrete benches. Hoops in the afternoon sun—playing outdoors in the open air. Alex looks to the top of the sky—a deep blue blotter—soaking up the air, all the oxygen. Maybe that's why he breathes so hard—why his lungs labor. But it's the first time in a while he's been out on the court. Thanks to his friend, he gets to stretch his legs—stretch his territory. Just down Bay Street from the university. This is about as close as he can get—suspended as he is, pending the outcome of his case with UCSC.

Toweling down—"Not too sharp today, Al, but that's no surprise. What a huge ordeal for you—"

Yeah, it is— The Academic Senate—the hearing's set next week with the Committee on Privilege and Tenure."

"So, who makes the call?"

"Ultimately, the Chancellor's in charge of disciplinary action. He works with the faculty, the Academic Senate—to come up with something."

"Well, I'm still shaking my head over what you did. All that tagging, then coming clean— Even though I get it now, I still worry for you." Reaching for two water bottles—he offers one.

"Thanks, Silk." Alex takes in an icy mouthful. "I've got no idea what they plan to do. Could be bad, really bad."

Out on the court, the next team faces off with the current winners. Guys going *shirts and skins* scramble to match up, man-to-man. It's a young group today—some college kids, a couple high school ballers.

"It's been hell on Lisa, too," he adds. "Been awfully quiet as of late. Guess there's not much she can say, really."

"Poor Lisa. What's the worst that can happen?"

"Losing my job, of course—my whole career. Being a burden to her— Those were some pretty outrageous things I did. Sometimes I can't even believe it myself."

The game starts—flows back and forth. The sound of the ball smacking concrete—that hollow sound—followed by a loud bang off the metal backboard—reverberation. Voices— More bouncing—then another rattle of rim. A pause, then the slick skid of a loose ball finding the peripheral grass.

"So, what about those strange things you've been going through?"

"Oh, I'm still having the occasional nightmare. It's getting a little easier to drive. I'm a bit more comfortable being in public and such. I mean—look at today. I'm here playing ball."

"Nita said it took a lot of courage to do what you did—to declare yourself like that."

"It really helped talking to her. She said it could take some work but would eventually get better. It's the public embarrassment—a big part of what's going on for me. The other day, I ran into a couple colleagues. I was sneaking some papers out of my office. They were diplomatic—cordial, even. I noticed though—the department chair across the way. He totally avoided me."

"Well, you can't stand the guy anyway."

"True."

As usual, now—Alex pays special attention to the point guard play. The guy on *shirts* runs fast, elevates quickly—is athletically gifted. But he's plagued with poor court vision—fails to see his teammate flashing into the lane—arms outstretched demanding the ball. Not making the pass, the point guard drives right into a double team.

"On one hand, I made a stupid mistake. On the other, I did exactly what I needed to do. And then, of course—I'm still processing it."

"You've got to keep working that narrative of yours. Keep defining it for yourself—make it progressive. There's integrity—a lot of strength in speaking your truth."

"Funny thing, really. I was the perpetrator in all this, and yet—I'm the guy who feels traumatized."

"Give it some time. You said you couldn't live with yourself the other way. I'm positive you'll rise above all this crap."

"Well, the Chancellor has real power. His decision could have enormous impact on me."

"Whatever Al, I've got faith in you. Nothing could be as bad as how you said you felt."

For the moment, Alex can't keep his eyes off a guy on *skins* who loves to shoot—a real *gunner*. Every time he touches the ball, he puts up a shot. Also slacking on defense—he's slow to find his man while getting down the court. The guy likes to lag behind—hoping for a chance to cherry pick.

"You know, Silk—I always thought I was a good team player. Maybe that was true on the basketball court. But when it comes to academia or my family life, for godsake—I've been a malcontent. I'm better off outside a system. Outside a team."

"But you and I—we've seen a lot go down at the university. We talk about stuff other faculty members—other *teammates*—would never share. Since we have each other's backs—to hell with the rest of them."

In the meantime, the game's about over and it's getting heated. One *shirt* shoves a *skin*. "Sure wish Joey was here to ref," Alex murmurs.

He notes how everyone's shadows have lengthened over time. It's as if two contests were going on at once. The guys on the court play a tough physical game all the while attached to another one played by shadows. A subtle, silent game of entanglements and quick separations. *Swish*—the game's over. The deficient point guard's team has beaten the team with the selfish shooting guard. The guy who sank the winning basket takes another shot just for fun—from way outside the three point line. *Swish*—it goes again. No clash with the backboard—no clatter with the metal rim. Alex muses—*The best shooters are usually the quietest.*

* * *

From The History of American Graffiti
    by Roger Gastman and Caleb Neelon

In 1970 and 1971, there were graffiti writers in a number of neighborhoods in New York: Crown Heights and

Flatbush in Brooklyn; Manhattan's Upper West Side and Harlem; and neighborhoods in the North and South Bronx. TAKI 183's Washington Heights was just one of them, and in all probability the earliest. What set TAKI apart was that he wrote not only near home but also smack in Midtown Manhattan. He was not trying to announce his presence to claim his neighborhood turf; he just wrote where everyone—including the movers and shakers of society—would see it.

And that is probably how TAKI's writing caught the eye of the *New York Times* in 1971. The resulting July 21, 1971, article, "TAKI 183 Spawns Pen Pals," marked graffiti's arrival, and feeling simultaneously that his flag had been planted and his cover blown, it prompted TAKI 183 to quit. Graffiti would soon become an art form, but TAKI was not interested in being an artist; he was ready to move ahead and be a responsible adult. While graffiti would soon run colorfully wild, TAKI had little interest in lording over the youth culture as some kind of father figure. He made his place in history and made a prompt exit, letting the half-truths flourish into myths: He tagged a Secret Service car! He tagged the Statue of Liberty! In the following years, the article would be alternately credited and blamed for starting the subway graffiti boom in the city, but really, it was just good journalism, bringing a new youthful phenomenon to adult attention. Graffiti's best advertisement, then as now, was graffiti itself.

* * *

Porter College

What does the koi pond have to say? Alex sets down his cardboard box, filled with indispensable items—books he wants nearby as he serves out the rest of his suspension. A box of books—how quaint. Standing in the courtyard, he finds himself beneath the pink-white canopy of cherry blossoms. Clearly, it's February in Santa Cruz. With such perfect weather, everything blooms early here. Today is ideal for a spray of beauty right in the middle of where he feels like an outcast.

Examining the water's surface, only gentle ripples emit from the small fountain. The silent fish seem to float about, seem to drift—seem to scatter. They remind him of tea leaves—even though so much brighter. *What does this mean?* he asks, as he tries to read his future. Maybe it means a *peaceful resolution*—but then again, maybe not. A bright orange fleck meanders about, then wafts away. A shiny black one appears, just as a white and orange one settles.

Lifting his box, Alex realizes he's standing where he and Whitney had met that special day. And the words he had tried to find back then were like the elusive koi. And where is Whitney now? No doubt she's working on her art. No doubt she's making the most of her last year on campus. Alex examines the flowering above—detects something deep inside himself he *knows* is Japanese. Something in his very genes, something encoded—a piece of knowledge, a certain exquisitely *sad* feeling. *Mono no aware*—literally "the pathos of things." He stands as witness to another season of cherry blossoms—like another graduating class of students. Another year, and yet another year. The same each time, yet entirely different. Once more, their gentle beauty overwhelms him thanks to that inborn sensitivity to cherry trees.

Alex's hands bracket his box—a concrete example of what he still controls. He leaves the courtyard and all the transient marvels behind. Turning the corner, he passes his father's memorial, once more pristine in the morning light—all but for a small gash on its side. And he wonders about the relative weight of it all. He wonders how his offense against property compares to what he's done to the people around him. Just behind him now, receding—a bronze and glass edifice weighing well over a ton. Across campus—across a forested ravine—he imagines a beautiful young woman readying herself for a new painting. And the woman is as rare and ethereal as the blossoms that have already vanished into his immediate past.

With visions of Whitney, Alex admits to a different form of indiscretion. Some would no doubt call it a crime. The words of the Code condemn a relationship, romantic/sexual, between a faculty member and someone who is a *current* or *future* student.

That being the case, Alex might view his timing as fortunate. Whitney was no longer his student when they became intimate. Going forward, she has no reason to be his student again. Once more, he places himself on the proper side of a technicality—right at the border, that infinitely thin boundary.

But Alex rejects his latest attempt at rationalization—*knows* that he's done wrong. Even so, he still finds himself wondering at times. A part of him will always believe that what he and Whitney shared spoke to a truth greater than the law and *morality*.

Alex readjusts his grip. He's finished with any leftover doubts about crimes committed against his father. He's claimed them now, has done so publicly—the guilt dwindles away. But with Whitney, he finds a new cause for remorse. In truth, it's not that he completely regrets the *romantic/sexual* involvement with her. Rather—he regrets his need to end it.

33

Downtown Santa Cruz

*H*ow Alex scrambles today—pushed by an internal pressure growing over days. An awkward rush downtown, driven in sudden spurts and stops. Parking in a two-hour zone on New Street. Bisecting the farmers market, he makes his way down Pacific Avenue. Feeling full and resolute, he presents himself at the Vault.

Inside, the bright lights and jewelry dazzle him. He hesitates, then follows the inviting voice of the saleswoman back to her desk. There, he spends the rest of his parking time equivocating. It's all about the choices that won't separate themselves into *good, better,* and *best.* He wants to make the right selection—wants his choice to be perfect.

In keeping with perfection, he drives next to Shoppers Corner, where he selects two peerless, succulent salmon steaks. He chooses nothing but the best organic produce for a flamboyant salad to be topped with marigolds. Smiling to himself—*This must be how retirement feels.* For the time being, a man of leisure—enjoying the luxury of creating a beautiful dinner for the woman he loves. And Alex's eyes know all about that love as they scan the displays of strawberries and raspberries freshly picked from Watsonville. And his fingers know all about that love as they select two perfect artichokes from a field farther south in Castroville. And Alex feels so sure of himself—partly because he's become so sure of his love for Lisa.

As much as his gold sedan limps along, he gets home early—two full hours before she does. Finishing up a business trip, she departs on another later this week. So now is the time for him to act—the opportunity he's been waiting for. This wonderful convergence when her schedule aligns with his lack thereof. This intersection of separate trajectories—this meeting of mutual desires—this confluence of physical realities. It's about time to bring them closer together—back to the way things were, if memory serves him right. And tonight whenever they make love, and Alex hopes they do—it will mean much more than just one body consenting to accommodate the other. It will be Alex and Lisa merging in a way where their respective arcs become one.

When Lisa arrives, the presentation amazes her. The candlelight and the rarely used china and crystal—silverware from the *chef's* mother. She lingers a bit before following her partner to her seat at the dining room table.

"A special occasion?" she asks in a tentative voice.

"Yes—a special occasion."

"I can't believe you did this for me."

"I did it for you, and I did it for the both of us."

Lisa doesn't know where to start—the splendid bloom of an artichoke, the brilliant salad, the glowing salmon? Probably the salad, she thinks—but lifts a glass of white wine to her lips instead. Back in Santa Cruz, back at home, if ever so briefly. She would never have guessed there'd be enough time for something this *incredible.* For some strange reason, she hesitates—feels suddenly *afraid* to try the food. Afraid of what? Afraid to disturb the beauty of the composition—to destroy the painstaking care of Alex's creation? In part, she's afraid the food will taste *too good*—will strike her as extravagantly delicious. But now the salad fills her mouth with a burst of the land that's become her stable resting place. And the fresh salmon mingles with her tongue, a reminder of the sea that has always attracted her.

"Alex, Hon—this is way beyond anything you've done before."

Nipping the edge of an artichoke leaf—"I'm so glad you like it. You look really happy tonight."

Quietly, the two continue to dine. As the candles shorten, Lisa begins to share details of her recent trip to Portland. Yesterday, she rode a fantastic gondola she'd never seen before. She rode it high up a hill to a hospital complex—a health-care business interested in what she had to offer. As her words spill out, Alex interrupts with a soft *hush*—accentuates with an upright finger before parted lips.

"I want us to go for a ride, too," he says. "In the car—"

"A ride tonight? A ride after all this?"

"That's right. Just a short one. Down to the wharf."

"But it's cold, Hon. Why don't we watch a movie instead?"

"That'll be for another time—"

Lisa consents, but wonders why they need to leave the warmth, the comfort of their home. "I'll get a wrap," she says—pausing as if to test his resolve.

Smiling, he crosses the hall—returns with a thick woolen coat for each of them.

It's the middle of the work week—not much traffic in keeping with his plans. Just a little jaunt through downtown to the Municipal Wharf by the Boardwalk. Looking out—the giant pier reaches a half-mile into the bay. Asphalt top—restaurants and shops border the entire right side. Alex wants all the elements to align tonight—wants a dramatic setting. He requires both darkness and deep water. And he wouldn't even mind a tinge of *fear*—venturing out so far from solid land. Gliding along, he cruises with his girl—his love—at his side. He drives as far as he can then parks in front of the last restaurant on the wharf.

"Let me get the door for you," he says—rushing out his side of the car.

She laughs but still can't guess what they're doing here. The wind proves bitingly harsh—a cold, heavy, wet wind. The chill draws them closer together as they meander to the very tip of what appears to be a deserted wharf. To the right, they spot the little brick lighthouse on West Cliff Drive. Only a dot of light periodically declares its solitary presence. Darkness completely surrounds the couple, as folds of black wind buffet them. No outline of the peninsula can be seen in the distance—nautical miles impossible to measure by sight.

"Let's go inside someplace," says Lisa—"I'm freezing."

She can't help it, but she's starting to feel a touch annoyed. Such a lovely, *loving* dinner—and now he has to take her to the very edge of the world, it seems. The two pass a row of open wells, resting places for several barking sea lions. Hurrying along one side of the pier, Alex strains for a panoramic view of the Boardwalk. No dancing summer lights—the rides are all closed at night until Memorial Day. Beyond the scene, the peak of Loma Prieta would stand tall, if they could only see it. The mountain top that gave its name to the big quake in '89—the one that led to so much sudden devastation. Unlike Lisa, Alex feels invigorated by all the natural forces brought to bear on the wharf. A powerful setting—perfect for what he has planned.

Tugging her partner by the hand, Lisa heads for Stagnaro's Restaurant. Once past the doors, she feels relief. She's definitely not hungry but wants something to warm her up—warm her quickly. The server points the couple to the tiny bar by a window facing the sidewalk. Choosing from a row of empty barstools, the two are the only ones present. The bartender—a soft-spoken man with shaven head—asks what they'll be having tonight.

Without hesitation—"An Irish coffee," Lisa says.

Alex ponders a bit before asking for a Campari with a twist.

Lisa looks glum. What had started off as a surprisingly beautiful evening feels miserable now.

Noting this, Alex banters—"Cheer up, Leese. It's going to get better. I promise."

He waits until the bartender delivers their drinks. Entertaining a mounting excitement, he watches the level of her coffee quickly sink. *The right moment,* he wonders to himself. *When's exactly the right moment?* It's been a wonderful evening—*perfect* he'd say, and now he's prepared to finish it off. He's all ready—ready for what—ready to *go for broke?* He places a hand atop Lisa's wrists, her fingers huddled about her drink. And with his other hand, he reaches deep into his pants pocket.

"Here Leese—this is for you." Without lifting the lid, he hands over the small felt box.

"What's this?" she asks.

"Go ahead—open it."

Lisa does, and when she does—she looks like she's not sure whether to burst into tears or laughter. "But there's no ring in it. I mean—this is for a ring, isn't it?"

"That's right, it is. After a lot of thought, I figured we should pick one out together. That's what the little note says—"

"So—so, what does this all mean?" Lisa's face struggles to find the appropriate expression.

"It means, Leese, I'd like you to marry me. That is—what I mean to say is, Lisa Keller—will you marry me?"

Silence— Alex waits on the silence—waits some more. His earnest smile begins to sag with Lisa's lengthening loss for words. She stares at the paper in the otherwise empty box in her hand. And then— And then, she shuts it. Without pulling it out to read the funny little note, she closes the box—places it on the bar.

"Alex," she says—and it's not clear if she's sad or simply stunned. Shocked, maybe—or could it be she's feeling something else? "You know—I've been thinking about things. Thinking about things for a long time."

More than confused, Alex feels dazed. All he can do is sit. He's aware of a strange sensation—as if he's starting to enter a dream—one of the bad ones.

"It means so much to me, that you would ask me to do this—to marry you." Trying to smile—"How long have we actually known each other?" The first tear forms, clings to an eye— "You probably don't know how long I've wanted to hear those words. There was a time, I'd say—I almost felt desperate to hear you say them." The first tear finds its way down a cheek. "But then, after all these years—"

Alex would like to wrap her in a hug. But of course, in a dream, the dreamer can't move.

Straining to meet his eyes—"Thank you, Alex—but I can't. I can't accept your proposal."

"But how can that be, Leese? How can that be? I love you— I love you, and I should have made that more clear. Should have made it more clear a long time ago."

Lisa's mouth tightens—"You're right," she says—her voice more bitter than she would have preferred. "You're absolutely right. You should have said that a long time ago. I never wanted to pressure you—never wanted to tell you—to make you say, 'I love you—will you marry me?' I didn't want to hear it unless you said it for yourself—" More tears, more anger now. "Sometimes, I had this feeling—like you were holding back—like you were just withholding something you knew I wanted. Something you refused to give to me—"

"But I'm saying it now, I'm making a commitment. I know who I am now. I know who we are together— Lisa, I know I love you. I'm sure you love me, too. All those times you were there for me. All the bad times—especially these past weeks. That shows me how you feel. That proves you love me—"

"I do love you, it's true. But somewhere along the line, loving you got all tangled up with—taking care of you. And there was all that time in between, when you just didn't seem to need me that much."

"But we have good times together."

"I agree—"

"Well then, let's work on things—whatever it takes. You don't have to marry me, if you don't want. Let's just work on things really hard, and later—we'll see what you think."

Lisa looks away—looks out the side window into a formless night. Glancing down at the bar, she swipes up the tiny napkin to stem the flow from her eyes, her nose. Embarrassed, she motions the bartender away.

"Why did you have to do it now? Why did you have to do it like this?" Angrily—"I'll never be able to marry you, Alex." Sadly—"Now, I'll never be able to marry you—"

"Well, if that's what you're saying—if that's what you believe—"

"You don't get it, do you, Alex? The reason I can't marry you is—I'm involved with someone else."

Feeling sure he's misheard—"What's that?"

No more new tears—the light of a neon sign turns the wet streaks red. "Some time ago—and I guess I should try and be more clear with you— But some time ago, I met this person. Someone special. It was through work—a guy who was in my department. He wasn't my boss or anything like that. Just a guy working—doing the same thing I was."

"So—what was it about?"

"It felt really good to meet someone like that. I mean, here was a guy—a man—who was excited about the same things I was. The same things were important—we talked the same language, kidded about the same things. We understood the products—shared in the development. We were placed in a position to put on shows together."

Alex registers a searing, visceral pain—one that barely overrides a *sick* kind of arousal. "So when did you start sleeping with each other? Where did it happen?"

Lisa shrugs her shoulders. Her voice softening—"It was at a trade show—just about what you'd expect, I guess—New York City. It was in New York—that's where we started."

Unable to contain himself—"I guess the *fucking* was pretty good—"

"Oh, Alex—" Lisa traces the lip of her coffee cup.

"So tell me, all the time you spent away— It wasn't all about business, was it?"

Touching her tongue with a fingertip—"Well, no. No, it wasn't."

"Was there really a trade show up in Portland?"

"Oh stop it. I don't know what the point is, asking me that—"

"Well, if it wasn't work, I guess it was all about *pleasure*. Tell me—how long has this little thing of yours been going on?"

Lisa catches her face in the mirrored flashing. "Some years now. It's three, actually—"

"*Three years? Three whole years?* So why didn't you go ahead and just end it with me?"

"I was confused. I know this sounds ridiculous, but I felt loyal to you. I felt this kind of old bond, holding us close together. I tried to balance things, the two relationships, the two of you. Santa Cruz felt like home, but over time—it turned into another version of Altoona. My home was here, and then there was someplace else."

"So that was it—you thought you were just, what—reliving your past?"

"That, plus his situation was complicated, too. That's all been taken care of now."

"When were you going to tell me, Leese?"

"I thought about it from time to time. Thought about it a lot—"

"And how close did you get?" Catching himself drumming his fingers—"How about recently? How about with all the problems I've been causing us?"

"Well, you know—being with you was getting harder all the time. It was feeling risky, crazy—*dangerous,* even."

"But I was open to big changes. I would have found work if I lost my position."

Shaking her head—"But it's something more basic than that. More basic than finances. It's like you always did what you wanted to do—for whatever your reasons were. And it's like you never really included me—never considered me in the equation. In the end, I can't trust a person like that."

"I'm sorry, Leese—"

"Well, I'm sorry too. I certainly wasn't being honest with you."

"So—I suppose you're in love with this guy."

Lisa exhales—"Yes I am, Alex— I am."

Stunned by the unequivocal answer—"What do you plan to do? Are you going to marry him?"

"Not for the time being. But after tonight, it'll just be easier for me to move out."

"Come on now—you've got to be kidding. You're not really going to leave, are you?"

"I have to now."

"Where will you go?"

"He's got a place."

None of Alex's logic can explain this truly surreal development. Tidying up, he pats his napkin flat. Then lifting his glass, he downs the rest of his drink. Asking for the bartender, he pays the bill—somehow tips a full 50 percent.

Alex and Lisa slide off their stools and head for the nearby exit. Side by side, they pass the server's station. Pushing hard—he opens the front door against the solid resistance of the wind. For him, the alcohol suddenly takes hold. But maybe he was already feeling drunk—drunk, asleep, in a dream. On a perfect night when all the powers that be—converge. Alex follows Lisa around the corner of the little bar at the end of the long pier.

He struggles with the truth he's managed to find a half-mile out over deep water, in a night much colder than he will ever remember.

"So—do I know this guy?"

"No, you don't."

"Have I met him before?"

"No—"

"Just tell me once, Leese— What's his name?"

34

From the Northwest Asian Weekly

"Japan recalls devastation of tsunami and earthquake one year later"
The Associated Press

Rikuzentakata, Japan— For 70-year-old Toshiko Murakami, memories of the terrifying earthquake and tsunami that destroyed much of her seaside town and swept away her sister brought fresh tears exactly a year after the disaster.

"'My sister is still missing, so I can't find peace within myself," she said before attending a ceremony in a tent marking the anniversary of the March 11, 2011 disaster that killed more than 18,000 people and unleashed the world's worst nuclear crisis in a quarter century.

Across Japan, people paused at 2:46 p.m.—the moment the magnitude-9.0 quake struck a year ago— for moments of silence, prayer, and reflection about the enormous losses suffered and monumental tasks ahead. In Rikuzentakata, which lost 1,691 residents out of its pre-quake population of 24,246, a siren sounded at 2:46 p.m. and a Buddhist priest in a purple robe rang a huge bell at a temple overlooking a barren area where houses once stood.

The memories of last March 11 are still raw for Naomi Fujino, a 42-year-old resident who lost her father in the tsunami. She escaped with her mother to a nearby hill, where they watched the enormous wave wash away their home. They waited all night, but her father never came as he had promised. Two months later, his body was found. "I wanted to save people, but I couldn't. I couldn't even help my father. I cannot keep crying," Fujino said. "What can I do but keep on going?"

* * *

Shaffer Street and Dover, Westside

The name of the guy, the name of the guy— Alex conducts the whole exercise in his head. He's promised himself never to write it down. He refuses to speak it aloud, and he swears never to say it even silently to himself. *The name of the guy*— But thanks to his mind's eye, that name seems to pop up everywhere he looks. He can't help but laugh at himself. It's just like a tag— just like graffiti. Wherever he goes, whatever he sees, the guy's name appears written all over. The man must be *all city*— He must be a *king*. And the guy has absolutely no idea. He's gotten himself up all over Alex's beachside town. Even here—walking down this little asphalt road.

Redolent fields of heather and grass stretch to either side. Rustic fence posts extend at least another quarter mile. In the distance, broad green hills frame a smattering of black cattle. Alex appreciates the lack of large buildings—their vacant walls perfect for imaginary tags. At least here, the rippling wind seems to buff the ubiquitous letters from the scene—disrupts the application of disturbing imagery. The *name* that continues to vandalize his life—

The harsh lilt of a redwing blackbird sounds. A three note call. He spies the bird as it perches on an upcoming bush. Looking small until taking flight—its red patches appear like the shoulder pads of a football player. Serves it well, as it chases a larger crow away from its nest. Alex walks and walks—has been walking this road for a while now. Almost every day this past week.

Soon he passes Natural Bridges Farm on the right—a community program run by the Homeless Garden Project. Tall poles with small wooden plaques designate the various plots. From *A* to *F* in a variety of bright colors—like the options a professor has for grading a student. But the first time he saw those totems, they taunted him, because two of their letters belonged to the guy's name. And of course, one of the letters belongs to Lisa. Lisa's name, her own tag—poses another degree of difficulty. Often enough, he finds it floating about right beside her lover's. Together they form a new composition, but not really. Three long years in the making, it's an arrangement perfected at various sites across the country.

By contrast, his own criminal campaign looks pathetically meager. How remarkable that he was completely blind to the possibility, had missed whatever the tell-tale signs. Lisa and her guy—a two-person crew. A two-person crew—just like Alex and Whitney. Certainly, *the-guy-who-shall-not-be-named* took advantage of a situation, but not of a person. Lisa appears to have been wholly complicit—not a victim of an unwanted seduction.

But the duration, the level of commitment—make Lisa's betrayal seem so much worse. Alex accepts the fact that he wasn't always the best partner. But he wonders exactly how long he was considered lacking. Was his a crime of five, ten, fifteen, or even twenty years? What duration coincides with a punishment of being cuckolded for three of them? Then again—maybe he's not *technically* a cuckold, since he and Lisa were never husband and wife. Frankly speaking, he tires of being so rational in his assessments. He appreciates how anger clarifies issues in a completely visceral way. Naturally, Alex is angry at Lisa's paramour—livid, angry at Lisa, too. Especially as he conjures up scenes of the man, spraying his scent all over the receptive surface of her skin. Drives him nearly insane, should the truth be told. And that special rage propels him into a kind of emotional ascendance, a soaring release—a kind of unexpected thrust toward healing.

Alex powers his way down the cracked pavement, past the farm—crosses a set of railroad tracks. How different this day is from that incendiary night, when the dock appeared to sway and the canyon beneath the bay dove deeper. After lying on his upstairs couch for a week, he's evolved from being flat on his back to fully upright. And for the past several days, he's gone from fully upright to walking Shaffer Street. Every time he feels like stopping, drooping, giving it a rest—he taps into the invigorating new anger—turns it loose.

And a day like today would have never happened if he hadn't told the world his truth. Even though his strange symptoms have failed to resolve completely. Having come clean has helped to bring his jagged pieces in line—stitched them back together, even if loosely at first. The internal mend made him strong enough to face the external pressures—had in fact, made it possible for him to propose to Lisa. And upon her rejection, he was forced to deal with everything alone, and somehow—he's managed to persist. To lose Lisa might have destroyed him before. But with his righteous anger, Alex—that erstwhile ragdoll—began to walk again.

So he takes a left onto the path that parallels Highway 1—a trail with a sign that reads, *Sensitive Wildlife Habitat/Avoid Creatures On Path*. Relishing the full reach and rhythm of his anger, he strides down this narrow lane that leads people beyond the city limits.

"Fuck the guy with 'the name!'" he says out loud. "Fuck Lisa!"

Then Alex reminds himself—that's just what the two lovers might be doing right now.

And—*Fuck the Chancellor! Fuck the Academic Senate while you're at it. Fuck the letter of censure, the dock in pay— the additional restitution for the damage I caused my father's memorial.*

Funny thing, and now his mouth unhinges to accommodate an actual belly laugh. It's virtually impossible to fire a tenured professor from the university. By now, Alex has heard some outrageous stories of wayward faculty flaunting rules in the most egregious fashion only to retire at the time of their choosing with full benefits. Gothic tales of convoluted relationships, sex and intrigue. Rumors of such going on even now. And—*toss the department chair into the fires* for the unofficial punishment being dealt. *What about the ridiculous paper I'm forced to write* about the 'broken windows theory of crime' and graffiti? What about the summer school course I'm forced to teach—a remedial class on art appreciation? And what about those snide looks and asides I endure for breaking the Code of Conduct?

And as for his own people, the Japanese American community? *To hell with the C.J.A.— I don't even live in my so-called community—haven't in a long time.* He anticipates no further action from legal jurisdictions in other parts of the country. In spite of political pressure, the crimes are only misdemeanors and apparently aren't important enough to pursue. *It's dying down—the whole thing's dying down.*

In time, Alex reaches a gentle dip in the rolling path. Poppies look optimistically bright orange. A redwing chases what looks like a starling. Interesting how much of its work occurs so close to the ground, and not while soaring. And as each time before, when he passes the sign on the left advertising a horse stable—when he passes a row of eucalyptus— When he reaches the quaint but working farmhouse—he turns around. Alex starts walking back toward Santa Cruz—a town in which he feels he still belongs. He travels back to familiar walls and open spaces—back to the task, the chore of buffing offensive graffiti from his mind.

* * *

Porter College

Rethinking his new class for fall quarter. "Contemporary Art— Art from the End of WWII to the Present." Includes the final throes of Modernism, the rise of Postmodernism, and what can be termed Post-Postmodernism.

Some basic points on the issue of "Meaning," given the zeitgeist of their times—

1. Pre-modern. Meaning passed down by authorities, tradition-bound, especially by the Catholic Church.

2. Modern. As a product of the Enlightenment, a humanistic rejection of tradition and authority in the form of reason and natural science. Meaning determined by the "autonomous individual."

3. Postmodern. Rejection of the "autonomous individual" as the source of Meaning and Truth. Rejection of the "grand narrative" of Western culture. Emphasis on the illusiveness of Meaning, because everything perceived, expressed, and interpreted is subject to gender, class, and culture. The assertion that all positions are relative and unstable.

4. Post-Postmodernism. Meaning?

Alex prepares an overview of the art coinciding with the last two entries above. Among other things, he will highlight Contemporary art's globalization and its use of new technology. "Post-Postmodernism" continues to evolve—the issue of "Meaning" yet to be clearly articulated.

But as Alex constructs his course, selects the important artists—another practitioner of art steps forward. His name is Alexander Arai, and he has absolutely no standing in the Art World that exerts control over such matters. He wonders if "Alexander the Creator," or *A.C.*, should be included in the treatment of Contemporary art due to his recent experiences in the field. It would be like bringing Mark Rothko back from the dead to elucidate Abstract Expressionism. Not really, of course—not by a long shot. However, in A.C.—who better to illustrate the fractured nature of these times? Why not interview the artist in front of class, in an auditorium full of students?

The interview might go something like this—

A.A. I think I'll start by asking you why you consider yourself a Postmodern artist?

A.C. Well, I actually began as a Modernist. You know—part of that Western fine art concept you lectured on. I really bought into that. A lot of heroic work—individual artists proclaiming new territory. New, new—everything new.

A.A. And that changed?

A.C. Well, it was that Duchamp lecture you gave. You know—the one in which you showed how he turned a urinal into art.

A.A. But of course I know.

A.C. You suggested he was the first conceptual artist and therefore, the first Postmodern artist.

A.A. I'm glad you were listening.

A.C. Well, I agree with conceptual artists that everything comes down to "concept." Whether it's the concept behind a cave painting, a Renaissance cherub, an Impressionist ode to light—the Cubism of Picasso and Braque— The painting, sculpture, the installation—is merely the illustration of the concept.

A.A. Is that so?—

A.C. Yes, and I've decided that the purpose of art is to stimulate the mind—often with visuals—specifically around an intellectual concept or construct.

A.A. But that's so generic—so non-specific. Concepts are every-where—involve everything. Most having absolutely nothing to do with art.

A.C. But, as you pointed out—*any* concept can be made into art, as long as there's someone like Duchamp to declare it so. For example, have you ever had those incredible experiences—pondering concepts like dark matter, the birthing of new stars—the existence of subatomic particles?

A.A. Well, yes—but I believe that involves a type of—*feeling* for me.

A.C. Emotions are optional. It's the mental stimulation that counts—that mental rush imagining a whole universe of things you cannot, and will never see. Let me just declare those experiences as examples of "art" for you, and there you have it.

A.A. All right, so it's clear that you like concept. What else makes you a Postmodern artist?

A.C. At this point, I prefer being referred to as "Post-Postmodern." I think artists like myself have long grown tired of Postmodern thought in the narrow, anti-Modern sense.

A.A. Oh, so you're beyond all that rebellion against the Modern era. I hear you actually retain some old-fashioned Modern values—like a trust in rational thinking and science.

A.C. Yes—so as you can see, I'm something of an amalgam. But mostly, I don't appreciate the fuzzy-headedness of Postmodern thinking. I would hate being so wishy-washy about what can be known. I hate to equivocate—that is, when I'm not obsessing. I'd say my new position is based primarily on "Meaning" for me, with the capital *M*—

A.A.   So, what exactly do you believe in?

A.C.   For me, God resides in Darwinian principles. God is a process, if you will. And I believe more and more people will turn to biology as a "higher power"—one that makes ultimate sense, or Meaning, of it all.

A.A.   And what does this "Process" do for you?

A.C.   It's an extension of the "meaningfulness instinct" you lectured on. Darwinians would agree that humans are hard-wired to seek Meaning—that to believe in something enhances survival and reproduction. Darwinian principles save us from the not-knowing of Postmodernism. Even existentialists, atheists, and nihilists find great Meaning in their positions. And every one of them has to live—practically speaking— day to day. Pragmatically, even those who don't believe in Meaning act as if they do. They eat, sleep, work, have sex. In other words, they support biological life. So apart from the suicidal, people behave as if they believe in life's primacy. And it's this de facto belief that smacks of ultimate Meaning.

A.A.   I'm impressed. Did you make that up all by yourself?

A.C.   I had help.

A.A.   Well, to change the focus— Your one big work, *Action Live,* turned out to have a large ethnic component to it. Do you see yourself accruing additional "Meaning" based on your ethnicity?

A.C.   Well, I didn't anticipate things getting so ethnic at first. It just turned out that way. As you know, my original concept had everything to do with correcting my personal narrative, specifically in relation to my father.

A.A.   But being genetically Japanese, do you think your authenticity as an artist ultimately resides in the Japanese American themes you highlighted?

A.C.   Not at all. In fact, I attacked traditional Japanese and Japanese American values when I did what I did. For example, I refused to conform to society—didn't do what was expected of me. I pursued self-expression, broke the law—became a criminal.

A.A. So—by attacking those ethnic values, could you be considered inauthentic?

A.C. I hope not. In a sense, by departing from my ethnic background, I became quintessentially American.

A.A. Right— You don't speak "the language" in either the literal or figurative sense—you hold to very few customs. You've become a generic American. Tell me—does that mean you produce authentic, generic American art?

A.C. I suppose—

A.A. But, you're still subject to people's stereotypes and pre-judgments. Walking down the street, people will make their suppositions. Don't you think you'll always be seen as Japanese American, or Asian American, at the very least?

A.C. True. But what ultimately counts is how I define myself. As with art—by virtue of Duchamp—my identity is in the *naming*. In my life, I believe I've gone beyond ethnicity, beyond being Japanese American. I'm not just the son of victims and heroes. I'm distinctly more.

A.A. Funny thing. In a way, you remind me of the quintessential Postmodern memorial—a receptacle for everyone's projections. From the majority culture, from your ethnic group, and others. A true case of ambiguous meaning—

A.C. Well, that I can't help.

A.A. You know—I think you should be very grateful for how your parents' and grandparents' generations comported themselves in this country.

A.C. I am. I sincerely am. Without them, I could not have become the completely acculturated American I am today. Without their actions, there would have been no solid ground to build on. By committing a crime, I busted up that ethnic narrative. I no longer feel like a hyphenated American. I'm no longer Japanese-dash-American. In fact, why don't you just call me a "Post-Japanese American"?

A.A. Well, then—I see you get your hyphen back— In any case, we're running out of time. I'm sorry I made things so personal—

A.C. That's okay, I understand.

A.A. All right, then—let's open it up for student questions.

A.C. Fine with me.

A.A. And by the way, thank you very much for taking the time.

A.C. Don't mention it.

35

Downtown Santa Cruz

*F*rom the perspective of skin—mostly accommodating, but within limits. The living fabric that defines the surface of a person and so much more. To a great extent, it keeps her safe—keeps her insides *in* and the outside world *out there*. It makes for a smooth interface with others—a highly sensitive, tactile boundary. Whitney thinks of all the things her skin can register, communicate. How it changes with the situation, the atmosphere—her emotional state. She thinks of how it responds when touched—how the little hairs rise, how goose bumps happen. She enjoys the thrill of an intimate caress. Sometimes she enjoys the thrill of pain. And the times she actually *pursues* pain, the pain doesn't really hurt. Sometimes the pain proves useful—necessary.

Whitney hears the buzzing—the intense sound of a swarm, a cloud of rapidly fluctuating movements. And the *bees* descend on her and start to sting. She makes no noise herself—doesn't move. The man in charge considers it more than business—considers it art. With her permission, he freely probes her skin. He works by inflicting exquisite pain—applies the stings in precise strokes. He performs a kind of penetration while never completely breaching her. He impregnates her skin with the fresh design she's conceived for this very purpose. Tilted on her side, she reclines on the bed—a stark white sheet drawn back to mid-thigh.

Each time the man stops to wipe off her blood, Whitney notes the difference. The lull in the pain feels odd at first— the silent numbness only temporary. When the bees return, she tries to sense how much of the design has morphed from *concept* to *permanence*. Time passes, measured in the man's rhythmic pauses. With the outline complete, he turns his attention to the shading. Whitney wants a 3-D effect—tells him to imagine a light source coming from her navel. She wants the shadows to point away from that physical remnant—that small, commemorative scar of her birth. Now the man introduces color—carefully colors between the lines. As he fills in the gaps, it feels less like stings than the burning aftermath of having been stung. It so happens, her favorite bees are honey bees. In her head, she imagines dead bees lying all over the floor. And half their bodies remain attached to the stingers imbedded in her skin.

The man finishes. The sharpest of the pains is over. What remains—that blistery, burning sensation on the raw outside of her thigh. Retracting the sheet, she leaves the bed—walks over to a full-length mirror. Her butt in profile, she examines the effect—likes what she sees. The latest tattoo is set the low-est—will clearly show when she wears a swimsuit. The fifth in the growing line of emblems. Each a record of a man—each a memorial to a relationship. And although each man has left his mark—the final design belongs to her.

She studies her latest work—her latest creation. In a circle of aqua blue—elegant black letters read *A, R* and *Y.* Surging up, they form a breaking wave—cresting in a whitecap, except the whitecap is actually red. And the red forms a *W* that, with its wings—takes flight from the middle of the name as it separates from the rest of the wave. The bird-like figure frees itself from the part that would cause it to crash back down. In the mirror, Whitney studies the cryptic text of five vertical symbols— approves each glyph and its special meaning. She likes her look, that bold look—the one that speaks to all she's learned about men.

* * *

Alex—

I remember we'd moved into the house a couple months before. A terrific house—better than anything we thought we could get. Not much furniture at first—couldn't afford it. Was practically empty for a long time. With its minimalist looks, Lisa and I could project whatever we wanted into that space—project our entire future together. We talked about furnishings—exciting pieces we could purchase up in the City. We talked over color schemes and the nature of surfaces. It was a large house, and somewhere along the line, I think we started populating it with potential kids. A backyard deck—room for a play set. Certainly somewhere we could entertain our friends in the meantime.

I know that particular day was just like any other for the two of us back then. Although it was fall, it was warm outside—an Indian summer kind of day. Lisa was home from work and making dinner—boiling a chicken to be exact. I was finishing up at the office—reviewing a paper written by one of my students. As I think about it now—the realization just kind of snuck up on me. The first thing I noticed was a hard shudder—thought to myself, *Maybe it's an earthquake.* Another shudder—*Probably an earthquake.* One more time—*Definitely an earthquake!* By then, I felt the whole room shaking—the corkboard in front of me flew off the wall. A small watercolor crashed to the floor. I remember the sound of breaking glass. By then, I'd jumped out of my chair—feared I'd be buried under the books behind me. Chunks of books broke off like pieces of glacier onto the floor. I got to the doorway and stood under the door jamb. It happened so fast—only my pounding heart let me know I was afraid.

Everything got really quiet—the earth was quiet, but then—it wasn't quiet outside on the second floor walkway. Everyone was out, and someone was crying. High-pitched voices—people were following the high-pitched voices down the stairs. I was one of them—trotting through the courtyard then out onto a welcome expanse of grass. By then, students were exiting the dorms—multi-storied structures that managed to stand their ground. I thought how great those buildings were—refusing to fall on people's precious children. And there was a lot of commotion—crowds of excited students, like ants scurrying about, greeting each other. And the energy was impossible to contain. For all of us—I felt how completely vulnerable we were, our soft human bodies so fragile under the tall trees and looming concrete.

So when exactly did I think of Lisa? It was early on, I know. It was somewhere back in my office—somewhere back between the initial jolts and fleeing for the door. An image of her—just enough time for an image only. No words, per se. But on the way to the grass—some huge feelings erupted—thoughts, words. *Oh my God—how's Lisa? Is Lisa okay?* A terrible sense of separation—already a feeling of loss. A desperate need to see her and to hold her close. The tangible Lisa—so unreachable. It was getting near dinner time—I knew she was home. After several minutes, I dashed back through the courtyard—flew up the steps. I entered the mess that was my office. Picking up the phone, I dialed our number—but the lines were down. I thought—here I am on campus—Lisa's less than two miles away. And it felt like some giant fracture had opened up in the middle of my life—something beyond whatever fault line had ruptured that day. A huge, yawning fissure, and there was nothing I could do to reach her.

I'd gotten a ride to work that morning—an older faculty member prepping me for an early meeting. But I couldn't find him in all the chaos. I thought I better start walking, and that's exactly what I did—I started for home on foot. Down from the hilltop campus—out the West Entrance. Along Empire Grade, Bay Street—Escalona. I walked fast—sometimes I ran. *What will I find?* I asked myself. Our house stands perched on the side of a steep hill. I had visions of everything having slid—or tumbled down at the worst. Nearly 6 p.m. and it still felt hot outside. The air was thick and heavy, and I soaked through all of my clothes. A few people lined the sidewalks. Actually, some were milling about in the middle of the street. People engaging each other—some agitated, some calm. I saw houses with shattered windows, warped walls.

One last neighbor's house, and then—there was ours. I ran all the way up the steep driveway—called out Lisa's name.

Why isn't she out on the street like everyone else? Bursting through the front door, everything seemed in place at first, mostly because there wasn't much to begin with. But when I got to the kitchen, I felt my feet crunching shards of glass. I saw cupboards flung open—spices everywhere. Cookbooks. Broken plates, cups. And I saw Lisa standing by the stove. I said something like—*Let's get out of here right now!* Her face looked stunned. She mumbled something about the chicken— the chicken she'd been boiling. *Glass in the chicken*— I grabbed her hand and we scrambled down the driveway to the street.

The rest of the evening, the citizens of Escalona banded together. Barbeques quickly appeared and food was offered freely. Neighbors sat in lawn chairs—listened to transistor radios. As night approached, everyone talked about sleeping arrangements—where they felt safe to sleep. Lisa and I agreed we didn't want to return to the house just yet. We looked up at the silent structure, and it felt so far away. All the dreams, all the wonderful plans—seemed unreal, so out of our grasp. I said to her, *let's take the car and drive off. Let's drive to someplace we know is safe.* At the time, I had a different car—another Volvo, but it was silver-gray. I made a joke of it—said we should check out the TV commercials—put the car's safety claims to the test. So we started climbing back up our driveway. Halfway up— another tremor. We just stood in place, hands interlocked— frozen. Eventually we made it inside—still terrified of aftershocks. Lisa and I threw toiletries and a change of clothes into one big suitcase. On the way out, we grabbed some bottled water, a loaf of bread, and cold cuts.

Electricity out—I opened the garage door manually. We got into the car and backed slowly down to the street. People waved as we drove off. *Where to go?* we asked ourselves. We'd heard the entire coast all the way up to San Francisco was hit. We'd heard that part of the Oakland Bay Bridge had collapsed—that fires were raging in parts of the City. We figured the quake must have been centered there. Little did we know—the actual epicenter was only nine miles away from us. Instinctively, I started driving to higher ground. *What if it's true,* I asked silently—*that the coast of California could fall into the ocean with the "Big One?"* As it was, wherever I looked, I saw toppled chimneys and an occasional house knocked off its foundation. I told Lisa—let's go back to the university. Let's go up to the top of the hills. I drove us through the East Entrance—took a left on Hager Drive. At the East Remote Parking Lot, I took a sharp right.

Entering the empty grounds, I drove to its southern edge. From there we could see a gentle field and then—the entire panorama of Santa Cruz and the bay below us. I felt we were atop the world—or at least atop California. Columns of smoke were rising from downtown, and beyond that was the hazy water, the hovering peninsula. And above it all was the darkening blue October sky. The sound of helicopters was vaguely reassuring, and for the first time, I felt I could relax.

Lisa was silent, then touched me with her hand—said something like, *Thank you— Thank you for knowing what to do.* Reaching into the back, I pulled out the water and food. We spent the next half hour or so just taking in nourishment— watching the sunset, that simmering vista. And I felt so relieved, and I felt so good being in that car with her. No big house—no pretensions to a grander life. It just felt right—the two of us sitting side by side, safe together—taking in this momentous event. And I'm sure I said it. I'm sure I said, *Lisa, I love you—* I'm sure I did—without her prompting me. I recall the feeling—a wonderful, close feeling as the clouds lit up in flame and the sky turned an ethereal orange. And I know—I know she was feeling the same way too.

And when it was finally dark—when the stars glowed like leftover embers from the sunset, we turned to each other. We hugged each other and we kissed. And we laughed because the gear shift kept coming between us. We laughed all the way down as we lowered our seats. When I squeezed over, it was so tight—I had to get on top of her. And although we kept most of our clothes on, we made love on that special night. And time passed, and periodically we heard the sound that was like the sound of a distant train. And each time after that sound, the earth shuddered again. And there was this kind of synchronicity—the earth's shuddering, then our shuddering. And finally there came a point when we stopped trying to tell the difference.

✱ ✱ ✱

Whitney B rides the bus. Her cell phone rings. It's Alex— She doesn't even bother listening to the message. Strange, the way he's been calling lately. What a time to re-boot communication. But she's already made up her mind—wants nothing more to do with him. She's completely done with the professor—is over him.

Sitting on the gritty seat, she doesn't hear the message that says, "I'm sorry, Whitney—I'm sorry I won't be able to see you anymore. It wasn't right—especially when I was about to make a new commitment to Lisa. It didn't work out with her, but you and I—we still need to come back down to earth. Hoped I could talk to you about it. Looks like you've made your own decision— Best wishes to you always."

Whitney stares out the glossy window as she rides the #71 bus to Watsonville. Heading south—crossing the bridge beside the Aptos trestle. Later this spring, she'll be traveling south once more—this time taking a plane. She's decided to visit her folks in Torrance—wants to discuss certain *things* about her past.

One spot over, her backpack carries both art supplies and lunch. She's included an old box of Conte crayons—thinks her new students might like the color and texture of the little sticks. Maybe she should take a fresh sketchbook when she flies to Southern California. Who knows what she's going to uncover while talking with her parents?

Whitney rehearses the directions to the Pajaro Valley Art Museum. She looks forward to working with the teens—those young artists coursing with creative energy. And soon, she hopes to create something new for herself—starting with the answers she'll find regarding the past she can't remember.

Whitney wonders if the kids might like to draw each other's faces. Maybe they'd like to look in a mirror and draw themselves. Maybe she'll ask them to draw pictures of their families— When imaging her own, she starts with the supportive, loving couple who saved her from a life of upheaval. Then she thinks of that crazy red-haired lady. The one who claims to be her real mother—the one people talk about only in whispers.

Children need freedom to express themselves and a safe place to do it. But for them to be good, they'll have to start learning technique. This summer, Whitney plans to learn something new as well. She plans to pursue any leads she finds in Torrance. She's determined to chart a new course—wherever it takes her—in order to find her biological father.

Whitney rides the bus to Watsonville. And the words in her head must be true, because the professor said they were. That to know yourself means knowing where you come from. Or *something* like that— She wants to reverse the clock—find the source of the traumatic events that stalk her—overpower her. She thinks of Alex—believes she's stronger now than before they met. But Whitney's not ready to thank him yet—and maybe, she never will.

✳ ✳ ✳

The house on Escalona Drive

It's morning, and Alex sits in his redwood chair, in front of his redwood burl table on the planks of his redwood deck. His mind feels clear and refreshed—the nighttime clutter gone. And it's a pretty day—purple and red azaleas enliven the jagged shadows cast by a warm sun. *What's different?* he asks himself. *What's not different?* he also asks. The house remains—redwood siding and all. The deck—the infamous Wall of Mistakes, the stream on the side of the lot. The basic structures have all survived. But looks are deceiving, or so it appears— It's like all the insides have been washed away by a tide. Or, it's like someone's dropped a neutron bomb—the kind that kills all the people but leaves the buildings intact. Alex surveys his property and its relatively de-populated state.

As he reenters his house, plenty of vacant square footage abounds. In the last two weeks, the bulk of the clothing has vanished—having departed hand in hand with its owner. Business and casual—an entire female wardrobe replete with shoes and accessories. Alex might welcome the extra room if only he could use it. How amazing to him—the incredible capacity of a newly-gutted closet. And as time passes, all the furniture will be leaving as well. Hauled off by professional movers to Goodwill and the Salvation Army. Since Alex plans to buy Lisa out, he's determined to restore the house to some primal state—something more austere than even a minimalist would like. He hopes to embrace a style so simple, it harkens to a time that's pre-cohabitation. In terms of design, he wants it back to some original architectural state—something close to blueprints.

And it's true—the losses keep adding up as he peers down an empty hallway. Lisa, of course. Whitney—even though he misses her, their artistic twinship would have ultimately turned out badly. And then, the matter of his father's death—the fact that someone else will write the intro to his retrospective. And how about the change in Alex's status on campus, the change in standing in whatever community? From time to time, he actually sheds some tears—especially when registering the full extent of the losses, when he finds himself utterly alone. It's a kind of controlled mourning, done in manageable increments.

The aftermath of devastation. So, what next? What to do with this freed-up floorplan? Certainly, opportunity knocks if ever so faintly. Maybe Alex can fill the vacuum with new athletic equipment. Maybe he can knock down walls—combine two of the redundant bedrooms into a yoga studio. Or—how about a den with a pool table? A bar? What about a smoking room? Carter would be just as lost in such troglodytic accommodations. And what about his art? What about more room for his art?

Alex finishes his review of contemporary matters. He'll probably take off for the coffeehouse once he checks his emails. Climbing to his loft, he looks about—experiences an unexpected benefit. He's already removed the shoji screen that once obscured his desk and any and all of his artwork. Now, his faithful drafting table claims the unlocked corner—glimmers in the beams of a steadfast northern light. The new tableau embodies acceptance—of a part of himself that should have always belonged in this space. Settling in, he logs on. He's not expecting much—but it's part of a new routine, to sit openly at his rightful station with the absolute backing of his room.

On the computer screen, he finds—

All Gone Awry

From Sendai Renewal Organization

Dear Sir:

As the cherry blossoms return, a beautiful wave passes over our country. We in Sendai apologize for not writing you sooner. From the news, we are sure you understand how busy we are in Japan. We are working very hard and making much progress in our renewal. We now look forward to the future.

We also provide our sincerest sorrow at your father's passing. As you know, we have had open communication with him for construction of a new memorial. In Japan, we have rebuilt our country many times. It is a good idea to make a memorial to help the people in their efforts. It will remind us how we must continue to endure. Most important, it will inspire the people to keep working in the present moment we have.

Before your father's passing, he contacted officials in Sendai and proposed a new memorial. His words sounded very excited and he sent excellent drawings of his ideas. We received them and planned to look at them at a different day. Our organization has now examined them and believe they hold much promise. In your father's notes, he wanted us to hear from you, the artistic professor and your own words. We believe your father wanted you to help with his designs, especially now after his passing.

Please find the attachments with the drawings. If you have some helpful comments, we would appreciate them. If all goes well, we will invite you to visit us in Sendai. You will be very interested in seeing the different sights. You will not have to worry about transportation and accommodations. We will make sure your visit is quite comfortable.

Whenever it is a good time for you, we look forward to hearing your response. Japan and America have been friends for a long time. Your country is standing by us as we rebuild. The memorial will be another help. The ideas of your father need to be further advanced. It is special for us and the organization to be working now with you. We hope you will be a true Japanese American artist just as your father was.

Sincerely,
Dr. Akira Yoshitani
Sendai Renewal Organization
Sendai, Japan

Alex absorbs what he's just read—welcomes the birth of a new concept, a new identity being offered him. He checks himself to see how it fits. It feels real—feels like a natural point in a lifelong evolution. A true Japanese American artist— plainly put, if not so simple. He gladly makes the designation his own. Returning to his computer, Alex responds—

Dear Dr. Yoshitani,

I have received your email. Thank you very much for your kind words. As soon as I finish with my father's drawings, I will gladly send you a more formal response. I have no doubt that we can enjoy a productive relationship. I look forward to providing you some original ideas of my own.

Sincerely,
Alexander Arai

Buoyant in his airy loft, Alex downloads the attachments, sets his computer aside—opens one of his artist's sketchbooks. He begins dismantling that final memorial—that last *collaboration*—with his father. He embraces the ideas that flow so easily now—all manner of possibilities in the use of materials. And the various permutations evolve so quickly, he can hardly keep track. His hand moves with the fluid freedom of a tagger, of a man determined to write his name in the interlocking forms of a graffiti piece. Using his favorite 4B pencil, he captures all that he can.

Gone now are the tortured figures and the towering wave of concrete and glass. Gone now is the sculptor, the father— *Kaz*. And through the flutter of pages, Alex undergoes his own transformation. He has yet to name that change, but his self-judging voice has diminished to a murmur.

Alex draws a hillside covered with trees. Atop its crest, his hand *discovers* the circular form of a great ceramic vessel. The size of a small amphitheater, its rim is uneven, at times—broken. The materials are simple, rough-hewn—forged in that *ring of fire* like the lands that circle the Pacific. A froth of blue-green glaze pours over the bisque-colored concrete walls. Metallic leaves and pine needles speckle the sides—all meant to rust from silver to brown. The effect is that of a ceremonial tea bowl, one so much a part of nature that it could have been found on a forest floor. And locked in its stillness is the very definition of the moment—of tectonic strike, of fragmentation—of the arrested violence of the sea. *Wabi-sabi*, the Japanese art of finding beauty in the imperfect, in the accidental—in life's relentless cycles—beauty in the fissured visage of age.

At the bottom of the enclosed pavilion, Alex sketches a pool of tranquil water. In filtered light, visitors may slowly ascend a ramp that spirals up the internal walls of the bowl. In this vortex of tragedy, their journey embodies a rising wave of its own. At spots, people can sit in sheltered coves to contemplate the void and the shimmering water below. At the top of the structure, visitors may step outside to a walkway circling the rim. After the relative dark, eyes will open to distant panoramas and a return to the immediacy of life.

For night visitors, Alex will design a series of holograms to illuminate the space inside. The images will morph in color and form, as well as in sound and voice. Viewers may experience the angry orange of an atomic explosion, the red of a newborn *rising sun*—the reassuring blue and white of the planet itself. Within the colors, they will find the faces of lost loved-ones as well as survivors—hear their stories.

As Alex creates, he welcomes a similar swirl of emotions—feels a deep kinship to all those living in the throes of upheaval. Laying down his pencil, he swivels in his chair—gazes out the windows of his loft. Extending his view toward the bay, the peninsula—he sends his vision out and back across the Pacific. Even the horizon holds no limits for him. No longer is it a barrier to what he can freely imagine. He feels gratitude for the foothold he has in this town—nestled on a beautiful coastline, one that forms the very edge of a shifting continent. As Alex looks to the future, he promises himself to remain nimble— knowing that each day, the world can change forever.

Acknowledgments

Thank you to the many people who contributed to this book.

To my fellow writers for your spirited critiques and friendship throughout the years: Jan Leininger, Kellie Monahan, Tim Woods, Susan Samuels Drake, and Sandy Raney. I enjoyed the comradery and all the good eats and drinks along the way.

To author Christine Z. Mason. Beyond your critical honesty, you were my steady guide on the path toward publication.

To friends and readers Dean Walker, Lorchen Heft, and George Ow for your early feedback.

To friend and reader, Dan Cavanaugh, for your thoughtful input and steadfast support through the long writing process.

To writer and editor Diane Wong who critiqued an early manuscript.

To Robert Sward, poet and novelist, a generous teacher who first suggested that I extend my poetry into larger forms.

To Patrice Vecchione, poet, non-fiction writer, artist, stage performer, and inspiring teacher. Your insightful, supportive instruction greatly helped my poetry.

To my editor Bryan Tomasovich and The Publishing World. Thank you for your astute guidance through multiple drafts. Your help encompassed both the craft of writing and the challenges of publication. Thank you also for your fine work on book design. I especially appreciate your patient, empathetic manner.

To Dr. Derek Conrad Murray, UCSC Professor, History of Art and Visual Culture. As the department's chief theoretician in the history, theory, and criticism of contemporary art, you provided me with expert analysis on Modern and Postmodern developments. You also shared many crucial insights into ethnic scholarship and academia.

To the late Dr. Albert Elsen, Stanford University Department of Art History and renowned expert on Auguste Rodin. He conducted his lectures with clarity, passion, and impeccable style.

To Stephen La Berge, attorney at law, for your valuable discussion of criminal defense and trial procedures, as well as for your kind encouragement.

To the late Bob Lee, former Santa Cruz County D.A. He was a passionate defender of the law who, among his many other accomplishments, enthusiastically fought graffiti vandalism through innovative programs for control and mitigation.

To Bill Ackerman, owner of Bill's Wheels. Through your sponsorship of "legal" walls, thank you for providing me access to local graffiti writers and the practice of their art.

To Lisa Brewer, who along with Randolph Bowes, founded Mission Art 415. After TORCH introduced us, I enjoyed our talk in Lilac Alley on a glorious spring day in San Francisco.

To the late George Tsutakawa, a seminal Japanese American artist whose "water sculptures" have always been inspirational. He kindly opened his studio to me when I was a young man.

To Taylor Reinhold, street muralist and founding member of MADE FRESH CREW. Working with you on the cover art was one of the highlights of this project. I appreciate your talent and creativity, along with your social awareness and activism.

To the graffiti writers who welcomed me into their culture:

NATE ONE, historic San Francisco writer and founding member of MPC [Masterpiece Creators] and famous for his meticulous "black books."

MONGO, "San Francisco born and raised." I had a lot of fun hanging out with you at Bill's Wheels watching you work. I loved your stories of life in Bernal Heights during a golden age in SF graffiti.

TORCH, from Queens, NYC, who first got up under the Unisphere at the world's fair site. Thank you for introducing me to Lilac, Balmy, and Clarion Alleys.

TITS Crew—"Time is Too Short." A group of legendary Santa Cruz writers and the very definition of a colorful crew.

To Dick and Phyllis Wasserstrom. Many thanks for the use of your house!

And finally, to my family, for the understanding and acceptance that allowed me to complete this project. To my wife, Carmen, for adding valuable cultural perspective to certain characters, as well as for your careful reading of drafts. To my sons, Daniel and Anthony, true believers in the creative process, even as you thought I was too old to take a graffiti writing class.

Andrew Kumasaka was born in Chicago and grew up in Seattle. An eclectic psychiatrist, he retired after thirty years in private practice. His poems have appeared in various literary journals. He contributed a chapter to *Flowing Bridges, Quiet Waters*, a clinical book about Morita Therapy, a Japanese form of psychotherapy. He and his wife live in Soquel, California with their border collie and two cats. They have two grown sons.

CPSIA information can be obtained
at www.ICGtesting.com
Printed in the USA
BVHW071416021221
623089BV00008B/219